OFF GRID

How Long Can They Hide From The Surveillance State?

J. P. Redding

This book is dedicated to freedom-loving people of all stripes. As Americans, our individual liberties, as enshrined in the Constitution, are at risk from the State which is encroaching on most aspects of our lives - well-intended or not.

CONTENTS

Title Page

Copyright

Dedication

Foreword

PRECURSORS TO PIVPAL™

PROLOGUE

PART 1   1

ONE   2

TWO   9

THREE   14

FOUR   19

FIVE   22

SIX   27

SEVEN   31

EIGHT   33

NINE   42

TEN   44

ELEVEN   51

TWELVE   57

THIRTEEN   68

FOURTEEN   71

FIFTEEN   77

SIXTEEN   82

SEVENTEEN   89

EIGHTEEN   94

NINETEEN   99

TWENTY   101

PART 2   104

TWENTY-ONE   105

TWENTY-TWO   112

TWENTY-THREE   118

TWENTY-FOUR   121

TWENTY-FIVE   126

TWENTY-SIX   132

TWENTY-SEVEN   138

TWENTY-EIGHT   146

TWENTY-NINE   150

THIRTY   157

THIRTY-ONE   163

THIRTY-TWO   171

THIRTY-THREE   176

THIRTY-FOUR   178

THIRTY-FIVE   182

THIRTY-SIX   187

THIRTY-SEVEN   191

THIRTY-EIGHT   197

THIRTY-NINE   200

FORTY   206

FORTY-ONE   211

FORTY-TWO   215

FORTY-THREE   218

FORTY-FOUR   222

FORTY-FIVE   228

FORTY-SIX   234

FORTY-SEVEN   243

FORTY-EIGHT   249

FORTY-NINE   254

FIFTY   260

FIFTY-ONE   267

FIFTY-TWO   273

FIFTY-THREE   275

PART 3   279

FIFTY-FOUR   280

FIFTY-FIVE   285

FIFTY-SIX   289

FIFTY-SEVEN   293

FIFTY-EIGHT   298

FIFTY-NINE   308

SIXTY   318

SIXTY-ONE   328

SIXTY-TWO   333

SIXTY-THREE   339

SIXTY-FOUR   346

About The Author   351

Request For Reviews   353

Cast Of Characters   355

FOREWORD

I started the outline of OFF GRID almost five years ago. At the time, several themes of the novel were showing up on the radar screen: surveillance of US citizens, censorship at universities, socialism entering the mainstream, identity politics, biased journalism, the nanny state, etc. As the years ticked by, I realized that if I didn't take action, I would be writing a history book instead of near-future fiction.

Fast-forward to Summer 2019. I finally sent out my manuscript for review. They liked it! They also had lots of recommendations... Anyway, I took the plunge into deep edit mode. Little did I know how deep that mode was. My original release date of Fall 2019 slipped - too close to the holidays. Okay. Then the new target date of New Year slipped. Hmm. I gave it one more shot - Spring of 2020. What could go wrong?

The COVID-19 pandemic was a double-whammy for this fledgling author: all bookstores were closed and a key element of the novel's plot - a disaster - was already unfolding. But this worldwide disaster has highlighted the primary theme of OFF GRID: *fear and control* - the tools of the totalitarian State - are upon us. God help us all.

J. P. Redding - May 2020

PRECURSORS TO PIVPAL™

1978: Foreign Intelligence Security Act (FISA) allows for unmasking of US citizens to facilitate foreign intelligence investigation.

1998: PayPal® establishes platform for secure financial transactions on hand-held devices.

2000: Location-Based Services proliferate with introduction of GPS-enabled mobile devices.

2001: 9/11 Terrorist attack. USA Patriot Act vastly broadens government powers for warrantless surveillance of phone, text, and email metadata of US citizens.

2004: Assisted GPS uses proximity to cell towers to calculate position of cell phones within feet of actual location when satellite-based GPS in unavailable.

2005: Real ID Act sets common security standards for state driver's licenses. Full implementation delayed until 2020.

2006: Personal Identity Verification (PIV) of federal workers requires 3-factor verification: what you have (smartcard), what you know (PIN) and who you are (biometric/fingerprint)

2007: Airlines accept high-capacity barcodes on smartphones as electronic boarding passes.

2009: Bitcoin launches as first decentralized cryptocurrency.

2012: Immigration and Customs Enforcement (ICE) reveals FALCON System to consolidate Personally Identifiable Information (PII) from multiple public databases, augmented with geo-spatial location mapping.

2013: The New York Times characterizes the FISA Court as "almost a parallel Supreme Court, serving as the ultimate arbiter on surveillance issues".

Eric Snowden leaks volumes of top-secret documents revealing National Security Agency (NSA) global networks and capabilities including surveillance of foreign nationals and US citizens.

2014: ICE approves Investigative Case Management (ICM) system to employ social network analysis to PII including address, phone records, social media posts, biometrics, birthmarks, tattoos, and physical location.

NSA completes Utah Data Center (UDC) to store massive collection of electronic surveillance records on Americans for the purpose of deep data mining.

Apple launches Apple Pay mobile wallet service. Android Pay and Samsung Pay soon follow.

2015: App/Cloud service enables tracking of first responders using smartphones as an ID, a locator, a unit collector, and an incident manager with syndication across jurisdictions.

2016: FISA surveillance is politicized in run-up to the 2016 presidential election leading to the unmasking of American citizens.

National Institute of Standards and Technology (NIST) awards grant to develop use of smartphones as trusted identities, including implementation as Digital Driver's Licenses.

2018: Major metro law enforcement agencies adopt Palantir's Gotham platform for predictive policing. Using social network analysis and data mining, potential suspects are targeted for preemptive intervention.

2019: FISA Court belatedly issues stinging rebuke of FBI for misrepresentation as well as withholding information detrimental to their requests for surveilling American citizens.

2020: China augments government control of the Internet with rollout of a national Social Credit System designed to surveil, grade, and rank citizens on conformance with Party dogma, resulting in rewards and penalties.

COVID-19 pandemic spurs multiple countries to use smart-phones for GPS tracking of real or suspected carriers, person-to-person contacts, and to enforce quarantines.

PROLOGUE

April 1975

Oak Ridge National Laboratory
Oak Ridge, TN

Lab Director Charles Loomis and his deputy Walter Bohr looked down on the test room from the second-floor observation deck, surrounded by bulletproof glass windows. Below, Jacob Schultz and his team were making final preparations on the prototype, which stood four feet off the concrete floor. Loomis thought the contraption looked like a cross between a jet engine and a Tennessee backwoods still—tubes and wires hung out all over the thing. After a few last connector twists and keystrokes, the white-coated scientists retreated to their observation booth on the testing floor. Before Schultz entered, the lead scientist caught the eyes of his administrative bosses and gave them a thumbs up. *Our nutty professor*, Bohr thought. *Good thing he's a genius with scores of patents to back him up.*

"What is this, test four or five?" Loomis asked.

"Five," Bohr replied.

Lights dimmed around the prototype, indicating that the test was moments away. As a precaution, Loomis and Bohr put on protective glasses to shield against any damaging light waves. In the booth down below, Schultz fine-tuned some knobs and then pulled a switch. Instinctively the managers backed away from the window. Nothing seemed to be happening. Then both men heard a deep hum. The prototype began to vibrate. Then they saw it, a jet of blue flame flaring out from the bottom. They watched in fascination as the blue jet continued to grow until it was licking the floor. The hum rose multiple octaves to a high-pitched whine. And then... BANG!

"Damn!" Bohr yelled. They both ducked for cover as shrapnel pelted the observation window. Assuming the worst was over, they raised their heads to view the test room. High-speed fans were quickly dispersing a cloud of smoke. The prototype itself was unrecognizable. A few smoldering remnants lay scattered around the test site. Schultz and his team came out of their observation booth to inspect the damage and retrieve data from various monitoring systems.

Loomis took off his safety glasses and looked at his deputy. "Shut it down."

"Are you sure?" Bohr was incredulous. "Have you read Schultz's whitepaper?"

"You mean *Net Energy from Intra-Plasma Containment*? Yeah, Walt, I've read it. Bury it," Director Loomis said with finality.

PART 1

The Party seeks power entirely for its own sake. We are not interested in the good of others; we are interested solely in power, pure power. What pure power means you will understand presently. We are different from the oligarchies of the past in that we know what we are doing. All the others, even those who resembled ourselves, were cowards and hypocrites. The German Nazis and the Russian Communists came very close to us in their methods, but they never had the courage to recognize their own motives. They pretended, perhaps they even believed, that they had seized power unwillingly and for a limited time, and that just around the corner there lay a paradise where human beings would be free and equal. We are not like that. We know that no one ever seizes power with the intention of relinquishing it. Power is not a means; it is an end.

George Orwell

1984

ONE

Present Day

I-75 MI – October 10, 7:45 am
Approaching Mackinac Bridge

Scott spurred his vintage Porsche to go faster, as if he could smash through a mounting wall of worries. Was Aunt Jenny going to be detained? Do they know about the plasma drive? How were they connecting the dots to his dad sitting in the US Congress?

The rare sight of another vehicle on the road jolted Scott out of his ruminations. The USDA food truck up ahead was one of the only signs of life he'd encountered in almost three hours on the road north. After a quick downshift, he punched the accelerator. The bright orange sportster closed on the truck with reckless speed. At the last second, he swerved into the passing lane to fly by the lumbering government vehicle. Scott caught a glimpse of the tag line emblazoned on the food truck's side panels: *A Fair Share for All*. What a load of bullshit, he vented.

Scott suffered a moment of anxiety, wondering if the truck driver might snitch on him, but he quickly dismissed the thought. Hell, he was being tracked anyway. What difference could it make? Besides, he had a Gold PivPal with Star—his official smartphone would affirm his elite status. Nobody was going to mess with him. Unless it was the Feds.

Of course, that was the problem. The Feds were on to Aunt Jenny, Tim, Jack—everyone he cared about. He needed to warn them, and there was no time to lose. Scott wanted to text or email, but that would be no different than turning them all in.

He comforted himself with the thought that he couldn't reach Jenny anyway. She didn't have a PivPal. She was off grid, and now she was a suspected rebel sympathizer to boot.

PivPal. What a stroke of marketing brilliance, Scott thought. He wondered how long they'd brainstormed before they'd figured out how to make "Personal Identity Verification Permitted Activity Log" devices sound like your friend, your best pal. A smartphone with everything you could ever need or want, free! Would PivPal have become the new opiate of the masses, Scott mused, if it had been marketed honestly as an electronic dog collar for humans? Come get your tether so we can track your every activity, communication, and movement, every purchase you make, every credit you earn, every gathering you attend, every bite of food you consume. You'll love it! And these days, they weren't just sampling metadata. They were storing content, too, and using sophisticated algorithms to dig deep into the gargantuan data trove that was growing exponentially day by day.

As if on cue, his oversized PivPal smartphone, or PIV for short, gave an audible chirp. By the tone, Scott knew he had been assessed a fine for speeding. What's a few more credits, he thought dismissively. Scott reached over to the cradle-mounted unit and cleared the penalty message. As the PIV refreshed, he had to admire the simplicity of the home screen design. Just six icons: Security, Comms, Entertainment, Health, Income, Expenses. For a Gold like Scott, Security and Income were the passport to privilege. One vouched for his elite status, the other attested to unlimited credits. Scott also admired the way PIV's architects had focused on income, rather than assets. No need for Golds to expose their true wealth in public.

"Map," Scott ordered. The PIV screen switched over to his trip map. He was approaching the bridge. Icons appeared for a security/toll booth and a mini-mart. Scott felt a wave of relief. There hadn't been any food or gas for 100 miles. You really had to plan your trips nowadays.

Nowadays. Scott chuckled at the refrain to soften the dread he felt. It seemed impossible that so much change had come so quickly after the terrorist attacks. The catchphrase for the economic ruin that followed the attacks was simply "The Crash." But it was the cleverly titled "Fair Deal" that irrevocably changed America's political landscape. As the government struggled to maintain control, a perfect storm of partisan horse trading ensued in Washington DC. Conservatives got a national ID and border control. Progressives got wealth redistribution and government program expansion. The people got guaranteed income and universal healthcare. Students got free college. And elites kept their preferred status. What's not to like? Scott opined. Everybody got a bone to go along with their tether! Except there were losers, too, like freedom, capitalism, the Bill of Rights, and the ballooning national debt —not to mention charities, churches, the working class, civil libertarians, independent journalists, entrepreneurs, charter schools, rural Americans…

Scott's list was cut short as he realized he was coming in a bit hot to the toll booth. He quickly braked and downshifted, the Porsche protesting with a high whine as it transitioned through lower gears. Only two lanes were open, Standard and Priority, and both were empty. Scott pulled up to the Priority booth and lowered his window.

"Good morning, Mr. Bennett. How are you today?" the oversolicitous attendant asked. She wore a freshly pressed, government-issued blue jumpsuit that attested to her authority.

"Fine, thank you," Scott replied. He knew she had been tracking him for at least the last half hour, and his Globally Unique Identifier, his GUID, had tipped her off to his Gold status. The Porsche was so low to the ground that Scott had to reach up to place his hand on the security scanner. Simultaneously, a camera affixed to the toll booth took a snapshot of his face. Even his Gold PIV didn't get him a pass on security protocol. They logged his exact location, checked that his PIV was online, and confirmed that his PIV authentication certificate was still valid. The interrogation was meant to confirm that he wasn't an imposter. His prints and facial image captured at the booth were compared against biometrics stored on his PIV and in the Cloud. A green light came on, and the guard gate raised.

Washington DC – 7:55 am
The Bureau Surveillance Room
Despite the early hour, Tommy Sutton was eating a candy bar. He took a bite, rolled up the wrapper, and tossed it at the trash can across the darkened room. It joined an assortment of other near misses lying on the office floor. He glanced up at one of his five flat screen monitors and saw that Bennett was stopped at the Mackinac Bridge PIV checkpoint. With a few keystrokes he brought up live video feed from the booth. Nice car, Tommy thought, looking at the bright orange Porsche that Bennett had been driving since 0500. When he'd started heading north from Grand Rapids, his PIV had tripped a geofence, and all the players had scrambled to pull up the mission. Entrapping Bennett would be a major coup—and it was all wrong!

After monitoring Bennett for over a year, Tommy knew his target intimately—who he talked to, what he bought, where he traveled, when he worked, everything that was available on the grid. Until recently, the tracking had been largely passive. Bennett had simply been a person of interest on the Department of Energy's watch list. Tommy had wondered why anybody would give a rat's ass about Bennett's startup company. That changed a couple of weeks back with the data mining hit and thermal imaging. Now he knew, and he was staggered.

What had started as a game of hide-and-seek had become deadly serious. Tommy's efforts to muddy the surveillance waters—even sending a note of warning—appeared to be for naught. Even worse, had his warning triggered this final stage of the game? He couldn't be sure, but he knew where this was heading: Bennett and his friends would be detained, questioned, and then they'd disappear, along with their work, their records, and everyone close to them. We've become a freaking Nazi police state, Tommy ruminated, and he was complicit.

It wasn't like he had a choice. He either played ball or it was off to federal prison for felony hacking charges. Jail was not a good place for a 23-year-old pacifist with long hair. Without his brother's connections at the Bureau, he'd be there right now. Or dead.

Tommy's thoughts were interrupted by the squawk of his intercom box, followed by the thick New Jersey accent of his boss. "Any updates on Bennett? I've got to brief the committee in ten minutes."

"Yes, Director Woods," Tommy replied with a tone of studied respect. "Bennett's going through a PIV check at the Mackinac Bridge. I've got two felony charges for speeding and reckless driving over the last hour. I've got the metrics and a USDA truck driver as a corroborating witness. You want me to alert the State Police to pick him up?" That might buy some time, Tommy hoped. Bennett is toast, but maybe I can still warn his associates.

"No, don't do a damn thing. We want the rabbit to run to its lair. My Do Not Detain order went out, right?"

"Yes, sir. Just the State Police and PIV checks. No sheriffs."

"That's right. I don't trust those damn sheriffs. Half of them are rebel sympathizers. Let me know if anything changes."

"Yes sir, I'll keep you posted."

What a tool, Sutton muttered to himself after he disconnected the intercom. Reginald Woods was a bureaucratic brownnose who didn't know squat about cyber-surveillance. He had just been promoted to Assistant Deputy Director, largely due to Tommy's work. Now he insisted on being addressed as "Director Woods." Despite his incompetence, or maybe because of it, Reggie was a rising star in Domestic Counterterrorism and not to be messed with.

Tommy looked back up at the monitor and saw that Bennett was on the move again. They figured he was heading for the Aux Baie area where his co-conspirators were holed up. Because his partners were off grid, the surveillance team had struggled to get a fix on their real-time whereabouts, and the local authorities had been less than helpful. But then they had uncovered a target site, and now Bennett was leading them right to the place where they could spring the trap.

If only he could warn Bennett—but how? He could use his prepaid burner phone, but that was squirreled away at home. He could route a message through various VPNs, but it still could be traced. Besides, any direct contact with Bennett would be flagged and they would arrest him on the spot. Tommy framed the problem in his head: How do I indirectly contact Bennett, right now, without using my own devices?

Reggie was about to brief the committee. That meant Reggie would be using the secure conference room. And that meant his office should be empty. A smile crossed Tommy's face as he unwrapped another candy bar, took a bite, rolled up the wrapper, and tossed it at the trash can. Nothing but net.

Straits of Mackinac – 8:00 am

"Thank you, Mr. Bennett. There's a mini-mart on the other side of the bridge. Please be careful of the potholes, we're still under construction. Is there anything else I can assist you with?" The attendant beamed, showing no sign of alarm at the Do Not Detain advisory that had flashed across her console throughout Scott's PIV check.

"No, I'm good, thanks," Scott replied, pleased that the attendant hadn't mentioned his speeding violations. He rolled up the window and quickly shifted through gears as the Porsche started to ascend the Mackinac Bridge. It was in a sad state of disrepair and was quite obviously not under construction.

Scott had been on the bridge before, but it never ceased to amaze him. Connecting the lower peninsula of Michigan with the state's Upper Peninsula, the Mighty Mac was over five miles in length and towered 150 feet over the Straits of Mackinac, which connected Lakes Michigan and Huron. At the top of the span, Scott looked eastward toward the rising sun. Driven by a brisk southerly breeze, white caps speckled the waters below. In the distance was Mackinac Island. He searched for, and found, the outline of the historic Grand Hotel, the island's signature building.

Before The Crash, the island had buzzed with tourists enjoying the novelty of a place without cars or motor vehicles. Everything moved by horse-drawn carriage or bicycle. Visitors and residents crossed between the mainland and the island on a fleet of ferries. Today, Scott didn't see a single ferry, or even a freighter, in the near shore waters. Commerce had come to halt, although the Grand Hotel was still used for high-level government consortiums. His dad had attended several of them.

As he sped forward to his destination in the Upper Peninsula, he thought back to the beginning of the journey that had brought him to this bridge at this moment. Just over a year ago, fresh out of business school, he'd gone to DC to ask for his dad's support of his startup business. That 22-year-old Scott had lived in a vastly different world. How had change come so fast?

TWO

13 Months Prior

Washington DC – September 11, 9:00 am
Rayburn House Office Building

"Unbelievable," Rep. Steve Bennett said as he hung up the phone on his immaculate desk. Due to his seniority, the conservative Congressman had one of the prize offices in the Rayburn Building, with a clear view of the Capital Dome. It was a fitting office for the ranking member of the House Committee on Homeland Security.

"What's going on?"

Steve turned in surprise to see his son, Scott, who must have sneaked into his office.

"I've been disinvited from the Elay University immigration roundtable," Steve said, shaking his head in disgust. "You'll never guess why: because of my stand on immigration! Their Student Action Council and some faculty signed a petition and made a stink. That was Chancellor Brown giving me the good news."

"I guess they haven't heard of free speech up there. What's the point of a roundtable if you don't have varying points of view? Someone should take a copy of *1984* and shove it up their thought police asses!" Scott said.

"You're reading George Orwell now?" Steve felt he knew his son well, but new developments in Scott's intellectual growth always had the capacity to surprise.

"Tim gave me a copy. He's using it in his first class today. Kind of depressing."

Steve's eyebrows went up. The fact that his son's business

partner was moonlighting was not a good sign. Maybe their cash position is worse than he thought...

"*1984* is depressing, but prophetic. College students and the professors who enable them often can't see the forest for the trees. Disinviting me is right out of a totalitarian playbook. Yet they're convinced they hold the moral high ground. In the name of pluralism and tolerance, they censure free speech and political debate. I have to hand it to them; their position takes some impressive doublethink mental gymnastics."

"You should publicly call them out on this," Scott said.

"That would be pointless. If the administration backed down and let me participate, I'd be shouted down. If the mainstream media got hold of it, they'd call it a progressive victory over intolerance. It's an upside-down world, Scott. People who defend free speech, individual liberties, and free enterprise are branded as intolerant. Meanwhile, people who promote censorship, identity politics, and a state-controlled command economy are called progressive."

"Why don't we fight back? Why don't we make a stink and protest at Elay?"

"Scott, I'm beginning to wonder if the professors at your fancy college gave you sufficient grounding in the fundamentals of American politics. With few exceptions, it's not in a true conservative's nature to join in group protests. We stress individualism and freedom, not collectivism. Progressive activists have more of a hive mentality. They band together to protest anything and anybody that is foreign to their worldview."

"Yeah, but we're a center-right country. Progressives are in the minority, but their voices drown out the rest of us."

"The real danger is progressives hide behind a veneer of fairness. Who can argue with fairness?" Steve spread out his hands to emphasize the point. "Problem is, their fairness comes with an all-encompassing administrative state to dole out the fairness, the entitlements, the welfare. Just scratch the surface, and underneath you'll find sheer power politics, with drones to bully and shame any individual who challenges their ideology."

"They're in it for sheer power politics?" Scott asked. "Some of the loudest liberal voices are people of privilege: movie stars, sports stars, billionaires, celebrities. They already have power."

"You know, I've thought long and hard about this. I think you can divide progressive activists into three camps. First among them are the genuinely altruistic people who want to help the disadvantaged. They devote their time and resources to making things better one-on-one in their own communities. I admire and respect them." Steve took a sip out of his coffee cup before continuing.

"The second group embraces the neo-Marxist ideology that a struggle between the haves and have-nots is inevitable. They confuse equal opportunity with equal outcomes. The way they pursue social justice fosters perpetual victimhood. They're the people who shout down college speakers, rough up conservative students, and cyberbully anyone who challenges their narrative. They remind me of the student-led Red Guards of Mao's Cultural Revolution who humiliated and punished everyone who didn't toe the Party line—the traditionalists, the middle class, the intellectuals." Scott's dad paused to grimace. "Can you imagine if they'd had Twitter back then?"

Scott shuddered.

"Then there's the last group, the ones who puzzle you the most, Scott. Some wealthy progressives—many of them politicians and celebrities—seem to suffer from some perverse form of privilege guilt. To inoculate themselves from being branded as rich elites or bigots or capitalists, they throw themselves into liberal causes. They demand reparations for past sins committed by the same America that gives them their power and prestige. They argue for a paternalistic nanny state that makes the poor dependent on handouts, diminishing the very people they claim to want to help."

"I know, but…" Scott was cut short by a knock on the door.

Marge, Steve's assistant, stuck her head in the room.

"I'm sorry to barge in, but John Bowden is on the phone. He's says its urgent, something about Israel."

"Okay, go ahead and connect him through," Steve replied. John Bowden, the DHS Under Secretary, was a no-nonsense man. If he said it was urgent, it was urgent. "Scott, why don't you wait in the conference room? This shouldn't take long, then we'll grab a bite to eat."

"Sounds good," Scott said.

Steve watched his son follow Marge out of the office before picking up the phone. "John, what's the problem?"

"Your father tells me you're working on an invention, cold fusion or something." Marge led Scott into the adjacent conference room.

"Oh, not cold fusion!" Scott chuckled. "We're experimenting with a new plasma drive that could revolutionize power generation. But we keep getting stonewalled by DOE—the Department of Energy. I thought dad might help cut through some red tape."

He smiled at Marge and met her eyes directly. She had been with Congressman Bennett since his beginnings in Grand Rapids and was considered family. Marge was old school, routinely dressing up in a skirt and high heels for work. As his dad's administrative assistant, Marge now traveled with him between Grand Rapids and DC.

"Well, he knows everybody," Marge said. "Introductions shouldn't be a problem. I'm sure he has connections at Energy. Who else is on your team?"

"My business partner is Tim Kelly. He's a serial entrepreneur. You might have met him at Uncle Sean's funeral. He was there with Aunt Jenny."

"Oh, that was such a tragedy," Marge furrowed her brow. "That poor couple was living under a dark cloud."

"Our chief scientist is Karl Schultz. He retired from Lockheed Martin a few years back. A bit crazy, but a brilliant inventor. The best part is he's on a mission to complete what a relative started back in the '70s. His Uncle Jacob was experimenting with a prototype plasma drive but was shut down for some reason. DOE denies there was even a project. But here's the thing," Scott lowered his voice to a conspiratorial whisper, "Karl's got his uncle's handwritten notes."

"Oh really!" Marge arched her eyebrows.

"Yes. All we need now is a breakthrough."

THREE

Despite the gusting winds and churning surf, it was eerily quiet. Jack crested the huge wave on his sailboard and prepared to reverse direction—to gybe—like he'd done a thousand times before. With a quick pump of the boom, he unhooked his harness from the boom line. He bent his knees and placed his weight on the balls of his feet to carve the sailboard into the trough behind the receding wave. As the board swung downwind, Jack released his back hand so the sail would flip over the bow and...disaster. As the sail released, the dangling boom line reattached to the hook protruding from his harness. With the sail now fully exposed to the wind and anchored to Jack, there was only one possible outcome: he and the sail were slammed to the water.

When he regained his bearings, Jack found himself under both water and sail. He tried to swim away, but a half twist had locked the boom line to his harness. Fighting a rising panic, Jack tried to loosen the line, but it was too tight. As the oxygen ran out from his last shallow breath, Jack had a moment of clarity. He grabbed the boom and pivoted his body back to its original position to unwind the twist. Free at last, Jack swam under the sail and grabbed on to his board, letting his lungs fill with life-saving breath. With the immediate threat over, Jack looked to shore for help.

Jenny Hernandez, his college lover, stood on the beach pointing at him, or was she pointing behind him? He turned around and could see land. It must be Wisconsin, although that was impossible! But there it was, and smoke was billowing across the water. He looked back at the shore. Jenny pointed behind him with increasing urgency. He turned around again and saw a young bear paddling toward him. Jack knew the cub would grab him to stay afloat. It came closer and closer. Just as the cub lunged forward to hug him, Jack used his lifeguard training to stiff-arm the cub in the chest. He then tried to grab the infant's arm and spin him around on his back, so he could apply a cross-chest carry. But he missed the arm and the infant started to sink, deeper and deeper into the dark water...

KABOOM! The thunderclap shook the house and woke Jack up. His heart was thumping, and he was in a cold sweat. The dream sequence was beginning to slip from his consciousness. He was windsurfing, there was smoke, and a bear, and he could see...Wisconsin? And Jenny?

BOOM! Another thunderclap shook the house and the meaning of the dream flashed into his mind. He could picture Jenny telling him the Legend of Sleeping Bear Dunes as if it had been yesterday. They sat high on the dunes overlooking the distant Manitou Islands. Her long, black hair flowed freely in the wind, tickling his face every now and then as she spoke.

"A massive fire in Wisconsin drove a mother bear and her two cubs into Lake Michigan. The cubs faithfully followed their mother as she swam for the distant shores of Michigan. Within sight of shore, the cubs were exhausted. One cub, and then the other, sank beneath the waves and drowned. Mother Bear made it to shore and turned around to wait for her cubs. Seeing her anguish, the Great Spirit Manitou created islands to mark the places where the cubs had succumbed and blew wind to bury Mother Bear in sand. To this very day, she waits for her cubs."

A wave of wistfulness overcame Jack as he thought of Jenny and their brief but intense college love affair. He grimaced as he realized that, while his memory of their day at the Dunes was clear, other memories were not. Too much partying back then, he conceded.

Forcibly clearing his mind, Jack looked at the clock on his nightstand. 9:00 am. Damn! He'd slept in. He had wanted to get an early start for what promised to be an epic day for windsurfing and kiting. Jack got out of bed, donned his blue jeans, and quietly walked down the hall past his daughter's room. Meg was sound asleep after a night out with friends. Jack had lain awake until she returned home around 2 am. Even though she was a grown woman, he worried. But Meg had her act together, certainly more than he had at age 22.

Once in the kitchen, Jack prepped the coffee maker. Coffee was one of his few remaining vices, and he indulged in it freely. As the coffee perked, he grabbed his smartphone and pulled up the news. Banner headlines warned of a *Middle East Meltdown*. Jack dismissed them with same shit, different day indifference and navigated to the current radar loop for the upper Midwest. The recent line of thunderstorms was departing east over Michigan. He was more interested in Wisconsin, where another line of storms was forming. Probably will get here midday, he noted with some concern. Everything pointed to gonzo conditions. A classic backdoor cold front was coming through with winds accelerating out of the southwest until the low passed. Small craft warnings were up, and it was already blowing 20 knots at the mid-lake buoy. Lake Michigan, or *Mishigami* as Jenny used to call it, would be rocking and rolling. Point Betsie was the place to be.

Jack drew a mental picture of the lake in his mind: 200 miles of fetch, or distance, from Chicago at its southern end to Point Betsie, which jutted out into the northern reaches of the lake. With the winds Jack expected today, ocean-like swells would march up the lake to reach 10, 15, or even 20 feet. If it got too big, he'd suggest to Meg that they go a few miles south to kiteboard in the lee of Frankfort Harbor's massive piers. But Jack wanted to hit Point Betsie. For sheer wind and waves, the Point was ground zero for windsurfing in northern Michigan. The Point was never crowded: beginners seldom braved it because of its wicked crosscurrent and a steep drop off from shore. If you got in trouble on the inside, you faced the crushing surf break and the metal jetties that protected the historic lighthouse. If you got in trouble on the outside, you faced a triathlete-level swim back to shore. Or, worse, you might be carried by wind, waves, and current out to the Manitou Passage, 20 or so miles in the distance. At least there was one consolation: no sharks in Lake Michigan.

Smartphone still in hand, Jack called his construction boss to confirm he was taking the day off. Rigs would understand—he was a former kiter who'd had to quit after blowing out both ACLs. The call connected. Jack turned on the speakerphone.

"Matt Riggins."

"Hey Rigs, it's Jack. As I told you, Meg's in town and..."

"I know, I know," Rigs cut him off. "Looks like it will be nuking out there today. Wish I could join you, but someone's got to work."

"You still got worker issues?" Jack asked.

"Are you kidding me? Half the guys won't work more hours because it would cut their benefits. The other half show up stoned out of their minds. So much for legalized marijuana; these guys are an accident waiting to happen. But they're all I got. I'm supposed to test them, but they'd all fail. The state legalizes pot and then expects me to police the stoners. How crazy is that?"

"I'm sorry Rigs." Jack didn't have the gumption to point out that the people, not the state, had passed the referendum to legalize marijuana. "I'll put in some make-up hours. I just can't pass on the opportunity to be on the water with Meg today."

"Don't sweat it. You're the only sober worker I have left. Have a great session and be safe. Say hi to Meg for me."

"Shall do. Thanks Rigs."

Jack ended the call and poured himself a cup of coffee. He walked down the hall and cracked open Meg's door.

"Hey Meg, time to get up. If it's blowin', we're goin'!" Meg greeted his goofy kiter's creed with a groan as she turned over and pulled a pillow on top of her head.

Meg had recently graduated from Grand Valley State with a degree in education and $30,000 in debt. She was trying to stay in the area but was finding it hard to pay the bills on the wages of a substitute teacher. Michigan continued to lose population and there were few full-time teaching positions open. Meg was sharing an apartment with a friend in Grand Rapids. She was near her mother, but two hours south of Jack's meager house in Traverse City. He'd hate to see her move further away for work.

Meg meant the world to Jack. After the divorce, his time with his only child had been limited. Now that she was of age, they got together much more often. She looked like her mother: blue eyes, dishwater blonde hair, and high Germanic cheekbones. But her disposition was more like Jack's: an adrenalin junkie who took things to the limit. She'd be as excited as he was about the day's conditions—if he could just get her out of bed.

FOUR

Traverse City, MI

Tim Kelly, co-founder of Plasma Drive Technologies, stood by the shore, his tall, lanky body silhouetted against the waters of East Bay. He adjusted his thick-lensed glasses, even though they were already on straight. He could see the faint glow of a sunrise trying to break through the rolling clouds of the departing thunderstorm. The bay was calm except for a slight undulation that made it look like liquid mercury. All was quiet except the caw of a seagull up the shore and the distant rumble of thunder.

The clean, almost chlorine-like smell of ozone hung in the air, and it was driving Tim crazy. It's all right there, he thought. Nature's atmospheric friction ionizing the air, loosening electrons and positive ions and, presto chango, lightning! Plasma on a huge scale leaving as a byproduct O3, ozone. If nature could do it, why couldn't his team? Karl Schultz, their chief scientist, had the inventive intuition. Scott Bennett, his business partner, had the political connections. And I —well I'm supposed to have the brains.

Tim took a deep slug of coffee from his travel mug. He'd spent a restless night brainstorming plasma drive next steps, fretting over the business, and reassessing the lesson plan for his first college class. The worries were all related, he realized. No dream of a plasma drive, no startup company; no startup company, no cash crunch; no cash crunch, no need to moonlight at Traverse University. He hoped Scott would have some luck in DC today raising much-needed investment funds.

He returned his attention to the bay and focused. One

of Tim's four degrees was in environmental biology. He saw things others didn't. This morning he focused on the record-breaking high water levels that were wreaking havoc for beachfront homeowners. Just eight years ago, he had visited Jenny Hernandez's cabin in the U.P. and water levels were at all-time lows, creating massive beaches. These wild swings were unprecedented for the Great Lakes and added credence to climate change theories.

Of course, time was a matter of perspective when considering climate change, Tim contemplated. Just 20,000 years ago, a mere blink of the eye in geological terms, two-mile-high glaciers had marched down from the north to carve out the Great Lakes. He could only imagine the impact this onslaught of cold and ice had on any indigenous people. As the glaciers retreated, they left in their wake quintillions of gallons of fresh water to fill the trenches they had created. The Great Lakes now hold 20% of the earth's fresh water. If global warming gets really bad, Tim thought pensively, the Great Lakes might become the last watering hole.

Tim's thoughts returned to Jenny. The sandstone cliffs protecting her cabin must be taking a beating with the high waters—just like the beating Jenny had taken over the years. Tim grimaced at the thought of Jenny's marriage to his college friend, Sean Bennett, and its horrible ending. He made a point of keeping in touch with Jenny. Besides being an old friend, he felt at least a tad culpable for her failed marriage and Sean's suicide.

In college, he and Sean would dive into great philosophical debates. As a dyed-in-the-wool determinist, Sean agreed with Bertrand Russell that free will is just an illusion, and everything is predetermined by circumstances. Tim took the side of free will and added a healthy dose of quantum mechanics; since we can't predict outcomes with certainty, and the best we can do is establish probability, cause is a moot point. He and Sean went back and forth over years of beers, neither willing to offer concessions. It was great fun and it honed Tim's debating skills. But he never saw or realized the depth of Sean's addiction. Even if he had, could he have made a difference?

Tim realized he was off on a tangent again, a self-diagnosed bad habit. He adjusted his glasses, which were still on straight, and looked at his watch, 9:00 am. He was running late. Class started in 30 minutes! His anxiety level went up a notch as he turned from the bay and strode briskly on long legs back to his nearby house.

Across the bay, and now far away, lightning pulsed in the high, roiling clouds of the departing thunderstorm—but Tim was too far away to hear the thunder.

FIVE

Aux Baie, MI
Jenny's Camp

Despite a sense of foreboding, Jenny cracked open the cabin door to let Toby out. The two-year-old black lab bolted through the opening and headed toward the bushes to take care of business. With no barking or growling, Jenny felt reassured there was no imminent danger. Still, she felt a general unease she couldn't quite put her finger on. Maybe it was last night's ominous dreams, the meaning of which eluded her. Or being the sole person on an 80-acre plot of wilderness... "This is silly," she told herself. She had been visiting or living in this cabin her whole life—there was nothing to fear.

With renewed courage, Jenny exited the cabin to inspect her compound. She walked by the side of the cabin to confirm her over-sized root cellar was closed and secure. Farther down the path, the detached garage with her family name "Hernandez" plastered on it looked undisturbed. Jenny approached her battery house to ensure the door was shut. In the distance, on a hill, she could see her three 5-kilowatt windmills standing still in the morning calm. Everything seemed to be in order.

Jenny continued her trek inland to check out her prize possessions; two 1,800-square-foot greenhouses wedged into a moraine that had been left by retreating glaciers. With southern exposures and solar panels, the greenhouses could produce well into the fall. They were Jenny's primary source of income and barter. She owed a tremendous debt of gratitude to her brother-in-law, Steve Bennett, who had sorted out her parent's estate to free up cash for the greenhouses. He didn't have to do that, Jenny figured, he was a busy congressman and her marriage to his brother had ended dreadfully with abuse, divorce, and suicide.

Jenny quickly shutdown her awful memories and entered one of the greenhouses. Warmth, humidity, and a rich, loamy smell greeted her. As she walked down the aisles, Jenny used her fingers to test the soil for moisture and greeted her plants with praise; "You look wonderful today," she greeted the tomatoes. "Are you getting enough water?" she asked the peppers and kale. "You are producing so well! Thank you for your gifts," she told the beans, which were plentiful and ripe. At first, her co-op friends—she jokingly referred to them as the Church Ladies—had laughed at her communion with the vegetables. But soon they began to mimic her, and the gardens and greenhouses were alive with song and praise.

As she exited the greenhouse, Jenny made a mental note that one of the LED lights was out in the greenhouse. She would have her maintenance man, Johnny-B, check it out. This summer they had started experimenting with low energy lighting to increase yield and extend the season. Like her father, Jenny was determined to remain off the power grid, so they were dependent on solar and wind. Since Aux Baie was smack in the middle of Lake Superior's snow belt, the solar panels were barely adequate. If she could just find another source of clean energy, Jenny thought, she could keep the greenhouses producing all year long.

Farther down the two-track, Jenny inspected her four acres of fenced in gardens. Although there were deer tracks around the perimeter, it looked like no raiders had managed to jump the eight-foot fence. Jenny made another mental note that some of the late season crops—sweet corn, tomatoes, sweet potatoes, and eggplant—needed harvesting. That meant rallying the Church Ladies and the 4H kids. And, with no cell service, that meant a trip to town.

Satisfied that her compound was secure, Jenny gave a loud

finger whistle to retrieve Toby and headed toward the cliffs by the shore. As a child, Jenny had often hiked this path with her dad who was one-quarter Chippewa. He was proud of their indigenous heritage and explained to Jenny how the tribal economy was centered on nature. He taught her to use the forest for bows and arrows, teepees, and canoes. He showed her how to differentiate edible mushrooms and berries from poisonous ones, how to identify and track an animal using footprints left in the dirt or snow, and how to net and spear fish from the lake. He told Jenny that the Chippewa live in harmony with nature and don't willfully destroy or kill without reason. "Why would we hurt Mother Earth?" he would ask her pointedly.

As she grew older, Jenny's father touched on more serious subjects: the arrival of Europeans, the subjugation of indigenous peoples, the clear-cutting of the climax forest to feed the white man's cities and economy, and the strip-mining of the land for copper and iron ore. She soaked it all up and blossomed into a naturalist. She loved talking with her father as they hiked the shores of Ojibwe *Gichigami* ("Ojibwa's Great Sea"). Now she walked the same shores with a different companion. "Come on Toby, we're almost there," she said, struggling up the last incline to her perch 60 feet above the water.

To her left were the remains of an old osprey's nest snug in the crook of a weathered cedar tree. To her right were several birch trees clinging tenuously to the side of the cliff. Strange how life found a way to hang in there, she pondered. Strange how she had done the same. Straight ahead, as far as she could see, stretched glistening water, all the way from her home in Michigan's Upper Peninsula to the distant shores of Canada far beyond the horizon. From this vantage point, nothing in her field of vision was man-made. She could imagine that she had been transported back to the days of her distant ancestors. It was Jenny's favorite spot to meditate. But not today. Not with this free-floating anxiety.

Having worked up a sweat, and noticing the dirt caked

under her fingernails, Jenny knew she needed to cleanup before venturing to town. "Come on Toby, let's take a dip." Toby
jumped up eagerly, tail wagging and ready to go. Retracing her
steps back down the path, Jenny reached a gully that ran toward the water. She carefully picked her way down the mossy
slope, weaving between immature trees and seedlings, until
she reached a cove dug out of the cliffs. Toby ran ahead to
smell, pee mark, and explore. With the high water levels, the
shore was mostly sandstone, but with a few patches of granu-
lar sand. Taking off her sandals, Jenny tested the water—cool,
but not bad for Lake Superior in September. The water still
held the heat of an unusually warm summer. Improved swimming was one benefit of global warming, she thought darkly.

Jenny walked to a nearby rock and started to disrobe, delighting in the early-morning sun. She slipped off her sweatshirt, placing it on a rock followed by her denim work shirt,
khaki shorts, and bikini underwear. At age 42, her body was
trim and well-toned, a testament to daily yoga and a healthy
diet. Her skin was supple, and her dark complexion revealed
just a trace of a farmer's tan from work in her gardens. She
waded into the water, the sandstone bottom like sandpaper
on her feet, until it was safe to dive. Under water, she felt in-
vigorated and cleansed; she thought of her swimming ritual as
a daily baptism in God's holy waters. Surfacing, Jenny pulled
her long black hair into a wet ponytail that draped down the
nape of her neck.

Hearing Jenny splash in the water, Toby came running down
the beach to join her. He jumped into the water and lunged forward until it was too deep, then started to dog paddle. As she
watched the furry ball of unconditional love approach, she
thought, as she often did, that it would be nice to share the joy
of Toby's company with a partner, with a child. Her thoughts
brought on a familiar pang of loneliness and sorrow, and a
wave of painful memories overcame her. Jenny dove back
under the water to stop the thoughts, but they came flooding
in anyway—her college crush on Jack Conrad, the clandestine

abortion, their breakup, her failed marriage, an empty womb. "Lord, please help me to stop thinking this way," she prayed as she waded back to the shore.

Toby followed Jenny out of the water. Finding a piece of driftwood on the shore, he came running to greet her, stick in mouth, an invitation to play that no child could have resisted. Jenny used her hands to brush off excess water from her goose bumped skin and then dressed, water patches darkening her shirt and shorts. She slipped on and latched her sandals and finally turned her attention to Toby, grabbing the stick from his mouth and tossing it out on the water. Jenny watched as Toby retrieved the stick, swam back, dropped the stick in front of her, and sprayed her with a full body shake. He would happily do this all day. She felt a moment of envy at the simplicity of Toby's existence: fetch and retrieve, run, pee, explore, eat, sleep, repeat. If only she could set her mind on some kind of instinctive autopilot. But, of course, she couldn't. Besides, she had to get to town to rally her co-op friends and pick up some groceries.

Jenny smiled at the thought of her closest friends. Mary DeVries, the Pastor's wife, who had brought her back to Christ and was now like a second mother. Cindy Beers who, like Jenny, was on Church Council but also had the best goat cheese in northern Michigan. A very pregnant Tina Cutler who, along with her husband, provided the surrounding area with the finest organic chicken and eggs. And, of course, Johnny-B— the kind veteran and only African American in town. Besides maintaining her compound, he was an endless source of fresh Whitefish and Lake Trout. After years of solitude and shame, Jenny was grateful for the community she was building. She might not have a mate, but that was okay—lovers had only caused her anguish.

SIX

Meg finally came out of the guest bedroom in her PJs, smartphone in hand. "Got any yogurt?" she asked as she grabbed a mug from the shelf and poured herself some coffee.

"Yeah. Bananas and granola, too," Jack replied. "Did you hear the thunderstorm?"

"Yep," Meg sat down at the small kitchen table and instantly became lost in her smartphone.

Probably checking Facebook and Twitter to see how many likes she racked up overnight, Jack surmised. Maybe he was just getting old, but he couldn't figure out Meg's social world. She had 2,000 Facebook friends, but she freely admitted she would only consider talking face-to-face with a few of them. Social media was her faux community, where friends and followers determined her popularity and standing, and it was all recorded for posterity. To Jack, it seemed narcissistic, bragging to everybody about the great time you were having, the cool people you were hanging out with, the amazing trip you were on, the great new toy you bought, the fantastic promotion you received, the neat relationship you were in. Hey, that's great! Good for you! The mere fact that he knew what FOMO meant confirmed his worries: the envy and jealousy generated by these posts was a real and negative force.

Fear of Missing Out wasn't something Jack grew up with. His social world centered around the kids in his neighborhood and the spontaneous games they played. They were always outside doing something. Each kid knew the rules of playground justice and who to pick for teams—who was fastest, who was smartest, who was a brat, who was a sissy, who was a bully. On the streets of his childhood, they'd figured out how to resolve conflicts and coexist with their peers. Otherwise, they risked the almighty hand of parental authority. These days, the way Meg explained it, when kids got together in person, it was all about diversity, inclusiveness, peer mediation, fairness, and the *everybody is a winner* drivel schools were dishing out. Maybe these kids would grow up to create a world of perfect harmony, free from conflict. If not, they were going to lack crucial social skills they'd need to survive in the dog-eat-dog world.

He shook himself out of his reverie. He could talk to Meg in his head any time. He was grateful she was here, now. He tried to engage his only daughter as he poured two bowls of granola and passed one over.

"Whatcha looking at?"

"Save The Date invite for Brad and Ian's wedding in March." Meg hadn't looked up once from her smartphone.

"Oh, great," Jack replied with thick sarcasm in his voice.

That made her look up. "You're homophobic," she said, knowing it would push his hot button.

Jack took the bait. "That's politically correct bullshit. Just because I don't believe in gay marriage doesn't make me a homophobe. Ian and Brad are great, I wish them only the best. I'm not afraid of gays, I don't hate gays, nothing like that. However, I *am* afraid of the progressive agenda to change our culture. And your generation has totally drunk the Kool-Aid!"

"What does that even mean?" Meg asked.

Jack wondered if he should bring Jonestown into his answer. "It means you've bought into the propaganda about redefining traditional marriage. Whatever happened to civil unions? I was fine with that. Acknowledging your commitment, inheritance, insurance. I get it. But calling it marriage? They've hijacked the word and its historical meaning."

"Dad, the Supreme Court and the majority of Americans approve of gay marriage. You're a dinosaur!"

Meg often took the devil's advocate position in their discussions, but those were fighting words. "Listen, most of the world still rejects gay marriage. Just because the US and Western Europe have trashed the traditional definition doesn't make it right. Since the dawn of time, marriage has been between a man and a woman. Then, overnight, it morphed into..." Jack searched for the right word. "Into a legal concept. But it's not abstract law, it's simple biology. And now there's all this gender fluidity stuff."

"So, marriage is just about having sex and producing children? It means nothing more than that?" Meg was not going to let it die. "Why can't two partners declare their love and have all the rights everyone else has, including the right to adopt and raise children? So many kids need loving parents, and so many gay couples have the means, the desire, and the love to provide great homes. It would be a crime to keep them apart."

"You miss my point." Jack was not ready to back down. "The existence of opposite sexes, male and female, is nature's blueprint for the procreation of the species. It's the yin and yang of the universe. It's a biological imperative, for God's sake." Jack took a deep breath. He knew he was losing his cool, but he couldn't help himself. "Growing up these days must be more confusing than ever. Now we've got kids running around trying to dial in their gender like it's some kind of self-controlled thermostat."

"Whatever," Meg replied. "It's unfair. It's a matter of civil rights. Besides, as Christians we should reach out to those who are discriminated against and bullied. What would Jesus do?"

"Listen Meg, Jesus brought grace, but he also brought truth. And the truth is that marriage is a sacred bond between a man and a woman. If progressives can redefine that, then there is no objective truth anymore."

"Yeah, just like your marriage to Mom was sacred."

Touché, Jack thought. "That was different. Your mother had every right to leave me. Let's change the subject."

They finished breakfast without speaking.

"We should leave in about half an hour," Jack said, breaking the silence. "I want to hit Point Betsie early. There might be another line of thunderstorms coming."

"Okay." Meg placed her dishes in the sink and headed for the shower.

Jack grabbed a cooler and stuffed it full of bottled water, Gatorade, granola bars, and snacks. He went outside to finish loading his infamous *surfmobile*, a trusty Subaru stacked high with boards and crammed full of kites, sails, and gear. The inside of the station wagon smelled unmistakably of skunky used wetsuits. But the old Subaru was all Jack could afford on his part-time construction worker wages. It had been a long time since he was on salary, way back in the old days when he was still drinking. He felt a pang of guilt knowing he'd failed Meg on college expenses. At least he could treat her to a day off at the beach. Damn! He wished they hadn't started off the day with an argument.

SEVEN

Washington DC
Rayburn House Office Building

"Can I get you some water or coffee" Marge asked.

"No, I'm fine" Scott said, although he was beginning to wonder why it was taking his dad so long to complete his call.

Suddenly, Steve Bennett burst into the conference room. "We've got a problem!" The concern etched on his face gave Scott a chill; his dad was not an alarmist.

"Scott, I want you and Marge out of DC immediately." Steve reached in his suit coat, pulled out his cell phone, and hit a speed dial icon. "I want you to fly back to Michigan ASAP."

"Dad, what's going on?"

"I can't get into specifics, but Israeli security has gone ballistic. They think a terrorist attack is imminent. Something big..."

Steve put his cell phone up to his ear. "Dan? Where are you? Good. Listen carefully, I want you to reposition the plane over to Manassas. File whatever flight plan you need to file and get over there ASAP. Scott and Marge will meet you there within the hour. Get them back to Michigan any way you can. There's a chance things might close down..."

Scott listened carefully, trying to sense what the hell was going on. Dan Fisher, his dad's pilot, was a battle-hardened veteran from Desert Storm. His involvement upped the ante.

"...yeah, you know what I mean. Might have to stretch some rules." Scott's dad ended the call with a simple, "Good."

"Dad, please tell us, what's going on?" Scott repeated.

"Hopefully, nothing, but Israeli security has picked up intel of Hamas agents fleeing Tel Aviv. They've never seen this behavior before. They're going apeshit and mobilizing forces. If it's a coordinated terrorist strike, we may be in play too. I want you out of DC now."

"Isn't this a bit extreme?" Scott's protest was cut short by his father.

"Marge, you're parked over in the garage, right? I want you to drive Scott over to Manassas Airport. Dan will be waiting with the plane. I want you to go now and go fast. Take Highway 66, it should be quicker. Okay?"

"Yes, sir," Marge said. "Are you sure you don't want me to come back to provide support?"

"No. If this blows over, you can fly right back. If it doesn't, I want you in Michigan. I've got to go, an emergency meeting with DHS. I don't want either of you to talk to anybody about this, okay? Top secret. No talk, no calls, nothing. Calling Dan was probably a mistake, people are listening, but I had no choice. Okay?"

"Sure dad," Scott replied. "Are you really that worried?" He searched his dad's eyes and saw the answer before he heard it.

"Yes. I am." Congressman Bennett stepped over and gave his son a hug. "Love you," he said.

"I love you, too."

Steve gave Marge a quick hug, whispered something in her ear, and then started to exit the conference room. He stopped and turned to meet Scott's eyes.

"Oh, and that plasma thing—drop it. There are some powerful people watching you." Steve turned and sped down the hall, leaving Scott and Marge in stunned silence.

EIGHT

Traverse University

Tim put his Nalgene on a shelf under the lectern. His heart was racing. He hoped he could present in a confident, direct, and bold manner with cold, clammy hands. He took a deep breath, straightened his glasses, and looked up at the class. They were too busy chatting and looking at their phones to even notice him. "Fear and control," Tim said louder than intended, but it had the desired effect—the class went dead silent.

"Good morning. I'm Tim Kelly and this is Political Ecosystems. This is my first class at TU, and I am going to take a rather unorthodox approach for this senior seminar. This class will be a PC-free zone, as in no political correctness. I am going to cover subjects that will make you feel uncomfortable, whatever your politics may be. I'm not a progressive, I'm not a conservative—I am a disruptor who intends to challenge your worldview. If you can't handle the discomfort I intend to cause with this approach, I suggest you drop this course now and try something else."

Tim felt all 30 sets of eyes in the room fix on him intently. Well, I've got their attention, Tim thought. At the back of the class, the Department Chairman, Ken Weaver, rolled his eyes. Tim hadn't expected that Ken would observe his first class. Oh well, too late to turn back now, Tim thought.

"The basic premise behind this class is elementary: humans yearn for a sense of well-being, and they organize political ecosystems to achieve it. Pretty simple, right? What's not so simple is the essential nature of man, and the fact that we've evolved from primitive cave dwellers to become masters of the earth in a relatively brief period of time.

"Faced with the existential triple threat of needing food, shelter, and safety, people organized families, churches, and communities. The well-being afforded by these groups allowed for the creation of ever-more powerful organizations. Kingdoms, empires, and nation-states leveraged bureaucracy and technology to create unimaginable wealth. Free market democracies unleashed the creative genius of capitalism and modern organizations. Very quickly, man found himself a long way from hunter-gatherer family groups.

"But the seeds of chaos were there from the beginning, embedded in the very nature of man and the organizations he creates. Our instinctive drive for more, the dynamo of capitalism, has led inexorably to the exploitation of our brethren and the environment. Organizations create and govern wealth, but they also become ends unto themselves; self-licking ice cream cones with the sole purpose of self-propagation."

Tim adjusted his glasses and shifted on his feet. Time to test the waters. "We meet here today in the most prosperous nation in history. Yet, ironically, our country has become rudderless, splintered, and full of oxymoronic paradoxes. We have lots of law, but little order. We celebrate in-your-face diversity while we bemoan a lack of commonality. We revere the environment yet condone the taking of emergent life. We preach about the rules of war—an oxymoron if ever there was one—while our missiles rain down on people all over the world. Our weapons fall from drones piloted by military personnel who sit at consoles in Kansas. When their shifts are over, they go home and have dinner with their families. Nice and tidy. But where's that in the rule book?"

Tim paused to scan the room. No one is doodling, no one is looking at a phone, no one is moving—all good signs, he thought. "Have I offended any sensibilities yet? If I have, it's by design. I am here to make you think critically, not to coddle you." He sensed openness and interest in the room, and hoped he wasn't imagining things.

"Today we're going to preview the semester ahead. First, we'll create a matrix to explore the range of political eco-systems. Then, we'll trace the roots of socialism, the resur-gent darling of many college students. Finally, we'll locate the American political ecosystem on the matrix and see if it tells us anything about its health or future. For instance, what if our political ecosystem gets body slammed by a man-made or natural disaster—something even worse than COVID-19? Do we have the moral compass to navigate uncharted waters?" Tim paused for effect, and then clicked his mouse to project an image on the large screen behind him.

Political Ecosystems Matrix

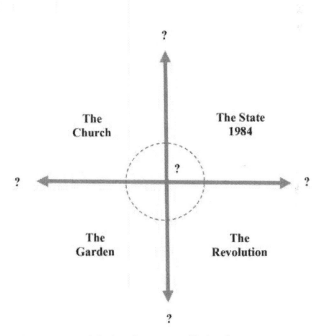

"I'd like us to think about political ecosystems using this frame. I've placed four archetypal political ecosystems on this matrix along with five question marks, one at the ends of both axes and one in the center circle. Anyone want to hazard a guess about how we might fill in the question marks?" His in-quiry was met by a prolonged silence. As he'd expected, no one was eager to go first.

Tim primed the pump. "Let's start by defining the terms on the chart. How about The Church?"

"Well, that would be organized religion. The term church is usually linked to Christian organizations, although I don't think that's your point here." An attentive adult woman sitting up front responded first. Tim silently applauded TU's continuing education program.

"Yes, exactly," Tim nodded. "For the purposes of our discussion, let's think of The Church quadrant on the matrix as representing theocratic political ecosystems, where religion dominates the political and economic discourse. Apart from Vatican City, there are no Christian theocracies left. A better example might be the Islamic Republic of Iran which is ruled by Sharia law. We could substitute The Church with The Caliphate. Same thing."

Seeing several nods, Tim moved on. "How about The State 1984?" More silence.

Eventually, a young man with a scruffy beard spoke up. "Well, *1984* was on our suggested reading list. A little out of date now."

"Right. It's a novel about the future, a dystopian future where the state controls all aspects of life. You should all read it." Tim scanned the class to reinforce the suggestion. "Big Brother watches every move people make. Individuals have no autonomy, no freedom. Thought police prosecute thought-crimes and even facecrimes. The title might be out of date, but the subject matter is very topical. In fact, the political eco-system described in *1984* is disturbingly analogous to things we're seeing today. In our matrix, The State 1984 represents totalitarian political ecosystems. OK, that leaves two more to define."

The enthusiastic student up front contributed again. "Is The Garden a reference to the Garden of Eden in the Bible?"

"That's right. The Garden is a utopian place where we are one with our brethren, the earth, the universe, our God or gods

—everything. For the purposes of this discussion, let's include in this quadrant the most basic of political ecosystems like hunter-gatherer societies. So, that leaves one term to explore. What do you think The Revolution represents?"

"I'm Tyler," a new voice spoke up. Young, tall, clean-shaven, and dressed all in white, it looked to Tim as if Tyler had the courage of his convictions. "Revolution means to overthrow the prevailing system. Radical change in how we are governed."

"Well said, Tyler. And thank you for giving me your name—I want to get to know you all by name. Okay, so we understand all four terms. Now tell me what you think the axes measure, and what you think the bullseye in the middle of the diagram represents."

The woman in front broke the silence again. "Wouldn't the far left of the horizontal axis be religion? I mean, you have both theocracy and the Garden of Eden on that side of the matrix."

"Excellent," Tim replied. "Name?"

"Oops! I'm Kristen."

"Okay Kristen. Religion is close, but let's use the term spiritual instead. That helps make it clear that we're not necessarily talking about organized beliefs on this end of the axis, but rather non-worldly, non-physical matters of connection beyond the self." Tim used his laptop to write spiritual over the question mark on the far left.

"So, if the far left of this axis is spiritual, what would the far right of the axis be?" Tim prodded the class.

"How about secular?" It was scruffy beard again.

"Name?"

"Sorry, I'm Joe."

"Joe, you are spot on. Secular is the opposite of spiritual, so let's fill that in." Tim completed the horizontal axis on his laptop. "Okay, that leaves the vertical axis and the bullseye. Any thoughts?" Tim was pleased. So far, he seemed to have generated some real curiosity in the class. Even the department chair looked interested.

"I'm Jodie," a fresh voice jumped into the discussion. "How about order for the top question mark?"

"Why order?" Tim asked.

"Well, both The State and The Church maintain order."

"Excellent. And how do they maintain order?"

"Well, I guess with religious dogma, laws, rules, police—that kind of stuff," Jodie replied.

"Good. Let me ask you this: Can you have order without laws?" No one offered a reply. Before the silence got too awkward, he pressed further. "Come on, any sociology or psych majors in the class?" More silence.

Finally, Jodie spoke up again. "Sure, societies can be governed by social mores and norms, by a commonly-held world view."

"Exactly Jodie!" Tim almost yelled in his excitement. His hands were not cold or clammy anymore. "Sociology 101: Societies are governed by widely accepted and internalized social mores and norms. In fact, law is the historical antithesis of order. When you have order, you don't need laws."

By the blank stares around the room, Tim could tell the class was struggling with this concept. "Let me give you an example. Tribal societies had few, if any, written laws or rules enforced by police or coercive forces. Acceptable behavior was passed on from generation to generation by example, custom, and verbal tradition. Official enforcement by elders or other authorities was the exception rather than the rule. Standards of conduct were internalized, not forced down from above."

"But isn't that the same thing?" A blond-haired, gangly young man posed the question.

"Name?"

"Nate. I mean, whether a law is written or a social expectation, it's still a law, isn't it?"

"I would argue that there is a qualitative difference between authoritative law enforced from above, and internalized social mores enforced from within the individual. But that's an excellent question, Nate. Let me ask you another question. Our Congress passes hundreds of laws each year. Do you feel any safer or better?"

"They're not passing anything this year!" Nate said, eliciting a laugh from the class.

"No kidding," Tim jumped in. "But my point is that laws and order have an inverse relationship. Societies with widely shared social mores tend to be harmonious. They don't need a library full of law books to keep order. I would argue that we're living right now in a society without a common moral compass, in a time of cultural relativism that rejects objective standards. We're hard pressed to come up with anything we can all agree on. Societies without agreed-upon objective truths or moral touchstones come to rely on lawyers, judges, and bureaucrats to Band-Aid their hemorrhaging social order."

Tim stopped and pulled himself back from further pursuing this favorite tangent and realized, as he took a breath, that he wasn't in the least bit nervous anymore.

"But I agree with Nate. Law is the best label for the top of this axis. And I think that was a successful first debate for our class. I intend that we'll have many more." Tim used his laptop to fill in the matrix.

"Okay, if law is at the top of the vertical axis, what is at the bottom? This should be a bit easier."

"How about chaos, or anarchy?" Nate asked.

"I don't think so," Kristen replied. "There was no chaos or anarchy in the Garden of Eden, at least not until Eve ate the apple."

"It's Kristen, right?" Tim asked, noticing with a jolt that he didn't really need to query her name. She stood out, and it wasn't just because she was the only adult student in the class. There was something about her eyes and the way she spoke that captivated him.

"Yes, I'm Kristen."

"Bingo! The Garden is all about order with man living in harmony with the world—that is, until the serpent comes along. The story of Adam and Eve eating the forbidden fruit is the mother of all allegories. You start with instinctive man, living in harmony with nature, enjoying the low-hanging fruit of a bountiful creation. He is the noble savage, the altruistic hunter-gatherer of Marxist ideology. Then along comes knowledge: rational man with the tools, laws, and weapons to crawl out of the cave, tame the wilderness, and relieve his existential fears. He is man as demigod with the knowledge of good and evil. But I digress. So, if it is not chaos or anarchy, what is the bottom of this axis? The top is law that restrains. What is its opposite?"

"How about freedom?" A new voice joined the debate. "Oh, I'm Justin."

"Justin, are you asking me or telling me?" Tim challenged.

"I'm telling you. The bottom should be freedom."

"Correct! Very good. We've labeled each axis: spiritual versus secular and law versus freedom. And we have four archetypal political ecosystems laid out accordingly: The Church, The State 1984, The Garden, and The Revolution. Now, what's in the middle? I will give you a hint—it's represented by a dashed line because it expands and contracts. When it expands, it creates coexistence among the competing systems. When it contracts, it sets the stage for conflict and extremism in multiple directions across the matrix."

"So, the center must be the economy, right?" Nate made the leap. "When it expands, everybody is happy. When it contracts, it sucks!"

"That's right, Nate. Eloquently stated." Tim chuckled. "The center is the economy. It's the sweet spot. When the sweet spot is big, everything and everybody is cool. When it is small, everything's bad and nobody is cool."

Tim entered economy in the center circle and looked up at the completed matrix on the screen behind him. He took a drink from his Nalgene and checked the clock, 10:15. He was running late, but his audience was hooked. Tim felt a rush of exhilaration. This is fun!

Political Ecosystems Matrix

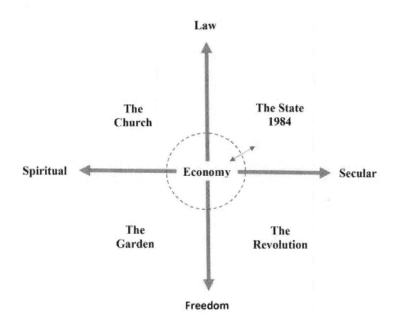

NINE

Washington DC – 10:15 am

As his limo raced through the streets of Washington DC, Steve Bennett's mind kept returning to his decision to send Scott and Marge home. Was he overreacting? The urgency of the summons to the White House couldn't be good—intel must be onto something imminent. Better to have them safely out of the city. An incoming call broke his thoughts. Steve looked down at his phone. The caller ID made his heart skip: Aaron Leibowitz, former Israeli Ambassador to the US. Amidst the deteriorating relations between Israel and the US, a back channel had been kept open between Israel and its friends in Congress. Ambassador Leibowitz and Representative Bennett as the ranking member of the House Committee on Home- land Security were key allies in the effort to preserve good relations, and friendship added to their effectiveness. Steve swiped his phone to connect and dispensed with any pleasant- ries.

"Aaron, how can I help? Are you in Israel? I am in transit to the White House for a DHS briefing as we speak."

"Yes Steve, my friend, I am in Tel Aviv now. We may only have a brief time. Do you have the latest intel?"

"I've been briefed on a CBRN threat and enemy agents leav- ing the city."

"Yes. I am afraid your government has emboldened Iran and its proxies to pursue the unthinkable. We are contacting Tehran, Hamas, Hezbollah, and others directly to explain the potential repercussions—if we are not too late. I suggest that your government pursue the same course of action. Also, we may not be the only target. You should take precautions."

"Of course, Aaron, I will..."

"Steve, my friend," Leibowitz interrupted, "do you remember our discussion over lunch at Tortilla Coast?"

"Yes, of course."

"I believe..." but before Aaron Leibowitz could continue, the call cut out, replaced by the fast beeps of the all trunks busy signal. Steve quickly hit redial and waited for the international call to go through without much hope of success. Steve recalled the lunch conversation Aaron mentioned with a rising sense of dread. They'd met on the heels of the Iran nuclear deal to discuss one topic: What would Israelis do if they suffered the existential threat of an Iranian nuclear strike?

TEN

Point Betsie, MI

It had been quiet in the car for a long time. Meg and Jack were both lost in thought. The scenery changed as they approached Lake Michigan, with small farms and fields giving way to the untouched stands of pines and hardwoods of the Sleeping Bear National Lakeshore. A few distressed maples were starting to turn, a harbinger of the fall color season that would draw tourists to the park. But for now the roads were mostly clear. Jack reached out to his silent daughter.

"Meg, I'm sorry I upset you this morning. Didn't mean to do that. I just get carried away sometimes."

"It's okay dad. A lot of what you said makes sense. But things have changed. You know, like I'm actually against abortion, but I don't dare call myself pro-life. My friends would shun me, and it would be even worse with the other teachers. You've got to watch what you say, or you'll get doxed."

"Doxed?"

"It's where someone outs you on the Internet. They label you as a bigot or something and give out your name, email, and address so people can publicly shame you."

"Oh great." Jack shook his head. "Listen, I'm proud of you and your convictions. Don't be bullied by a bunch of morons. Just because some things are legal, it doesn't make them right."

"Dad, you just don't understand. It's complicated. I really don't want to talk about it right now."

"Okay."

Before the silence went on too long, Jack turned on the

radio, preset to NPR. *"Israel is mobilizing its reserves in response to escalating violence in the Gaza Strip and West Bank..."*

Jack quickly changed the band to the NOAA weather station. *"And now the near shore forecast from Manistee to Point Betsie..."* Jack turned up the volume. *"Gale warning from 6 pm Friday to 10 am Saturday. Today, south winds 15 to 20 knots increasing to southwest gales to 35 knots with gusts to 45 knots this evening. Waves 5 to 8 feet increasing to 12 to 15 feet. Chance of thunderstorms..."*

Jack briefly turned his head to engage Meg. "Whoa, sounds perfect! Maybe a closeout later. Do you want to try Point Betsie, or just go right to Frankfort?"

"Let's check out PB. If it's too big, we can head down to Frankfort."

Soon they reached the Point Betsie turnaround. Tourists and a few kiters filled most of the parking spots. To their right was the majestic Point Betsie Lighthouse, a photo op prize for out-of-staters. In front of them, the waters of Lake Michigan roiled.

"It's lit up!" Meg smiled at the sight of the breaking surf.

Once outside the car, they appraised the conditions. Over the roar of the waves and wind Jack yelled, "It looks big, maybe 20 knots. You still want to try?"

"Sure. I'll rig my 7-meter. You windsurfing or kiting?" Meg shouted.

"Windsurfing!"

They started gearing up in the parking lot. Since the water was still warm, they both pulled out their shorty wetsuits. As Jack rigged his 4.5-meter high-wind sail in the parking lot, he saw some guys checking them out. There weren't a lot of female kiters in Michigan and Meg had drawn their attention. Instinctively, Jack gave the young bucks a glare that said, "Back off." At the same time, he saw the parked cars of some of his old kiting friends, Bubba and Gordy. That's good, Jack thought. They can help keep an eye on Meg while she's kiting.

With their gear assembled and ready, Jack locked the car

and hid the key. Meg slipped on the kite backpack and grabbed her harness and twin-tip board with her free hands. Jack balanced his sailboard on his head, using his two hands to steady it and keep it pointed into the gusting wind. He would come back later for his sail. They wound their way down the little path to the shore. As they walked up the beach to separate themselves from the metal breakwaters protecting the lighthouse, several tourists stopped what they were doing to stare at the sight of father and daughter, headed off to battle the surf.

They hadn't gone more than twenty yards when Meg stopped in her tracks, dropped her equipment and leaned over to pick up a Petoskey. Often referred to as a stone, Petoskeys are actually remnants of prehistoric reefs. Rounded and sanded over the millennia, they have a cell structure mosaic that is beautiful when wet or polished. After a quick inspection, Meg gave the pebble-shaped fossil a lick to reveal its pattern. She turned it over to inspect the backside, which was almost flawless. "It's a beauty!"

"Definitely gem quality. We will be rich beyond our wildest dreams!" Jack smiled at his daughter's childlike enthusiasm.

Meg walked up to a nearby tourist. The overweight middle-aged man was scouring the beach in a futile effort to find one of northern Michigan's most sought-after souvenirs. "Looking for a Petoskey?" she asked. "Here, have this one," she said, and handed him the prize.

"Thanks!" the tourist smiled and waddled over to his wife to show off the treasure.

Meg retrieved her gear and they continued up the beach, smiling together as the sun, surf, and wind combined to create a moment of pure joy. "It's going to be a wonderful day," Jack promised his daughter.

Jack stood close to shore holding Meg's kite in launch position, waiting for her thumbs up. Years of experience enabled him to hold the C-shape of the kite perfectly into the wind, with no buffeting. The 7-meter kite would fit Meg's height and weight, given today's 20 knots of wind and higher gusts. Jack saw friends on the water with 12-meter and 10-meter kites, but they were 180-pounders.

Jack watched protectively as Meg attached her safety leash to a single line so that she could completely depower and flag the kite in case of emergency. Next, she positioned the chicken loop on the hook protruding from her harness and inserted the crudely named donkey dick to prevent the loop from falling off accidentally. Approving Meg's completed preparations, Jack walked back a few steps to take the slack out of the two front lines and two back, or steering, lines. This allowed him to visually inspect the lines and ensure they weren't crossed. Nothing like crossed lines to start off your session with a so-called *kitemare*, Jack always said.

Everything was looking good. Meg gave the thumbs up, and Jack released the kite. It quickly arced up into the sky, putting force on the lines and lifting Meg slightly off the sand dune and toward her dad. She landed like a cat and walked up to Jack. With the kite now fully extended 22 meters overhead, Meg did a couple of quick test turns to generate force, each time rising a foot or so off the beach before landing with control. Jack had taught her this warmup maneuver to assess the strength of the wind.

"I'm good," she said and reached over for the kiteboard her dad was holding. Similar to a wakeboard, it had open heals to allow you to slip your feet in and out with ease.

"Be careful," Jack said. "Gordy and Bubba are out there if you need help. And, keep an eye out for thunderstorms. I don't like the looks of that," he pointed toward the west, where blue sky was giving way to darkening clouds. "Don't hesitate to dump your equipment if you get in trouble. You're more important than the gear. Do you have your knife?"

Meg patted the knife attached to her harness. If things got dicey, she could use the knife to cut her lines and free herself from the kite.

Jack pointed up the sand dune. "There's a self-landing strap up the dune if nobody's here to land you."

"I know, I know. See you out there!" Meg strode into the water, left hand holding the control bar, right hand gripping the center handle of her board.

Despite a strong crosscurrent and an incessant shore break, Meg managed to time a lull in the waves, drop her rear end into the water, and quickly slip her feet into the board. Jack watched as she dove the kite down toward the water through the wind window to generate force. Up she popped, rapidly leaving the shore break behind as she headed for the much bigger waves of the first sandbar, rising four to five feet high.

Jack grimaced as a big wave broke and came barreling toward her. She instinctively brought her kite up overhead near the 12 o'clock position to provide lift, tilted the front of the board up to meet the incoming white water, and let her bending knees act as shock absorbers against the impact of the breaker hitting her board. She rose several feet into the air with good forward momentum and landed in control on the other side of the wave. Dipping her kite toward the water again to regenerate force, Meg quickly escaped the cauldron of the first sand bar.

Damn! Jack thought. She's gotten good.

Confident that Meg was safe, Jack headed down the shore toward his sailboard. He positioned himself between the board and the downwind mast that were laying on the beach. Feeling his heart rate and respiration increasing, Jack took a moment to calm his mind. Then he picked up his rig and waded into the shore break to time his launch, scanning the incoming waves. A water start was the only way to start his small, 85-liter sinker board. Jack waited for a series of waves to crash on the shore and then waded in further.

In a movement orchestrated by years of experience, Jack quickly swiveled the board so its nose faced the incoming waves and laid it on the choppy water. Simultaneously, he circled around the back of the board and pulled the mast and boom over the board so he could reach them with both hands. Without hesitation, he dropped his butt into the water, propped his heels on the board, tilted the sail to catch the wind, and let the sail pull his body up and out of the water onto the board.

In the strong wind, the board immediately came on plane and darted toward the first sandbar. He took a wave head-on, sending a spray of water high into the air as it hit his board and chest. Perfectly balanced, Jack survived the strike. He connected his harness hook to the dangling boom line, providing much relief to his arms. Using a keen eye, he saw an opening among the massive breakers of the second sandbar and scooted through to escape the danger zone.

With the immediate threats behind him, Jack took a moment to size up the situation. He was now about a quarter mile out in waves ranging from five to ten feet. Closer to shore, he could see Meg playing in the safe space between the first and second sandbars. She seemed to be doing fine and was near Gordy and Bubba. He was out far enough to see the lighthouse down south at Frankfort. Jack was certain that expert kiters would be doing a downwinder on an epic day like today. A group would leave one vehicle at Point Betsie and use another to taxi the kiters upwind to Frankfort. The payoff was a five-mile, downwind session, darting in and out of waves to surf or catch big air. But they would have to be on guard today. The horizon was beginning to look ominous.

Jack turned his attention to the north. In the distance, he could see the Sleeping Bear Dunes with Mother Bear still glistening in the sunshine waiting for her cubs, and beyond her, in the distance, South and North Manitou Islands. Jack flashed back to his morning dream, and to Jenny. But she was a powerful distraction he couldn't afford. He shook his head to forcibly clear his mind and brought his focus back to windsurfing. Every now and then, he stole a glance toward shore to check on Meg. But soon his conscious mind retreated, and he entered The Zone.

Jack couldn't explain The Zone, it wasn't rational. It didn't make sense or follow the rules of his everyday life. But it was as real to him as Meg was. He'd heard extreme skiers talk about venturing into no-fall zones, where the smallest mistake would mean severe injury or death. In those moments, they said, it was as if time itself slowed down. They were able to move in harmony with the slopes, foreseeing every check, turn, and jump. They were outside of mundane existence; they were in The Zone. At its best, windsurfing was like that for Jack. He called it the Zen of Windsurfing, for lack of better words. His senses were heightened, and all distractions receded. His mind and body became one with the wind and waves. He was hyper focused, able to anticipate changes and undulations *before* they occurred. In The Zone, he was connected to the air and water as if by an invisible field. Time and sound fell away, and he experienced once again the immersive, blissful feeling of being part of something much larger.

ELEVEN

Route 66 Approaching Manassas, VA

"Let's try Talk Radio." Scott reached over from the passenger seat to switch the band to AM and searched for a channel.

After a hurried exit from the parking garage, Marge and Scott had made good time navigating the late morning traffic around the beltway. They were just 20 minutes out from the airport. Marge focused on driving while Scott scanned through radio stations and checked his smartphone. So far there was no breaking news. Scott was beginning to wonder if it was all just a fire drill. But his dad had been adamant, even scared. He couldn't discount that.

"Scott, I am going to drop you off and head back to the office," Marge said as she wove expertly through traffic. "If your father's fears are confirmed, he will need all the help he can get. I am going to be there for him."

Scott's antennae went up at her tone, and her words. "All right," he replied. Scott searched his memory for any signs of a relationship between his dad and Marge that he might have missed.

A relationship would not bother him at all, he decided. Mom had been gone for several years now. His dad had been through a terribly tough few years, Scott thought—first Uncle Sean, then his mom. They were finally beginning to recover. He hoped his father would get back in the game. Scott took a chance.

"Pardon me for asking, but are you and my dad seeing each other?"

"Hm," Marge breathed, as her eyebrows shot up. She turned

her head to meet Scott's gaze. "Better to ask your father about that." Her face was beginning to blush.

"Okay," Scott replied. "Anyway, if you were, that'd be great." He tried to process this unexpected change in family dynamics. Unsure what to say next, Scott continued to channel surf until he hit a station announcing the market report. "Here we go," Scott said. "The proverbial canary in the coal mine."

"The Dow is now off 1,300 points on breaking news out of the Middle East. The S&P 500 is off one hundred points. Let's bring in Bob Reynolds from the New York Stock Exchange. Bob, are you there?"

"Yes Tim, the markets are tanking on reports of a terrorist attack in Israel. The Dow is now off 2,500 and plunging. Wait..."

Marge and Scott could hear a loud commotion and yelling in the background. *"Oh Lord, the ticker says there are reports of a dirty bomb in Tel Aviv!"*

Manassas Regional Airport – VA
Glancing now and then at the TV for any breaking news, Dan Fisher—Steve Bennett's pilot— paced anxiously in the lobby of the private plane hangar. The Cessna 182T stood on the tarmac, fully fueled and ready to go. He had already entered his flight plan back to Michigan. All he needed now was passengers—and a little luck. While Steve Bennett had been vague on the phone, you didn't need to be a genius to figure out that there was a substantial threat. Private airport operators were still semi-exempt from the stifling security measures mandatory at commercial airports. But if the Feds closed the airspace, it would impact all craft, not just commercial jets coming out of Reagan and National. Scott and Marge needed to arrive soon.

On cue, Dan saw a white Audi S4 pull up in front of the large lobby window and Scott and Marge Stevenson exit the car. The man behind the counter turned up the volume on the TV. Regular programming had been interrupted and a national news anchor filled the screen. *"I repeat, we have confirmed re-*

ports out of Israel that they have suffered a dirty bomb attack in *Tel Aviv. I'm sorry, please standby."* The news anchor appeared to be receiving an update. Several people in the lobby crowded around the TV.

Dan did not wait for details. He rushed out the front door and greeted his passengers with a terse, "We have to go, now!" From the look on their faces, he saw they were already aware of the news.

Marge gave Scott a prolonged hug and then turned to Dan. "I'm not going with you. I'm headed back to DC."

"What?" Dan's brows furrowed with concern. This wasn't part of the mission.

"It's fine. Dad needs the help," Scott said.

Dan hesitated a second, digesting the change in plans. "Okay, let's go."

"God speed," Marge said as she watched them head for the lobby doors.

Dan led Scott through the lobby, disregarding the huddle around the TV. But they were both stopped in their tracks when they heard over the TV, *"We have now confirmed that a drone was used in the dirty bomb attack on Tel Aviv. There are now reports of drone strikes in New York City and London. We do not yet know the nature of the New York and London attacks. But we fear we are seeing a coordinated terrorist attack on the anniversary of 9/11."*

Drones. Dan could feel his body switching over to fight or flight mode. They'll certainly close the airspace now, he thought. "Got to go," he said, pushing Scott through the door from the lobby to the adjoining hanger.

They trotted past some parked planes and exited through the large hanger doors to board the awaiting plane. Dan yelled to Scott to take the co-pilot's seat. Dan shut and latched the door and ignited the single engine, still warm from his repositioning flight. He put on a set of headphones and motioned for Scott to do the same.

Dan contacted the tower. "November 43820 requesting

taxi to runway 16R for departure."

He was already rolling the plane when the tower replied. "November 43 cleared to taxi on A1, halt at 16R."

Dan kept the plane at a faster than normal taxi speed and soon they were just short of the runway. "November 43820 at 16R, request immediate departure." Dan scanned the horizon for any incoming or outgoing traffic. All was clear.

"November 43 hold at 16R."

Not good, Dan thought. "November 43820, hold for traffic?"

"Negative November 43, waiting for system clearance," the tower replied.

"November 43820, Roger that," Dan said as he turned off the tower channel, revved the engine, swung the plane on to runway, and went full throttle.

As they lifted off the runway, Scott could see Marge standing by her car, waving. He felt a wave of unexpectedly strong feeling for, what appeared to be, his dad's new partner. Scott turned to look at the control tower and could just make out the local air traffic controller with his nose to the tinted window, arms up in a WTF gesture.

"Well, we're in deep shit," Scott said on the intercom channel.

"Better to ask for forgiveness than permission," Dan replied, and banked the small plane to the north.

***

Marge watched the small plane recede into the distance. She felt an odd mix of emotions: shock over the attack on Israel, regret for having broken the news to Scott, longing to be with Steve, rising fear. Reflexively, Marge switched over to work mode. Back in the car, she texted Steve, keeping it cryptic just in case: *Package delivered and on its way. I'm heading back to office.* He's not going to like that last part, she thought. Marge waited for the text to send, but it was hung up. It will go eventually, she thought, and started driving back to DC. The roads were clear. Nobody was going back into the city.

***

As they left DC airspace, Scott tried to compose himself. Things were happening too fast. The mad dash from his dad's office, news of the terrorist attacks, Marge's revelation. And then there was his dad's cryptic comments about the plasma drive.

Of all the problems before him, the plasma drive wasn't an obvious priority, Scott thought, but what the heck? Sure, he knew the Department of Energy had intended to stonewall them from day one. First their correspondence had been ignored. Then their request for a research grant was summarily rejected with a terse reply: Project not commercially viable. With help from his dad, Scott and Tim had finally been granted a face-to-face meeting with the DOE's Technology Incubator Division. The meeting was particularly telling, Scott recalled.

The government administrators had dismissed their detailed plasma drive proof of concept out of hand. DOE scientists were already working on plasma solutions, they explained, as part of NASA's next generation space exploration program. They insisted that the engine Tim and Scott proposed would require more energy than it would produce, and they likened it to crackpot cold fusion concepts. The meeting was thoroughly demoralizing.

Afterwards, as they were walking out of DOE headquarters, their escort opened up to them.

"You realize that your proposal is a threat to the DOE, don't you?"

"What do you mean?" Tim had asked.

"Well, half of those guys in the meeting were consultants or part-time researchers for DOE. You come up with a solution, they lose their jobs. The last thing they want is a solution. Really simple. Also, any solution you come up with is going to be directly in the crosshairs of fossil fuel, solar, and wind lobbyists. You think they want to see a commercially viable alternative? They'd shit their pants!"

"But isn't the DOE responsible for regulating the industry, for coming up with green solutions?" Scott had asked.

"Right," their escort's voice dripped with cynicism. "Just remember, they win when oil is controversial and taxable, they win when renewable energy is debatable and expensive. They lose if there's a no-brainer winner. Understand?"

As they sped toward Michigan, Scott tried to make sense of it all. One thing was certain: The terrorist attack was going to set everything back—the economy, the stock market, and investment in their fledgling startup. His business partner, Tim, and chief scientist, Karl, needed to hear about his dad's warning soon. And they needed to figure out what the hell to do next.

TWELVE

Traverse University

"Okay, we're behind schedule so buckle up for a whirlwind tour of socialism and then our own political ecosystem. Wherever possible, we'll use our matrix to explore political dynamics." Tim noticed that the four strongest students— Kristen, Jodie, Tyler, and Justin—were now dominating the discussion. Not what he wanted, but it might speed up the class.

"To really get at the roots of socialism, we'd need to go back to the 1789 French Revolution and trace it through Hegel and Marx. But we're going to jump ahead to the world's first constitutionally socialist state, the USSR. The Union of Soviet Socialist Republics was formed in 1922, after the 1917 Bolshevik Revolution and the resulting civil war. Does anyone know what's left of this Union?" Tim asked.

"I'm Justin. Russia is the only republic left."

"That's right, Justin. Which gives us a hint as to the success of this grand social experiment." Tim noticed Justin's head nodding in agreement—maybe a closet conservative?

"Anyway, the 1917 proletarian revolution in Russia led by Vladimir Lenin came at a tipping point," Tim said. "All the right pieces were in place. Tsar Nicholas II was the last in a line of absolute monarchs who ruled in alliance with the Russian Orthodox Church. Despite terrible deprivation and poverty at home, the Tsar had sent unit after unit of men to pointless slaughter at the hands of the Germans on the Western Front of WWI. Defeat had left the Russian army in a state of disarray and mutiny. A corrupt state, a collapsing economy, and lack of effective law enforcement all helped pave the way for revolution."

Tim paused to adjust his glasses. "Lenin promised desperate Russian workers bread, land, and peace. They would own the means of production—the land, raw materials, tools, machinery, and buildings—the capital of capitalism. There would be no ruling class of aristocrats, land barons, and emerging industrialists to exploit their labor. The church would no longer take their money in return for promises of heavenly rewards. Lenin promised The Garden of Marxist theory, 'from each according to his ability, to each according to his needs', where the creation and distribution of goods and services would be totally fair. And Lenin further argued that, once the workers gained a fully collective and socialist conscience, the revolutionary vanguard of the party would wither away.

"So, what happened?" Tim asked. "Did the revolution succeed?"

"No," Tyler said, "but that doesn't mean the ideology was wrong. The movement was hijacked by dictators and strongmen!"

"Any counterargument?" Tim scanned the class and reached for his Nalgene to wet his throat.

"Socialism was flawed from the beginning," Justin said. "It assumes all people will work just as hard as their comrades. But that isn't the nature of man. Just as you said, man's instinctive drive for more is the dynamo of capitalism, to profit from the fruits of one's own labor. It was the Protestant ethic of hard work, self-reliance, and savings that drove the explosion of free market democracies—not socialism. Socialism just leads to runaway government bureaucracies with unelected technocrats telling us what's good for us. They produce nothing, they just redistribute other people's income!"

"Can you tell us how you really feel?" Tim joked to relieve the growing tension. He was greeted with some laughs.

"Actually, Justin, I agree with much of what you've said," Tim said. "We've seen other socialist experiments across the world in China, Cuba, Venezuela, and now California—just kidding about California." A few more laughs. "But in every case, the revolution fails, and we end up with an impoverished, totalitarian state. Look at China. They even tried to institutionalize the revolution; how about that for an oxymoron? But China's Cultural Revolution and Great Leap Forward only solidified the iron fist of their dictator, Mao Zedong, resulting in tens of millions of citizens murdered, imprisoned, or reeducated."

"I'm sorry Professor Kelly, but you're cherry-picking history to fit your argument," Tyler said. "Socialist programs have been successful in Western Europe and Canada where they have universal healthcare and secondary education. Even in the U.S. we have socialized institutions; k-12 schooling, libraries, the national postal and park services, Medicare, Medicaid, and Social Security. And, personally, I'm sick of hearing about the Protestant ethic. Jesus would have been a socialist!"

"'Whatever you do for one of the least of these brothers and sisters of mine, you do for me.'" Kristen added in agreement. "This is an important lesson in the Bible. I can't speak for Jesus, but if he were forced to choose sides, I imagine he would lean toward socialism. I mean, he was the original social justice warrior."

Tim nodded. "Let's keep in mind that there isn't just one definition or type of socialism. Winston Churchill offered this definition of Christian socialism: all that is mine, is yours. This is bottom-up charity: I will take what I have and give it to you. I'm sure many of you have seen examples in your own communities of people reaching out to help others in an informed, direct way, and doing enormous good. Churchill contrasted that with the top-down socialism of England's Labor Party: all that is yours, is mine."

"So, you're saying government doesn't have a moral responsibility to help the vulnerable—the children, the elderly, the sick, the disabled?" Tyler broke in, red faced. "We have to rely on individuals, acting alone, bottom-up, to somehow see and address the scope of the want, need, and inequity across our nation? We're the richest nation on earth. Conservatives are okay when the government uses its powers to subsidize profitable corporations, wage war across the world to protect oil interests, or set regulations favorable to business interests. But when government is directed toward helping the least among us, they say that's wrong? They say that's the job of the private sector. You know what that is, really? That's conservative B.S.!"

Tim was taken aback by the vehemence of Tyler's response. He thought it might be wise to bring the emotional temperature of the room down a few degrees. "I believe we can all agree that government has a role in assisting the disadvantaged. I think what Justin and others like him are worried about is the steady growth of government on the one hand, and the steady erosion of civil liberties on the other. It happens incrementally over time, so we don't see our loss of freedom until it's too late. Can you see why many Americans are worried about government overreach, and fear that the all-powerful state of *1984* is fast approaching?"

"You keep referencing *1984*," Tyler said. "I did read *1984*. You've got it all wrong. Orwell was an avowed democratic socialist who was lambasting the warfare state, not the welfare state. You're twisting the message of his book in support of a particular set of political ideas. Is that the point of this class?"

"Respectfully, Tyler, I'm afraid you may be twisting things," Tim said quietly. "We've explored a lot of political ideas today with the goal of making us think critically. Here we are looking at two ways of addressing inequality: from the bottom-up, based on the Christian idea that all that is mine is yours, versus the big government top-down approach, based on the Socialist idea that all that is yours is mine. This is not just a play on words. I know this is tough to grasp. But if your mind shuts down and can't consider another point of view, you might have a blind spot."

Tim paused for a second, and then rashly continued, "Or, you could simply walk out of class and flee to your safe space, so you don't get triggered by these topics."

The minute Tim said it, he regretted it. "I'm sorry Tyler, that was uncalled for." Tim bowed his head and exhaled. For the first time in the long class, he heard shuffling of feet and shifting in seats.

"That's okay Professor Kelly," Tyler replied. "But I thought you wanted us to debate."

"Yes, I do. And I don't want to succumb to the divisiveness plaguing our nation, however, I do want us to understand its roots. But we have gotten way ahead of ourselves. Let's first close out our discussion of socialism, and then we can aim the matrix at our own country's political ecosystem." Tim felt he was starting to lose the class. He needed to reengage them, make them part of a constructive debate.

"So, in summary, the roots of socialism as manifested in the Bolshevik Revolution are easy to trace on our matrix. The State had become illegitimate in the eyes of the masses. The Church, which was in league with the Tsars, became guilty by association. Lenin took advantage of this breach in the social contract and promised the masses The Garden. The ensuing Revolution resulted in tens of millions of deaths and imprisonments. And, after all that, the Communist Party did not wither away—it simply replaced The State. The Communists perfected the use of fear-based propaganda, restrictions, and enforcers to control the country and expunge counterrevolutionaries. You can see this pattern repeated throughout history."

Tim took a deep breath and reached for his Nalgene, only to find it was dry. He looked up and saw the Department Chairman, Ken Weaver, rise from his seat with his smartphone held against his ear. What did that mean? He looked at the clock, 10:40. Time was running out.

"Okay. Let's turn our attention to the United States. Our national ethos is based in the Protestant work ethic, individual responsibility, talent, and ingenuity. We have been a world leader in technological advancements. We have a lot of land that is rich in natural resources, giving us a lot of space to move and grow. But we must also acknowledge the role of slavery and the taking of indigenous peoples' land as part of our early economic growth—bitter roots indeed. He locked eyes with one student after another. They met his gaze with steady seriousness. "For all these reasons, both good and bad, we benefit from a large economic sweet spot at the center of our system.

"In fact, I theorize that because our economy has been so large and powerful, and has given our system so much stability, it has enabled us to accommodate multiple political ecosystems within our larger system. To paraphrase Ronald Reagan, America is 'a shining city on a hill' that has attracted multitudes."

Tim looked around the room, raising a quizzical eyebrow at each student in turn.

"So, let's test my theory out. Let's go one by one through the four systems we have explored on our matrix and see how they relate to our political ecosystem. To start, how do we accommodate The Church within our system?" Tim asked. He hoped Kristen would weigh-in.

She didn't disappoint. "The freedom of religion the Puritans sought in the New World was foundational to our Bill of Rights," said Kristen. "The Church has flourished in many forms within our borders. The Mormons even found enough space to set up a territory. At the same time, separation of church and state prevents us from being pushed toward theocracy."

"Excellent points," Tim agreed. "Americans are able to practice any religion we choose, or none, and the government can't officially recognize or favor any religion."

Tim continued. "How about those who seek The Garden? How do we accommodate communal systems within our complex political ecosystem?"

Jodie took on The Garden question. "We have communes, communities for hippies and environmentalists. You might have to go west to find your people, but they're out there. Sometimes waaaay out there!"

"Good, Jodie, thank you," Tim said amidst laughter. "Many people live long and fruitful lives in counterculture communities in America. Some communes share everything, and live simply off the land, modeling themselves after the Garden of Eden.

"And The Revolution? Do we accommodate that, too?" Tim asked.

Justin joined the debate. "I think we do, in a way. We have freedom of speech, freedom of assembly, and freedom of the press. And I'd say over the course of our history, we've used them fairly regularly and effectively to bring about change in our system."

Tim approved. "The fact that our founders built protest into our system of government allowed abolitionists to demand the end of slavery, for women to demand the vote, and for citizens to demand civil rights to give a few examples. But I must ask, where are the mass protests today? Before I was born, dramatic Vietnam War protests happened around the nation and changed the course of American foreign policy. Today, people seem equally upset, but they don't take their ideas to the streets. What's different?" Tim asked.

As the silence dragged on, Tim gave the class a prod. "Marx has been paraphrased as saying 'religion is the opium of the masses'. Do we have a new opium affecting our masses?"

Kristen picked up on the clue. "Well, our culture worships stuff—consumer goods, new toys, fancy food, coffee bars, smartphones and social media. The list goes on and on."

"That's right, Kristen. Capitalism has delivered the goods, and it drives neo-Marxists nuts. What else has kept the lid on the pot of revolution?"

"The democratic socialist programs I previously mentioned, and that you dismissed, have also kept the lid on the pot," Tyler said. "But that could change, and rapidly."

Tim did not rise to the bait to argue. He was just glad to see Tyler participating again. "That's right, Tyler. Welfare programs and our social safety nets have blunted the need and anger of the poor—at least for now. Okay, last, but not least, do we accommodate The State into our system?"

As expected, Justin jumped in. "Not only do we accommodate the state, we've put it on steroids. Our government is intervening in every aspect of our lives at the local, state, and federal level. As *I* previously mentioned, we have runaway government bureaucracies with unelected technocrats telling us what's good for us—a welfare state where we become wards of the state. The poor have already become dependent. We've all heard the adage *give a man a fish, he will eat for a day, but teach a man to fish and he will eat forever*. What happens when we give a man a fish every day and tell him it's all right because he has been, is, and will always be a victim? What happens to self-esteem and motivation under these conditions? Are we really helping the poor here?"

Tim wondered if Justin was making this up on the fly or it was buried deep in the suggested reading list. "Justin, I think you have summarized the conservative argument against the so-called nanny state and attendant culture of victimhood where minorities and other identity groups are seen as deserving of special treatment and amends for current or past discrimination.

"But here's the broader question: If we have a huge economic sweet spot, if capitalism has delivered the goods, if we have welfare programs to support the underprivileged, if we have freedom of religion, then why is there so much divisiveness in our country? Rich against poor, black against white, rural against urban, liberals against conservatives, young against old, secularists against the religious?" Tim let the question settle in.

"Does this mean our matrix is wrong? Or might we explain what is happening despite our strong economy by looking at the strong forces of law and secularism that are straining the system and pushing it to extremes. Have we gone too far away from freedom and spirituality on the axes of the matrix?"

Tim paused, looking at the consternation on his student's faces.

"For generations, the nuclear family and organized religion were foundational institutions in America. Think of the family as the car of society, and spirituality as the roadmap to a purposeful life. Relative freedom in family units balanced the law of the public space. Spirituality in churches and other groups balanced the secularization enshrined in the Constitution. Since then, the nuclear family has practically disintegrated before our eyes, and the church has become increasingly irrelevant. No wonder so many Americans feel we're headed in the wrong direction—we have no car, and we've lost the map!" That earned another laugh from the class.

"If you've ever been with a group that got lost, you know how ugly it can get. People often vent their fear and anger by striking out viciously, looking for a scapegoat. Now imagine if large swaths of our society felt *morally* lost. Who would they strike out at?

"Could that explain why rural, working class Americans as a group have been pilloried as *deplorables* who cling to their guns and religion? Really? Most of these people are salt of the earth who would give you the shirt off their back. And their tormentors? Progressive elites sitting in their gated communities on the coasts who, arguably, have already won the cultural wars. Nice victory dance." Tim scowled.

"Who will be the next group to be stigmatized and cyberbullied by opponents on the other side of an argument? Will immigrants be the next group blamed for all of America's problems? Seriously? Except for the few remaining Native Americans, we're all immigrants. Or will the tables be turned, and the new face of the enemy will be privileged white males and their ignorant wives. Where will this identity politics and vitriol stop?"

A hush fell over the class. Some students sat frozen with their mouths agape.

Realizing he had slipped into personal opinion, Tim tried to reel the argument back in and close out the class. "You know, we've been talking around the extremes of our political spectrum: the welfare state versus the warfare state, capitalism versus socialism. But the remarkable thing about America..."

Tim stopped short. Smartphones throughout the room began to simultaneously emit ominous warning alarms. Everyone except Tim hurriedly reached for their devices. Ken Weaver, the Department Chairman, rushed back into the classroom and addressed the class.

"I'm sorry to interrupt, but the University has activated the emergency notification system. It appears there has been a major terrorist attack on the United States. There is no immediate threat on campus, nor are we locking down the campus. However, we urge all students to monitor the emergency notification system for further information. Tim, could you please turn on the TV so we can get the latest news?"

Tim stood, dumbfounded. Moving slowly as if he was surrounded by thick fog, he adjusted his glasses and blinked. All eyes were on him, expecting action. He shook himself, pivoted to the TV console, and fumbled ineffectually with the controls, completely flustered. "Here, let me help you." It was Kristen, Tim realized. She quickly found the right remote and turned on a newscast, then led him gently back from the set so the rest of the class could see.

"... at 10:30 am today. The attack appears to be coordinated with similar attacks in Tel Aviv and London. The Department of Homeland Security has instructed all citizens to remain on high alert for additional terrorist activities. Any suspicious behavior should be reported to local authorities at once. To repeat, the President has declared a state of emergency. An evacuation has been ordered for Lower Manhattan, the site of the dirty bomb attack on the Financial District. Other citizens in New York City have been ordered to shelter in place so as not to hinder the evacuation or emergency *responders. Washington DC has also been locked down. Citizens should shelter in place until further notice."*

As students filed out of the classroom to greet a changed world, Tim stared at his matrix on the big screen. His opening comments now seemed prophetic. Tim tried to think—what would happen if our country got body slammed?

<u>Political Ecosystems Matrix</u>

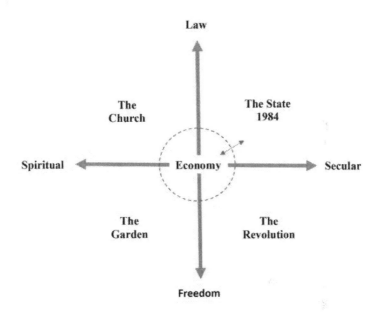

THIRTEEN

Washington DC – 11:00 am
White House Briefing Room

Steve Bennett's phone buzzed with an incoming text. His associates in the briefing room glared at him as he pulled out his phone to get Marge's update. He gave a sigh of relief, but then grimaced as he learned of Marge's intention to return to DC. He did not try to respond to the message—he had already broken enough security protocols. Steve returned his attention to the briefing. His friend, DHS Under Secretary John Bowden, was standing to the side of a big screen world map showing red circles around New York, London, and Tel Aviv.

"To summarize," Bowden said, "we have confirmed worst-case scenario dirty bomb attacks on three of the world's top strategic targets: New York City's financial district, London's financial district, and downtown Tel Aviv. In each case, two drones were used to spread radioactive agents. Same type of drones used for crop dusting. Israel shot down one drone before it reached Tel Aviv. The others reached their targets. The President has declared a state of emergency and we are mobilizing National Guard in all 50 states. We are on full alert for a possible strike in DC. We think Brussels, Paris, and Berlin may also be at risk. FAA has ordered all airports closed and the Capitol Police are locking down the city."

Steve took advantage of the pause to interrupt. "How is Israel responding?"

Bowden turned to Steve. "DOD and State have opened up communications, but so far the Israelis are playing it close to the vest. As you know, the immediate casualties from a dirty bomb, particularly a drone-delivered aerosol, are minimal. But the long-term radiation and psychological damage can be devastating. At this point, we don't expect them to go nuclear, although they could decide to hit Iran's nuclear facilities. Highest probability scenario is that they strike back in kind. The question is, where? Dirty bombs deployed in close proximity targets like Gaza, the West Bank, and the Golan Heights could be as harmful to the Israelis as they are to the targets themselves."

"What about New York?" another congressman asked.

Bowden used a laptop to bring up multiple feeds from New York City: a news report, live video from surveillance cameras, and a plume analysis showing a spreading pink blob over Lower Manhattan.

"Latest intel is that two drones released radioactive material over the financial district, and then crashed near the New York Stock Exchange and the Federal Reserve. We expect the radioactive material was plutonium or cesium isotope—we'll know soon. The Emergency Broadcast System has been activated. We are evacuating the lower part of Manhattan. DMAT and CBRN teams have been mobilized and medical surge capabilities are coming online at Bellevue, Presbyterian, and St. Luke's. We're getting reports of absolute chaos as everybody tries to get off the island—we estimate close to two million people." For emphasis, Bowden clicked on video feeds from the New York Stock Exchange, Times Square, and Grand Central Station showing masses of people rushing for exit and shelter. "So, we're depending on self-presentation by people who were exposed."

"Are you going to quarantine Manhattan?" Someone interrupted.

"No," Bowden replied. "Our protocol for a dirty bomb is to set up a perimeter around the hot zone and channel exposed civilians to the surge hospitals for radiation scans. But we have no perimeter. Everybody is fleeing the financial district. First responders are overwhelmed. The good news is that our preliminary plume analysis indicates less than 100,0000 people have been exposed to harmful levels of radiation. We won't know for sure until we get confirmation from the monitoring stations and CBRN units."

Bowden pulled up the plume map of Lower Manhattan on the big screen. "The threat of civilians spreading lethal radiation is minimal. The real threat is chaos, people panicking. But anyone who comes into direct contact with the radioactive materials should be quarantined and treated at once. Cleanup of the district could take years, and the cost will be astronomical."

"And the markets?" another committee member asked.

"All exchanges have closed. All markets were down 20% with a $5 trillion loss in market value before Level 3 circuit breakers halted trading. We are not optimistic that US markets will reopen any time soon. Same with Europe and Asia. The world's markets and central banks were just recovering from the COVID-19 pandemic—this might send them over the brink."

"Do we know who did this yet?" Steve asked.

"We are waiting on analyses from NSA and the CIA, and intel from Israel. The strikes were highly coordinated and sophisticated. The likely suspects are proxies of Iran. But there's a counterargument that this might be a resurgence of ISIS. Some are even eyeing China. Nobody has claimed responsibility at this time. Israel's reaction might be telling. Right now, we have more questions than answers," Bowden said. "I am afraid this is just the beginning."

FOURTEEN

Aux Baie, MI

To get to the main highway and town, Jenny had to carefully navigate a long, two-track driveway. Toby rode first class in the passenger seat, tongue lolling out the window, delighting in all the smells. At the boundary of her expansive property was a gate. She exited the pickup, quickly closing the door before Toby could jump out. As she opened the gate, her gaze was drawn to reminders of the past—her father's carved wooden fish with *Welcome* painted on it, nailed to the gate near his handmade bird house marked *Hernandez*. Faded and water-marked though it was, the little house was still structurally sound. Jenny could feel wistful memories welling up, but they were arrested as she amusingly recalled Tim Kelly's last visit. As brilliant as he was, he had totally missed these signs and took the wrong fork in the road. Tim ended up lost at the aging, but still serviceable, guest house a quarter mile past her cabin. She still ribbed him about that.

Hopping back into the pickup to continue her trip, Jenny felt this morning's sense of foreboding creeping back. She tried to concentrate on gratitude, a lesson she had learned from Mary DeVries. Mary said if you are filled with gratitude, then there's no room for fear or resentment. Wise woman! Jenny started to tick them off. She was grateful for her father who had the foresight to buy lakefront property in the '60s and build the cabin. For Steve Bennett and his son, Scott, who helped settle her parent's estate and modernize the green-houses. For Johnny-B who kept everything up and running. For her co-op friends, the Church Ladies. For her constant companion, Toby, who rode shotgun next to her. And, of course, she was grateful for Mary herself, who had lovingly heard her confession about her painful past and had absolved her.

Jenny's reverie was broken as she came to the intersection with CR550. She was about to enter the highway when the blaring sound of sirens stopped her in her tracks. She watched as a Michigan State Police car sped toward downtown Aux Baie, followed closely by a Baraga County Sheriff's car. Toby whined anxiously at the sound of the sirens. Probably an accident, she guessed. "I hope everyone is okay." Jenny offered a silent prayer. She reassured Toby with soothing tones and then turned to follow the official vehicles, a safe distance back.

Entering the outskirts of town, Jenny noticed a commotion at the bank. The lot was full, and lines had formed at the entrance and at the outdoor ATM machine. That's odd, she thought. It looked like a proverbial run on the bank you'd see in Depression-era movies. Fighting the urge to stop and get in the queue herself, she kept driving toward the grocery. Maybe they'll know what's going on with the bank, she hoped. As she turned onto Main Street, her jaw dropped. The grocery store was a mob scene. People were running in and out of the small supermarket like ants whose nest had been toppled.

Jenny realized she had caught up with the state trooper and the sheriff's officer. She was happy to see it was her good friend, Sheriff Jim Larson himself. Standing by their cars near the entrance to the parking lot, Sheriff Larson and the Michigan trooper yelled back and forth animatedly before the trooper ran off towards the grocery, his firearm drawn. Jim reached through his open window and grabbed his police radio mic.

Jenny pulled over and parked a short distance from the chaos. She cracked the window for Toby, got out, locked the truck, and ran over to Sheriff Larson. "Jim, what's going on?"

"People are hoarding supplies in case this thing spreads," he said, pointing toward the store. "You better hurry before things run out."

Larson listened to a staticky transmission coming in on the radio, affirmed "10-4" into the mic, then hunched over to await a reply.

"What thing?" she asked in confusion.

Larson looked up sharply. "Lord, haven't you heard? Israel, New York, and London have been hit by terrorists—dirty bombs, radioactive stuff."

Jenny's body seemed to react before her mind, with adrenalin pushing her toward a panic attack. She heard herself utter, "What?"

Sheriff Larson didn't hear her. He was listening to a message coming in over the radio.

Distantly, she registered that someone was calling her name. "Jenny! Jenny!" Johnny-B ran up and grabbed her by the hand. "Come on," he said, "we've got to get supplies. This could get bad. You're the naturalist, what do we need for the long haul?" He pulled her toward the store entrance.

Jenny stumbled forward uncomprehendingly, until the sight of a pistol stuck in Johnny-B's back pocket broke the spell. "Wait!" Jenny shouted, finally grasping the situation. Johnny stopped abruptly and turned in her direction.

"Let me think this through," she said. "Okay, listen. Get all the sugar, salt, honey, and pectin you can find. That's your number one priority. Next, bags of dried rice and beans, as much as you can haul. If you still have room, throw in some canned tuna and peanut butter, if there's any left. Forget any processed foods, perishables, snack foods, or other crap." She pulled her hand away from Johnny's grasp. "I'm going to Brogan's. Meet me there when you're done. If I'm gone, meet me at the cabin."

"Okay," Johnny replied. "Be careful. I'm afraid this could get ugly."

"Got it," Jenny said as she turned and rushed back toward her pickup. Toby was pacing back and forth on the front seat, panting heavily. Jenny slid in next to him, started the engine, and peeled away from the chaos. She hit the main highway, accelerating to top speed. She needed to get to Brogan's Farm and Feed before it was overrun, too.

Jenny was relieved to see just a handful of vehicles populating Brogan's lot, many belonging to friends. She saw Tina and Cal Cutler loading up bags of chicken feed. Nearby, Cindy Beers' flatbed trailer was being loaded with bales of hay. Probably reserve food for her goats, Jenny thought. Jenny got out of her vehicle, leaving Toby safe inside. She ran up to Tina, who was grimacing as she worked to get the 50-pound feed bags into her pickup.

"Tina, you shouldn't be lifting those, you're pregnant. Let me help," Jenny said.

"Thanks Jenny, but I'm fine. Cal's doing the heavy lifting. Hopefully, this will all blow over, but we don't want to take any chances."

As she spoke, Cal came out of the large side door pulling a handcart filled with more bags of feed. "Jen, better get in there quick if you want seed. Some guys are piling up bags and guarding them until their truck comes. Total bullshit."

"Thanks Cal," Jenny replied as she entered the store and almost ran over Bruce Brogan, the family store's aging patriarch, who was trying to help load handcarts.

"Bruce! I'm so sorry!" Seeing that he was all right, she turned her attention to the store, which was far more crowded than she'd expected. A queue had formed at the checkout counter, and people she had never seen before were piling bags of seed and feed in a corner.

"Jenny! It's getting crazy in here. The guys in the corner are trouble, so watch out," Bruce said, flicking his head in their direction. "I don't like the looks of those guys. What do you need?"

"Don't worry about me, Bruce. Just one thing—do you have any seed potatoes?"

"Over by the cooler," he said. "Take what you need, Jenny. Your credit is good here." Bruce turned and walked toward the checkout counter where his son and daughter-in-law were ringing up a growing line.

Jenny didn't hesitate. She grabbed a handcart and went straight to the seed potatoes, loading several ten-pound bags. Next, she went for other root seeds including beets, carrots, radishes, and parsnips. These will work in the garden late into the year, she thought. Then she moved on to hearty, fast growers including squash and zucchini. Finally, Jenny concentrated on produce that could thrive in the greenhouses. She loaded her overflowing cart with seeds for several varieties of lettuce, cucumbers, kale, spinach, and various beans and peas. Having gathered almost everything she needed, she strained to pull the overloaded cart toward the exit.

"Get the hell out of my way!"

Jenny had been too focused to notice the growing confrontation in the corner of the store until it exploded. She turned in time to see a young man shove Bruce Brogan backwards. He tripped against a handcart and went sprawling to the concrete floor, hitting his head. A tense silence filled the store as Bruce struggled to get up.

"Hey, mister, what's your problem?" Cal and Tina Cutler were now inside the store, and Cal came to Bruce's defense. He helped the elder up and turned to face the stranger. Bruce pressed his hand to his head, and it came away covered in blood. He was shaking.

"Mind your own business, asshole," the young stranger said, as an older, bearded man moved to his side for reinforcement.

"Cal, let's go," Tina Cutler said. She stood at the store entrance, biting the side of her lip in fear.

Jenny sized up the situation. She was almost certain the bearded man was armed. His right arm was hanging by his side, near a bulge in the back of his pants that was partially hidden by an untucked shirt. Cal was probably in mortal danger. Jenny decided to act.

"What are you guys looking for?" she shouted in their direction. Everybody in the deathly quiet store turned to stare at her. "I have some great seeds if you need them."

"We got what we need, lady. Shut the hell up," the bearded man said. He turned his attention to Cal, who stood his ground, bristling with anger.

Drawn inside by the shouting, Cindy Beers moved to stand next to Jenny. "Why don't you guys take what you have and leave? Isn't that your truck out there?"

"We can help you load your truck." Jenny added.

The generous offer confused the strangers for a second. The older, bearded guy looked out the window to confirm their truck had arrived.

"Yeah, great idea lady. You can start by taking your cart outside and putting your shit in our truck."

Jenny grimaced as he saw the stranger reach around his back for what she took to be his gun.

FIFTEEN

Point Betsie, MI

A subconscious mental alarm went off as Jack surfed the outside. He snapped his attention to near shore waters, searching for Meg. Relieved, he located her on the beach helping other kiters land their kites. Just a phantom signal, he thought. Jack performed a gybe, turning to head back out. But there on the horizon, and closing rapidly, Jack saw the source of his premonition: the unmistakable signature of a squall line. He focused on the rolling clouds and saw embedded lightning. Bad news. Time to head home. The deep rumble of thunder drowned out all other sound and the wind picked up. Jack switched to survival mode.

Jack knew better than to trivialize the force of a Lake Michigan squall. Many times, his father had told him the story of the 1967 Coho Fever disaster that had happened on the very same waters he now needed to escape. Coho salmon were introduced into Lake Michigan in 1966. When they became mature, everyone with a boat went trolling by cabin cruiser, rowboat, canoe, whatever. On September 23, 1967, more than 1,000 craft were on the water. Few had weather radios, and almost none had radar. Driven by strong thunderstorms in Wisconsin, the squall hit with surprising suddenness and force. Lucky boaters saw the telltale signs of the squall line and hightailed it for the protection of Frankfort Harbor. Some minimized the threat by riding out the storm with their bow to the waves. Others were totally oblivious to the approaching storm until it was too late.

Winds hit the flotilla of boats with gusts exceeding 50

miles per hour. Driven by storm force winds, waves quickly built to 20 or even 25 feet. Within an hour, over 150 boats were beached, and many more were capsized or in distress. Despite the nearby Coast Guard station at Frankfort and the air/sea rescue helicopters in Traverse City, local authorities were overwhelmed. Larger boats and local citizens on shore did the best they could to help foundering craft and crews. But, on that fateful day that started sunny and calm, 16 people drowned within sight of shore.

Jack set up his gybe to turn around and flee the approaching squall. But the one gybe he needed to hit, he missed. Maybe he let his mind be distracted by thoughts of lost bear cubs, maybe the wind changed—whatever the reason, as Jack charged up the oncoming swell, he lost his balance in some side chop and splashed hard in the trough between swells. He tried to hold on to the boom, but it was wrenched from his grasp.

Most of the time when you fall while windsurfing, the sail goes in the water and acts as a sea anchor. However, maybe one time in a hundred, the mast and boom land on the board, and the sea anchor fails. In moderate conditions, it's no problem; the sail eventually rolls off into the water and you can swim to catch the board. But in near gale conditions… Jack watched as his board careened away, driven by swell and gusting winds. Finally, the sail hit the water, but the board was a good 20 yards downwind. Even then, it continued to drift further away. "Damn!" Jack floated a quarter mile offshore, with no life vest, and an approaching squall line bearing down on him.

The scene on the beach was chaotic. Blowing sand stung any exposed flesh. Beachcombers grabbed their kids and fled to the safety of their cars. Kiters who had raced to shore looked for helpers to land their kites in the gusting winds. Some panicked and pulled their quick-release latches, crashing their kites in the surf. To rescue the swamped kites, kiters had to reel them in by hand on one line, risking deep, raw cuts if the kites relaunched or were yanked by the surf break. One kiter disconnected entirely, abandoning his kite to the mercy of the wind and waves. He watched it tumble downwind toward the lighthouse on its way to the Manitou Islands.

Meg ran up the shore to help Bubba land his kite. Usually Meg could execute the routine maneuver in one smooth attempt. Today it took three tries to catch the erratic kite at its midsection and flip it over safely on the sand. Meg scooped several handfuls of sand on the leading edge of the kite to keep it in place. Bubba came running to help secure the kite.

"Thanks!" he yelled. "Where's your dad?"

Meg looked out over the darkening waters and saw no sail. She scanned the beach and saw no windsurfer. Her dad was not on shore. "Oh God, please don't take him away from me," she prayed, as she continued to scour the churning waters.

A loud clap of thunder acted like a starter's gun as Jack sprinted to catch up with his board. Adrenalin and instinct took over as he pushed his body to its limit. His board was the only chance he had to get out of harm's way. And in the worst case, if he couldn't ride out, he'd need it as a flotation device. He cursed the seat harness that slowed his progress. Between strokes he saw that the wind was picking up spindrift from the waves, a sign that the wind had increased to gale force. The sun was now fully obscured by dark, menacing clouds; the water was dark gray, speckled with white caps. With a final push, he finally reached the sailboard and grabbed the rear foot strap.

Jack was completely exhausted by the effort, but knew he had no time to rest. The board had drifted downwind from the sail, the wrong side for a water start. Letting go of the board, he worked his way along the foot of the sail until he reached the end of the boom. He used his remaining arm strength to lift the end of the boom and clew out of the water so the wind could catch it. Immediately, the sail was picked up by a gust and flew over, and downwind from, the sailboard. Once again, Jack had to sprint to catch the board. He realized he had finally caught a break: the boom was in a reasonable position for a water start.

The storm was almost on him. He figured he had the time and strength for one attempt at a restart. Jack brought the boom over so it rested on the very back of the board. With one hand on the back of the board and one hand holding the boom, he swung the boom up and over the stern, allowing the sail to catch the wind. Years of doing water starts paid off as he found the elusive angle of sail to wind; just enough to raise him out of the water, not too much to catapult him over the board.

He was back up.

Jack took a deep breath and quickly assessed the situation. The wind and rain line of the squall was only a couple hundred yards away. Lightning and thunder were now continuous. He had drifted north, but he still had an angle of attack that could get him to shore upwind of the lighthouse. If the storm line hit, he would be done. Jack pulled in the sail to gain momentum, placed both feet in the board straps, and immediately came on plane. He would race the storm to shore.

Meg held back tears as she trotted down the beach with Bubba and Gordy. If she didn't cry, it would be okay, she thought. Suddenly, Gordy stopped and pointed. "Look, a sail!"

"The squall's going to hit him!" Bubba shouted. All three stood transfixed, watching Meg's dad ride to escape the storm.

Jack's sail was barely visible as he raced between two huge waves at the second sandbar. As he barreled into the first sandbar, he caught air, launching off the backs of the breakers. Too exhausted to slow down, Jack had just enough energy to unhook his harness as he crashed through the shore break. The board smashed against the beach, breaking its fin and sending Jack flying onto the rock-covered sand, bruised and cut.

Meg rushed to his side while Bubba and Gordy dropped their equipment and grabbed his board before it washed out to sea. They pulled it up on shore just yards short of the lighthouse. The squall line hit the shore with a violent gust of chilly wind and stinging rain. "Let's get out of here," Gordy yelled.

Meg helped her father to his feet, and they staggered up the dune to the Subaru. Jack was too exhausted to speak as Meg retrieved the hidden key, opened the car door, and let her dad slump into the driver's seat. She ran around and got in on the passenger side. Rain and hail pelted the car.

"Thank you, God." Rain and tears were spilling down Meg's face. She took a towel and blotted blood off her father's arms and legs.

Minutes later, after the initial fury of the squall had passed, Bubba approached the car in his wet suit. He cracked open the front door. "Damn man, you okay?"

Jack, still slumped over the steering wheel, looked up. He replied with fake bravado, "Yeah, still breathin' air."

"Good. Turn on your radio, Jack. Things are really messed up." Bubba shut the door without further explanation.

Meg grabbed her phone out of the door pocket. She let out an audible gasp as she read the headlines.

"What is it?" asked Jack.

"It says that New York, London, and Tel Aviv have been attacked with dirty bombs," Meg responded, trying to grasp the enormity of the news. "Are those nuclear bombs?"

"My God." Jack straightened up and started the car. "We've got to get home."

"What about our gear?" Meg asked.

"Damn," Jack swore. He contemplated the trade-offs for a few seconds. Even with the world falling apart, the equipment was too expensive to leave on the beach. He was in debt, his daughter was buried in student loans, and he could only afford a rusty Subaru. "Let's pack it," he said, and opened the door into the receding squall. The temperature had dropped twenty degrees and he began to shiver. Jack noticed that he and Meg were alone in a deserted parking lot. A rising sense of dread hit him, harder than the storm had done. The world had changed. Nothing would be the same.

SIXTEEN

BOOM! The 12-gauge shotgun went off in the store with a deafening blast, shattering the plaster ceiling.

"Don't move!" Bryce Brogan, Bruce's son, shouted from behind the counter. He pumped another round into his shotgun and aimed it directly at the stranger. The bearded stranger froze, his hand just short of reaching his concealed gun. He slowly raised his hands, unprepared to argue with the open bore of a 12-gauge.

"Turn around and lie face down on the floor. Slowly," Bryce said, wagging his shotgun to the left, away from the accomplice. The bearded man complied. "You too," Bryce waved the shotgun at the young accomplice. "On the floor, face down." The second man followed his companion. Bryce came out from behind the counter to cover both prone captives. "Cal, check his waistband for a gun." Bryce gestured at the back of the bearded man with his shotgun. Cal lifted the man's shirttail and removed a semiautomatic pistol.

"You know how to use that?" Bryce asked.

"I do," Cal replied, and chambered a round in the Glock.

"Okay. Pat down the other guy," Bryce said, as he turned to look out the front door for the truck driver, another potential threat. "Dad, how many of them were there?"

"Maybe three," his elderly father replied. Linda Brogan handed her father-in-law a towel to blot his head wound.

"He's clean," Cal said. He stood by the strangers, keeping guard.

Bryce saw the truck driver exit his vehicle, gun in hand, and walk slowly across the parking lot toward the store.

"Damn!" Bryce considered the options. "Linda. have you called 911?"

"I keep getting a busy signal," she said, cell phone to her ear.

Bryce returned his attention to the parking lot. The truck driver was now within range. "Stop right there and drop the gun," Bryce yelled. "We have both of your friends disarmed."

The truck driver stopped in his tracks, raised his pistol, and aimed it at Bryce, steadying it with both hands. To Bryce's dismay, a fourth man exited the crew cab of the truck with his own shotgun. The odds were even.

"Let our guys go now!" shouted the driver. The fourth man pumped his shotgun to chamber a round. The distinctive sound made everybody in the store flinch.

"Take cover," Bryce yelled, sensing that a shootout was imminent. "You," he kicked the bearded guy. "Get up and kneel in the doorway."

"Screw you!" The bearded man didn't move. Instead, he yelled, "Joe, come get these rubes. They've got my gun and a shotgun."

This was not what Bryce had expected to hear. He was a hunter, not a cop or a killer. Bryce looked over at Cal, and asked quietly, "Should we let them go?"

"Either that or I think there'll be some shooting," Cal whispered. "I can use this thing, but I'm no good."

"Last chance!" the truck driver yelled from outside.

"Okay, you two, get the hell…" Bryce started.

"Stop!" Jenny but up her hand. Johnny-B's pickup swung into the lot and parked next to the armed mens' truck. Johnny jumped out of the truck holding a military-style, assault rifle. He took cover behind the truck and let loose a couple of rounds at the feet of the man with the shotgun.

"Hey guys, next rounds go in your chest!" Johnny yelled with the authority of a trained soldier. "You won't like how they come out. Drop your weapons. Now!"

"Cal, cover them. If they move, shoot their legs," Bryce said.

He looked out the front door to size up the situation. The gunmen were in the open and defenseless against crossfire. "Hey Johnny!" Bryce yelled, raising his shotgun to let Johnny know where things stood. "We have two captives in here. Cal has their guns."

"I'm not asking again!" Johnny shouted at the men outside. The driver, and then his companion, dropped their weapons and raised their hands. Johnny approached with his weapon trained on them. "Move away and lie on the ground," he said.

"Listen mister, we're just here for some supplies cause of this dirty bomb thing," the driver said as he lay down.

"Right." Johnny kicked their weapons out of reach. "Bryce, bring the other two out here."

"Let's go." Bryce goosed the two captives with the shotgun muzzle to get them up and out the door. "On the ground with your friends."

"God, Johnny, am I glad to see you!" Jenny said as she exited the store with Cal, Tina, and Cindy. The other shoppers headed to their vehicles and sped away, some with supplies, some empty handed.

"Is everybody okay?" Johnny asked.

"Dad has a gash on his head, but he'll survive," Bryce said. "What the hell are we going to do with these guys? Can't reach 911."

Johnny motioned Bryce and Jenny over and out of ear shot of the captives. "Everything is jammed up, and the police have their hands full in town. I'd hate to let them go, but who is going to lock 'um up and watch them?"

"I've got an empty storage shed." Bryce nodded toward the side of the store. "We can tie them up and lock them in there."

"You going to watch them and feed them?" Johnny asked. "Could be days before order is restored around here."

"Maybe you're right, Johnny. I don't have time for this crap," Bryce said.

Johnny walked back to the captives. "Okay, wallets and cell phones out and take off your shoes," he said. "Cal, go check their truck for weapons, phones, IDs, whatever."

"Mister, we don't want any trouble," the driver said. He was obviously the leader. "Just let us go and we won't be back. We're just here for some bird hunting and the casino, nothing more. This dirty bomb thing got us scared."

Johnny inspected their driver's licenses. "Chicago, that figures. You know, we don't take too kindly to strangers coming up here and assaulting our elders." With that, he slammed the butt of his rifle into the ribs of the young man who had roughed up Bruce Brogan, eliciting a deep groan.

"Johnny, stop it!" Jenny rushed over and grabbed Johnny's arms. "We can't sink to their level."

"Okay, here's the deal." Johnny stood over the captives who lay prone on the dirt. "We are going to keep your wallets, phones, shoes, and weapons. We'll give them to our county sheriff. His name is Jim Larson. You want them back, you explain to him what happened up here. Now, get up, get in your truck, and get the hell out of here. If we ever see you again, you'll be the birds we'll be hunting." Johnny threw the truck keys in the dirt in front of them and glared.

"Sure mister," the driver said as he scrambled up, grabbed the keys, and walked barefoot with his pals toward their vehicle.

As Cal and Bryce escorted the thugs from the property, Johnny turned to address the circle of women who had gathered around him. "Jen, I was afraid of this. Law and order can break down in this mess. The grocery store wasn't much better, lots of fights and yelling. Good thing the police showed up."

"Did you get what I asked?" Jenny looked over at Johnny's truck.

"Got as much as I could. Sugar, salt, and all their pectin. Peanut butter and canned stuff were already gone."

"This is not good," Tina Cutler said. "What are we going to do?"

"Not sure how bad this thing is going to get," Johnny replied.

"My friends on the net say it's 50/50 that Israel is going to go nuclear. If that's right, all bets are off. Could be the start of World War III, or at least another Depression. Currencies, including the dollar, may well crash. We might be headed back to bartering and trade."

They all stood silent for a minute, imagining the worst, until Jenny interrupted their grim reflections. "Listen, we're going to stick together as a community. There will probably be more outsiders to deal with," she said, looking up the road their recent tormenters had used to exit. "We've got plenty of food if we combine forces. I've got all the vegetables we could eat. Tina, you've got chickens and eggs. Cindy, you have your goats and cheese. Johnny, you bring in fresh fish every day. The forest is thick with deer. We can get by if we stick together." Jenny turned to look each one in the eyes, seeking confirmation.

"We're just a seed and feed distributor," Linda Brogan said. "What do we bring to the table?"

"If I were you, I would close the store and preserve your supplies—money might mean nothing tomorrow" Tina said. "Besides, you have horses and feed crops, those could come in real handy. Jenny's right, we can expand our co-op."

"Okay, is everybody in?" Jenny asked. The members of the small circle nodded. "Good. We need to meet to discuss this more. See what is happening in the world, how we should react. How about we meet at the church tomorrow morning, say 9 o'clock? Afterwards, we need to harvest the gardens— they're your vegetables too! Cindy, can you let the other gals know?"

"Sure Jenny, we'll all be there," Cindy replied. Tina and Linda nodded in agreement.

"Okay, Jenny," Johnny said. "After I chase down the Sheriff, I'll drop off these supplies at your place. I'll also monitor the net, but I expect that'll crash, too. I'm using my shortwave to reach out to others. We may have more problems than food to deal with. I know you're a pacifist, but we need to talk about self-defense. These city thugs could just be the beginning."

"All right," Jenny said. "We can talk about that as a group. Church, tomorrow at 9 am."

The group broke up. Tina and Cal drove off to put their chicken feed in secure storage at their farm. Cindy headed down the road with her bales of hay to supplement the feed for the goats. Johnny helped Jenny load her seed bags into the pickup, and then took off in search of the Sheriff. Jenny and Linda went into the farm store to check on the severity of Bruce's head injury. They decided Bruce was in need of medical attention and probably some stitches. However, he insisted they close up the store before they left for the clinic. Once everything was stored and closed, Linda loaded Bruce into their pickup and headed toward the only medical clinic in Aux Baie. Bryce stayed to watch over the store in case any other trouble arose.

Jenny approached Bryce before leaving. He looked grim. She decided a little levity was in order. "Nice job on the ceiling," she said, looking up at the damage caused by the shotgun blast.

"Guess I kind of got carried away." Bryce chuckled. "But, listen Jenny, thanks for the help. I know what you did to distract them. You saved my bacon. He was going for his gun, sure as the sun will rise."

Jenny gave Bryce a quick hug. "I'm just glad you're safe. See you tomorrow?"

"Yep. Linda told me about your plan. We should know more by then. But we'll be there, we're all in."

"Thank you. God bless."

Jenny turned and walked toward her pickup. Toby barked at her approach. He'd been safe through the firestorm, but he'd also been cooped up without food or water for hours. When she let him out to relieve himself, he jumped up on her with frantic licks and nuzzles before running off to the edge of the woods. As she watched him do his business, she fought a growing pang of loneliness. Today, even more than most days, she wished someone she could talk to was waiting for her at home. Toby returned and jumped up into his seat. Jenny started the truck and headed back toward her camp.

SEVENTEEN

Traverse City, MI – 3:00 pm

Operating on the borrowed energy of an adrenalin high, Jack insisted on driving home from Point Betsie. Meg repeatedly tried to call her mother, but the cell networks had become hopelessly overloaded. The Internet had become intermittent too, so they turned to the radio for news. It only increased their anxiety; a mass exodus from New York City, fear of escalation by Israel, and the first signs of looting and rioting in the cities. All the while, Meg asked questions that Jack couldn't answer. He thought about stopping for gas and food, but every mini-mart they passed on the road was already overrun by hoarders.

Once they reached Jack's place, he was able to strip down and, with Meg's help, clean and bandage his more serious cuts and scratches. He would clean off the blood in the car later.

Meg was finally able to reach her mom who insisted that she return to Grand Rapids at once. Jack protested that the two-hour trip was far too dangerous. But in the end, Meg made the decision to head home.

"Are you going to be okay?" Meg asked.

Jack imagined that he looked like shit. "I'll be fine. I'm more worried about you. Are you sure you don't want to take my gun?" Feeling the beginnings of an adrenalin crash, he took a deep swig of the stiff coffee he had brewed the minute they got home.

"Dad, I don't even know how to use a gun. Besides, I don't have a permit."

"I can teach you really quick. It's just aim and shoot."

"I'll be fine. It's just down to Grand Rapids. There will be police on the road, and I have my cell phone. I'll call you the minute I get there."

Privately, Jack conceded that Meg was probably safer traveling unarmed than with his gun. He dropped the subject. "Okay. I'll pack you a cooler for the ride. It might be a while before stores get back to normal." He refilled the cooler with the snacks and drinks they had taken to the beach that morning... in another lifetime, Jack thought.

"All right. I'll pack my stuff," Meg said and went off to the guest bedroom. Before long, she was back with a suitcase crammed full of assorted sports gear. Jack helped carry the bags to her rusted-out Honda. He placed the cooler on the passenger seat so she could reach it. He was close to tears as she gave him a big hug and told him that she loved him. When she turned to get in the car, he quickly dragged his sleeve over his eyes.

"Don't stop for anybody," Jack said. "And call me when you get to the highway, okay?"

"Sure dad. I'll be fine." She started the engine and backed slowly down the driveway.

"Love you!" Jack yelled out, but she was already too far away to hear. As she drove down the street, she gave a quick wave and toot of the horn before turning out of sight. Their familiar farewell ritual was too much for Jack. Tears welled up uncontrolled.

Before going back inside, Jack looked up and down the street for someone, anyone, to talk to. But it was ominously quiet. Everyone must be hunkering down, he figured. Back inside he found his cell phone and put it in his back pocket, so he'd be ready for Meg's call. He turned on the TV for breaking news.

"Our sources at the Pentagon now confirm that Israel has launched retaliatory strikes targeting Tehran, Damascus, parts of Beirut, and the Gaza Strip. The nature of these attacks is unknown. However, it is speculated that the Israelis have responded in kind

with some sort of dirty bombs. There is no indication of any nuclear response at this time. There is mounting concern that the situation will continue to escalate in the Mideast. We are told that the President has been in contact with Israel, Russia, Pakistan, and Saudi Arabia regarding the situation. Let's check in with Chris Cummings at the White House..."

My God, it just keeps getting worse. Jack muted the TV and sat in stony silence. Meg, her mother, and Jenny—all the women he loved, or had loved, were out of his reach and protection. Jack had a passing thought about finding some alcohol, but quickly dispelled this notion as a disastrous choice. If he got drunk, he would be of no use to anyone, not even to himself. Instead, he turned his mind toward action, to prepare for whatever might come. Jack poured himself another cup of coffee and headed toward the garage.

He rummaged through his old camping gear: a tent, cooking utensils, water purification, a hunting knife, fishing gear, and an oversized duffle. He brought it inside and threw it on the bed. From his closet, Jack pulled out his hunting camo, down sleeping bag, and some all-weather gear to add to the growing pile. He found cans of tuna, some ramen, and granola bars in his sparsely stocked pantry. From his bed stand, Jack retrieved his .38 Special revolver. Out of his lockbox, he inspected his stash of emergency money: 10 hundred-dollar bills and two tubes of gold coins inherited from his father. Jack used to laugh at his dad's gullibility and fear of doomsday scenarios. He wasn't laughing any more. The $5,000 in gold could be worth a fortune soon.

After another slug of coffee, Jack went down to his poorly lit basement and opened the gun cabinet. Like millions of other Americans, he stocked up on guns and ammo whenever liberals were set to take control in DC. Jack considered the small arsenal he'd assembled over time. He pulled out his Remington 12-gauge shotgun and a case of buckshot shells. He also grabbed his lever-action Marlin 1894C, conveniently chambered for either .357 Mag or .38 Special. Besides being cool, it had great utility for deer or small game hunting.

Finally, he grabbed his first firearm—the single-shot .22 rifle of his childhood. He'd learned to shoot at his great uncle's farm in North Carolina. Everybody knew how to shoot down South. Later, Jack became a great shot while attending YMCA summer camp. He got so good he could knock the bullseye out of a target with just four bullets and use his fifth bullet to shoot the clothespin holding his counselor's target. The counselor went crazy trying to find the culprit. He couldn't go by how many hits each target showed, because the cluster on Jack's targets were too tight. Thinking about it now, he realized his counselor probably knew it was him all along. The same counselor had given his testimony around the campfire about being a Christian. He had said he didn't fear death, and it had made a huge impression on Jack. Can't do that at the YMCA anymore, Jack thought. He figured most people didn't even know that YMCA originally stood for *Young Men's Christian Association*.

Leaving his .22 behind, Jack grabbed the Remington, Marlin, and a bag of assorted ammo and returned upstairs to add it to the pile on his bed. He carefully packed everything into his large bug-out duffel bag. He'd be ready if he needed to flee. But flee to where?

He thought of Jenny's camp. It was out of the way, off the grid, self-sustaining, and Jen had enough gardens to feed an army. Of course, he hadn't seen her for years. Would Jenny even want him at her cabin now? His cell phone ringing interrupted his thoughts. It was Meg.

"Meg, you okay?"

"Yeah, Dad. Just got on the highway. Everything's fine. There's almost no traffic. Are you okay?"

"I'm fine. Do you have enough gas?"

"Half tank. I should be good," Meg replied. "Did you hear about Israel's retaliation?"

"Yeah. Not good, but I'm not surprised. Let's pray it stops there. Please call me when you get home. Are you going to see mom?"

"Yes, she's freaking out. I'll text you then."

"Okay. Drive safe. I love you."

"Love you dad."

The call ended, and so did Jack's muscle control. He staggered over to the couch to lay down, his entire body aching from his ordeal on the water. He would take just a short rest, and then get back to... back to what? Preparing for the coming apocalypse? Jack was sound asleep when a soft chime indicated he had received a text message: Meg was safely home in Grand Rapids.

EIGHTEEN

Traverse City, MI – 6:00 pm

Tim propped open the screen door, balancing bags of groceries while Kristen worked the key into the lock of her one-bedroom apartment. As they entered, they were greeted by the pitiful cries of a gray cat who rubbed its arched back against Kristen's legs and then, after a brief review, rubbed against Tim's legs too.

"That's Smokey," Kristen made introductions. "He's a five-year-old Russian Blue mix. He has his claws, so fair warning."

Tim gingerly walked around the cat and followed Kristen into her small kitchen to place the grocery bags on the counter. "Bathroom?" he asked. Hours in a crowded grocery store full of panicking people had taken its toll on his bladder.

"Just down the hall on the right," Kristen said as she opened her refrigerator and started storing perishables. "It's Smokey's bathroom too, so apologies—it's a bit stinky."

Tim scoped out the small apartment as he headed toward the bathroom. Quaint, tidy, and feminine. Family photos placed prominently on the walls. A small bookcase full of hardback books and keepsakes. On the coffee table in front of the sofa, a well-tended plant and a Bible. A flat-screen TV hung on the wall across from the sofa. Tim stole a glance into Kristen's bedroom and saw a nicely made queen bed, with everything put away and in order. Smokey sat on the bed, eyeing him suspiciously. Hope he's not territorial, Tim half-joked to himself as he entered the bathroom.

Tim looked in the mirror and took deep breaths to gather himself. The afternoon had been a blur. Leaving campus, he somehow found himself teamed up with Kristen: he had a car, she had a plan. They spent hours fighting crowds at the local grocery store, using a divide and conquer strategy, separately rushing down the aisles before everything was taken. Then came an interminable wait in the checkout line, fighting to maintain their place in the queue. The wait gave them time to get to know each other a bit.

Kristen's last name was Campbell, she was 34, and she worked as a registered nurse at the hospital. She was an only child whose parents still lived in California. Over the last 10 years she had been a traveling nurse, holding every nursing job imaginable: emergency room, critical care, school nurse, nursing home, even a stint as a public health nurse flying in to remote Inuit communities in Alaska. A friend recommended Traverse City as a place where she might settle for a few years. She decided to pursue a degree as a physician's assistant and had picked up Tim's senior seminar to earn some elective credits.

As Tim washed his hands, he considered the cursory bio he had provided. Certainly not enough for Kristen to know him in any real sense. Did anybody really know anyone else? Tim ruminated as he exited the bathroom. Kristen was still in the kitchen. Tim saw the TV remote and decided to get caught up on the latest news. He was able to activate the right channel quickly, quite different than his fumbling attempts in class today, he bemoaned. The news was all bad: looting in cities, runs on banks and grocery stores, retaliation and threats in the Middle East, and rampant doomsday speculation. At least the blame game had not started. Everybody on TV was united in the face of a common threat.

"Anything new?" Kristen asked as she came out of the kitchen.

"Israel attacked Tehran. Now they're worried about Iran retaliating." Kristen walked toward him, coming quite close, and looked at him intently. He felt his face warm up. "Perhaps I should go home and stow my groceries."

Kristen looked hurt. She tilted her head to the side and softly responded "Oh no. I was hoping you would stay for dinner. I can quickly put something together." She touched his arm.

Kristen's soft touch was brief, but it left Tim's skin tingling in anticipation of more. He tried to compose himself—it had been such a weird day. He took a deep breath. "You know, that sounds great. How can I help?"

"Well, I have a bottle of local wine that we could open. I hope it goes with tuna salad."

"As long as it has a cork, we should be fine."

Once Kristen had finished preparing the meal, Tim turned down the TV and they sat across from each other at her small dining room table. The close proximity bothered Tim at first, but as Kristen told her story, he found his eyes finally fixing on hers.

"I was ready to start a family," she said "and then a friend from church told me he'd been cheating on me. It was so embarrassing. I didn't believe it at first, but it all made sense—the late nights and lame excuses." Kristen rubbed her forehead before continuing. "Anyway, I finally confronted him and, well, he blamed me." She paused, picked up her napkin and dabbed her eyes.

"I'm sorry," Tim didn't know what else to say. "You don't have to relive this."

"No, I'm fine. Anyway, the divorce got really ugly with lawyers and all. I moved in with my parents for a while and then started to travel. But, as they say, wherever you go, there you are. I guess the only constant in my life has been my faith."

"Do you plan on staying here in Traverse City?"

"It's a beautiful place. I don't know. I've been searching around for a church community. It's tough for a single woman —not a lot of chances to socialize outside of the bar scene. How about you? Any special person in your life?"

Tim could feel his face blush again, but he didn't avert his eyes. "I've had a few girlfriends, but no one serious. If you haven't guessed by now, I'm kind of a nerd." He chuckled. "I guess knowledge became my obsession. I've got four advanced degrees, multiple patents, and several startup companies under my belt and, you know, I still don't have a clue."

"About what?" Kristen tilted her head again in her endearing way.

"About life. Why we're here. Why anything is here!"

"I see," Kristen said. "I guess that's where faith comes in."

"Are you so sure? How could a loving God allow evil and misery in the world? Look at today's terrorist attack. It's a byproduct of religious extremism. It's been the same throughout man's history."

"What about today's class, 'all that is mine is yours' and Christian socialism?" Kristen asked.

"That was just to prove a point. I mean, Christianity has some noble precepts, but on the matter of God, where's the proof?"

Kristen got up from the table and started to clear their dishes. "Our lives and God are certainly a mystery," she nodded slowly. "But isn't that the whole point of faith? Besides, if we aren't part of God's creation, then what's our purpose? Just a cosmic accident? Might as well be a nihilist."

As Kristen headed to the kitchen, Tim thought about how he should respond. He'd had this same discussion thousands of times before and wasn't about to renounce his agnosticism. But tonight, Kristen's point of view shed a different light on the argument. Faith alone didn't make sense. Yet there was Kristen in the kitchen, calmly cleaning dishes, oblivious to— or perhaps at peace with—the fact that the world was falling apart. It's always falling apart. What did she know that he didn't?

He sat frozen.

Smokey appeared under the table, rubbing against his leg looking for affection. A flashback from today's class welled up, "Yes, I'm Kristen." Her eyes had invited him in, or was he mistaken? Despite the risk, he had to know. He found himself standing behind Kristen, embracing her closeness and scent. The desire was now unbearable. He took the chance, his hands enveloping her waist.

She hesitated.

Oh no...

Kristen reached over for a towel to dry her hands, and then turned to accept Tim's embrace. The world fell away as he was consumed by her willing lips.

NINETEEN

It was getting dark when Johnny-B finally got back to his cabin. He'd located Sheriff Larson and briefed him on the armed robbery at Brogan's. Jim now had the wallets, phones, and guns of the foursome from Chicago. Afterward, he'd dropped off the supplies at Jenny's cabin. Now he was glad to be home. Johnny leaned his assault rifle against the wall in the mudroom—he would clean it later. First, he wanted to find out what the hell was really happening. He grabbed a beer from the fridge and walked past his TV to the Kenwood shortwave radio set up in the corner of the living room. Johnny sat down and brought the radio to life.

"WW5BT, WW5BT, this is K8JNB." He waited for a reply, fine-tuning his frequency to take out some static. He didn't have to wait long.

"WW5BT at your service. Well Johnny B., is this a crock of shit or what?"

"10-4 Big Texas. How are things down there? Over."

"People are ornerier than a hornet in a tar bucket. I mean, we got looters in the cities, we got preppers heading for the hills, we got doomsdayers readying for the end times. I'm telling ya, we're back to beans, bullets, and booze! How 'bout up there? You Yoopers seceded from the union yet? Over."

"Pretty bad. Broke up an armed robbery at the local farm and feed store just now. Seriously, what are you hearing? Over." Johnny knew this was all just an opening monologue for Big Texas, aka Ben Sutton. He was actually a serious guy: ex-Special Forces coms specialist with a Purple Heart. No family now, except his brother Tommy who worked for the Bureau.

"Actually JB, nothing good. Got some sources who think Israel is going to take out Iran's enrichment facilities. Not sure how, but if they do, we might have a shooting war. If Iran has an ace up its sleeve, the shit could hit the fan. Over."

"You hear anything from Europe? Over."

"Yeah, same shit. It's early morning over there but they've already closed the markets and banks indefinitely. Some vigilante attacks on Muslims in France, Belgium, and Germany. We got a real mess on our hands, Johnny. Over."

"I think the Internet and cell service are going to be FUBAR," Johnny said. "I want to set up a news network, maybe just for veterans. You in? Over."

"That's a big 10-4 JB, a vet-net! I'll reach out to some other HAM-bones. I agree, good information might become a rare commodity. Over."

"I was thinking of transmitting at 12 midnight. The later the better for wave propagation. Same frequency. Over."

"I'll be all ears, Johnny. By the way, got any gold you can send me? Over."

"On its way. Don't spend it all in one place. K8JNB over and out."

"WW5BT. Good night."

TWENTY

As he entered his office, Steve Bennett didn't realize his shoulders were hunched over. Marge greeted him by putting a hand to the side of his face while she searched his eyes. He felt comforted as she gave him a long, hard hug—as if she was part lover, part mother.

They remained silent until they finally released.

"How did you get here?" Steve asked. "I thought the city was locked down."

"I have my ways," Marge replied, waggling a photo-ID smart card that hung by a lanyard around her neck.

"Oh yeah, I forgot about our PIV cards."

"Did you hear from Scott?"

"Yes. He's in TC, thank God."

"He asked about our relationship on the way to the airport. I told him that he'd have to talk with you—I didn't know what else to say."

"Oh, really?" He looked at Marge anew, trying to imagine how his son might see her. How had he reacted? Would he wrongly suspect that he had an affair while his mother was still living? It was all too much—this wasn't the time for family melodrama. "I need a drink."

"Are you done for the night?" Marge asked before heading over to the wet bar.

"Not sure. I have a meeting at 7 am but could be called at any time." Steve took off his coat and tie. He watched Marge pour a couple of stiff scotches and return with his drink. They sat down together, nursing their drinks, looking out the window at the brightly lit Capitol Dome.

"I assume you heard Israel retaliated with dirty bombs?" Steve asked

"Yes, Damascus and Tehran, right?"

"They also took some potshots at Hamas and Hezbollah."

"You need some sleep. Should we head back to your condo?"

"No, I've got to stay close. I'll try a nap on the couch. Why don't you go home?"

"I'll stay, if you don't mind," Marge replied.

"Sure. You want the couch?"

"The chair is fine. I'll check your emails." Marge went over to the desk, drink in hand. Soon she was navigating his computer for incoming messages.

Steve rose from the couch and went to the bathroom for a quick spit bath. He returned with his shoes off. After finishing his drink, he propped up a pillow on the couch. Soon he was stretched out on the couch, snoring softly.

With Steve asleep, Marge sought comfort from the Bible she pulled from the bookcase. She knew where to go, flipping pages until she reached Psalm 27:1. *The Lord is my light and my salvation; whom shall I fear? The Lord is the stronghold of my life; of whom shall I be afraid?* She continued to read, finding solace in the eternal Word, until her eyes grew heavy.

The hard knock broke Steve's slumber, his whole body flinched as if he was falling in a dream. He looked at the doorway. Jerry Belinsky, his legislative aide, had stuck his head in. "Sorry boss, but we've got more problems."

"What now?" Steve asked. He sat up on the couch, rubbing his eyes.

"Israel just took out Iran's enrichment facilities. Looks like some sort of new tactical nuke. We've got seismic confirmation as well as..."

Steve sprung from the couch, hyperalert. "Did you say nuke?"

"Yeah, they think it was a shaped charge, bunker buster. Low yield, low plume, but it was a nuke. They need you at the briefing now!"

Steve dashed toward the bathroom, hardly acknowledging Marge whose face was etched with fear. "Any response from Iran?" Steve yelled, feeling his heart starting to race.

"Just happened Steve—you're getting this in real time," Belinsky shouted back.

"I'll be right there."

"Okay, meet you at the tunnel," Jerry said, before heading to the corridor that connected the Rayburn Building with the Capitol.

As Steve splashed cold water on his face, his mind flashed through the possible scenarios: Defense of Israel? A regional exchange of nukes? An inevitable escalation into nuclear war? He looked at his cabinet holding spare underwear, shirt, and socks—no time for that or a shave.

Marge was waiting with a giant carry cup of coffee when he exited.

Steve grabbed it and headed for the door. "Not sure when I'll be back."

"I'll be praying for you, and our country," Marge whispered.

Her words caused Steve to abruptly stop and turn. Summoning up a grateful smile, he simply said, "I love you."

And then he was gone.

PART 2

Those who would give up essential Liberty, to purchase a little temporary Safety, deserve neither Liberty nor Safety.

Benjamin Franklin

1755 Letter of Reply to the Colonial Governor

TWENTY-ONE

Post Attack

Washington D.C. – September 16
The Bureau Surveillance Room

With Assistant Attorney General Maxwell "Max" Hunter following him down the hall, Reggie Woods couldn't help but feel nervous. Why so soon after the attacks? Why was the Department of Justice involved? And why did Hunter break protocol, going around my superiors to engage me directly? It didn't add up, but he wasn't about to challenge this powerful man. They reached the surveillance room and Reggie gave a perfunctory knock before entering. It took a while for their eyes to adjust to the darkness. Tommy Sutton's face glowed from the reflection of multiple monitors. Reggie scanned the room to make sure Tommy had cleaned up his candy wrappers as ordered. He had—now that's a good boy. Having a Cal-Tech IT whiz kid on staff was nice, even better when you had a suspended sentence hanging over his head.

"Tommy, our visitor would like a quick demo of the Deep-Sea program we've restarted." In the wake of the attacks, the legislative and judicial handcuffs had quickly come off their surveillance programs—despite the earlier failings of the FISA Court.

"Sure. Do you want a general sweep, or a specific target?"

Reggie turned to Hunter. "Do you have a person you would like to search? It could be anybody—family, friend, opponent —anybody you want. We will delete this after the demo."

"Steve Bennett."

"Congressman Steve Bennett?" Reggie couldn't help but raise his eyebrows.

"That's right. Is that a problem?" Hunter asked

"No, no problem at all. Tommy, please do a standard dump on Congressman Steve Bennett."

"You might want to come around behind me," Tommy said as he typed in and entered the target's name. It took about 10 seconds before a standardized form appeared on the screen with boilerplate information about Stephen J. Bennett.

"Hell, I can get that information from Google," Hunter said.

"Please note that this is just page 1 of 18," Tommy replied. He then scrolled through the pages and Hunter's eyes began to widen. "We can tell you his criminal record, his medical records, his education records, his tax filings, his extended family relationships, what he buys, what websites he visits, what he posts on social media, who he communicates with and how often, where he's traveled. You want me to go on?"

"No, I see—very powerful."

"Tommy, do a Level Two Criminal Screen," Reggie said.

Several entries popped up on the screen. Tommy provided a summary. "Let's see. Minor in Possession, University of Michigan, September 8, 1993. Expunged after one year."

"I thought those things were erased from the database," Hunter said.

"Nothing is erased from the database," Tommy replied. "Okay, here's another one, his company was sued for negligence in 1998. A subcontractor got hurt at a work site; settled out-of-court by his insurance company. A Michigan Employment Security audit in 1999, hmm, looks like he wrongly claimed employees as subcontractors; paid back taxes and a penalty. What else... A couple of speeding tickets. He had a brother with two DUIs, committed suicide. Maybe they have an issue in the family?"

"All right." Reggie interrupted. "Bennett's pretty much a Boy Scout. Let's show our visitor the geospatial and Level One Associates".

"Okay, let's see where Mr. Bennett is right now." Tommy entered some keystrokes and a map came up showing lower Michigan and a white star near Grand Rapids. He zoomed in and overlaid a satellite image of the terrain. It looked like a downtown office building. "Let's see who is close to him. I will use 100 yards." A few more keystrokes and a cluster of yellow dots surrounded the white star. "Okay, I am screening for peer-to-peer communication, people that have previously connected with Bennett's smartphone." The population of yellow dots narrowed down to eight. "Let's check one out." Tommy hovered over one yellow star and double-clicked. Up on the screen came *Marjorie Stevenson 555-989-3245*. A couple more keystrokes and an extensive phone call history between Stevenson and Bennett appeared. "Must be a family member or something," Tommy said.

"Marge is his assistant," Hunter said. "That's amazing! How can you do that without GPS or Location Services authorized by the user?"

"We've had this capability for years," Tommy replied. "We have access to the CSLI—that's cell site location information —of the public carriers. Or we can set up our own fake cell towers to capture this information. It's called a Stingray. The rest is just database searches and correlations. Our G5 capability will be even better. We will use smartphones, with a trojan horse app, to track other smartphones that are in proximity; in effect setting up a distributed grid independent of the public carriers. The phones don't even have to be on—just have power!" Tommy looked over this shoulder at his audience with a gleam in his eye. "Users already do this when they link or pair their phones. We'll do the same thing, just covertly."

"Let's do a deep dive, a top 50 connect list for the last year," Reggie said.

Tommy's fingers raced over the keypad and up came a list of 50 names, cell phone numbers and number of times they had connected with Steve Bennett over the last year. Marge was near the top along with Bennett's immediate family.

"Okay," Reggie said, "screen for charitable deductions to a church." A few more keystrokes and the list was reduced to about 40 names. "Quite the religious circle!" Reggie snickered. "Let's see how religious they really are. Screen for visits to porn sites or escort services."

Tommy complied, and the list shrank to five names.

"Jesus," Hunter whispered.

"Hmm, I wonder if their churches are aware of this activity?" Reggie asked. "Let's try one more screen. Tommy, does anybody have itemized deductions exceeding two standardized deviations from the mean?"

After a couple of keystrokes, the five names were reduced to two.

Reggie laughed. "Now that's something the IRS might be interested in. Maybe they're deducting their escort services?"

"My God, this is powerful!" Hunter said.

"And it doesn't stop there," Reggie replied. "We can monitor Bennett and his associates in real time and setup any flags we want. Also, we're evaluating a new program to rate people based on their social consciousness, or SCR for short."

"A what?"

"A Social Consciousness Rating," Reggie said. "We grade people based on various criteria such as political affiliation, gun ownership, church membership, pro-life, PAC donations, school affiliations, websites visited, group memberships like the Tea Party or NRA, use of key words in phone, text, or email. For politicians, we also factor in their voting record. Anyway, we have about two-dozen criteria identified so far to grade a person from 0 to 100. Any rating in the top quartile we consider a potential domestic threat."

"What's Bennett's score?" Hunter asked.

"I was hoping you would ask. Tommy, can you oblige our visitor?"

Tommy went back to working the keyboard. A single line came up on the screen; *U.S. Rep. Stephen J. Bennett, R-MI, SCR = 84, Risk = High*.

"Son of a bitch! What's this info used for?" Hunter asked.

"The original plan was to use this as opposition research for the next election," Reggie said. "The idea of rating a person seemed to be a logical extension so we could prioritize threats."

"Interesting." Hunter took off his glasses and placed a stem in his mouth, staring into the distance. "Can you also look up a company?"

"Sure," Reggie said. "What company?"

"Plasma Drive Technologies." Hunter put his glasses back on.

In a matter of seconds, Tommy had the company's boilerplate on the screen, including its principals.

Hunter leaned in to better see the screen. "One of the Cofounders, Scott Bennett, is he related to Congressman Bennett?"

Tommy hit a function key to cross-correlate Steve Bennett's info with that of Plasma Drive Technologies. "Yes, Scott Bennett is his son," Tommy said. "Do you want a dump on him?"

"No, that's okay. But their Chief Scientist, Karl Schultz," Hunter used his finger to point at the screen. "Can you show me his family tree? Close relatives?"

"Piece of cake," Tommy said.

Hunter remained quiet as he perused the list. Reggie leaned in to see if he could glean what Hunter was searching for.

"Hmm." Tommy whispered.

Reggie heard the murmur. "What is it Tommy?"

"Well, these files have been recently accessed."

"By whom?" Hunter asked.

"Well, most recently, DHS. Let's see." Tommy hit a couple function keys and brought up the chain of custody for the files. "DHS was John Bowden on August 25. Before that DOE accessed the files on August 19 as well as in June and May. A Sarah Wong."

"Really," Hunter said. "Are they authorized to view these

files?"

Reggie thought that was a strange question coming from a person who was breaking protocol himself. "Correct me if I'm wrong, Tommy, but I believe these corporate files were non-classified even before the attacks."

"That's right, sir."

"I see," Hunter said. "One last thing, can you show me who Steve Bennett talked to on September 11th?"

"Sure, no problem," Reggie replied. "Tommy?"

A few more keystrokes and a list of about ten entries appeared.

"Zoom in and scroll those entries," Hunter said. "Stop. So, at 9:51 am Bennett called this Dan Fisher. Who's he?"

Tommy did a quick search. "Looks like a pilot, veteran of the Gulf War."

"Interesting. Do you have a recording of that call?" Hunter asked.

Reggie stepped in "Yes, but we can't access it without going through channels. I'm sure your office could clear the way by..."

"This entry at 10:15 am." Hunter interrupted. "Looks like an incoming call from Aaron Leibowitz, the former Ambassador from Israel. I'm sure we can get that transcript. What's this?" Hunter pointed at another entry on the screen with a time stamp of 10:48 am.

"That's a text message from Marjorie Stevenson." Tommy replied. "I can give you the transcript on that one." He double-clicked the entry: *Package delivered and on its way. I'm heading back to office.*

After a moment of silence, Hunter said, "I've seen enough."

Walking out of the government office complex, Hunter turned to Reggie. "This meeting never happened. Also, I may need your participation on an interagency committee—I'll get back to you."

Yes sir." Reggie tried to conceal his smile. An alliance with Hunter could be career changing.

As Assistant AG Max Hunter walked away, Reggie saw him place a call. He wondered if this muckety-muck knew his smartphone was being tracked too. Always wise to have something on everybody.

TWENTY-TWO

Traverse City, MI – September 18
Plasma Drive Technologies, LLC

Scott sat at the head of the conference room table waiting for his co-founder, Tim Kelly, to arrive. Instead of an all-hands meeting, which was a stretch with only five employees, he had only invited Karl Schultz. Affectionately called their mad scientist, Karl was all of 5'5" with unruly, gray hair. A widower with grown children, he was all in with their little startup company. Karl knew a bad news meeting when he saw one. He had seen many at Lockheed Martin before retiring a few years back.

"So, how did the meeting go last week?" Karl fiddled with the height adjustment to his swivel chair. "Or, is that a moot question with the terrorist attacks?"

"Let's wait for Tim before we get into the details, okay?" Scott replied

"Sure, it'll give me time to check on my 201—I mean my 401k." Karl snorted. "I dumped everything yesterday, I'm going to T-Bills and cash."

"Are you kidding me? You're just locking in your losses. The markets are back up today."

"Listen, I'm tired of fretting over it. Besides, I think the markets might not recover this time. The Euro is crashing, and I think the dollar will be the last domino. Time to hunker down."

Before Scott could respond, Tim came into the conference room carrying a cup of coffee and shut the door.

"Sorry I'm late, had to drop Kristen off at the hospital."

"Who's Kristen?" Karl asked.

"I guess you would call her my girlfriend," Tim said, his cheeks starting to blush.

"Oh," Karl raised an eyebrow. To the best of his knowledge, Tim had never had a girlfriend before.

"Anyway, let's kick this thing off." Scott interrupted. "When I met with my dad last week, he told me to drop the plasma drive research. He said, to use his exact words, 'there are some powerful people watching you'." Scott paused to let that sink in.

"Hmm," Karl murmured, "I bet it's Energy or maybe even Defense. Have you gotten anything more out of your dad?" Well, this ups the ante, he thought. Never had to worry about stuff like this at Lockheed Martin...

"No. He's totally swamped with the emergency right now. Besides, I got the distinct impression that we should avoid any electronic communication in case we're under surveillance."

Karl nodded his head. "That seems prudent."

"Okay, so what are we going to do?" Tim asked.

"Well, I talked to our investors yesterday, they're in total risk aversion mode now. So, we've got about two months of working capital left, and then it's on us. Other than that, things are great!" Scott said with a rueful smile.

"Are you suggesting we close the business?" Karl asked. After everything they'd been through, it would be gut punch. "Don't you think there's too much potential here to back away? And we're really getting close. If it makes any difference, I'm willing to work for free. What else do I have to do?"

"Thanks for the offer, Karl." Scott patted his old friend on the back. "But I really don't know what to do. If my dad is right, and we are under surveillance, then we might need to close the facility. Hell, we won't be able to pay rent in a couple months anyway. Tim, how big is your basement?"

"Not big enough" Tim replied. "But let's back up. Karl, are you hiding something from us? What do you mean we're really getting close?"

Karl had a cat that ate the canary grin on his face, and he tented his fingers over the conference table. "Well, I made a little progress the other day."

"And..." Tim egged him on.

"Well, our little engine that could had plasma flow—at least for a while." Karl let that hang in the air.

"You what!" Scott said. "You actually had ignition?"

"It's activation Scott, not ignition," Tim said. "Plasma can ignite things, just like a spark plug, but actual plasma is activated by free radicals."

"Yeah, whatever, but you actually created plasma?" Scott asked, turning his attention back to Karl.

"Activation is not the problem," Karl explained. "The problem is to sustain the reaction and buffer the engine from the superheated plasma while using nominal energy so we can generate a *net energy gain*. Otherwise, what's the point? Anybody can create plasma by throwing enough energy at it."

"So, what's your approach moving forward?" Tim asked. "Were you able to glean anything from Uncle Jacob's notes?"

"His chicken scratch is worse than mine, but I've deciphered a couple things. First, he hypothesized that a microjet of air would be hypersensitive to ionization, vastly reducing input energy. Furthermore, he theorized that one might contain the plasma in a bubble by regulating the electromagnetic fields of the plasma itself. It's called a Skyrmion, the same thing that contains ball lightning. That would eliminate the need for huge, external super magnets. You know, I had a dream the other day."

His statement garnered the effect Karl expected—both Scott and Tim went silent, giving him their rapt attention.

"I dreamt of my granddaughter blowing bubbles. If she blew too hard, they immediately collapsed. If she blew too soft, they never formed. But, if she blew just right, a chain of perfectly-sized bubbles would form like they were playing follow the leader—almost as if they knew how to behave! Formation, pinch off, independence, and then collapse. If I could repeat that process with plasma bubbles, we might superheat the air without blowing up the engine! It's all a matter of quantum harmonics."

"Well, I'm glad you put it in layman's terms!" Scott snorted. "Tim, does that make sense?"

"It sounds promising," Tim replied, deciding not to challenge Karl's anthropomorphic characterization of bubbles as *knowing* how to behave. "Karl, what do you need from us?"

"What I need is some peace and quiet, access to a high-voltage battery array, and three microturbines: one for a proof of concept and two more to move toward a pre-commercial prototype. I am going to have to conduct open heart surgery to modify the compression chamber to squeeze air through a micro-input port and..."

"Karl, you can spare us the details." Tim interrupted. "Where can we order those?"

"From a second-tier auto supplier out of Toronto. They're using the microturbines to generate electricity for next-gen hybrid cars. The thing is only two feet long and 75 pounds but can generate up to 70 kilowatts of power. I'm ordering factory seconds, but they still cost over $1,000. Can I order more?"

"Absolutely," Scott said. "I'll pay for them. Might need to jump some hoops—half the country is cash only, the other half is credit. Not sure where Canada stands. The real question is where to ship them? Are they still meeting their shipping schedules after the attacks?"

"I don't know—the whole supply chain is screwed up," Karl said. "Since they're factory seconds, they might still have some in stock."

"Well, we're committed on rent through October unless we break the 30-day notice clause in our lease." Scott said. "I know it's a bit risky, but I say we ship them here and then find a new location, somewhere out of the way." Scott turned to Tim looking for approval.

"I don't know," Tim adjusted his glasses. "Karl, how quickly can you disassemble and pack your essential apparatus? Also, what are we talking about for transport: a car, a van, a truck?"

"Depends on the battery array," Karl replied. "If you skip that, we're talking a day or two and a van would be more than adequate."

Tim turned back to Scott. "You know, your Aunt Jenny has a battery array. It's charged by solar and wind—she's totally off grid.

"That's right!" Scott's face brightened. "She also has a backup diesel generator."

"I think the system has a standard 12 Volt to 110 Volt inverter," Tim said. "But I imagine we could step that up as needed. There's a guy up there, a veteran, who maintains the entire system."

"When's the last time you talked to her?" Scott asked.

"It's been months," Tim replied. "As you know, Jenny's cabin is in a dead spot—no cell coverage. She checks her messages on occasion when in town. Do you want me to reach out to her?"

"Yes, better you than me," Scott said. "I don't want any connection to my dad. Maybe you should communicate indirectly in case we are being bugged?"

Tim nodded in agreement. "I'll use Kristen's phone. They won't be monitoring that."

"Even better," Karl said, "just buy a burner, use it once and throw it away. But guys, if we're under surveillance, we've got bigger problems. All our data is in the Cloud."

"Shit!" Scott said. "Can we shut that down?"

"Yes," Karl replied. "We still have an in-house server we could use as a backup, but the damage might already be done."

"All right," Tim said, looking back and forth between Scott and Karl. "I'll contact Jenny to see if she would be open to us setting up shop up there. Karl, put everything on our server and shut down the Cloud. Also, order those microturbines. And, make a list of everything you need to continue your research and prototyping. Assume we have access to a battery array."

Karl smiled in response. Their dream of a plasma drive—clean, distributed energy—was alive!

"I agree with Scott," Tim continued. "We should stay put at least through October. That will give us time to devise a plan to get up to Jenny's, assuming she'll take us in. Scott, can you reach out to your dad and get more info on who is watching us and why?"

"Shall do," Scott said. He placed his elbow on the table and propped his head in hand as he concentrated. "But I'll have to be careful, very careful."

"One small thing," Karl said, his smile fading away. "Your Aunt lives up in the U.P, right? You don't expect me to move up there? In the winter?"

"Well…"

TWENTY-THREE

Washington D.C. – September 19
The Bureau

Assistant Deputy Director – Domestic Counterterrorism. Tommy Sutton read the placard on his boss's desk in disbelief. Nobody in the Bureau self-promoted like that. Of course, nobody was like Reggie Woods. Tommy wondered if Reggie had incriminating info or photos on higher-ups that explained his fast-track promotions. Didn't make sense, the guy was a loser.

Reggie completed his phone call and turned to Tommy. "What do you have for me?"

Well that's nice, Tommy brooded, didn't even acknowledge me by name. "They just took down their Cloud."

"Oh really. We've got a copy, right?"

"Yes, the Cloud host was more than happy to comply with our request—didn't even need a warrant."

"Okay, I assume they'll use a local server. We may need to inspect their offices. Where are they located again?"

"Traverse City, Michigan, right here." Tommy held up the back of his hand to simulate the shape of the Mitten State and pointed to the top of his pinky finger. "About two hours north of Grand Rapids."

"Middle of nowhere," Reggie said. "Where are we on the phone and email taps?"

"We're now fully active with expanded coverage on both Steve and Scott Bennett."

"Is John Bowden, the DHS Under Secretary, covered? He's a buddy of Steve Bennett's and on Assistant AG Hunter's shit list."

"Yes, he's covered. We also added Scott Bennett's co-founder..." Tommy looked at his tablet "...Tim Kelly, and their top scientist, Karl Schultz."

"What's their stories?"

"Kelly's 45 years old, single," Tommy replied. "He's a serial entrepreneur, but also a brainiac with four degrees, including Engineering from MIT. Previously, he was with Ion Carb, a company which claims improved fuel efficiency by ionizing gas as it enters the carburetor. He's also moonlighting at the local university, Traverse University, teaching Political Eco-systems."

"Hmm," Reggie murmured. "Maybe we should give the University a little nudge—put the fear of God in them? What about Schultz? Hunter certainly seemed interested in him."

"Yes, he's more interesting. A 69-year-old widower. Retiree from Lockheed Martin. Was a project leader in their Basic Research Lab. Field of expertise, Electromagnetic Plasma Dynamics. Top-secret rating now expired. Advanced degrees in Physics and Engineering. He's the real thing."

"Yes, need to watch him closely. Any family?" Reggie asked.

"Two grown kids on the west coast. A son in Portland and a daughter in Seattle. They look pretty benign."

"All right. And keep me posted on any pushback from Con-gressman Bennett. That son of a bitch is cagey. He still has a lot of friends on the Hill and at the Bureau."

"Got it." Tommy got up to leave.

"Oh, one last thing," Reggie stopped him in his tracks. "Add an IRS screen on all of them, state tax too—might come in handy."

"Yes sir!" Out in the hall Tommy muttered, "What a shit-head." What they were doing was far worse than the lit-tle hacking episode they were holding over his head. All he did was access the U.N.'s website and add a fake page for a fake country! Tommy had gotten serious accolades from the hacker community for adding *Freedonia* to the U.N. roster, complete with the country's flag and national anthem.

After Tommy had left, Reggie used his encrypted email system to send a brief update to Assistant AG Hunter, including Tim Kelly's link to Traverse University.

TWENTY-FOUR

Traverse City, MI – September 25

Tim took a sip of his coffee and placed the cup next to his laptop. He leaned down and gave Smokey a scratch under his collar. The cat purred and rubbed against his leg, begging for more. Tim had to admit that he had become fond of the kitten since Kristen had moved in. Now if he could just get the cat to stop using his sofa as a scratching post!

Refocusing his attention to the laptop, Tim perused the latest headlines. All were *Breaking News* and *News Alerts*, as if the audience needed any more agitation. It had been two weeks since the attacks and dominos were still falling across the world. The immediate impact was the lack of essentials. People were not going to be caught short like they had during COVID-19. Shelves were stripped bare within 48 hours. The President had issued emergency orders to ration and price-fix essentials, but the horse had left the barn—stockpiling and black markets were endemic. Tim wondered if Kristen could borrow some toilet paper from the hospital, but then cringed at his own devious thoughts.

As bad as the shortages were, Tim was more concerned about the financial markets. Already weakened by the COVID-19 bailouts and stimulus, the financial systems were now seizing up, and in unexpected ways. The promise of direct payments to Americans to jump-start the economy were not moving the needle—people wanted essentials, not luxuries. And, for the first time in recent history, the dollar was weakening as trading partners lost faith in the U.S. and its $30 trillion in debt. The end result was *biflation* as too many dollars chased too few essentials while consumers cut back on discretionary spending out of fear or unemployment. Tim grimaced at the thought of where those negative feedback loops might lead...

Tim was thankful that the University was reopening—he needed the money and the distraction. He had decided to tweak the subject matter of his senior seminar to probe freedom of speech in a post-truth America. It seemed topical as the pundits tried to spin this latest disaster to their political advantage. Tim was just starting to type his new course outline when his smartphone chimed with an incoming text message. He expected a text from Kristen but was surprised to see it was from Ken Weaver, his Department Chairman. All it said was, *Meet me at my office at 11 am.* At the bottom of the text was a link to Twitter. Tim touched the link with his finger to access a recent tweet. He felt a wave of vertigo as he read the header.

PolyTu@PolyTu. Professor Supports Slavery, Slams White Males, Shames Student. #TU #Bigot #Racist #Fascist. Youtube.com/watch?v0832.

Who the hell is PolyTu? Tim asked himself. Tim looked at the stats; 43.3k views, 27.7k retweets, 5.8k comments. All since 9:13 this morning. Oh no, he thought. He touched the link and a grainy cell phone video showed Tim at the lectern during his first class. He turned up the volume to clearly hear his own words. *"But we must also acknowledge the role of slavery and the taking of indigenous peoples' land as part of our early economic growth..."* The video then cut to later in the class. It looked like the picture was taken from one of the back rows. Tim could see Tyler's back in the video. *"...the new face of the enemy will be privileged white males and their ignorant wives?"* Tim felt bile moving up in his stomach as he watched the last clip taken from earlier in the class. *"Or, you could simply walk out of class and flee to your safe space, so you don't get triggered by these topics."*

Tim walked into Ken Weaver's office expecting the worst. Judging by the frown on Ken's face, his fears were well-founded.

"Please shut the door and have a seat, Tim." Weaver gestured to one of the side chairs in front of his desk. "Listen, I'm not going to beat around the bush. You've seen the videos. Hell, everybody's seen the videos. They've now been picked up by cable news. The University is demanding immediate action."

"Ken, my remarks were completely taken out of context," Tim said in an even voice. "My comment on slavery was qualified as being *bitter roots* of our economic growth. I admit that chiding Tyler was a mistake, but I made an immediate apology. You were in the room. You heard what I said." Maybe they'll want me to issue a public apology? Tim wondered.

Weaver slowly shook his head side to side. "Tim, your class was fascinating, but it was politically incorrect. What about your comments on privileged white males and their ignorant wives? I wasn't in the room for that one."

"It's the opposite of what it appears," Tim replied, his voice rising in intensity. "My whole point was that progressive elites continue to demonize white, working class and rural Americans as deplorables. The video was edited, and I can provide witnesses."

"Like Kristen Campbell?" Weaver fired back.

"What does she have to do with this?"

"Besides the video, we received pictures of Kristen entering your house and exiting the next morning. Presumably, you two are having an affair. That's strictly prohibited by our code of conduct."

"She's a grown woman for heaven's sake!"

"Listen Tim, I don't want to get into your personal life, but the optics are horrible. Here we have a male professor who has lopsided power over a female student. You could show favoritism. You could take advantage of her. You just can't do that anymore! The University has a zero-tolerance policy." Weaver said crossing his arms over his chest.

"Well, what do you want me to do?" Tim asked.

"If it was my call, I'd have you issue a public apology to your class and through the school newspaper. But the administration is demanding your immediate resignation. I argued against it but..."

Tim felt the foundations of his world crumbling around him. Everything he believed, everything he worked for... And then, anger rose in his throat. Keeping his voice as controlled as he could, Tim said, "That's unacceptable. I did nothing wrong and you know it. This was a cyber hit job plain and simple!"

"Tim, I'm sorry. I recommended you, but now I'm in deep trouble. The University is not looking to negotiate. You either resign or you'll be fired." Weaver looked down at a document sitting on his desk.

That was the last straw for Tim. "Well, I think you are going to have to fire me so I can sue your sorry asses! Let's see...libel, defamation, collusion. I'm not a lawyer, but I know lack of due process when I see it!"

"You might want to rethink that Tim. If you resign, your record will remain clean. Also, you won't drag Kristen through this mess. As far as I know, her photos haven't gone public yet. Finally, and I'm telling you this as a friend, you might have bigger problems. The FBI has contacted the University about your job status."

"What?" Tim's jaw dropped.

"You heard me. The FBI is looking at you. Don't know why. Don't know if they got the videos or what. But you might have bigger fish to fry than suing us," Weaver said. "The University has prepared a letter of resignation for you." Weaver pushed the document on his desk toward Tim along with a pen.

Tim tried to make sense of it all. He could hear Weaver's clock ticking from its position on the wall. He felt his rage retreating, replaced by a sick feeling in the pit of his stomach.

He didn't have the money for a protracted legal battle. And the FBI? A shiver went down his spine.

"Is there any package if I resign? A couple months' salary? How about COBRA medical benefits?" Tim knew it sounded pathetic, but the harsh reality of his situation had started to hit. He adjusted his glasses. He had to do something with his hands.

"Tim, if it were up to me, I'd give you a package. But it isn't. You're part time and still under probation. We legally owe you nothing. Besides, the administration is feeling anything but charitable. From their point of view, you've trashed the University's reputation."

Tim looked down at the document and tried to concentrate on reading it: Waiver of Rights, Confidentiality, Indemnification. Despite his high IQ, it all seemed nonsensical. He picked-up the pen and signed the letter of resignation and pushed it back to Weaver.

"Thanks Tim. This is the best way. Let me get you a copy. Oh, I need your ID card and parking pass."

Tim walked out of Weaver's office without looking at any of the office workers who probably knew what was going on. A frigid wind greeted him as he stepped outside, scattering fallen oak leaves across the faculty parking lot. Tim tried to let his mind go numb, but the dread of an FBI investigation kept circling around his brain.

Tim got into his car and drove away from the University for the last time.

TWENTY-FIVE

Traverse City, MI – October 26

"I'm sorry Mr. Conrad, but with the current market, your house is worth less than your loan." Jack eyeballed the bank officer—cleanly shaved, a freshly pressed white shirt, striped tie. I wonder what I look like to him. Probably pathetic.

"Under these conditions, I'm afraid a home equity loan is out of the question." The banker looked down at the report he had pulled on Jack. "Also, as a reminder, the federal moratorium on mortgage payments expires at year end. You're currently two months in arrears." Jack averted his eyes and stared at the giveaway pens artfully arranged in a mug on the banker's desk.

"But there might be some good news on the horizon," the banker continued. "There are rumors that the Feds are looking at buying out distressed mortgages and garnishing wages and social security to pay them down. Is there anything else I can help you with?" The banker ended with a perfunctory smile.

"No, thank you." Jack replied. He got up and left the banker's office, hearing a belated "have a good day." On the way out, Jack passed by the bank's center island grabbing a handful of mints.

Within 20 minutes, Jack was jogging toward Old Mission Peninsula. He wore a headband to fend off the chill and keep his earbuds snuggly in place. Jack adjusted his iPod to play *Gael*, the theme song from *The Last of the Mohicans*, in a continuous loop. The rhythmic and repetitive fiddle runs, and soaring crescendos, set a perfect pace for Jack. Jogging was one of the few tools left in his toolkit to relieve anxiety. But, after the bank meeting, the squirrel cage in Jack's mind was working overtime. What am I going to do for money? How am I going to pay bills? Will they cut off my utilities? Can they do that—with winter approaching? Despite his best efforts, Jack could feel his resentment growing. Frigging bank!

With light traffic, Jack had no problem crossing roads until he reached Peninsula Drive headed north up the west arm of Grand Traverse Bay. Keeping a steady physical tempo, Jack could feel some of his tension bleed away. The sky was overcast, and a brisk wind blew out of the north, but soon his body warmed from the exercise. He passed miles of orchards and vineyards, the trees and vines now skeletal, having been harvested earlier in the fall. The once thriving tasting rooms were now vacant or closed, nobody had the transportation or money for such luxuries. He thought about all the bottles of wine neatly stacked inside. Without warning, he felt a moment of euphoric recall of the relaxation a drink would bring. Stop it!

Jack had no illusions that he could ever successfully drink again, not even high-end wine with dinner. Besides, what was the point? He drank for effect, not taste or bouquet, for God's sake. One drink and he would be off to the races with no end in sight. No, Jack knew he could never drink again—unless he got a bad case of the screw-its.

Jack kept his steady pace and tried to concentrate on gratitude, a tool learned from Alcoholics Anonymous. He was thankful that Meg was okay down in Grand Rapids, even though he might not see her this Christmas. He was thankful for his health, although he was losing weight. He was thankful that, despite his worst fears, the world had not ended with the dirty drone attacks. No, it was more like watching a slow-motion car crash; mass retaliations in the Middle East, a crashing stock market, food and gas shortages, looting and riots in the inner cities... Stop it!

After a ten-mile loop, Jack returned home feeling a degree of serenity, or was it exhaustion? He started a fresh pot of coffee, his answer to an empty refrigerator and pantry. As the coffee brewed, he changed into some dry clothes and returned to the kitchen. Jack loaded his coffee cup with sugar, poured in the coffee, and sat down at the table, cell phone in hand. He searched his contact list. Jeff Johnson—he hadn't tried Jeff yet. He took a deep breath, touched Jeff's contact icon, and engaged the speakerphone mode. After a few rings, he got a pick up.

"Johnson's Custom Cabins, Jeff speaking."

"Hey Jeff, Jack Conrad. How ya doing?"

"Hey Jack, getting along, you know. How about yourself?"

"Well, to be blunt, I'm looking for work. You got any projects going on? I need some hours bad. Things are pretty tight." Jack braced himself for the answer. He had done excellent work for Jeff in the past, but things were different nowadays.

"No shit," Jeff responded. "I don't have anything going on. No new starts, no remodels, nothing. I'm getting by on a few repair calls. You know I'd throw you a bone if I had one."

"I know, that's okay."

"I'm sure you've tried Matt Riggins. How about Perkins Construction?"

"Yeah, they're basically shut down too."

There was a brief pause before Jeff continued. "You know, I've heard that the government is hiring for some remodel projects on schools and other government properties, part of that emergency infrastructure bill. Do you have your U.S. Works card yet?"

"Jeff, that's welfare. Not sure I'm ready for that."

"Might as well take it. Hell, you paid your taxes all those years. Get some back."

"Yeah, maybe. If you hear of any work, let me know. How are Melissa and the kids."

"They're fine. Melissa is helping down at the church; they've opened a new food pantry. The kids are okay. They've got counselors at school helping them with the crisis and all. I don't know, certainly different than our school days. How about Meg?"

"Still down in Grand Rapids, trying to get a full-time teaching position. At least that's a growth business." Jack said with a tone of heavy sarcasm.

"Yeah, we got in the wrong line—should've been a postman!" Jeff snorted.

"No kidding. Anyway, thanks for taking my call."

"No problem Jack. Good Luck."

"Yep, Bye." Jack ended the call and sat back in his chair. His guts growled from too much coffee on an empty stomach. He considered going to the ATM and grocery. Or, maybe he should check out that new food pantry Jeff mentioned. How embarrassing would that be? Or, he could bike down to the U.S. Works office and just give up. Frigging bank!

That evening, Jack rode his bike over to the nearby Lutheran Church for a much-needed AA meeting. He was pleased to see many regulars, but also quite a few newcomers. As the basket was passed for the voluntary donations, typically a dollar, Jack was surprised how few people contributed. Of course, the best he could do was four quarters—another lesson in humility. Many attendees were struggling with the same issues: no work, no food, no hope. Not a good situation for an alcoholic. But knowing he wasn't the only one made Jack feel a bit better. After the hour-long meeting, Jack pulled an old AA friend aside.

"Hey Bill, how goes the battle?"

"Hi Jack. I thought you might have graduated or something!"

"Yeah, right." Jack chuckled at the old AA bromide. "Well, I'm still sober, but a little short on serenity. What's with all the new people? Is the hospital sending rehab patients over again?"

"No, it's their ticket for a free meal over in the fellowship hall. A lot of them are homeless. You coming?"

"Are you going?" Jack asked.

"Yeah, my pride is no match for my stomach. Come on, you look a little bony yourself."

Jack's face flushed with embarrassment; he had never asked for a free meal before. But, heck, it was a church, he was there for a good reason, what was there to be ashamed about?

"Sure, show me the way." It was nice to have Bill as an escort.

As they approached the fellowship hall, Jack could see a queue forming at the doorway. No hiding now, Jack thought. The queue moved quickly and soon he had a tray and was in the meal line. It was only then that Jack saw Tim Kelly serving food. Shit! He tried to turn away and leave, but Tim had caught his eye and given him a nod. Damn! Nothing to do but press on. Jack tried to come up with some excuse, but his mind went blank. Although they were acquainted from high school, things had gotten awkward when Tim's best friend, Sean Bennett, had married his college crush, Jenny Hernandez. Jack slid his tray down and was soon in front of his old friend.

"Hi Tim. I was at a meeting and heard about the free food."

"Hey Jack. Long time no see." Tim put a large helping of coleslaw on Jack's plate. "You doing okay?"

"I guess. Can't seem to find any work nowadays. How about you?"

"It's been challenging." Tim nodded in agreement. "Oh, this is Kristen." Jack looked over at the woman standing next to Tim. Her kind eyes met his gaze. "Kristen, Jack Conrad, an old friend from high school."

"Nice to meet you Jack," she said and placed a roll on his plate.

"Thanks," was the only thing Jack could muster. Tim's introduction and Kristen's body language left Jack with the distinct impression that they were an item.

"Oh, have you heard anything from Jenny? Is she still up in the U.P.?" Jack asked, looking back at Tim as he slid his tray down the line.

"Yes," Tim replied. "Why don't you drop by my office and

we can talk."

"Sure, where you located?"

"I've got a business over on Hastings, 3224 East Hastings. How about next Tuesday, say 12 noon?" Tim shouted, so Jack could hear him as he moved down the line.

Jack stopped to yell back an answer. "Sounds good."

"Come on man," a bearded guy next to Jack bumped his tray.

"Sorry!" Jack pushed his tray forward to close the gap with Bill.

As he sat next to Bill and savored the ham and scalloped potato meal, Jack considered Tim's invite. What was there to lose? Besides, he was anxious to hear anything about Jenny.

TWENTY-SIX

Washington D.C. – October 29
Department of Energy (DOE) Conference Room

"Unlike most magnetohydrodynamic plasma engines which suffer from Hall Effect losses, this device appears to..."

This interagency committee meeting smells like a trap, John Bowden brooded. The DHS Under Secretary half-listened to the presentation while scanning the attendees around the table to discern the hitman. Kohl, the Energy Under Secretary, was a likely suspect. Bowden had already told his friend, Congressman Steve Bennett, that the DOE was surveilling his son's company. Maybe a backdoor attack on Steve himself? Then there was Assistant Attorney General Max Hunter, a well-known political foe of conservatives, including Steve.

"Stop!" Hunter shouted, almost as if he had read Bowden's mind.

The DOE Analyst, Sarah Wong, halted her presentation at once and looked for direction from Hunter.

"Would someone please give me a primer on this? How about plasma for dummies? I have no idea what the hell you're talking about!"

Richard "Dick" Kohl, Under Secretary of Energy, jumped in to rescue his staff member. "Sarah, would you please provide Assistant Attorney General Hunter a brief overview of plasma, how it is used today, and then we can discuss this patent application and its implications. Okay? Just the ABCs." Kohl loosened his blue tie.

Bowden watched the interaction, trying to pick up on physical cues. Kohl looked seriously agitated.

"Of course," Wong replied. "I'm sorry. I can get carried away with tech talk."

Bowden could tell Wong knew who the power players were. She directed her attention to Hunter, Kohl, and himself. The other handful of attendees were hacks from the NSA or the Bureau.

"There are four states of matter." Wong began. "You're all familiar with solids, liquids, and gases. Plasma is the fourth state. Although little understood, plasma is the most common material in the universe since all stars are primarily plasma. Examples of plasma are all around you: plasma TVs, a welder's arc, fluorescent lights, even spark plugs. Plasma occurs when atoms or molecules become highly ionized, losing electrons when acted upon by a high-energy source or electromagnetic field. For instance, the nuclear fusion of the sun superheats hydrogen and strips away electrons to form plasma. The friction of water molecules in a churning thunderstorm ionize the air to form lightning—plasma. Perhaps as a child you rubbed your feet against a rug to ionize yourself so that when you touched metal a spark was emitted—mini-plasma."

"Okay. I get that," Hunter said. "Now, please explain the use of plasma for defense and energy."

"Yes sir," Wong replied. "For defense, a plasma weapon is still in the realm of science fiction. We don't have phasers or light sabers or anything like that. The closest thing we have are high-powered lasers which can be directed at targets and, through superheating, create plasma at the point of impact. Certainly, there is high potential with lasers, particularly for our space defense initiative."

"I see," said Hunter.

"With respect to energy, there are various plasma engines that have been developed in laboratories. NASA is researching various ion thrust and plasma propulsion engines for deep space exploration; the first real test may be our missions to Mars. DARPA—that's the Defense Advanced Research

Projects Agency—has been researching plasma jets for use in air vehicles. At Energy, we are working with a consortium of nations to explore plasma fusion. It may represent a clean and renewable source of energy. Essentially, plasma fusion attempts to recreate the nuclear processes taking place in the sun, but in a controlled, laboratory setting. Immensely powerful magnetic fields are required to control and buffer the superheated plasma. In any case, we are years away from having anything remotely close to a viable plasma fusion reactor."

"Thank you, Ms. Wong," Hunter said. "Now, could you please explain what this new plasma invention is and why it's a threat to national security?"

"Of course," Wong replied. "As a reminder, we have not seen or tested this invention. All we have is a patent application and some…"

"You've killed that, right?" Hunter interrupted.

"I'm sorry?"

"The patent application."

"Um, it's already in the public record," Wong said.

"Well, then change the damn record!" Hunter grimaced.

"I'll talk to Commerce." Kohl flicked his hand aside. "They can lean on the Patent Office. Sarah, you can continue."

"Well, um." Wong stopped and took a sip of water. "We've seen the patent application and preliminary drawings. It's entirely speculative. That being said, what they are claiming is a plasma drive engine that ionizes compressed air, O2N2, to create plasma. This plasma superheats the residual compressed air in a combustion chamber which results in expansion. The expanded gas is directed out through exhaust turbines like an ordinary turbine engine to provide thrust and/or electrical generation."

"Are you saying they've invented an engine that burns air?" Hunter leaned forward on the table; his hands flat on the surface.

Bowden watched the faces of the participants for any physical tell. Except for Kohl, they all looked sincerely shocked.

"Actually, burning is a misnomer. What they claim is an engine that can activate plasma using ordinary, compressed air that is exposed to an electrical arc. Much like a welder's arc creates plasma to weld metal. But, in this case, the plasma superheats and expands the air to drive turbines to create thrust and energy."

"Is that even possible?" Hunter asked.

"Any one element of their claims is possible. Certainly, you can employ electrodes to ionize air to create plasma. And certainly, superheated air does expand and could power a turbine. But to engineer a fully operational plasma drive engine is highly unlikely. We know, we tried something similar in the mid-70s and mothballed the project."

"Why did you do that?"

"Well, we kept having catastrophic failures."

"What do you mean catastrophic?" Hunter asked

"The engines kept blowing up," Wong replied. "The list of reasons is long. We couldn't throttle the reaction. We couldn't shield the plasma chamber from the superheat. The internal mechanicals and ball bearings couldn't handle the RPMs and forces. Besides, we couldn't overcome the First Law of Thermodynamics."

"Sarah, could you briefly refresh the audience on the First Law of Thermodynamics, in layman's terms?" Kohl asked.

"Certainly. In simple terms, it stipulates that energy can neither be created nor destroyed, only changed. For example, when we burn coal, oil, or gas, we are changing the stored-up energy of carbon into heat for internal combustion engines or to drive turbines to generate electricity. While the hydrocarbon ceases to exist, its stored-up energy lives on as mechanical, kinetic energy or heat. It quickly boils down to a matter of efficiency of energy change. With our plasma drive prototypes, we calculated that the electromagnetic energy required to activate plasma exceeded the resulting kinetic energy. So, what's the point!" Wong concluded with a smile.

John Bowden's ears perked up. "Excuse me," he spoke for the first time. "If you knew you couldn't overcome the conservation of energy, why did you even pursue a plasma drive?"

The smile slowly disappeared from Wong's face. She turned to her boss for direction.

"I'll answer that," Kohl said. "Back in the '70s we were dealing with dated technology and a bias toward large-scale energy production, which dictated large-scale prototypes. As Sarah said, we kept failing. Before we canned the project, we were following a promising path to miniaturize the entire plasma drive based on a theory developed by one of our top researchers. In simple terms, the theory hypothesized that as one approaches the atomic limits of a highly compressed gas, plasma formation could be extremely efficient. Also, if you could buffer the drive using the electromagnetic fields of the plasma stream itself, you might eliminate the need for super magnets. In combination, this might allow a net gain of energy, not unlike the dream of cold fusion."

"Okay, then what was the real reason you stopped?" Bowden asked.

"It was a political decision, plain and simple," Kohl said. "If we were able to develop an efficient plasma drive, it would be totally disruptive to our existing energy sector. Not just Big Oil, but also our public utilities and massive investments in green alternatives such as wind and solar. Furthermore, it would let the genie out of the bottle for any third world country, community, or even a private citizen to become an energy producer. There would be no way to control it, regulate it, tax it. It could potentially disrupt the entire geopolitical order of the civilized world."

"What was the name of your top researcher?" Hunter asked.

John Bowden's antenna went up. Here we go, time for the big reveal.

"I believe it was Jacob Schultz," Kohl replied.

"Would that be the uncle of Karl Schultz, the chief scientist with Plasma Drive Technologies?" Hunter asked. "And Scott

Bennett, co-founder of the company, would that be the son of Steve Bennett, ranking member on the House Committee for Homeland Security?" There was silence in the room.

Hunter turned to face Bowden. "John, I believe Congressman Bennett is an associate of yours—or should I say a friend?"

"Yes." Bowden matched Hunter's stare. He could sense the impending trap.

"Does he know the thin ice he and his son are treading on?"

"Yes, I believe he does," Bowden replied, knowing his neck was now fully extended.

"Given your relationship with Congressman Bennett, wouldn't it be prudent to recuse yourself from this committee?"

SNAP went the trap.

Nice hit job, Bowden had to admit. It was a two for one; implicate his friend Steve Bennett while neutralizing himself.

But the game wasn't over—not by a long shot.

TWENTY-SEVEN

Traverse City, MI – November 2
Plasma Drive Technologies, LLC

Jack used his fat-tire bike to pedal through the early November snow over to Tim's small office on Hastings. Seeing no doorbell, Jack knocked on the glass door, noticing a lingering shadow of a recently removed stencil: Plasma Drive Technologies, LLC. After waiting several minutes, Jack was about to leave when a small man in a white lab coat came to the door and opened it.

"I'm sorry, but we're closed. Is there anything I can help you with?"

"I'm Jack Conrad. I was supposed to meet Tim Kelly here. Is he around?"

"No, have you tried calling him?"

"Not yet," Jack replied.

"Well, come on in. It's getting nasty out there!" Jack entered and brushed the snow off his coat and stamped his feet. "I'm Karl Schultz," the small man offered his hand. "How do you know Tim?"

"Oh, just old high school friends," Jack said.

"I see. I was just making some coffee, care for a cup?"

"Sure. Let me send a text to Tim first." Jack tapped out the message, then put his cell phone back in his pocket.

"Come on," Karl said and led Jack down a partially darkened hall to a small kitchen area. He started loading coffee into the filter of an old Bunn coffee maker. "Everybody has gone to those newfangled one-cup brewers, but I still like the old-fashioned ones," Karl said as he poured water into the reservoir.

"So, are you just closed for the day?" Jack asked.

"Well, the short answer is we're closed until further notice. With the financial crash, we lost our investors and had to let our employees go. I'm working pro bono. More of a hobby than a job. What do you do?"

"Not much right now. I was working construction, but that's gone. Before that, I had a corporate job in high-end marine electronics. Degree in Electrical Engineering from MSU." For some reason, Jack felt compelled to tout his credentials.

"Really," Karl replied. "You might be interested in our little invention. Did Tim tell you about our project?"

"Nope."

Karl managed a hot-swap with the coffee maker, removing the partially filled pot and placing a spare mug under the still-dripping coffee. He filled two other mugs from the pot and then reversed the hot swap, sending a few drops of coffee sizzling on the hot plate. "I'm a bit impatient." Karl explained. He handed Jack one of the mugs. "Cream, sugar?"

"Sure," Jack loaded his coffee with sugar and creamer. He hoped Karl didn't notice the slight tremor in his hand.

"Come on, I'll show you the lab while we wait for Tim." Karl led Jack farther down the hall into a well-lit, large room. Work benches filled most of the room along with a battery array and canisters of compressed gas. A couple of odd-looking machines stood in the corner.

"Whoa! Is that a plasma globe over there?" Jack asked. "We had one in my high school physics class."

"Very observant. We use that for investor presentations. Our real invention, I call it the doomsday machine, is over here." Karl walked over to a jury-rigged contraption. It looked like a miniature jet engine clamped to a steel bar rising from the floor. The top of the engine was covered except for a protruding steel tube connected to a canister of compressed gas. Various electrodes and wires hung from the side of the engine.

"Okay. I give up. What's it supposed to do?" Jack took a long slug of his coffee. His phone chimed with the message that

Tim would be over soon.

"Well, at the risk of sounding grandiose, we hope to revolutionize energy production using plasma. The reason I call it a doomsday machine is that it spells doom for the fossil fuel industry." Karl took a sip from his coffee mug, looking over the rim for Jack's reaction.

"Really," Jack said with skepticism in his voice. This is crackpot stuff, he thought. "So, how does it work?"

"Not too well right now." Karl snorted. "But I'm close!"

"Okay, how's it supposed to work?"

"Well, with an electrical engineering background, you're probably familiar with plasma mechanics, right?"

"Yeah, I know some basics," Jack replied.

"All righty then. So, the theory behind a plasma engine is actually quite simple. Take your basic turbine engine, but instead of compressing air and atomizing fuel in the combustion chamber for an explosive expansion, you ionize the compressed air, creating plasma to superheat the air into an explosive expansion."

Dumbfounded, Jack just stared at Karl. He tried to remember his physics from high school and college. "How do you ionize the air? Wouldn't that take more energy than you would produce?"

"Ah, you're sounding like the Department of Energy now." Karl laughed. "Actually, the energy draw is nominal once the engine is running—it's just a matter of stepping-up the voltage. Of course, like any turbine or jet engine, we have to jump-start the damn thing."

"What's your optimal scale? This is pretty darn small. Not exactly a nuclear reactor, if you know what I mean."

"Funny you should ask." Karl took another sip of coffee before continuing. "You know, the nuclear industry made a fatal mistake going all the way back to the '50s. The first nuclear reactors were naval reactors built for submarines. These naval reactors were over-engineered to provide very safe energy, for a very long time, with a very small footprint. At the time, there was heated debate in the emerging industry on whether to adopt a distributed grid featuring small, naval reactors or a centralized grid featuring mega-reactors with cooling towers and all. Well, we know who won that argument! Of course, that led to large-scale fiascos like Three Mile Island, Chernobyl, and later Fukushima. If our brain trust had selected the distributed grid, we would probably have virtually unlimited, safe nuclear power today."

Karl paused and looked away from Jack as if contemplating what to say next. "Our design is the polar opposite. We seek miniaturization for two simple reasons. First, a micro-jet of compressed gas is highly responsive to electrical fields for plasma activation. Second, at a small scale, we might have a chance to buffer the superheat created by the plasma by creating a Skyrmion, the same thing that contains ball lightning. We are exploring the intersection of quantum mechanics with classical Newtonian mechanics in hopes of generating energy literally out of thin air!" Karl snorted at his own joke. "Get it? thin air!"

"Fascinating. So, how far along are you with the prototype?"

"Actually, I was about to conduct an experiment when you interrupted."

"I'm sorry..."

"No, no, no! I would love to have an observer, and maybe you could even assist." At that moment, Tim Kelly and Scott Bennett walked into the room. "Gentlemen! Perfect timing." Karl greeted them. "I was just about to turn on the doomsday machine."

"Sorry to keep you waiting, Jack," Tim said. "We had a meeting with some irate investors. I see you've already met our mad scientist."

"Actually, Karl's given me quite a headache. I mean, this is fascinating stuff." Jack waved his hand at the prototype.

"Scott, this is Jack Conrad, an old friend of mine from way back," Tim said.

"Your name sounds familiar," Scott said as he shook Jack's hand.

"Jack dated your Aunt Jenny in college," Tim said.

"Of course. Nice to finally meet you, Jack."

"So, you're Steve Bennett's son?" Jack asked.

"Guilty as charged!"

"No, I admire your father. Wish we had more like him."

"Thanks."

"Okay guys, enough with the pleasantries." Karl broke in. "You ready for the grand experiment?"

Tim looked over at Scott "You have any problems with Jack observing? I imagine it's going to be a dud anyway."

"No, I'm good. Jack, please treat this as confidential. I don't think we need to have you sign an NDA or anything. Okay?"

"Sure, Scott."

"Okay then," said Karl, taking charge of the demonstration. "I'm not sure how this thing is going to react, so I suggest we take some precautionary measures." Karl put down his coffee mug and went over to a cabinet, pulling out several pairs of safety glasses and handing them out. "Just in case the thing blows!" Karl laughed. "Okay, everybody over here." Karl gathered them around a workbench. "Scott, this switch is to jump-start the engine injecting high pressure air into the engine intake; I'll tell you when to flip it. Jack, this switch is to activate the high-voltage superconductor to ionize the air; wait for my signal. Tim, here is the kill switch for the engine just in case. Also, you're in charge of the fire extinguisher. I'll manage the voltage regulator."

Karl walked over to an adjoining desk and adjusted a camera tethered to his notebook computer. "Got to record this for posterity!"

"Karl, you're worse than the kid that got a chemistry kit for Christmas!" Tim laughed.

"I know, I know. I used to burn up all the stinky stuff in the kit before the parents were even awake." Karl replied as he went over to the wall and turned off the lights.

"Okay, everybody set?" Karl asked.

They all nodded and focused their attention on Karl.

"Okay Scott, hit the air."

Scott complied and flipped the compressed air switch. A high-pitched hiss emanated from the nozzle affixed to the air intake chamber on top of the engine.

"Okay Jack, hit the juice." Jack flipped the electrical switch, which resulted in a low buzzing sound.

"Nothing's happening," Scott said.

"Hold on," Karl replied as he turned a dial to regulate the voltage flow to the prototype.

Suddenly, the engine started to whine like a mini jet engine. At the same time, blue flame came shooting out of the exhaust. The entire team stood transfixed as the engine rapidly increased its RPMs and screamed under protest. Simultaneously, the blue plasma exhaust doubled in size.

BANG! The engine exploded and sent shrapnel flying across the lab.

"Holy crap!" Jack yelled as they all ducked for cover behind the workbench. Tim belatedly flipped the kill switch, but there was nothing left to kill. He came around the work bench with the fire extinguisher, but all that remained were a few parts of smoking metal.

"Oh, my God," Tim summed up the entire team's reaction to a successful, but cataclysmic experiment.

"You know, I believe the throttling mechanism still needs some work," Karl said.

"Ya think?" came Scott's reply as the smoke alarms went off in the room. Despite the annoying sound, they all were smiling.

After cleaning up the mess, the team gathered in the conference room to discuss next steps. With no protest, Jack tagged along. There was something important happening here, and he wanted to be part of it.

Tim kicked things off. "Karl, that was incredible, but it

doesn't change our predicament. I can't sleep at night knowing the FBI is looking at me, probably at us! Besides, our lease is up next week so we've got to close the facility." He turned to Scott. "Unless you've got something up your sleeve, I think we're broke. Our investors are certainly done. I've got a few bucks left in my 401k, but I'm going to have to rely on Kristen until I can find work."

"I'm tapped out," Scott replied. "Those turbines took my credit card over its limit. I can't ask my dad for help; he thinks we're closed. But what about Jenny's? You said she was good with us heading up there." Jack's ears perked up at the sound of Jenny's name.

"That's not the problem Scott," Tim replied. "How are we going to transport all our equipment, including the turbines, up to the U.P.? They're doing ID checks at the Mac Bridge, and the same at state lines, so we can't go around the lake. If the FBI is tracking us, we'd be caught. Besides, it's already winter up in the U.P."

That got Karl's attention. "I agree with Tim. In any case, I need time to finish the quantum equations for the Skyrmion. If we can't create bubbles to contain the plasma, we're just going to keep blowing up engines. I can do that work anywhere, even Florida." Karl smiled. "Anyway, I say we stash the turbines and key equipment in my storage bin and revisit this in the spring."

"All right" Scott said. "I can't argue with your logic." He turned to Jack. "You're in this now. Everything needs to be kept confidential, agreed?"

"Sure. But I think I can help. There may be a way to get up to the U.P. without being tracked." Jack's mind turned to Lake Michigan...

"Okay, keep Tim posted with any ideas. In the meantime, I need to divorce myself from this entire project. I can't risk incriminating my father. Although, I'm still not sure what we are doing is wrong."

"The world has changed," Tim said. "It's no longer a matter

of right or wrong, just whose side you're on."

Tim's words cast a pall of silence over everyone in the conference room as they contemplated this disturbing new reality.

TWENTY-EIGHT

Washington D.C. – November 17
House of Representatives – Homeland Security Committee Room

Ron Taylor, the powerful Congressman from Texas, slammed his hand down on the conference table. "Dammit Paul, when is this going to stop!" Taylor's rage was directed toward Paul Ruiz, the liberal from California. "We've failed to secure our borders, we missed the 9/11 attackers, and now this—illegal aliens attacking the heart of our financial district!"

Steve Bennett and the remaining committee members remained silent, not wanting to get into the brawl.

"Ron, we can't…"

"Shut up!" Taylor yelled, breaking any semblance of decorum. "Don't give me this crap about immigrant rights and privacy. We won't have a country left if we don't fix this mess! Look at the polls. Almost 80% of Americans want to secure the borders and enforce a national ID."

It went dead quiet in the conference room as Taylor and Ruiz glared at each other.

Finally, Steve broke the awkward silence. "Ron is right." He supported his fellow conservative. "We need to do something; the country is demanding it. If we don't step in, the President is going to go around us anyway."

"Steve, we don't want to be obstructionists," Ruiz said in a measured voice. "But you, of all people, should appreciate that our individual rights and freedoms are at risk here. We lose those, then the terrorists have won. What is your side proposing?"

"I'll answer that!" Taylor's face was flushed. "First, we put an indefinite moratorium on immigration until we sort out a vetting process. Second, we identify—and tag—all illegal immigrants, undocumented residents, HB1 visa holders, and any other non-citizens. And we enforce this with zero tolerance! If a business hires an illegal alien, if an agency helps an illegal alien, if a church shelters an illegal alien, then it's a felony, plain and simple! Third, we institute a standardized, national ID for our citizens."

"Are you talking about mass deportations of undocumented immigrants? That's not going to fly." Ruiz countered.

"Let's find them and tag them first, then we can decide," Taylor fired back. "We don't even know who's in our own country!" Silence shrouded the committee room.

With the meeting going off the rails, Steve jumped in again. "Okay, let's try crafting an approach that will be acceptable to the public. Paul, will you accept identifying all noncitizens if it's not linked to deportations?"

"What about asylum seekers? Will we still process those?" Ruiz asked.

"Listen Paul!" Taylor interrupted. "With the world economy imploding, we're going to have everybody and his brother trying to come here to suck us dry! What about our own citizens? What about legal immigrants who have patiently waited in line for years? Are you going to put illegal aliens ahead of our own citizens? You're nuts!"

"Hold on Ron, let me finish," Steve said. "No deportations of noncriminal, undocumented immigrants. But we stop catch and release of asylum seekers into the country while their cases are pending. They stay out of country until DHS makes a determination. Heck, most are not showing up for their hearings anyway."

"They'll still be at risk without our protection," Ruiz said. "It's immoral to keep families stranded at our borders without food, shelter or medical care."

Taylor turned to face his liberal adversary. "It's also immoral to tempt these illegal aliens to make the dangerous journey up here with the false promise of welfare, healthcare, and driver's licenses. You might as well put sugar out to attract ants!" Taylor ranted. "But we all know your real plan, give them the vote so they can keep you in office!"

"You're right, Ron." Ruiz replied sarcastically. "We should just let these undocumented residents, who you call ants, be exploited as off-the-books, cheap labor by your major donors. They don't dare complain about work conditions, not with ICE on speed dial!"

"Okay, stop it!" Steve interrupted. "We obviously have some differences to iron out on immigration. Let's try to find some common ground. Back to a national ID. How about we require all states to issue a standardized ID to all residents, citizens and undocumented immigrants alike?"

"If it is not linked to deportations or reducing benefits, we're okay with that," Ruiz said.

"Any law we pass would have to be enforceable," Taylor said. "I suggest any state that doesn't comply loses all federal funding. Or, we just federalize the entire process."

"Do you really want the federal government to usurp more power?" Steve asked. The lessons learned from COVID-19 were still fresh in his mind.

"Maybe not," Taylor conceded. "But we need more than an ID card, we need to address electronic proxies too."

"What do you mean?" Steve asked.

"Smartphones, tablets, PCs, whatever. Terrorists use them to conduct transactions and transfer monies. Hell, they're using them to set off bombs and pilot drones! They must be part of our identity verification and security programs."

"Okay, electronic proxies too," Steve said. "I believe we have enough of a consensus to draft a new National ID Act. It would be great for our country if we showed a united, bipartisan front." Steve slowly turned to look at each committee member in the eye. "Do we have a deal here?"

At that moment, Steve's aide, Jerry Belinsky, entered the closed-door session. All eyes turned to him. "I'm sorry to interrupt, but I need to talk to Congressman Bennett immediately."

"Jerry, can't this wait?" Steve admonished.

"Sir, I don't think so, it's a matter of national security."

"Well, then the entire committee should know."

"If you say so. Treasury just called. The Chinese are dumping T-Bills, the dollar is crashing."

"That's insane," Ruiz replied. "They're shooting their own foot!"

"Treasury says they've launched their own cryptocurrency, the *Laohu*." Belinsky elaborated.

"What the hell does that stand for?" Taylor asked.

"Tiger."

"Oh shit!" Ruiz succinctly captured the sentiment in the room.

TWENTY-NINE

"I'm sorry, I wish there were some other way. But we can't make a living here. God bless you all." And with that, the church president, now ex-president, walked out the conference room door.

Jenny looked at her fellow Church Council members. Cindy Beers and Bryce Brogan were slowly shaking their heads in disbelief. They had just lost a pillar of the church. The Council turned their attention to Pastor DeVries for direction.

"Okay. I'm not going to sugarcoat this, it's a blow to our church family," DeVries said. "But we must carry on. The first thing we need to do is find a replacement. Cindy, you know the bylaws. What's the process going forward?"

"Pastor, our normal process would be to establish a nominating committee, create a slate of candidates, and then take it to the congregation. But these are not normal times…"

As Cindy droned on, Jenny's attention was distracted by the scenery outside the conference room window. It was midday, yet it was already dark gray. The lake-effect clouds and snow concealed any light from the low, November sun. She thought about her greenhouse solar panels being starved from life-giving energy, just like the church and community were being sapped by the economic crash. From her vantage point, Jenny could see the parsonage where Mary DeVries had taken her confession a couple years back. It was all a coincidence, she pondered…or was it?

Jenny had been delivering vegetables to the casino when she saw an elderly woman helping a drunk wallowing in his own puke. Despite her revulsion, Jenny offered to help. One hour and an emergency room visit later, Jenny found herself in a spare set of clothes while Mary threw Jenny's soiled garments in the washer and started coffee. Soon they were at the small kitchen table of the parsonage talking like old friends. After discussing Good Samaritans, schooling, and family backgrounds, Mary looked hard at Jenny. Seeming to intuitively understand her pain, she asked a simple question. "Jenny, are you okay?"

It was as if Mary had lanced a boil. Everything spilled out in a complete catharsis: Jenny's wild college lifestyle, the ill-timed pregnancy, the abortion, the failed relationship, the rebound, the failed marriage, Sean's suicide, her parents' passing, and the inescapable loneliness and depression that followed.

When she finished her story, Mary pulled Jenny up off her chair and gave her a long, loving hug. "Oh, my dear child. You will learn to let go of this guilt and shame." Mary paused, and gently opened the hug to look Jenny directly in the eyes. "Remember, Christ came not to judge you, but to save you. Your sins have been forgiven. You are a child of God and he loves you as a father. He longs for you to commune with him, to bring you peace." Then Jenny cried, as if she were a newborn coming out of the womb.

"...so, we don't even have a quorum on the Church Council. Besides, we are losing members in groves. We only had 53 in attendance last Sunday. Nobody is going to jump on this sinking ship... I'm sorry Pastor, bad metaphor." Cindy concluded.

"No, that's all right Cindy, I share your qualms," DeVries said. "But I'm sure that God hasn't take us this far to abandon us. This could be a time of rebirth for our church. With these troubled times, we are now the focal point of the community.

Can't we bend the rules a bit?"

"Well, our bylaws allow for acting officers. Although, I'm not sure anyone would want to step into the breach." Cindy looked around the table for reactions.

"Listen, we are the church," Bryce Brogan said. "We can make or break any bylaws we want. Who's going to stop us?"

"Are you volunteering?" Cindy asked.

"Are you kidding me? I'm totally swamped at the store, Dad hasn't been the same since his concussion, and now Linda is homeschooling. Besides, I freely admit I don't have the temperament. We need someone who can bring people together, a healer, not a blowhard." Bryce turned his attention to Jenny. "Hey Jen, how 'bout you?"

"I'm sorry, what?"

"Would you take the job of church president?" Bryce asked.

"Oh no, not me. I'm not a leader."

"I beg to differ," Cindy said. "You've formed our co-op, you've organized the 4H kids, you know practically everybody in town. And you're young—we need to attract young families, they're our seed corn. I think you'd be great!"

Before Jenny could protest, Pastor DeVries piled on. "You know, Cindy's right. People are naturally attracted to you Jenny. And your faith is on fire. Would you please give it thoughtful consideration?"

Jenny looked around the table at her friends. They needed her, the church needed her, the community needed her, but it was all too much. "I'm sorry, I have to decline."

Cindy was not to be denied. "Jenny, how about just *acting* president until we can find a replacement?"

A sudden gust of wind made the ancient church shutter. Outside the window, a snow devil formed, gathering loose flakes into an ephemeral cyclone.

"Let me pray on it."

***

"Can I help you with that?" the old timer asked as he opened the door for Jenny.

"Thanks, but I'm fine," Jenny said, as she carried the heavy box of vegetables into the general store. "Hey guys!" She addressed the town's coffee clutch, eight idle guys sitting around a large table shooting the breeze. Most were recently laid off. Quite a few knew a trade but were now on the dole.

"Hey Jenny," they replied in unison.

Jenny took her box of vegetables and left them on the checkout counter. She toured the few aisles of the little store and browsed the dairy section. The shelves were poorly stocked, and the dairy was out-of-date. There was no fresh fruit to be found.

"How bad is that, this town can't even support a bar!" A voice spoke up from the clutch.

Jenny couldn't help but overhear the banter. Obviously, the topic de jour was the rumored closing of the town's only bar. Certainly, a sign of the end-times!

"Do ya think it'll open in the summer?"

"Nah, they can't even keep a waitress," the former postmaster said. "Charlie, you're just going to have to drink more!" The entire table broke out in laughter which soon subsided.

"That Jenny is one fine looking woman," one man whispered.

"Shh, she can hear you," another murmured.

Jenny shook her head and returned to the checkout counter where the owner had appeared, inspecting her produce. "Hi Jenny. Looks good, how much?"

"Fifteen bucks should do it." That was a bargain, but she knew the store was struggling. "Is it true about the bar?"

"I'm afraid so," the owner replied. "Keith says he's had enough. Barely breaks-even in the summer, and now this. I thought bad economic times were good for bars!"

"What about you?" Jenny asked. "You hanging in there?" The store catered to about everyone; part gas station, part mini-mart, part souvenir store and, of course, fishing tackle and bait. In the summer, ice cream.

"I don't know Jen. We had a surge when the grocery closed,

but between the summer folk gone and people moving away, we're hurting for sure. Those that stayed are driving to Houghton for their groceries. If I didn't have the free labor of my wife and kids, I'd be sunk. Now, the state wants me to clean up the leakage from our gas holding tanks. That's not my fault, it wasn't disclosed when I bought this place!"

"I thought the state had a superfund for that," Jenny said.

"They do, but I'd have to pay thousands of dollars for their deductible, and probably hire a lawyer to boot. I don't have that kind of money."

"I'm sorry. We certainly need you in this town."

"I'm trying to stay Jenny, but even the distributors are threatening to drop me—not enough volume. They've already cutback to biweekly deliveries."

That explains the spoiled dairy, Jenny thought, and no fruit. "Well, you know, a little prayer and support wouldn't hurt. We'd love to see you back at church, you and your entire family." So much for attraction versus promotion, Jenny chuckled.

"Yeah, maybe. I'm pretty busy on Sundays, but I'll think about it."

"Great! Either way, you and your family are invited to a Christmas Eve dinner at the church. We're asking the whole town. Don't have to bring a thing, just show up at 6 pm."

"Well, that's truly kind of you Jenny. I'll tell the wife for sure."

On her way out the door, Jenny stopped to address the table of men. "Don't know if you've heard, but the church is hosting a Christmas Eve dinner for the whole town. We'd love to see you and yours there, 6 pm. Oh, and Eugene, you're one *fine* looking man," Jenny said with a wry smile.

The whole coffee clutch burst out in laughter, some laughing until they cried.

***

Despite the early cold snap, Aux Baie harbor was free of ice. The charter fishing boats had been pulled a long time ago,

154

mostly due to the lack of clients after The Crash. Only two boats remained operational—George Russell's gill net boats. George's family had been fishing these waters for generations. His grandfather started with one boat and one net for subsistence fishing back in the day. It was his father who built a nice commercial business with a fleet of boats, an icing operation, and distribution throughout the upper Great Lakes. But the business was floundering since the attacks. Now they were down to two boats to harvest Lake Trout and Whitefish. Despite his non-tribal status, Johnny-B was part of the crew due to his mechanical skills. He kept the boats running. Jenny found him on the *Peggy Sue* working on a winch.

"Johnny," she yelled.

"Hey Jen, just a second," Johnny shouted back. He tested the winch, shook his head, and turned it off. He used a towel to wipe his hands and then jumped over the gunwale onto the pier. He approached Jenny. "Is there a problem?"

"No, no. Everything is fine. I was just in town and I thought I'd see if you were around. I wanted to bounce some ideas off you, about the Tribe."

"You're more Native American than I am, but what's on your mind?"

"Well, with the grocery closing and all, I thought the Tribe might be interested in trade or bartering with our co-op; their fish for our veggies, cheese, chicken and eggs. We even have some maple syrup."

"Maybe. Did you hear they're closing the casino?" Johnny asked. "That's going to hit the Tribe hard. Heck, that's going to hit you too, isn't it?"

"Yes, I was selling quite a bit to the casino. Most of my cash business is disappearing—no grocery store, no restaurants, no tourists for our food stands, and now the casino. That's why I am trying to expand trade in Aux Baie."

"I can't speak for the Tribe, but here's the man that can." Jenny followed Johnny's pointed hand and saw George Russell walking up the pier.

"Hi George," Johnny said. "You know Jenny Hernandez, don't you? She's got a business proposition for you."

"Yes, we know Jenny," the boat owner said with a smile. "How can I help?"

Jenny was surprised by George's reply, *we know Jenny*. She couldn't remember ever talking with George before. But he, or they, seemed to know her. "I was just telling Johnny that our co-op has a surplus of produce, including vegetables, eggs, cheese, syrup. What we don't have is a fresh supply of meat and fish. So, we were thinking that maybe you, and the Tribe, might be interested in bartering?"

"You know, that might make some sense," George said. "Our markets are shutting down, so we have a surplus. We either cutback or start throwing away fish, which would be wasteful. I'd just as soon keep some crews working for barter. With the casino closing, more people are going to be out of work. I hate to see us depend more on the Feds. How would we set pricing? One fish for an egg?" George laughed out loud, the crevices in his weathered face deepening with the effort.

"Haven't gotten that far," Jenny said. "But I'm sure we can work out something that's fair. I just wanted to see if you were open to the idea."

"I'm interested. I'll talk with some others in the Tribe. While I own the boats, the harvest is for all. You know, we also hunt deer and rabbit. Would you trade for that?"

"Absolutely!" Jenny smiled. "One other thing; the church is having a Christmas Eve dinner for the entire town. You and the Tribe are all invited. And, you don't have to bring a thing." Jenny saw George frown. Oh no, have I offended him?

"Jenny, you know some of us are Christian, some are mixed, and many follow our traditions."

"That's fine George, all are welcome!"

"I know. But if we come, we won't be empty handed."

THIRTY

Jack looked around the U.S. Works office as he shuffled forward in line. He was surprised to see all sorts of people: farmers in bib overalls, businessmen in suits, young adults and students tapping away on their smartphones, moms keeping their kids corralled. People busily typed in information at computer terminals. On the far side of the office one-on-one interviews were taking place. Jack could feel his tension rise a notch. On the wall was a U.S. Works banner with the simple tag line: *Working Together*. The line slowly moved until Jack was next.

"Driver's license or ID," the female attendant asked. Jack got out his wallet and handed over his driver's license. She put it in a scanner that stripped data from the weird barcode on the back, and maybe optical character recognition on the front? Jack wasn't sure about the technology.

"First time applicant?"

"Yes," Jack replied.

"When was the last time you worked?"

"Oh, I don't know. Maybe August…"

"Just give me an estimate," the attendant interrupted.

"Okay, August."

After some quick keystrokes, a sheet of paper came out of a printer next to her desk. She handed it to Jack along with his driver's license. "This is your temporary case number. Use it for all data entry or inquiries until you get your card. Next."

Jack went over to the next line to wait for a computer terminal to free up. It gave him time to estimate the number of computers. Let's see, five rows, 25 computers per row, that's... Damn! The simple math confounded him just a second too long, increasing his anxiety. After 20 minutes, he made it to the front of the line.

"C 24. Follow the instructions on the screen," the attendant said as he waved Jack forward. After finding Aisle C and Computer 24, Jack took a seat in front of the monitor and printer. There was a prompt on the home screen to enter his temporary case number, which he did. A screen popped up with *Welcome Jonathan Paul Conrad to U.S. Works Registration.* It showed the info from his driver's license as well as his social security number. Pretty standard stuff he thought. What caught his attention was the warning message on the bottom of the screen highlighted in red:

IMPORTANT INFORMATION – PLEASE READ CAREFULLY

By submitting this application, I am authorizing U.S. Works to obtain and disclose information related to my income, resources, and assets foreign and domestic, consistent with applicable privacy laws. This information may include, but is not limited to, information about my wages, account balances, investments, benefits, and pensions. I understand that U.S. Works has prepopulated this application with data sourced from federal, state, and local agencies, including but not limited to...

There were more than two dozen agencies listed ranging from the IRS and ACA all way down to Friends of the Court and his local bank. "What the hell," Jack uttered to himself. Fearing the worst, Jack quickly scrolled through the application to see what info had been prepopulated. It started with Criminal Offenses. Damn! There it was, *DUI, May 18, 2009.* Next, Jack opened the Work History section and saw his reported earnings. He grimaced at the steep drop five years ago when he'd lost his corporate job. Crap! His last five years were highlighted in red with an asterisk and note; *Unreported Cash Income?* Jack clicked on one last section, Health. He perused the information he had provided ACA years back. Yep, they had Prozac listed as a prescription—he was off it now, but this digital record could last forever. Lower on the screen it showed he was three months past due on insurance premiums.

Jack looked up from his cubicle and focused on the area where the one-on-one interviews were taking place. Some of the discussions look animated if not downright hostile. Shit, are they going to quiz me on this stuff? Jack's heart started to race, and his hands became clammy. He took a deep breath and whispered the AA Serenity Prayer; "God, grant me the serenity to accept the things I cannot change, the courage to change the things I can, and the wisdom to know the difference."

It took him over an hour to finish the registration form. He clicked the box affirming that, to the best of his knowledge, the information he had provided was accurate. *Congratulations* popped up on the screen, followed by a notice that he had been selected for a follow up interview. A wave of instant anxiety engulfed Jack. A slip of paper automatically came out of the printer. He was #79 and instructed to take a seat in the waiting room. He looked over to the other side of the large office and saw #52 on a monitor above the rows of interviewers. Darn! He took the printout and found an empty seat in the waiting area. People looked either extremely bored or stressed like himself. It didn't help that the fluorescent lights were buzzing incessantly. Probably bad ballast, Jack thought.

Finally, Jack's number was called and he was waved over to an open station. Jack sat down across the desk from a male clerk. *T. Williams* was typed on his U.S. Works name tag. Williams had his eyes fixed on the monitor to his side, ignoring Jack. After a minute or so, he finally looked up.

"So, construction. When's the last time you worked?"

"August, I think," Jack replied

"Independent contractor?"

"Yes."

"Do you receive 1099s? Have you been filing taxes?"

"Well…" Jack hesitated. Williams just stared at him, probably trying to trap him in a lie. Since he had joined AA, Jack realized honesty was the best policy, even if it hurt. "Actually,

I have been getting mostly cash payments."

"Yeah, I thought so. Lots of you off-the-books guys are coming out of the woodwork these days," Williams said with disdain. "Your last four years of tax returns look pretty suspect. How are you buying food and paying bills?"

"That's why I'm here. I'm basically broke and can't find work."

"What about utilities?"

"I'm late on everything, but they haven't cut me off yet. Oh, I'm current on my cell bill." Jack realized how pathetic that sounded.

"It says you're registered for healthcare, but you're late on premiums?"

"Yes, once again, I don't have the cash. Thankfully, I'm healthy."

"That can change. So, you own your house, why haven't you gotten a home equity loan?" Williams asked.

"I tried. The bank rejected me. They said my house is worth less than my loan."

"Do you have any other financial assets other than your," Williams took a look back at the monitor, "$118.33 in the bank?"

"No, that's it," Jack lied, not mentioning his emergency cash or gold coins. So much for honesty...

"Have you been receiving any aid or meals from churches?"

Jack thought that was a weird question. "Yes, I've gotten a few meals, why do you ask?"

"HHS, that's Health and Human Services, wants to make sure they are serving food that's up to code. Don't want to get a Norovirus outbreak or something. Which churches?"

"Well, a couple at Trinity and St. Francis." Jack watched as Williams entered the data into his terminal.

"Okay, you've got some serious issues here, but we're here to help you, not bust you. Your daughter's student loan has been forgiven, so we can take that off the list," Williams said with a smile. Even though it was a gratuitous smile, Jack felt himself relax a bit.

"This is how it works," Williams continued. "First of all, you are now registered with U.S. Works. We will be issuing you a smart card that you can use for allowable purchases, including approved groceries, utilities, medical, and public transportation. A full list of allowable purchases is available on our website. In exchange, you must actively seek work and report on your job hunt. Also, you must report any wages, tips, or cash payments you receive. USW Form 100 is an activity log that needs to be submitted weekly. You will be assigned a case manager with biweekly meetings. Any extended travel must be reviewed with your case manager. You are required to attend any job training that is recommended. Also, you agree to make U.S. Works custodian of your financial assets, in this case, your bank account. Not a bad exchange, right?"

"Yeah, I guess so, I mean, I only have a hundred bucks. So, I just use the card to buy everything on credit?"

"That's right, but it's more like a debit card with set limits for allowable purchases. It's all explained on our website," Williams said. "One other thing. You qualify for the new Fair Access Net package. You'll get a free FAN browser and U.S. Works app that's tied to your account in the Cloud. So, you can manage your activity log, check out approved purchases, and monitor spending limits, all from your cell phone. And, we'll pick up the bill and provide you unlimited data. Interested?"

"Sure!"

"Okay, we need a few signatures before we issue your card." Williams slid a couple of forms in front of Jack. "Right here, here, and here," he pointed out the signature lines for Jack and handed him a pen.

Jack thought about reading the fine print, but what was the point? They had him by the short hairs and he knew it. He signed on the three lines as instructed, feeling self-conscious about the slight tremble in his hand.

"Can I have a copy?" Jack asked feebly.

"There will be a PDF copy accessible from our website,"

Williams replied.

"Is that it?"

"You're almost done. Head over to the card issuance line, take your temp case number with you." Williams gestured to the queue down the hall. "You should be out of here in 10 or 15 minutes. Any questions?"

Despite the fact his head was spinning, Jack simply said "No, I'm good."

"Good day then," Williams dismissed him with a wave of his hand.

Thirty minutes later, after being photographed, finger-printed, and having his cell phone updated by a tech, Jack walked out into fresh air with his U.S. Works card. He wrestled with conflicting emotions; the raw humiliation of failure coupled with the relief of letting go. Almost like when he surrendered to his alcoholism and asked for help. He unlocked his bike and headed for the nearest grocery store. He was starving.

Before Jack had even made it to the grocery store, his record was added to the FAN database joining millions of other new welfare recipients. His activities on the FAN browser would now be aggregated to identify internet usage patterns and buying habits. HHS policies strictly prohibited using an individual's private data unless, of course, there was reasonable cause.

THIRTY-ONE

There were somber mumbles as Steve joined other dignitaries to file into the Cabinet Room. The gravitas of the room never ceased to amaze Steve; the busts of Washington and Franklin stood in niches on either side of the fireplace, a rendition of the signing of the Declaration of Independence hung above the mantel, french doors and arched windows stood as silent witnesses over the large mahogany table where history was made.

Besides the Cabinet, the leadership of Congress from both parties was present. In an unprecedented move, the Chief Justice of the Supreme Court was also in attendance. As the ranking member on the House Committee on Homeland Security, Steve had a second-tier seat around the walls. He gave a brief nod to his friend, John Bowden, who sat on the opposite wall. A few chairs down from Bowden was Assistant AG Max Hunter. Steve momentarily locked eyes with his nemesis.

The mumbling stopped as President Rodgers entered and took his seat at the center of the table. He didn't mince words. "Our nation stands at the precipice. We need to take bold action. As President, I have emergency powers to act unilaterally. However, for the sake of our country, I am looking for broad consensus across the three branches of government. Time is of the essence. Our very survival as a nation is at stake." He paused and slowly looked around the entire room. "Robert, please provide a summary of where we stand."

Robert Gould, Secretary, Department of Homeland Security, cleared his throat. With his perfectly quaffed silver hair, black suit, and requisite blue tie, Gould oozed authority. "Thank you, Mr. President. It has been almost three months since the attacks, and our country is in a freefall. Most of this is public, but let me summarize:

"The stock market is down 65% since the attacks. That's $25 trillion in lost capitalization. Our GDP has plummeted over 50%. Unemployment is rising so fast we can't keep track, but our best estimate is 40%. As we enter the holiday buying season, retail is dead. Our price freeze on essentials—food, fuel, medicines, and paper products—has triggered hoarding and an exploding black market.

"Worse still is our financial system. We were already over-extended from the COVID-19 stimulus packages when this hit —and now the dollar has collapsed. Countries are flocking to the Chinese Laohu as its reserve currency. In short, we've lost our monetary weapons to combat this crisis.

"Finally, the National Guard has been deployed in 23 states in response to rioting and looting, mostly in our major cities. With this chaos and open borders, we are sitting ducks for another terrorist attack. Our domestic security apparatus is overwhelmed at all levels." Gould paused and looked at the audience. "Are there any questions at this point?"

Steve looked around the room. Nobody had the guts to speak, including himself. Nobody wanted to take the first harpoon. It was the oldest trick in the meeting book. If you were leading a meeting with potential naysayers, then the first adversary to speak would receive a verbal harpoon to discourage other sharks. Steve got the distinct impression they were gathered here for advice, not consent.

"All right then," President Rodgers broke the silence. "All is not lost. Since the COVID-19 pandemic, we've had an interagency working group in place to draw up contingency plans in the event of a complete economic collapse. Some of the plans need to be tweaked, and you may consider some of them draconian, but grave times demand bold action. Stu, please summarize our recommendations."

"We have three basic objectives," began Steward Friedman, the Secretary of the Treasury. "Stabilize our currency, stabilize our economy, and improve domestic security." Steve was amused by Friedman's rumpled suit and crooked tie, the stereotypical Ivy League professor. Friedman was brilliant, but today his darting eyes betrayed nervousness. "We want to meet these objectives as soon as possible with the tools and technologies at our disposal today." Friedman paused as an assistant handed him a folder.

"Okay. We are recommending four actions for Congress to consider, provisionally labeled as Acts. However, we are prepared to pursue Executive Orders if necessary," Friedman threatened. "Collectively, we are calling them the Fair Deal, a name borrowed from the Truman administration.

"First, THE CURRENCY RESTORATION ACT. We recommend adoption of a cryptocurrency to replace the dollar. Unlike current cryptocurrencies which use distributed blockchain ledgers, all transactions would flow through financial institutions controlled by the Fed. We can use proven Public Key Infrastructures to provide strong authentication. This will securely match citizens to accounts and prevent any errors or piracy. The Fed will have visibility on all transactions to eliminate fraud, money laundering, and terrorist or foreign interference. We will still be able to increase or decrease the money supply by mining and minting our own crypto-dollars. Our citizens will enjoy the safety and security of processing deposits, payments, and transfers right from their own smartphones or computers—with no need to handle potentially contaminated paper money or coins like we did with COVID-19.

"Second, THE INFRASTRUCTURE PROTECTION ACT. We recommend nationalizing key industries including food products, utilities, healthcare, and banking. We also propose the Internet becomes regulated under the FCC. We can't allow foreign Internet Trolls and Bots to sew discord in our nation as they did in the 2016 election. We can't permit thugs to coordinate flash mobs to loot stores. We can't allow terrorists to maintain sites for recruitment, propaganda, or dirty bomb specs. Nor can we afford to have our energy grid or financial systems hacked. We got along just fine without the Internet; surely we can survive with a regulated Internet." Secretary Friedman looked around the table to see if there was any protest.

Nationalize industries? Steve started to squirm in his seat. He glanced at the other attendees and was greeted with an increasing number of frowns.

"Third, THE WEALTH EQUALIZATION ACT. We concluded it was a matter of homeland security that we narrow the income inequality in our nation, to defuse a ticking time bomb for civil unrest. The keystone will be guaranteed income for our lowest tier of citizens, along with free universal healthcare and secondary education. We foresee three tiers of income earners. Bronze would be the lowest tier with a living wage of about $40,000 for an individual. This tier targets the unemployed, under-employed, disabled and retirees who represent about 50% of our population. This living wage would replace Social Security. The Silver tier would target the working-class population, perhaps 35% of our citizens. This would include manufacturing, agriculture, services workers, the trades—we are still refining the demographics. The target average income for an individual, $100,000. I say average in that a newly created Commerce department, the *Job Equivalency Board*, will create salary bands for each job type. Finally, the Gold tier addresses the remaining 15%. These would be our professionals, government employees, educators, and high-wealth individuals. Average income for a Gold, $200,000, once again subject to salary bands. By the way, $200,000 is the average salary for members of Congress."

These guys aren't kidding, Steve thought. They had broached several political taboos, but still no protest from the table, just a series of rumblings.

"A couple more important points. Target incomes would be

subject to family formation as well as a progressive tax structure. Accumulated wealth—stock, bonds, real estate, and savings—would remain untouched." Friedman let that settle in with the audience who, undoubtedly, were high-wealth individuals.

"Now, I know this is a lot to digest, but let me ask you a simple question. Would you rather have our inner-city residents collecting benefits from five different welfare programs or transfer $40,000 to each individual while taxing it and tracing it? Remember, these will be crypto-dollars with each transaction archived and visible. Think about it; no more underground economy for drugs, prostitution, money laundering, gun purchases, you name it!"

Steve saw some nods around the table. Clearly, Freidman was scoring some points.

"Finally, THE NATIONAL PIV ACT. PIV stands for Personal Identity Verification. This is a no-brainer. All U.S. citizens will be required to carry a certified smartphone, PIV for short. It will be used to verify their identity and status, process cryptocurrency transactions, access universal healthcare, and provide traditional smartphone functions such as communication and Internet access. When you register for PIV, you also register to vote. So, we should have universal voter registration..."

A mental alarm went off in Steve's head. Universal voter registration? Electronic voting was sure to follow. The Liberal's dream of harvesting votes on a national level will be a reality. My God, they will just keep voting for bigger government!

"...you've all seen the COVID-19 Spring Break video? Anonymous tracking of student cell phones, from just one Florida beach gathering, showed the exponential spread of the virus as students returned to the upper Midwest, the U.S., and the world. We see PIV as a *National Health Imperative* for tracking citizens during pandemics and quarantines."

The mumbling began again in earnest. President Rodgers

jumped in to quiet the room. "I know we've thrown a lot at you. I urge you to look at the big picture. These recommendations address both conservative and liberal hot buttons. They even touch the third rail of politics; Social Security and Entitlements. The intent was to provide a balance between partisan priorities while offering a path of recovery for our country." With the room back under control, the President cracked open Pandora's Box, "Okay, now for questions."

"When would we cut over to a cryptocurrency and what would it be called?" a Senator asked.

Friedman fielded the question. "We are targeting a mid-February cut over with all accounts converted to e-dollars, although *credits* will probably become the common lexicon. We will use our network of accredited banks to ensure all citizens have a valid account for electronic funds transfers. Banks will also be used to exchange hard cash for e-dollars for a period of time."

"How will you manage distribution of this new PIV smartphone?"

"Beth, why don't you handle this one," DHS Secretary Gould deferred to his Under Secretary, National Protection and Programs Directorate.

"Thank you, Mr. Secretary. We have already reached out to our domestic smartphone manufacturers for proposals. You can imagine who the lead contenders are. The manufacturers are ecstatic about churning their base; they have been facing market saturation for years. This will be a huge boost to our manufacturing output with over 250 million new smartphones or PIVs. That will take some time to roll out. Thankfully, about 70% of current smartphones are PIV-compatible. So, in the interim, we are looking to run apps on these existing platforms. In fact, we are already beta testing some key apps through HHS and their U.S. Works program. E-wallet can be used to track SNAP expenditures, more commonly referred to as food stamps. Geolocator can help verify attendance to training programs as well as monitor any restricted travel or suspected black market activities. As far as physical distribution of new PIV units, once again we'll use our network of banks to ensure proper registration and EFT links."

Steve couldn't stand it anymore. Harpoons or not, he had to address the elephant in the room. He stood up. "Mr. President." All eyes were now fixed on him. "What you propose is an unprecedented overreach by the federal government into virtually every aspect of our citizens' lives. All monetary transactions would be surveilled. Our economy would become a command economy and the Internet would be censored. Your income proposals would institutionalize a tiered society. Finally, this PIV Act would put an electronic tether on each citizen at the expense of our liberty and privacy. Is this what we really want? An end to our individual freedoms?" Steve sat down, his heart racing, questioning his rash action.

A hush fell over the room as attendees waited for the put-down, the harpoon. It came from an unexpected source. John Bowden, Under Secretary of Homeland Security, and Steve's longtime friend, responded.

"Steve, you know I share your views. But here's the thing, we already track large or suspicious monetary transactions and the IRS already has our financial records. We already regulate most industries—agriculture, communications, banking, utilities, healthcare—and the government has been picking winners and losers for years. We already have a de facto two-tier society; 50% of all income and 80% of all wealth is controlled by just 20% of the population! Finally, we already enforce identity verification and the NSA has been monitoring everything for years. For the average citizen, if you haven't done anything wrong, you have nothing to fear. What we propose is dealing with the new reality, fine tuning it, making it more efficient. But, at the end of the day, if we don't secure the homeland and our economy, we won't have a country."

Steve knew John's arguments were sound, but it was just too painful to admit. We have crossed the Rubicon, he brooded. Steve didn't think President Rodgers was some present-day

Caesar. That tyrannical role had been assumed by the Deep State, unelected bureaucrats who were rapidly crossing the river to rule the country. There was no turning back. However, he could fight a rear-guard action. But he would need help. After the meeting was adjourned, Steve sought out the Chief Justice. Regretfully, he was already engaged with the President off in a corner of the rapidly vacating room.

"Mr. President, I understand the urgency here. But I must warn you, the Court may have severe reservations about imposing an electronic collar on our citizens, as your PIV initiative suggests. It's a direct invasion of privacy. You should expect resistance."

The President's face remained impassive. "Thank you for your guidance. To be honest, we expected some pushback. We're considering letting our citizens opt into the program, just like they do today with subscriptions or apps. Might that sway the Court?"

"We'll see, the devil's in the detail," the Chief Justice replied as he turned and exited the Cabinet Room.

Steve noticed that the Chief Justice was frowning as he left. Was that good or bad?

THIRTY-TWO

"Thank God, we were about to send out a search party!" Bryce Brogan said as he grabbed some bags of potatoes from Jenny who was entering the backdoor of the church kitchen.

"It's a blizzard out there, hope we still get a crowd," Jenny replied as she dusted herself off. A mélange of cooking smells evoked fond memories of her mother's holiday dinners.

"Don't think that's going to be a problem," Bryce opened the swinging door to the crowded fellowship hall, abuzz with conversation. "Go on out and greet some people. Heck, this was your idea! We've got this covered." Bryce swept his hand across the kitchen where helpers were busily preparing the meal. Cal Cutler was minding two huge pots of venison chili bubbling on the stove top. Bryce's wife, Linda, mashed potatoes using an industrial mixer. An elderly woman stood in front of the open commercial oven basting broiled Whitefish supplied by the Tribe. Several pans of apple crisp were cooling on the counter.

Properly excused, Jenny took off and stowed her snow gear. She slipped on some comfortable shoes, fixed her hair, and made her entrance into the fellowship hall. Jenny took in the whole scene, her heart filling with gratitude. There were 15 colorfully decorated folding tables each with seating for 10. A large Christmas tree stood in the corner. Various handmade wreaths adorned the wall. People were already sampling the punch and nibbling on Cindy Beers' cheese platters. Children dashed about the room, laughing and giggling. These are my friends; this is my family.

Tina Cutler came forward to greet Jenny, carrying her four-week old in a sling. "Jenny! Isn't this great?"

"Oh Tina, you brought Noah!" Jenny said as she leaned over to get a better view of the infant. The baby greeted Jenny with a precious yawn.

"Would you like to hold him?"

"Oh yes." Jenny gently took the infant from Tina, carefully supporting his head. She instinctively rocked back and forth humming a nearly forgotten childhood song. The baby briefly opened his eyes and scrunched his face. "He smiled at me!"

"I think he did," Tina said.

"Oops," Jenny reacted as Noah spit up some milk on her sleeve.

"Here, let me relieve you," Tina took Noah back and handed Jenny a burp cloth.

"Can I hold him later?" The unexpected urge surprised Jenny. She consciously stopped where that train of thought might take her...

"Of course, Jenny, anytime."

Mary DeVries interrupted the two women, giving both a hug. "Merry Christmas!"

"Merry Christmas," Jenny replied. "Looks like we are going to have a full house despite the blizzard."

"David has corralled some boys to bring up some extra folding chairs and trays from the basement. I think we'll need them."

Tina and Mary started chatting, giving Jenny a chance to continue her rounds, greeting everybody in the room. Johnny-B was there. Members of the Tribe. Sheriff Larson and his niece, Sally. The whole Brogan clan as well as the Beers and Cutlers. Probably 75 active members of the church and a matching number from the community. People were already reserving spaces by leaning chairs against the tables. Pastor DeVries was busy directing the placement of spare chairs around the periphery of the room. A parade of tired but happy kitchen workers carried large pots and trays stacked high with food into the fellowship hall. They placed the bounty on a long buffet table against the wall.

Pastor DeVries put his two outside fingers in his mouth and silenced the room with a piercing whistle. "Okay people, form a circle and hold hands."

Everybody jockeyed to the periphery of the large room and held their neighbor's hands. Jenny squeezed in between Johnny-B and Sally Larson. Before closing her eyes, Jenny saw nonbelievers, newcomers, and agnostics alike looking for cues from their Christian brothers and sisters, bowing their heads out of courtesy.

"Dear Lord, we gather tonight to celebrate your wonderous gift to us, our Savior, Jesus Christ..." The pastor's calming prayer continued in stark contrast to the howling of the wind outside. Every now and then, a gust would elicit a groan from the aging church. "...In your Son's name we pray—and all God's people said..."

"AMEN!" was the collective response as people squeezed each other's hands. As people started to get in line for the banquet, a commotion arose at the front door. It opened and three big men in military parkas entered the room along with a blast of frigid air. They each carried two, 20-pound bags of oranges.

"Greetings from the 107th Engineering Battalion!" one soldier announced.

"Oranges!" The crowd called out in glee.

Nobody had seen fresh fruit for months. Bryce Brogan was just ahead of Jenny and Pastor DeVries to greet the men.

"Kurt, I'm so glad you came!" Bryce put his arm around the leader's shoulders and turned to make introductions. "Jenny, Pastor, this is my cousin, Lieutenant Colonel Kurt Brogan from the Guard unit in Ishpeming."

"Ma'am, Pastor DeVries." With his hands full, Kurt acknowledged each with a polite nod. He turned to his comrades. "This is Sergeant James Banks and Corporal Greg Miller. They both have family 'round here."

"Welcome and Merry Christmas!" Pastor DeVries offered. "Where did you get those oranges?"

"Well, the base is still getting some fresh fruit on occasion. We thought we would share the wealth." The Colonel turned to face his cousin. "Besides, I know Bryce is crazy about oranges; our grandma used to hand them out as treats."

"Thanks Cuz!" Bryce replied.

"Here, let me help you with those," Jenny grabbed a couple of the bags. "Follow me," she ordered as she turned for the kitchen.

"I know the way," Colonel Brogan replied, "I was baptized and confirmed in this church."

"Really! Then welcome home. How did you guys ever make it through the storm?"

"Ma'am, there's not much that can stop a Humvee. We were not going to be late for Christmas Eve dinner!" Corporal Miller replied as a relative came up and gave him a big kiss on the cheek.

After the meal, Jenny grabbed a cup of coffee and joined Pastor DeVries and Cindy Beers at a corner table to take in the scene. Someone had found some candy canes and the kids were decorating the tree and sucking on broken ones at the same time. Across the way, Jenny could see Colonel Kurt Brogan and his cousin, Bryce, engaged in animated conversation with Johnny-B and Sheriff Larson. An occasional laugh or guffaw emanated from the group. Probably telling old war stories, she figured.

Pastor DeVries turned to Jenny, "This had been a wonderful evening. Thank you for your inspiration and leadership."

"Pastor, it was the whole church that made this happen," Jenny demurred. "And remember, I'm the *acting* president, we need to find a replacement."

"Of course, Jenny. But you know, I've been thinking that we need to utilize the church more. It doesn't make sense to use it for only two hours on Sundays." Pastor DeVries took a sip of coffee. "Take tonight for example. The whole community chipped in and we had more than enough. What if we had a community meal, say, every Saturday night? Maybe a soup kitchen midday during the week? I know our food pantry is empty, so we would have to rely on the generosity of others— like both of you, the Cutlers, Johnny, several of the hunters in our congregation. What do you think?"

"Pastor, I'm a bit worried about the yield of our green-houses," Jenny said. "But maybe we can find a way to boost our harvest. I know there are lots of deer out there. And we seem to have plenty of Whitefish and Lake Trout. I can't speak for Cindy and Tina, they've been so generous with their cheese and eggs, but I like the idea!"

"We can spare more cheese," Cindy said. "But this community has other needs. With the school closing, we have a lot of families in a fix; do they send their kids on a two-hour round trip to Marquette or homeschool? Also, parents who are still working have no childcare. Marilyn closed her place last month and went back to Milwaukee. Maybe the church has a role. We used to run a Vacation Bible School during the summers, back when membership was high."

Pastor DeVries agreed. "Those are great ideas! Let's bring them up at Church Council next week. Perhaps we can kill a couple of birds with one stone."

Their conversation was interrupted by a ruckus near the kitchen. Somebody had retrieved Toby from the garage and put blow-up antlers on him. He came charging in the room barking and chasing children and children chasing him! It was a hoot. Everybody started laughing.

"Pardon me while I go rescue my reindeer." Jenny excused herself and joined the chase.

THIRTY-THREE

Washington D.C. – January 18
The Bureau

Although it was only nine inches of snow, the January snow-storm had crippled the Capital. All schools were closed as well as government agencies except, of course, Tommy's. He sat in front of Reggie's desk waiting for him to finish reading the brief he had prepared.

"So, they shut down?" Reggie asked.

"It looks that way," Tommy replied. "They've shuttered their doors and the building's up for lease. We got a Michigan OSHA inspector in there and confirmed it was cleared out. We also checked out some of their investors. They cut off funding right after the attack. The only loose end is a couple of microturbines they ordered from Toronto—they're MIA. Perhaps the whole thing was a scam?"

"Maybe. What about the team?"

"They're scattered to the four winds," Tommy replied. "Bennett is working for his dad in Grand Rapids. Schultz is down in Florida. Kelly is still in Traverse City but got canned from his job at the University."

"Really, maybe our friends at the DOJ gave the school a nudge?"

"Actually, he was caught on video spewing all sorts of politically incorrect comments. Some hothead doxed him."

"Serves him right," Reggie said with a rueful smile. "Anyway, I think we can put Plasma Drive Technologies on the back burner."

Tommy saw the opening. "Should we cut back on surveillance? At least Kelly, he looks like a loser."

Reggie hesitated for a second. "Yeah, that makes sense, but keep surveillance in place on young Bennett and Chief Scientist Schultz—Energy seems particularly interested in him."

"Got it." Tommy inwardly smiled at his small victory. Surveillance data on Kelly would no longer be automatically *pushed* to the Bureau. An authorized IN, Information Need, would be required to *pull* surveillance data.

"With this plasma crap going dormant, they want us to narrow our focus on Steve Bennett. I've got the green light to expand our Deep Sea program to investigate possible abuse of power, obstruction of justice, and sexual harassment."

"Sexual harassment?"

"We have reliable sources who say that Bennett is sleeping with his assistant, Marge Stevenson."

"Oh." Tommy tried to keep his face passive. You would think they had better things to do!

"Also, Hunter wants us to dig deeper into events on 9/11. Remember the communication log we showed him?"

"Sure."

"Well, he wants details on how, when, and why his son, Scott, left the DC area. Also, he wants us to investigate the Congressman's communications with his girlfriend, pilot, and the former Israeli Ambassador—that could be a violation of the Logan Act."

"Okay. What's the timetable?" Tommy asked.

"I want you to get started on this right away. However, we might sit on the info for a while. Assistant AG Hunter will orchestrate the timing of any disclosures."

"All right, I'll start work today." Sounds like a political hit job to me, Tommy thought, as he exited Reggie's office. And targeting Bennett's girlfriend? What type of scumbags am I working for?

THIRTY-FOUR

Washington D.C. – February 15
House of Representatives

They chose Friday, February 15, at 9 pm ET, for the Special Address to the Nation, well after the markets had closed. The House Chamber was deemed the appropriate venue, but there was no pretense that the State of the Union was good. In fact, the country was broken. After briefly rallying around the flag, the nation had devolved into a nightmarish landscape. *The thin veneer of civilization* had become the new catchphrase.

It would be the most widely viewed event in the nation's history, far surpassing the last episode of *MASH*, the Super Bowl, or even the 1969 Moon Walk. Curiously, only one network would carry the address. At the time, it was argued a single voice was needed to avoid confusion and fake news. But, for conspiracy theorists, it was prophetic. Regardless, the nation was in desperate need of reassurance and the President delivered. "My fellow Americans..."

***

Marge listened to the President's speech with resignation. Afterwards, she tolerated the pundits' spin for a while and then switched off the TV. This was not news to her; Steve had already provided a preview of this coming behemoth. His efforts to derail it by forging an unlikely alliance with far-left civil libertarians had been to no avail. Except for the PIV opt-out, which had support from the Chief Justice, they had gotten steam-rolled. Mainstream Republicans and Democrats had voted overwhelmingly for the Acts. Steve had derisively called them ruling class lemmings—but weren't they themselves also part of that ruling class? Regardless, he would be devastated tonight. Marge made a pot of tea and waited for his return from Congress.

***

"Unbelievable!" Tim lamented as he turned off his TV. He turned to face Kristen and their guest, Jack Conrad. "Say good-bye to our free market democracy."

"What other choice did they have?" asked Jack.

"I don't know," Tim replied. "But it smells like totalitarianism to me. I mean, all monetary transactions going through the Fed. Everybody's required to have an electronic tether. Adopt a command economy model. My God, there will be no privacy left."

"Sounds like you can still buy a premium education and healthcare if you've got the money," Kristen said.

"Did you notice the part about all Internet transactions will be subject to national security considerations?" Tim asked. "That sounds a lot like what China is doing with the Internet. Also, what's with only one network carrying the address and commentary? *Fox News* wasn't even transmitting!"

"We gotta get out of here," Jack said.

"Got any clever ideas?" Tim asked as he paced the floor, running his hands through his hair.

"Yeah, in fact I do," Jack said.

As Jack laid out his plan, they were oblivious to the surveillance they were under. Using the app provided by U.S. Works, Jack's phone had used Bluetooth communication to probe his friends' phones for MAC and IP addresses. At the default one-hour mark, the data was routed through various VPNs to the NSA's Data Center. Their identities were now linked in a spatial-temporal association. A seemingly meaningless bit of information unless someone was actively data mining. Results from the U.S. Works pilot program would be used to fine-tune the roll out of the app on PIV and PIV-compliant units. The smartphone suppliers were more than happy to follow the

Homeland Security mandate. Jack was clueless as to why the battery on his smartphone was always draining so fast.

***

Meg Conrad turned off the TV with renewed hope. She got her laptop and quickly accessed the new usa.fairdeal.gov website, frantically scrolling through the freshly posted job tiers. She found it. "K-12 Public School Teacher, Gold Level, Mean Income $200,000 E-Dollars," she read out loud. "I'll be rich!" Her enthusiasm was curbed when she read the footnote, income subject to probation and tenure. Besides, she was only a substitute teacher; full-timers would have a lock on these positions. Still, she had a leg up on others. Meg tried to formulate an attack plan. How could she differentiate herself? What was her dad's old axiom? Oh yeah... "Find out what they want and give it to them."

***

"Well, I'm not sure about guaranteed income, but it's about time for universal healthcare," Pastor DeVries said. He and the Church Council had watched the address in the fellowship hall and were trying to figure out the impact on the church.

"I'm not so sure this is all good," Cindy Beers said. "How will we collect e-dollars, or whatever the darn things are, in a collection plate?"

Jenny agreed. "Cindy brings up a good point. Also, did you catch the part about no itemized deductions? That's going to kill charitable giving!"

The Council members looked to Pastor DeVries for guidance. "God will provide."

***

"Did you notice they didn't say a thing about accumulated wealth and unearned income?" Johnny snorted over the radio.

"That's a big 10-4 Johnny", Ben Sutton replied. "Wouldn't want to catch the elites with their knickers down! Also, sounds like we're going to have Big Brother right up our ass. Whatever happened to covert surveillance? Hell, they practically told everybody they're gonna be tracked!"

"No shit, Big Texas. I was surprised they didn't go after our guns."

"Stay tuned Johnny. If Texas is an indicator, they'll be knocking on your door soon! Listen, I got to go. I'm working with my wife on a new casserole for Easter brunch. Over."

Johnny's ears perked up. Ben Sutton was single and certainly not a cook. "Oh really? Mind if you share the recipe. Over." Johnny leaned over and turned on his computer to accept the input of the shortwave carrier.

"No problem, Johnny. You ready? Got a pencil and paper? Over."

"Good to go. Over."

"Okay, preheat oven to 350. Stir cheddar cheese, eggs, bacon, red pepper, onion, mild garlic, salt, and black pepper together in a bowl until well-mixed. Pour into a prepared baking dish and bake in a preheated oven until eggs are set. Takes about 20 to 25 minutes. Over."

"Thanks, Big Texas. Does it keep? Over."

"You can refrigerate, but it's probably only good for a couple days. Over."

"10-4 Big Texas. Can't wait to try it. WW5BT over and out."

Johnny chuckled as he ran the shortwave carrier input through his demodulation algorithms. Only Ben Sutton would send a digitally encrypted message through a *scrambled* egg casserole recipe. After a few minutes, Johnny read the decrypted message. It was about creating and operating AM radio transmitters—and powerful 50-Kilowatt ones to boot! That was the highest wattage allowed by the FCC, a so-called clear channel. They could easily broadcast across states in the daytime, and across the country at night when the sun's electromagnetic interference was low, and the atmosphere cooled to become stable. Johnny put his chin in his hand and tried to figure out what Ben was up to. Why would we need a clear channel? Unlicensed use would be illegal...

THIRTY-FIVE

Aux Baie, MI – March 10
Community Church

Jenny's hands were full, so she had to knock on the church kitchen door with a kick. Cindy Beers was right behind her cradling blocks of cheese. "Hey, let us in!" Jenny yelled.

Mary DeVries opened the door to let them enter, along with a raw, biting wind. "Oh dear, it's freezing out there!"

"Well, it's only March. Spring doesn't start up here until July!" Cindy joked as both women put down their packages of food and got out of their winter coats. The delightful aroma of a pot of vegetable, egg drop soup boiling away along with venison chili filled the kitchen. A couple servers carried dishes back and forth between the kitchen and the fellowship hall.

"How's our numbers?" Jenny asked as she put her veggies in the refrigerator.

"They keep growing," Mary replied. "We've got 15 in daycare, 20 homeschoolers, and by my last count, 35 for lunch."

"That's great!" Jenny exited the kitchen into the fellowship hall. To her right was a little buffet line with volunteers serving the soup, some store-bought crackers, and lemonade. There were only five tables set up, but they were all packed. Jenny recognized most everybody; a mix of seniors, rural poor, the Tribe, and regular folks who had fallen on hard times. Although diverse, they did have one thing in common; they had all opted out of the Feds PIV program and had lost their benefits. For many, it was a matter of privacy. For others, it was a matter of pride. For the elderly, it was the intimidation of PIV and e-wallet technologies. Besides, they said, there were no stores open anyway to spend these newfangled e-dollars!

Jenny walked over to the table where several of the Tribe were seated. She saw some fresh faces. "How's the soup today?"

"Soup's good, chili's better," a man replied. "It's got my deer in it," he smiled.

"Thank you so much for your hunting. It's meant all the difference in the world." The Tribe had been more than generous with their game.

"You're Jenny Hernandez, aren't you?" an ancient, shrunken woman asked. "I knew your grandmother. You look just like her!" The woman looked to be pureblood, although that was increasingly rare.

"Oh really. Please tell me more." There was a void here that needed to be filled—with her family gone, she had lost her roots. Jenny pulled up a spare chair next to the old woman.

"Oh, she was a beautiful woman, just like you, long black hair. And she kept a big garden, just like you. She would join us at powwows and celebrations. She was not ashamed of her ancestors. Oh, and her husband was so handsome! All the women were jealous," she giggled like a little girl.

"And what's your name?" Jenny asked.

"Wenona. It means first daughter."

"That's beautiful. I'm a first daughter too. I would love to speak more with you Wenona. I didn't know my grandmother. She died when I was just a baby."

"I know. We will talk."

Jenny smiled and moved on to a table of a young couple with a child. Newcomers, she thought. "Hi, I'm Jenny Hernandez, welcome to our church!"

The husband stood up and offered his hand. "Al Federico. And this is my wife Maria and Pepe, our four-year-old."

"I'm so glad you could join us. Are you new to the area?" Jenny asked.

"We just got here from Chicago," Al said. "It took us several days, but we made it. A nice family in Iron Mountain told us we could find food and help here."

"Really," Jenny replied, surprised the word had spread so far. "Why did you leave Chicago?"

"I lost my job, but I refused to go on welfare."

"I'm sorry," Jenny said. "What was your job?"

"I'm a plumber," Al said with a trace of pride. "But our owner got in trouble with that new Job Equivalency Board."

"Well, we certainly could use a plumber in Aux Baie if you choose to stay. We also have several abandoned houses in the area that can be claimed. See the woman in the dress over there?" Jenny pointed toward Mary DeVries. "She can help you with any questions you might have."

"Thanks Jenny," Al replied. "We're also looking for a church. The authorities closed ours down in Chicago—they said we were discriminating. I don't get it."

"What?" Jenny was incredulous.

Before Al could answer, Jenny noticed a couple had walked in the front door, looking for help or direction. "If you'll excuse me..." Jenny walked over to greet the new guests. They were well dressed, but Jenny decided not to draw conclusions. "Welcome. Are you here for the free lunch?"

"No, we're from the Department of Health and Human Services, Marquette Office," answered the man. "We're here to inspect this facility. Can you tell me who's in charge?"

It was late afternoon by the time the Church Council had gathered for an emergency session. They sat around a table in the fellowship hall: Pastor DeVries, Jenny—the acting president, Cindy Beers, and Bryce Brogan. Pastor DeVries had a stack of paper in front of him. It was the inspection report that had been printed by the HHS inspectors before they left. He leafed through the various findings with a growing frown. "This looks bad. There must be twenty or so violations here," he bemoaned. "Cindy, can you make us some copies?"

"Our copier broke last week," Cindy replied "and no one's

going to come up here to fix it. I'm sorry."

"Let me take a look," Bryce said. DeVries slid the packet over to him. All eyes were trained on him as he leafed through the report. "Okay, there's a lot of stuff, but here are the bad ones. Expired food service license. No daycare license. No school licenses. Unlicensed medical facility. Expired boiler inspection. Harboring undocumented residents..."

"What?" Pastor DeVries interrupted.

"They asked some of the Tribe for IDs, and nobody had one," Jenny said.

"Oh, I see. Sorry to interrupt."

"No problem," Bryce said. "The rest is just crap, like out-of-date fire extinguishers."

Jenny reached over and grabbed the report. She leafed through the sections until she found what she was looking for. "We have 30 days to remedy, or we risk being shut down." Jenny looked at the front of the report which had the business cards of the two inspectors. "Amber Johnson is MIOSHA, that's state. This guy Peter Furman is HHS, that's federal. What the hell is he doing here! Oh, pardon my language."

"That's okay Jenny. I share your opinion. So, what are we going to do?" asked DeVries.

"There's not much we can do," Bryce said. "I mean, each of these licenses would probably take months to process through the state bureaucracy. They know that. They aim to shut us down."

"I can't believe they would stoop so low." DeVries shook his head.

"Pastor, this is not a random attack," Bryce narrowed his eyes. "You know the Bernards? They moved here from Pine River because the Feds shut down Trinity Lutheran. And the Riveras left Providence because they closed the Catholic school. They're systematically targeting churches and private schools as havens for off-gridders, or OGs as they now call us."

Jenny nodded in agreement. "I spoke to some visitors at lunch who said their church in Chicago got closed down too—

something about discrimination. This is crazy!"

Everyone went quiet, staring off into the distance. Pastor DeVries broke the silence. "We can't shy away from this, the community depends on us. Let me see those papers." Pastor flipped a few pages without focusing. "Cindy, can you start on the license applications? I'm sure Mary is willing to help. Maybe if we show some good-faith efforts, they'll cut us some slack."

"Yeah, right." Bryce said

Pastor DeVries repeated what had become his mantra lately. "God will provide."

THIRTY-SIX

Aux Baie – March 18
Johnny-B's Cabin

"Hey!" Johnny-B shouted. "Let's get this thing started." Someone had brought a 12-pack of beer and the gathering was deteriorating into a party. There was one last "pssssch" of a can being opened before the self-appointed, community defense team quieted down. Johnny noted it was a diverse group: Bryce Brogan and Cal Cutler from the church, Sam Aishkebay and George Russell with their sons from the Tribe, Sally Larson and a few others who, along with himself, were allied with the nascent Resistance.

"Okay," Johnny said. "It's been six months since the attacks and our town has done pretty well—at least with self-defense." He took a swig from his beer. "But that could be changing. The church was inspected last week, and the Feds are tightening the screws on PIV and ID checks. Also, we're getting closer to tourist season, which means outsiders. Bryce, tell us what happened at the church."

"As you said, we were inspected, but it wasn't just county and state inspectors. The Feds were also involved." Bryce paused to appraise the audience. Johnny wondered if he was getting cold feet associating with the rabble rousers. "Anyway, they wrote us up for a bunch of violations including unlicensed food service, schooling, and medical care. There's no way we'll be able to meet their deadlines."

"They know that," Sally Larson sneered. "I've worked with these people before. They're setting you up. It's happening all over the state."

Bryce agreed. "That's what I told the Council. So, what are we supposed to do?"

"Fight back," said Sam Aishkebay, the tribal elder. "We wouldn't let them do that on tribal land."

"I wish we had your protected status," Bryce replied. "Anyway, we're a church. We're not going to fight these guys."

"If we don't resist now, they'll just walk all over us," Sally spread her hands to emphasize the point.

"How about your uncle?" Cal Cutler asked. "Can the Sheriff help us?"

Before Sally could answer, Johnny stepped in. "He's cool. If push comes to shove, I think he'll break our way. But I don't want to get him stuck in the middle—at least not yet." Sally nodded in agreement. "Where does the Tribe stand on all of this?" Johnny asked.

George Russell, Johnny's boat captain, addressed the question. "I'm tempted to say it's not our fight, but that's not true. Jenny, the co-op, and the church have been more than fair to us. Besides, our people are now being harassed with ID checks."

"Who's scanning you?" Sally pressed.

"State Police, Indian Affairs, we're even being *helped* by Health and Human Services. I think we face a common foe."

George Russell's answer silenced the gathering. He had finally named and framed the adversary, the foe. Johnny broke the silence. "This is just going to get worse. I hear they're going to force people to use PIVs to buy anything, including paying for utility services. How many of you are registered with PIVs?" Johnny scanned the group. He already knew the answer but wanted to test some loyalties.

"Cal and I are PIV-compatible," Bryce said. "So is the leadership at the church, except for Jenny."

"Okay," Johnny said. "Listen carefully. You should assume that you are being tracked, even if it is just an ordinary smartphone. Whether you know it or not, the Feds have been loading tracking apps for months. Isn't that right, Sally?"

"That's right. I know for certain that tracking apps are being used for SNAP food purchases. I think the Feds have forced smartphone manufacturers to add a trojan horse app—you don't even know it's there. I destroyed my phone a while ago."

"Think about that," Johnny said. "If they want to, the Feds can track what you bought, where you are, who you're talking to. Anyway, you might think twice about owning a smartphone. And to repeat, no smartphones allowed at our meetings, right?" Everybody nodded in the room.

Bryce leaned forward in his chair to face Johnny. "What are you proposing? How would we buy things without PIVs? How would we communicate? How do we fight this foe?"

"All right." Johnny looked around the room, meeting each person in the eye. "We're all in this together. I'm working with George and the Tribe to setup a little black market with our Canadian friends so we can buy critical items in secret—stuff like guns, ammo, walkie-talkies—anything the Feds are tracking." Johnny could see Bryce and Cal shift uncomfortably in their seats.

Johnny took a sip of beer before continuing. "We should increase trade and barter within our community. Also, if you've got friends or family that have a PIV, they can buy things to share with others. Just remember, those purchases will be tracked." Johnny turned to fix his eyes on Cal and Bryce. "One last thing. You can tell the church that we've got your back. We're not going to do anything stupid, but if you need our help, we're here. If I can find some walkie-talkies, I'll get you some for off grid communication. Okay?"

"Sure Johnny, thanks," Bryce replied.

As the meeting broke up, Sally approached Johnny-B. "You think they get it?"

"Don't know. They're pacifists at heart. Although Bryce certainly knows how to handle a shotgun." Johnny thought back to the confrontation at Brogans months ago. "Whether they get it or not, I think trouble is headed their way."

"Yep." Sally agreed. "You know, the snowbirds will be re-turning soon. Most of them are rich. Some of us have been thinking about sharing the wealth." Sally paused for reaction.

"You mean some Robin Hood action? Don't think your uncle, the Sheriff, would approve."

"Just a thought."

"You be careful, girl!"

THIRTY-SEVEN

Traverse City, MI – April 20
Municipal Boat Ramp

West Bay was placid and the skies were clear. That's good, Jack thought, looks like we picked the right day. Despite his anxiety, he kept a steady pace on his bicycle as he approached the boat ramp. Jack felt naked without his PIV, but they had all agreed to trash them before they congregated. He could see Tim and Karl by the ramp, but no boat! Jack abandoned his bike at a public rack and approached his friends.

"Where is he?" Tim asked, echoing Jack's fears.

Jack scanned Grandview Parkway for any oncoming traffic. "I don't know, we agreed to 7:30." He could feel his chest tighten, a harbinger of rising panic.

"Maybe he stiffed us," Karl said, rocking back and forth.

"He knows he gets his second payment when he delivers the boat." Jack tried to reassure them, and himself. They had loaded the turbines, lab equipment, and personal effects into the boat last night—and the owner had gotten his first gold coin. The second coin was in Jack's pocket.

"Is that him?" Tim gave a nod toward the access road to the ramp.

"Yes! Thank God," Jack replied. Despite the relief, he still felt like a bug under a microscope. He scanned the area for any police or municipal workers.

The pickup made a quick semicircle so that the trailer was pointed toward the ramp. Jack ran out on the ramp dock to help tend the aging, *Bayliner* cuddy cabin. Within minutes, the boat was bobbing in the water and tied-up. Without saying a word, the owner jumped into the boat, lowered the drive unit, and cranked the engine. It started as promised! The owner climbed out of the boat and approached Jack.

"It's got a full tank of gas. I scratched out the serial numbers and scraped off the old license stickers. It's been off the books for a while. As far as I'm concerned, this boat was stolen years ago." And with that, he held out his hand.

Jack dropped the remaining gold coin into the owner's hand and simply said "Thanks." By the time Karl and Tim had gotten on the boat, the pickup and trailer were already leaving the ramp area. "Untie the lines," Jack ordered. He put the boat in gear and steered a course heading due north up West Traverse Bay. It took all his self-control to keep the boat at a moderate cruising speed as they fled Traverse City.

Washington DC
The Bureau Surveillance Room
"What the hell!" The alarm on the tracking monitor had startled Tommy. Karl Schultz had gone off grid! This was not good. If was a major alarm, so it would be pushed to Reggie's attention. He had to think fast. First, he checked the obvious—a malfunction or power outage. But the diagnostic feed showed Schultz's PIV was fully functional before it went dead. Was he on the run? I wonder what Schultz's associates are doing. Before he could investigate, Reggie was on the intercom.

"Tommy, what's with Karl Schultz? I have an alert that says he's off grid."

"Yes sir, I am checking on that right now. Probably a power outage or malfunction. I've already double-checked his recent communications and travel, and he has had no contact with Scott Bennett who remains on grid down in Grand Rapids." That should buy some time. "I'll get back to you with an update. Anyway, I've got some juicy data and photos on Congressman Bennett's girlfriend."

"Really? I'd like to see those."

What a twit, Tommy thought. Like a dog chasing a squirrel.

Tommy compiled the routine surveillance on Marge Stevenson. Before leaving his office, he initiated his secret tracking routines to pull data on Schultz's associates. He was particularly interested in Tim Kelly and friends.

Mackinac Bridge, MI

Kristen drove her SUV toward the Mackinac Bridge, her cat, Smokey, complaining in the back seat. She was towing an enclosed snowmobile trailer—in April. Might as well write *I'm guilty* on it, she thought. Kristen could feel her pulse quicken as she entered the PIV check lane, stopped, and rolled down her window.

"PIV." The male attendant demanded in a flat voice.

Kristen complied and reached out the window with her smartphone. The attendant used a wand to read her PIV and looked intently at Kristen and then the image on his monitor to confirm a match. "What's in the trailer?"

Kristen's heart skipped. "It's empty. I'm going up to Marquette to pick up my dad's snowmobile. It broke over the winter."

"Lucky you. That's 14 credits with the extra axles," the attendant said as he automatically charged Kristen's e-wallet on her PIV. "Have a nice day."

The toll gate rose, and Kristen let out a deep sigh of relief as she drove onto the Mackinac Bridge. She looked west out her window at Lake Michigan and wondered how Tim and the rest of the crew were doing.

Lake Michigan

With calm water, the little cabin cruiser performed like a champ. Exiting the mouth of Grand Traverse Bay, they could see the Manitou Islands to the southwest, the Fox Islands to the Northwest, and far in the distance, the end of the ancient archipelago, Beaver Island. Jack's serenity started to ebb as they approach the large island which was inhabited and had boat traffic. He decided to give it a wide berth, keeping it well to starboard. With no radio, no flares, and no PIVs, if they broke down now, they'd be goners—the water temp read 39 degrees.

Karl remained below deck, looking very pale. But Tim stayed in the cockpit with Jack making light conversation.

"You know the story about Beaver Island?" Jack asked.

"What story?"

"It used to be run by a Mormon King in the mid-1800s. King Strang, self-appointed leader of the Strangite Mormon Church."

"You're joking, right?" Tim asked.

"No joke. He had close to 12,000 followers at one time."

"Wish I had known that for my class at the University. I was looking for examples of theocracies. What happened to him?"

"It's a crazy story. Some members of his congregation shot him in broad daylight at the island's harbor. Anyway, the assassins were taken up to Mackinac Island for a mock trial, fined $1.25 each, and let go! I guess life was pretty cheap back then," Jack concluded.

Before long, in the distance, they could see the underbelly of the Upper Peninsula of Michigan. Tim kept the compass on a steady northwest heading as they approached the shoreline.

Washington DC
The Bureau Surveillance Room
With Reggie properly diverted, Tommy had time to check his covert tracking routines. He got a hit right away; Tim Kelly had gone off grid within 30 minutes of Schultz. Too close to be a coincidence. Tommy continued to pull on the thread, looking at one-off associates of Kelly. Another hit! Kelly's girlfriend, Kristen Campbell, had gone through a PIV check this morning at the Mackinac Bridge. He pulled up that record and looked at the video history. Hmm...looks like she was pulling a snowmobile trailer. Tommy's excitement grew as he accessed the X-ray data of the trailer scan. But, it was empty? That didn't make sense! He pulled up his tracking map and saw that Campbell was still online. She was heading west on U.S. 2

toward Manistique. Why there?

Tommy was about to shut down the routine when he got one last peripheral hit; a Jack Conrad had gone off grid this morning about the same time as Schultz and Kelly. Of interest, Conrad had previous contact with Kelly and Kristen Campbell —his U.S. Works PIV had made an association. I wonder how he fits in. It dawned upon Tommy that he was rooting for the bad guys. Heck, he was already running interference for them!

Manistique, MI
Municipal Harbor

"Thank God you made it," Kristen said as she grabbed the mooring rope from Tim's outstretched hand.

Jack killed the engine and jumped on the dock to secure the ropes to the dock cleats. His head pivoted as he scanned the harbor and adjacent marina for any threats. All was clear. He approached Kristen who had just finished hugging Tim. "I need the car keys." Within minutes he had the snowmobile trailer backed down close to the boat. "Okay, let's do this as fast as possible," Jack said. "We can talk later."

Tim and Jack handled the heavy lifting of the turbines while Karl and Kristen transferred smaller cases and duffle bags. Karl was about to pick up the largest duffle bag when Jack intervened. "I've got that one." He picked up the overweight duffle knowing it contained his rifles, ammo, and a last-minute addition—a kiteboard and kite. It joined the rest of their equipment in the snowmobile trailer. Soon, the transfer was complete, and Jack felt his tension subside. He was closing the trailer doors when he saw a man approaching from the marina. Oh shit! "Guys get in the car. I'll manage this."

Jack walked toward the approaching man to maintain some distance from the trailer. The elderly man had an old, plaid wool coat on. He had gray whiskers and a weathered face. "Hello," he said in a friendly greeting. "Are you mooring for the day or overnight? Twenty credits for a day pass."

"I'm just dropping off some people," Jack replied. "And then

I'll be on my way. Is that a problem?"

The man looked back and forth between the boat and the snowmobile trailer. He raised an eyebrow. "Kinda early for boating, and kinda late for snowmobiling. Where you guys from?" He nodded toward the SUV where Karl, Kristen, and Tim stood watching the confrontation.

Jack didn't like where this was going. But the guy wasn't acting hostile, more like a hustler. He took a chance. "You know, we're just passing through. It would be great if someone could look after our boat."

"I might be able to do that," the man replied. "But I don't have my payment terminal," he spread his hands open.

"Here," Jack tossed the boat keys over to the man. "If we're not back within the hour, the boat is yours."

"The old man eyeballed the keys, and then the boat. "Well… that works for me," he said with a twinkle in his eye. "You all have a good day now." He turned and walked back toward the marina.

Jack watched the old man retreat. He hadn't copied down their license plate or used his smartphone, or anything. This smelled like a small town shakedown, or maybe a sympathizer? Didn't really matter. He walked back to join his friends. "Let's get out of here!"

As they drove away from Manistique, Karl asked for Kristen's PIV. Using the pliers on his Leatherman, he wrenched the PIV until it cracked open. He removed the motherboard and twisted it in half. The various pieces and battery of the PIV were thrown out the window to litter the road.

They were all off grid.

THIRTY-EIGHT

Aux Baie, MI
Jenny's Camp

The last two miles of the trip were the worst. Jenny's two-track was a rutted, muddy mess from the spring thaw and run-off. With Tim driving, it gave Jack time to reflect. Except for the confrontation at the marina, his plan was proceeding flawlessly. The problem was, the closer he got to Jenny's property, the more anxious he was. Tim had let Jenny know that he was tagging along, but would she even want him there?

"This is the turnoff I missed last time," Tim interrupted Jack's thoughts. He pointed to the *Welcome* sign and *Hernandez* written on the wooden birdhouse. "We're almost there."

Jack bit his lower lip.

The guest house was stick built with a basic design; kitchen, bathroom, and main room on the first floor and two bedrooms on the second floor. The focal point of the main room was a fireplace surrounded by a couch and two easy chairs. A colorful rug with a few burn holes completed the conversation area. A fire had been set which they lit to take the chill out of the air. Jenny had put a few staples in the refrigerator and cabinets.

Tim and Kristen moved their stuff into the master bedroom with the queen bed which left Karl and Jack the guest room with the two single beds. After nervously casing the joint, Smokey hid under the queen bed. Everybody took turns in the bathroom to tidy up, each marveling at the indelible rust stain in the sink from the iron laden water. It was 6 pm when they gathered in the main room before heading over to Jenny's cabin.

"Let's just walk over," Tim said. "It's only five minutes."

"Why don't you guys go ahead," Jack replied. "I am going to take a walk to clear my head—it's been a long day. I'll catch up later."

"Yoo-hoo," Tim called out in a falsetto as he knocked on the cabin door and let himself into the main room.

"Tim!" Jenny ran to greet him giving him a big, long hug. "Oh, it's great to see you!" Toby came charging out of a back room barking and sniffing the visitors, begging for attention.

"It's been too long," Tim said. "You don't look a day over 30."

"Right," Jenny said, pointing to some stray, gray hairs in her otherwise gorgeous black mane.

Tim pivoted to introduce his friends standing in the entryway. "Jenny, this is Kristen, my girlfriend, and Karl, our mad scientist."

"Welcome!" Jenny walked over to the entryway and gave both a quick hug. She gave Tim a quick glance, subtlety rising her eyebrows. "I hope you had a safe journey."

"We're so happy to be here," Kristen said. "Thank you for taking us in."

"I'm just happy to be on terra firma!" Karl added. He looked around the great room with its massive fireplace, log pole rafters, and windows with peek-a-boo views of Lake Superior. "This is even neater than Tim and Jack told us. Did your family build this?"

"Yes, my dad designed and built it with the help of local friends. By the way, where is Jack? He came with you, right?"

"He went out for a walk," Tim replied. "He said he needed some fresh air, which is odd since we just had a five-hour boat ride."

"Well, I'll just have to find him," Jenny said. "You guys make yourselves at home, *mi casa es su casa!* Plan on dinner here tonight. I won't be long." Jenny slipped on a down vest and headed toward the door giving Kristen a light touch on the arm as she passed.

Jenny followed the main path to the ridge rising above the shoreline. The warm sun glinted on Lake Superior which was calm today. On a hunch, she headed left down the path on the ridge line toward her secret cove. Jenny stopped at a clearing above the cove. She was right, Jack was below. Did he remember? Our beach fire so long ago? Jenny warmed at the memory. She fought off an urge to call out to him. Instead, she just stood still, hands in her vest, watching his body move as he skipped stones across the glassy water. Graceful, balanced, instinctive—it that what attracted me? Or was it just a college crush? Even though he had broken her heart, something still stirred inside her. Jenny carefully descended the bank and approached her ex-lover.

Jack was bending down to pick up another stone when he noticed her. He dropped the stone and smiled. "Hi" he said as he walked toward her. She hasn't changed.

"Hey."

Jack looked into her familiar eyes as he approached—soft, warm, open. His pulse quickened. Take it easy, he told himself, it's just Jenny. Even so, his hug seemed awkward till the scent of her hair brought back powerful memories. Jack held her closer, and still closer until she melted into his clutch. Jenny seemed to be swaying with him, each breath drawing her nearer in a slow dance. He had forgotten what a perfect fit she was...

Time seem suspended until Jenny released the hug. She held Jack's arms at a distance. Her gaze had become guarded. "We've got a lot of catching up to do."

THIRTY-NINE

Aux Baie, MI – April 20
Jenny's Cabin

That evening, they all sat around the long, rustic log table enjoying a dinner of venison, fish, potatoes, and some of Jenny's choice vegetables. The large fireplace was roaring, and Toby lay splay-legged on the wood floor enjoying the heat. Jack watched Jenny from across the table, trying to make sense of their reunion on the beach. *She seemed happy to see me, and the hug was real. So, what happened?* Jack tried to retrace events in his mind. *Did I say or do something wrong?*

"So, how do you buy or pay for anything if you're off grid?" Karl asked. "We destroyed our PIVs yesterday."

"It's a mixed bag," Jenny said. "Some of us were already self-sufficient, but now we pool our resources to help others get by. The church is the focal point for our co-op..."

Jack was still lost in his thoughts when he heard his name mentioned. "Jack, do you want some wine?" Jenny asked, holding up a half gallon of cheap white wine.

He waved his hand across his glass. "No thanks, I'll pass." Jenny raised her eyebrow. *She doesn't know I've stopped drinking,* Jack thought.

"Don't you have to get some store-bought stuff too?" Karl asked between bites.

"On occasion," Jenny replied. "Thankfully, we have friends who stayed on grid that share essential items with us. We also do a lot of bartering. Our biggest challenge is church finances since they prohibited gifting e-dollars. But we get by. If I need gas, someone will fill up legally and then we'll siphon. If we need medicines, someone will head over to Houghton to buy and then donate to the church."

"Can you drive without a PIV?" Tim asked.

"Well, you're not supposed to, but our local sheriff is turning a blind eye as long as you have a driver's license. I guess they're going to start issuing new IDs for us so-called undocumented citizens," Jenny pursed her lips.

"This venison is great," Tim said. "What else does the church provide?"

"Well, all the services a community might need: child care, schooling, a community meal and food pantry. Regretfully, we were just audited by the state and they claim we're not licensed to provide any of these services..."

"That's bullshit." Jack interrupted. Dang, not what I wanted to say!

Jenny gave Jack a sideways glance. "It is, but it's the new reality. They've given us 30 days to remedy, which is impossible."

"What are you going to do?" Kristen asked.

"We've started the license applications and hope they don't bust us. Right now, under Pastor DeVries' directions, we're continuing our mission."

"How can we help?" Kristen asked.

"That's kind of you," Jenny said. "I'm afraid you'll be helping more than you think. We practice a bit of tough love here. We expect everyone to work. Our community needs the labor, and it helps teens stay busy and out of trouble. Kind of common sense."

"Has Tim told you I'm a registered nurse?" Kristen asked. "How are people getting medical care up here?"

"You're a nurse! Thank God, you're an answer to prayer." Jenny was ecstatic. "We could set up a room at the church and maybe even have designated days or hours when you're available."

"Sign me up." Kristen smiled.

Jenny turned to Jack who was staring down at his plate. "Are you still in construction?"

"Yep." He looked up with a half-smile.

"We need you," Jenny leaned forward on her seat, eyes fixed on Jack. "The church is in disrepair and we're trying retrofit some houses for off grid operation. The craftsmen in town are great, but they lack leadership. We also need hunters for deer and community defense."

"I might be able to help," Jack said, perking up. "But it's off-season for hunting. Maybe small game, but deer season is over, and it might never come back."

"The Sheriff doesn't care; he calls it subsistence hunting. And the DNR hasn't been an issue, at least not yet. I think they're afraid to come out here in the sticks," Jenny said.

"What's everybody doing for power?" Karl asked.

"Now that's become a problem," Jenny replied. "My camp and greenhouses are designed to be off grid. I've got solar and wind power to feed a battery array. But even with all that, I can barely keep the greenhouses warm in the winter. The problem is even worse for the off-gridders in the community. Many have to burn wood for heat. Now we have a smog issue, but what else can they do? Actually, that might attract the DNR faster than the poaching."

"Well, maybe Karl and I can help there," Tim said. "That invention I mentioned, it's designed to provide local, decentralized power."

"Is it clean?"

"We think so. We've only tested a prototype, and that exploded...."

"Oh great," Jenny interrupted. "Is it legal?"

"Well, that's a good question," Tim said. "The reason we're up here is because we think the Feds might see our invention as a threat."

"To what?" Jenny asked

"I don't know," Tim said. "Maybe to the fossil fuel industry or maybe they just don't want communities to be self-sufficient."

"If it can help this community, then I'm all for it," Jenny said. "Particularly if we can reduce wood burning. I still have some conservation friends who would be fascinated by a clean energy alternative. Perhaps they could offer you support."

"It's best to keep this under wraps," Tim replied. "We want to stay off the Feds radar screen."

"Okay then, what do you need from me?"

Karl jumped in. "We need access to your battery array and maybe a small building to set up our lab gear. Preferably heated," he added with a smile.

"I see," Jenny replied. "You need to meet with my maintenance guy, Johnny-B. He knows all the ins and outs of my camp."

"Since Karl is doing the heavy lifting with the invention, I might have some spare time," Tim said. "I could help out with teaching. Of course, I got fired from my last job."

"You got fired?" Jenny's eyes widened.

"Yes, I guess I wasn't progressive enough for them—isn't that a hoot?" Tim rolled his eyes.

"You've got to be kidding me. You're Mr. Liberal!"

"Yeah, but I'm a classic liberal which, I'm afraid, is now on the wrong side of history."

Jack saw an opening back into the conversation. "Okay, what's a classic liberal?"

"Well, I guess most people would define a modern liberal as one who is open to new ideas, willing to discard traditional values, and use government to affect social and political change. On the surface, sounds pretty reasonable." Tim adjusted his glasses before continuing. "However, if you look at the etymology, liberal has the same Latin root as liberty, which is *liber*, meaning free." Tim explained. "The classic liberal sought freedom from one's hedonist desires, material wants, and religious authoritarianism. But this freedom wasn't the end game. Rather, it allowed citizens to pursue loftier virtues, to be good and righteous in the eyes of the community. Virtues of wisdom, self-control, charity, courage, and justice to name a few. These are traditional values not to be willfully discarded!"

Kristen interrupted. "I think you forgot a couple of Christian virtues, including faith and hope."

"I stand corrected," Tim said. "Anyway, progressive activists have warped liberalism into an odd mix of self-actualization and identity politics; the individual is free to pursue one's selfish bliss, but they look to big government to mete out welfare and social justice to the community. Perhaps well-intended, but where is the cohesive, social norm? Where is the buy-in from individual citizens versus 'let the government do it'? Also, the risk is real of simply replacing religious dogma with progressive dogma—a tautological narrative that allows no challenge. If you dare to differ, you're castigated as a *deplorable*." Tim looked at his audience. "I'm sorry, I get carried away."

"Really?" Jenny ribbed. "Anyway, being let go is no fun. And, yes, we would love to have you help us at the school."

With a break in the conversation, Jenny got up to clear dishes. Kristen took the cue and joined the effort, almost tripping over Toby who was at their feet waiting for any floor-kill. Karl and Tim discussed the challenges of operating a laboratory in the wilds. Jack tended to the fire, poking the embers as he brooded over Jenny. She was cordial, but something had changed. *I guess neither of us are college kids anymore...*

Jack's deliberations were broken as Kristen and Jenny brought hot tea and a surprise dessert to the table; strawberry preserves served with light goat's cream. Sitting around the rustic table, they all raved about how delicious the concoction was. After dessert, Jack turned to Jenny. "Do you still know how to play Euchre?"

"I might be a bit rusty, but yea, I think I could," she smiled. "Let's see, there's a Big Bower and a Little Bower, or something like that." She giggled.

"How about the rest of you guys?" Jack prodded.

"Not me," Kristen replied, "games make me nervous."

"I'm in," said Tim. "Karl, how about you?"

"Never played."

"You've played trump games before, haven't you?"

"Sure, Bridge, Oh Heck..."

"You'll be fine," Tim smirked at his brilliant associate. "Let's do a trial hand for Karl's sake. Who wants to be partners?"

"How about Jenny and me against you and Karl?" Jack said.

Tim agreed. "Sounds good, where're the cards?"

They played late into the night, enjoying the crackling fire and chortling over humorous accusations of table talk. Every now and then, Jack would steal a glance at Jenny—smiling and laughing, she was as beautiful as ever.

For a moment, life had returned to normal.

FORTY

Steve Bennett entered the DHS Domestic Terrorism Mapping Center, informally referred to as the War Room. John Bowden, his friend and escort, closed the door behind them. As ranking member of the House Committee on Homeland Security, Bennett had top-secret clearance and unfettered access to the DHS. But this large amphitheater was new to him. It reminded him of Mission Control at NASA with banks of monitors, including a big screen positioned front and center on the back wall.

"Impressive," Bennett said.

"Yes," Bowden said, "and this is just the tip of the iceberg. Most of the data is coming out of Salt Lake. We need some Congressional oversight on this, the pendulum on domestic surveillance has swung too far. I can't show you our Predictive Policing analytics, but I can show you our nationwide metrics and mapping. You should be able connect the dots from there."

"No problem," Bennett replied. "I understand your situation. Just show me what you can."

"Okay." Bowden walked over to one of the analysts sitting behind rows of monitors and asked him to bring up the summary report for pacification.

"Yes sir." After a few keystrokes, the analyst pulled up a map of the United States shaded with blues and reds, with most of the country looking pink.

"My God, John, that looks just like the electoral map from

206

the last election!"

"I thought you would see the resemblance." Bowden chuckled.

"So, let me guess. The dark blue metro areas are pacified, the dark red splotches are active resistance, and the large swaths of pink are passive or mixed resistance?"

"Excellent summary, Steve. We have an aggregate 85% adoption rate of PIV or PIV-compliant platforms. But it's lopsided; the metro areas have a 95% adoption rate but only represent 15% of our counties. The remaining 85% of our country is pink or red with adoption rates of 50% or less. That's where we see the Resistance hanging on. Ironically, that's not where the violence is. Looting and rioting remain metro issues, the so-called passive areas."

Bowden asked the analyst to overlay the National Guard deployments. A few more keystrokes and military icons appeared over the major metro areas.

"So, Texas is as bad as I've heard," Bennett said. Military icons spread all over the state.

"Probably worse than you've heard. Obviously, we are keeping the situation under wraps, but it's almost a full-blown civil war down there. We even have some split loyalties in the National Guard. The President is considering regular military, but that would be another constitutional crisis to deal with. Besides, I'm not sure SCOTUS would allow it. Hell, they had a tough enough time with the PIV Act!"

"John, I know this is stating the obvious, but we have become a bifurcated nation. The only common element is fear. We have half the country afraid that big government won't do enough to protect them, while the other half is afraid of big government itself. I don't see a happy ending here."

Bowden nodded in agreement but remained silent.

"Could you zoom in on Michigan?" Bennett asked.

The analyst moved the cursor over Michigan and double-clicked. The state now covered the entire big screen with individual counties highlighted in color. As expected, Detroit,

Lansing, Ann Arbor, and Grand Rapids were dark or light blue, but the rest of the state was pink and red. Except for Marquette County, the entire Upper Peninsula was red, including Aux Baie.

"Hmm," Bennett murmured.

"Looks like you have trouble brewing up north," Bowden said. "Listen, why don't we take a stroll, we can talk more freely."

"Sounds good to me, my calendar is open for the rest of the day."

It was unusually hot for mid-May so both Bennett and Bowden draped their suitcoats across their shoulders as they walked down the bustling sidewalk. As they approached the Washington Monument, Bennett marveled at the paradoxes of DC. Despite the collapsing economy, the streets were abuzz with activity and commerce. No depression here, he thought. In fact, employment was up in the Beltway as the government pivoted toward a command economy and welfare state. In contrast, just blocks away were some of the most dangerous and drug infested neighborhoods in the nation. When added to the graft and corruption of DC, it left Bennett with the feeling that the country was rotting from the center out.

"How's the crime rate in DC after the Fair Deal and the new cryptocurrency?" Bennett asked.

"Not what we expected," Bowden replied. "With cash off the table, we thought the gangs would lose their lifeblood. But they just changed currencies to hard assets; guns, drugs, gold, and black market vices like liquor and tobacco."

"I thought we let Bronze citizens buy liquor and tobacco with their allowance."

"We do, but it comes with such a heavy tax and health plan penalty, we've created a new black market." Bowden explained. "The good news is that we've completed and linked our Predictive Policing program in the major metros so we've got the gangs in our sights. The bad news is these guys aren't dumb. They've abandoned their PIVs and rely on face-to-face communications. We've made tampering with a PIV a crime, but it kind of defeats the purpose if they just ditch them and forfeit their benefits."

"Another unintended consequence," Bennett said. It didn't surprise him. He never thought gangs were about wealth anyway. Gangs provided a sense of belonging, albeit a poor substitute for an intact family. And, with black males being incarcerated at alarming rates, it was a vicious cycle with few, if any, exits.

They turned a corner and the monument grounds opened before them. Bowden did a quick glance around to make sure they were alone. "Listen Steve, I wanted to give you a heads-up on what I see as a disturbing development. With the urban areas pacified, they are extending the Predictive Policing programs to combat rural resistance."

"Oh great," Bennett said. "What criteria are they using?"

"Well, it mirrors the metro program: biometrics, contact mapping, crime history, aliases, phone records, social media posts, location mapping, etcetera. But here's the thing, for Operation Heartland…"

"There's actually a named program?" Bennett interrupted.

"I'm afraid so. Anyway, they're also tracking gun ownership, church membership, homeschooling, military background, political affiliation—such as Tea Party or Libertarian —as predictors of the Resistance. If it follows the metro program, it could eventually lead to preemptive intervention."

"You mean detention and re-education," Bennett said. "And now they're targeting rural churches?" *My God, where is our country headed? Bennett brooded. How will I explain this to Scott or Marge?*

"They're monitoring anything that could provide a focus for the Resistance. I guess that includes churches," Bowden said as he looked up at the Washington Monument. "Our Founding Fathers must be rolling in their graves."

"What ever happened to 'if you haven't done anything

wrong, you have nothing to fear'?" Bennett dinged his friend for his comments in the President's Cabinet Room so long ago. "You know, rural folk might be clinging to their guns and religion, and I don't blame them. They're not bitter, they're fearful. Fearful that our government—originally founded on Judeo-Christian ethics and a standing militia to oppose tyranny—could become the tyrant itself."

Bowden furrowed his brows. "Five months ago, I would have laughed at that. I'm not laughing anymore. That's why I'm talking to you. This has gone too far; we need to scale it back. Can't you rally your allies in Congress to fight this?"

"I don't know," Bowden replied. "Since The Crash, even staunch conservatives have bought into big government intervention. It's the same thing we saw with COVID-19; the response was well-intended, but we never reeled the government's tentacles back in after the threat had passed."

"Well, I'm just telling you that I, and a lot of other guys at DHS, are appalled at where this is heading. Let me know if we can help in anyway."

"Thanks John. I'll do my best."

"Oh, one last thing. Your son shut down his business, right?"

"Yes, Scott is working for me at my Grand Rapids office."

"That's what I thought, and it confirms what I've seen in the database. Thing is, Scott's associates went off grid last month."

"Really?" Bennett raised his eyebrows. "That committee you were kicked off of, is it still operational?"

"Yes, which means the case is still open," Bowden said.

"Thank God Scott's not involved."

FORTY-ONE

It was hot and humid. The midday sun beat down on the greenhouse turning it into a steam room. Jenny felt sweat slipping off her nose and saw the drop land in the soil she was weeding. She straightened her back to relieve the ache and then used her arm to push herself up and off the foot stool. She grabbed the stool and moved it a few feet down the aisle to work on the next section. This is stupid, she thought. Should have done this in the cool of the morning instead of working the fields. But the 4H kids had needed supervision and, besides, I'll be done soon.

A bark from Toby broke her thoughts. She looked down the aisle and past the door. "Oh damn," she said in resignation. Toby had left the shade of the picnic table to greet Jack who was heading her way. Jenny quickly appraised herself; damp marks under her breasts and armpits, hair a mess, and she was sure there was dirt smudged all over her face. So what, she thought. He's seen me worse. Heck, he's seen all of me! She remained seated and used her free hand to clear strands of hair and moisture off her brow.

"Hi Jack. What's going on?"

"Just taking a lunch break. We're putting in a stove at Smith's, although I'm not sure they need the heat right now!"

He walked right up to Jenny, standing over her. She could detect a slight sweaty smell, or was that herself? "Yes, finally got some summer, but I'm not complaining." Jenny caught Jack eyeing her partially unbuttoned shirt, which had folded open, exposing her breast. She blushed, and stood up to face him, a bit too quickly.

"Whoa!" Jack quickly gripped her shoulders. "Are you okay?"

Feeling safe in his grasp, Jenny let Jack slowly sit her down again on the foot stool.

"Put your head down between your knees," Jack said. He ran over to get her water bottle and returned. "Here's some water."

"I'm sorry…"

"Nothing to be sorry about, it's like an oven in here." Jack grabbed a handkerchief out of his back pocket, wetted it from Jenny's bottle, and gently wiped her face.

"Thanks, I don't know what happened."

"Let's get you outside," Jack said. He offered his hands and pulled Jenny to her feet, put his arm around her waist, and let her lean into him as they exited the greenhouse. He helped her to sit down at the picnic table by the entrance.

The fresh air helped immensely, and soon Jenny was sitting up straight and alert. "Well, now I've left a mess," she pointed to the weeds and clippings littering the aisle of the greenhouse.

"Let me get those," Jack said. "Is there a rake around here?"

"Just inside the door on your right, trash can too."

Jack retrieved the implements and got to work, every now and then looking up to check on her. Jenny took the opportunity to button her shirt and tidy herself. She drank deeply from her water bottle. Soon, Jack came out of the greenhouse rolling the partially filled trash can.

"There's a compost pile around back." Why is he here? Jenny pondered.

After dumping the debris, Jack returned to face Jenny, putting a foot on the table bench to prop himself. "You know, we've got several newcomers looking for housing, so there are two crews working on refurbs now."

"Isn't that great? Nice to see people making Aux Baie their

home again. You still installing wood burning stoves?"

"Yep. That's the only choice right now for off-gridders," Jack replied. "The grace period for utilities ended May 1. Tim is helping me design a do-it-yourself catalytic converter for the older stoves. That would really cut the air pollution."

"That'd be great. I just wish we had an alternative to burning wood. How's Karl coming along with the prototype?"

"Hard to tell. Karl is optimistic, but he's always optimistic. I think he's working on the air intake of the compression chamber. To be honest, it's beyond me." Jack pulled out the hanky he had used on Jenny and wiped his own brow.

"What else have you been up to?" Jenny asked, sticking to small talk.

"Well, I'm doing some hunting with Johnny-B and the Tribe in the mornings. You know, I'm a good shot, but these guys are natural hunters. They know how to track and read the terrain, and they honor the game they kill. Certainly makes the whole experience more intimate."

Jenny approved. "My dad used to tell me we should never take an animal's life except for food and nourishment, what the community needs."

"Anyway, after hunting, there's always a project going on somewhere. Then, I'm chairing the evening AA meetings. By the time I get home, I'm dead!"

"Your AA meetings have been such a blessing." Jenny fixed her eyes on Jack. "The Crash has led to so much addiction, the whole community is indebted to you."

Jack remained silent, acknowledging the praise with a forced smile. Finally, he averted his eyes, pushed away from the table, and took the trash can back inside the greenhouse. When he returned, he took a seat directly across from Jenny.

Okay, let's see what he really wants...

"With it warming up, I thought we might have a beach fire, just like old times." Jack smiled.

Jenny's mind exploded in a tangle of memories and emotions. Is he hitting on me? After all these years? She fought to keep the intimate memories of their last beach fire at bay. Her silence was becoming uncomfortable. She looked at his expectant eyes. "You know, I think it's still a bit early in the season for that. Maybe when things get warmer, we can get a group together."

"Sure Jen, that makes sense. Can I walk you back to the cabin?"

"I want to finish up here before lunch. You go ahead without me."

"You sure you'll be okay?" Jack held her gaze.

"Yes, I'm feeling much better now. But thanks for the help!"

"No problem." Jack reached down to give Toby a pat. "I guess I'll see you later." He turned and walked down the path toward the guest house.

Jenny watched him retreat into the distance, head down and shoulders slumped. That's how I felt after you graduated and dumped me, she scolded him. And you didn't even know I was pregnant, she groaned.

With your baby, Jack.

FORTY-TWO

Aux Baie, MI – June 5
Community Church

"I don't understand this making amends stuff." The newcomer had cornered Jack outside the church after the AA meeting. "I've already told my wife I'm sorry. What more can I do?"

Jack took a step aside to escape the cigarette smoke that was floating his way. "Well, that's a good start," Jack said. "And just staying sober is a huge amend for your wife and family."

The newcomer took a deep drag from his cigarette and continued. "That's the problem. I made a total ass of myself last Christmas with her family. I don't remember much, but my wife said it was awful. It's really been bugging me. Every time I see them, I'm embarrassed."

"If it's bugging you that much, you've got to get it off your chest. Have you told your sponsor?" Jack asked.

"Yeah, he said to apologize to them. But they might just spit in my face!"

"That's always a risk. But, in my experience, most people are forgiving. Particularly if you're staying sober. You can't control how they will react, but you can keep your side of the street clean. Know what I mean?"

"I guess," the newcomer replied. "To be honest, I'm scared." The newcomer smashed his cigarette butt into the urn outside the church.

"You know, we weren't scared when we staggered in and out of bars," Jack said. "You can do this, it's the next right thing to do. And, remember, making an amend is as much for you as for the person you offended. I know that sounds selfish, but you can't carry around this shame and stay sober."

The newcomer frowned, took out another cigarette, and lit it. "Thanks, Jack." He walked away to talk with some of his buds. Jack gave him a 50/50 chance of staying sober.

On his way back to the guest house, Jack started thinking about Jenny again, as he had every day since he'd arrived. Even more so now after she had rejected his overture. Were they done? Should I seek out other women? No—I want Jenny, but what can I do? And then the light bulb came on. "Of course, you stupid idiot." The simple realization brought immediate relief, and then fear.

***

Jack didn't waste time. The next day, after dinner, he walked over to Jenny's cabin and knocked on the screen door. "Hey Jen, you around?" His heart started to race.

"Just a second," Jack heard from inside the cabin. Toby came running up to the door to greet his new friend, tail wagging. Jenny soon followed. "Hey Jack, what's up?"

"Do you have a minute to talk?"

Jenny searched Jack's eyes before answering. "Sure, let's get some fresh air. How about a hike to the cliffs?"

"Sounds good to me."

Jenny grabbed her hoodie and slipped it on. "You stay here," she told Toby and slid out the door to join Jack.

Soon, they were winding their way down the path toward the shore. With the sun still far up in the sky, it remained warm and the soft breeze carried the scent of pine needles. The sound of an earnest woodpecker could be heard in the distance. Jenny took an unfamiliar route, scrambling up what looked to be no more than a deer track. "You know, my dad and I used to visit this overlook all the time," she said.

"I wish I had gotten to know him better." Jack winced at his own comment. Not only was it a cliché, it was a lie. Jack could only imagine the impression he had left on Jenny's dad—a young drunk dating his daughter. An only daughter, just like Meg. With no chance to make amends to Mr. Hernandez, the least he could do was treat his daughter right. Here and now.

Jenny remained silent as they approached the perch over-looking Lake Superior and sat down. Mustering his courage, Jack sat close, feeling her long hair tickle his face as it blew in the breeze.

"So, what's on your mind?" Jenny kept her eyes focused out over the water.

Despite rehearsing his speech many times, Jack's mind went blank. He spoke from the heart. "Jenny, I um…I just want to apologize to you for any harm I may have caused in the past. To be honest, I can't remember how or why we split-up. I was drinking way too much back then. I'm an alcoholic. Still, no excuse for whatever I did. You've always held a special place in my heart. I hope and pray you can forgive me?" Jenny had turned to listen, but now turned away, looking back out over the water, slowly shaking her head. Oh no, was this a mistake? What is she thinking?

Jenny contemplated opening up about the pregnancy, the abortion—her infertility. But, while it might assuage her regrets, it would only hurt Jack. "You know, we both made so many mistakes back then. We were so young." Jenny stared at the water glistening in the distance, trying to remember their romance. "I'm not sure what we were thinking, maybe we weren't thinking at all." After a period of silence, she turned back to face Jack. "For a long time I was adrift. I didn't know God's plans for me. But I've been blessed in more ways than I ever expected. So, it's okay." Jenny used a finger to dab a tear in her eye.

Before Jack could think of a reply, Jenny began to rise signaling the conversation was over. As Jack jumped up to join her, he noticed a large nest wedged in an old cedar tree clinging to the cliff. "Is that an eagle's nest?"

Jenny turned to look. "No, that's an old osprey's nest…" Jenny stopped, fascinated by the sight of new branches and twigs that had been added to the aging nest.

FORTY-THREE

Washington DC – June 8
Department of Justice

Assistant AG Max Hunter turned up the volume on his computer so he could hear better. Congressman Steve Bennett's impromptu press briefing was being carried live from the steps of the Capitol Dome.

"...I am 100% behind the lawsuit filed by the state attorney generals. The Fair Deal is an insult to our constitutional rights..."

"Crap!" Hunter fumed. What sites and networks are carrying this? They will pay a price! Not that it matters, the lawsuit by the 24 state AGs wasn't going anywhere. He continued to watch Bennett on his monitor.

"...the first 9/11 attacks resulted in the Patriot Act. It certainly seemed reasonable at the time. But look at the resulting surveillance abuses—government spying on its own citizens. And then we got hit by COVID-19. It demanded bold action. But, once again, look at the unintended consequences: crushing national debt, abuses to our freedom of assembly, and the start of a national health registry..."

"Shit!" Hunter went to split screen and started typing in orders to his underlings. First on his list, demand that all social media, search engines, and web browsers delete the video. There might be some residual bootleg copies, but they would eventually censor those too. It sounded like Bennett was wrapping up.

"...and now the Fair Deal. Our government has become Big Brother, using PIV to track us 24/7. And, if anybody complains—civil libertarians, conservatives, the religious—they're branded as intolerant and then censored. In fact, I implore you, make copies of my statements before they are erased from the Internet."

"Dammit!" Hunter screamed out loud. He went to his encrypted email account and sent a two-word message to Reggie Woods at The Bureau: *Release it.*

Grand Rapids, MI
Congressman Steve Bennett's District Home Office

When the live stream ended, Scott turned off the app on his computer. He now had a nice backup file of his dad's news conference in case they censored it. The small District Office staff were waiting for the blowback. There would be calls from ardent supporters as well as vitriol from partisan foes. Scott himself felt split; he was proud of his dad for standing up for his principles, but what was the point? The tide had already turned; time to go with the flow.

Scott used his mouse to cruise various social media sites and political blogs. Only a few were carrying the video. Comments on his dad ranged from "true patriot" to "fascist pig". Then, before his eyes, the video started to disappear from the few sites that carried it, replaced with the ubiquitous statement *This Video is No Longer Available*. Scott frowned. The censorship was quicker than he expected. And soon, they would block the keywords to search for his dad's speech. It would disappear as if it had never happened—just like the plasma drive.

It had been more than eight months since his last meeting with Tim, Karl, and Jack. He had heard through a friend of a friend that his team had made it up to the U.P., but they might as well be on the Moon. Neither could risk communicating with each other. And, even if they did succeed with the plasma drive, there was no avenue to promote or commercialize it. The Feds would simply stomp on it, and his team, and his father. If any word got out, it would be trivialized—relegated to the tabloids along with space aliens, divining rods, and the

Loch Ness Monster. So, what's to gain? Why risk their privileges, their Gold status, on a pipe dream?

Scott's musings were abruptly halted as the news banner on his computer changed: *Breaking News – Congressman Steve Bennett (R-MI) Under Investigation.*

Washington DC
Rayburn House Office Building
Steve Bennett tried to maintain his equanimity. He knew this was coming. Still, to see it in print on the Internet was disquieting: *According to DOJ officials who spoke on condition of anonymity, Bennett is under investigation for his actions on the day of the attacks. Areas of concern include disclosure of top-secret information, Abuse of Power, and violation of the Logan Act. Representative Bennett (R-MI) is the ranking member of the House Committee on Homeland Security. He has been a vocal critic of the Fair Deal. Most experts agree that the Fair Deal saved the country from complete collapse during The Crash. Recent polls show that Americans overwhelming support the Fair Deal. In a related story, the House of Representatives has opened an ethics inquiry into Representative Bennett. Sources close to the inquiry deny that Bennett is under scrutiny for nepotism and sexual harassment. Bennett's son, Scott, works out of his District Office in Grand Rapids, Michigan. Bennett's Administrative Assistant, Marjorie Stevenson, has been a constant companion of the Representative since his election in 2012. Bennett's wife, Lisa Jones Bennett, succumbed to ovarian cancer in 2020.*

Bennett turned off his computer, stood up, crossed his arms, and started to pace back and forth. Was it worth it? The report had one thing right; Americans, at least those in the cities, seemed to be in love with the Fair Deal. Was he on a suicide mission? He didn't care about himself—but his family and loved ones? This B.S. will be posted all over the Internet within hours, maybe minutes. Bennett stood in front of the window that framed the Capitol Dome where he had just spoken. He propped his arms on his hips, stood up tall and slowly twisted his head, listening to the crackles in his neck. He was not going down without a fight! Bennett turned at the sound of his office door opening.

The look on Marge's face, with tears running down her cheeks, was crushing.

FORTY-FOUR

Aux Baie – June 10
Community Church

Crumbs littered his To-Do list. Tim took his last bite of the homemade muffin and washed it down with a swig of coffee. It was delicious! He folded the single sheet to corral the crumbs and dumped them into his waste basket. He put the list back on his desk and considered this day's attack plan: 1.) Jenny gift, 2.) Jack specs, 3.) Kristen database, 4.) Karl prototype, 5.) Lesson Plan.

Tim considered Jenny and smiled. Who would have thought? His old college friend, the quiet naturalist who liked to party, had blossomed into a leader. There was no other word for it. Tim wanted to show his appreciation for the food and shelter she had so freely given. But it was more than that, Jenny had provided them a community. And for Tim, a chance to be useful again. How funny was that? The brilliant agnostic was now the Headmaster of a church school! Tim looked around his makeshift office and chuckled. His lesson plan, The Seven Dialectics, was outlined on a flipchart next to a shelf of hymnals. And on the wall was Jesus himself looking down on him. Tim connected the odd dots of his own mind and laughed out loud. He was climbing Maslow's Hierarchy of Needs!

Jenny's food and shelter met his *physical needs*. The community supplied at least a modicum of *safety*. Kristen brought him *love and belonging*. His new job offered a chance to reclaim *self-esteem*. Finally, his Seven Dialectics promised the *self-actualization*, or arrogance, of answering life's mysteries. What does that leave? He looked back up at Jesus. Oh yes, *transcend-*

ence. Kristen would approve of that one!

It all took him back to his class at Traverse University and the nature of political ecosystems. Aux Baie was a study in contrasts, half commune, half Wild West capitalism. Order without the coercive state. Once again, he had to tip his hat to Jenny. Without her co-op roots, the community would have died some time ago. And it was a hard-fought battle for Jenny; convincing producers to not only barter and trade with each other, but also apportion a share for non-producers like himself, Karl, Kristen, and others. Of course, that was not entirely fair. Kristen was providing healthcare, Karl promised to provide energy. And he, well, he was tasked with teaching the community's youth. I wonder what Marx would have thought —*from each according to his ability, to each according to his needs?*

But this was not a Marxist nirvana, far from it. People owned private property and their tools of production. The hunters owned their guns. The Tribe had its fishing boats. Jenny managed her greenhouses. Even he and Karl possessed an idea, an invention, that might change everyone's lives. The glue was a universal expectation that everybody worked, and everybody shared, so that the base of Maslow's pyramid of needs was met—food, shelter, and safety. Anything beyond that was gravy. Tim didn't know whether to laugh or cry at the irony. Aux Baie was meeting the needs of the community, the original charter of organized government. But it was organized government that they now feared. Would the state shut down their food services? Close the school? Bust Plasma Drive Technologies? Would it shutter the church itself? Since the HHS inspection, these were constant, if unspoken, threats hanging over the community.

Tim's thoughts were broken as Kristen walked in, carrying her own cup of coffee. "You look lost in thought," she said.

"Yes, off on tangents again. I can help you with the database after lunch."

"No hurry. I've got my hands full storing some PPE, that's Personal Protective Equipment, we got from our underground friends in Marquette. Sounds like they have a glut of PPE and ventilators now that COVID has subsided. Ironically, they can't afford to maintain the ventilators. They'll be worthless in a year or two."

"Maybe someday we can repay them," Tim said.

"I'm sure they'd love a plasma drive. How's Karl coming along?"

"Better than expected. Johnny-B has been an incredible resource! He's got Karl all setup in Jenny's garage, including a conduit to the battery array. Somehow, he got his hands on a step-up transformer so we can power up the prototype. Also, Johnny introduced Karl to an old tool & die guy who closed shop when the iron industry collapsed. Anyway, he's helping Karl configure a concave input port for the compression chamber. Even better, this guy's nephew has a job over at Michigan Tech and he has access to industrial lasers! So, we can ablate micropores in the input port." Tim stopped, seeing Kristen's eyes glaze over. "Sorry, it's just so exciting."

"That's okay." Kristen chuckled. "Do you have a target date for completion?"

"Still probably a couple months away. I'm working on designing an exhaust chamber to withstand the heat from the plasma discharge. Later today, Karl and I are going to review his quantum equations. He's way beyond me on this one. All I can do is check his logic and math."

Their conversation was interrupted by a loud hammering noise. "What's that?" Kristen asked.

"Jack's working on some church repairs," Tim replied. "He and I are planning on meeting later today. We're trying to design a catalytic converter to retrofit existing wood burning stoves to make them more efficient and cleaner." Maybe that's the gift I can give Jenny, Tim reflected. She's always complaining about the wood smoke.

"You mean like a car?" Kristen asked.

"Very similar, except you are burning the residual smoke of the fire. You funnel the smoke through a ceramic honeycomb coated with platinum or palladium. The coating drops the ignition point of the smoke from over 1,000 degrees to about 500 degrees. Our challenge is to come up with a one-size-fits-all solution so we can apply it to different stove types."

"How are you buying those without a PIV?"

"Johnny-B and his black market. I think Jack's financing the purchases with gold, the same gold he used to buy the boat to get us up here. Anyway, it keeps us off the grid in case the authorities start to crack down on wood burning stoves."

"Maybe we can use Jack's gold to payoff Health and Human Services?" Kristen asked with a rueful smile.

"Yeah, how's that going? Any progress with the applications?"

"It's like going through a maze. I have my nursing certification for Michigan, but the church is not a qualified educational organization. So, before I can legally practice medicine, we need to apply to the state Board of Education to qualify as a school. That has its own set of regulations and licensing, even if you are a private or charter school. Cindy is at wits' end about the whole application process. Besides, the people she has talked to are not exactly fans of private schools. She's getting no help."

"That's convenient," Tim said. "I understand the need for licensing and best practices, but it sounds like the state has a monopoly on education and healthcare."

"What about your classes?" Kristen asked. "I thought you were concentrating on the basics: math, science, civics." She pointed to the flipchart. "That doesn't look basic to me."

"I've got a couple hot shots that are pushing me on philosophy, so I thought I'd introduce them to the classics: Aristotle, Plato, Descartes, Kant and, of course, Kelly!" He snickered. "Back in college, I tried to distill all philosophical debate down to seven dialectics. Behold, my creation!" He waved his hand at the flipchart: 1). Creation vs. Evolution, 2). Nature vs. Nurture, 3). Determinism vs. Free Will, 4). Subjective Relativism vs. Objective Truth, 5). Individualism vs. Collectivism, 6).

Quantum Uncertainty vs. Persistent Reality, 7). Mind vs. Body Enigma.

Kristen considered the bullet points. "Okay. I get the first three. They all have a streak of religion in them. And I presume number four means my truth might be different than someone else's truth?

"Close enough," Tim said. "Are truth and morality relative to time and culture, or are there absolutes?"

"Number five looks like it pits democracy against socialism," Kristen said.

"Have you been reading my notes? Very topical as we slip toward socialism. Is the power of society limited by unalienable individual rights, or are individual rights constrained by what is best for the collective group?"

"Okay, I can buy that. But you've got me totally lost with quantum uncertainty versus persistent reality." Kristen tilted her head, furrowing her brow. "What's that?"

"How much time do you have?" Tim laughed. "Albert Einstein summed it up best with his quip, 'Reality is merely an illusion, albeit a very persistent one'. Quantum theory suggests that nothing is certain, just a probability. That the universe is indeterminate until observed. As creative observers, are we really separate from the universe? Or are we part of a self-aware and irreducible field that isn't constrained by space or time? On occasion, we catch a glimpse of the bigger reality; like intuition, or Karl's inventive trances, or being in The Zone like Jack talks about."

"Or spiritual awakenings and epiphanies?" Kristen asked.

"Yes, I think those qualify too." She is tenacious if nothing else, Tim chuckled. "Which leads us to the last dialectic, the mind/body enigma. In short, are our thoughts, even my seven dialectics, constrained by neurological processes within the material brain? Or is there a higher consciousness, a self-awareness and ability to imagine the future that transcends our bodily limits? Independent, pure, and eternal—like mathematics."

"I think you just touched upon the soul," Kristen said. "How about adding spirit to your enigma? Remember your class and The Garden? You never really explained that quadrant. But isn't that the bigger reality we seek? And haven't we caught glimpses of The Garden?"

Tim rested his chin on his hand trying to digest her multiple questions. "I'm not sure I understand. Give me some examples."

"Okay. How about the saving grace of Jesus, the abolition of slavery, or the power of prayer? Aren't those spiritual awakenings? Can you explain those away with just mind and body?"

Tim remained silent for a while, staring off into space. He thought about challenging her on Abolition, which seemed to be as much about political expediency as spirituality. But he wasn't up for arguing, not with Kristen. "Body, mind, and spirit. I guess it comes down to who's driving the bus—man or God?"

FORTY-FIVE

Aux Baie – June 19
Jenny's Camp

"Watch out!" Kristen yelled. But it was too late. Karl's perfectly roasted marshmallow was ablaze. Worse still, it drooped off his stick and plopped into the beach fire.

"My God, it's the Hindenburg!" Karl cried out. Jack and Jenny as well as Tim and Kristen broke out in laughter.

"Here, let me get you a new one," Kristen said as she reached into the bag of semi-stale marshmallows she had found in the church pantry.

As the calendar approached the summer solstice, warm weather had returned to the U.P. And, being on the far-west of the Eastern time zone, the sun stayed up forever. They didn't start the fire until after 10:30 pm and there was still a glow in the west. Jenny's secret cove was the selected site. It was a glorious evening with a cloudless sky and softly lapping waves.

Everybody studiously avoided the latest news; several churches in the U.P. had been raided for unlicensed activities and sedition. Restrictions on assembly and speech, first explored during the COVID-19 pandemic, were now migrating from urban to rural areas. They kept the conversation light, regaling each other with childhood memories and exploits. As the sky finally turned dark, Jack captivated his audience with his knowledge of the stars that his father had taught him.

"Okay, there's the Big Dipper, Ursa Major," he pointed his finger to what looked like a ladle. "And if you look at the last two stars, they point to the North Star, which is the end of the handle of the Little Dipper, Ursa Minor," he used his finger again to sketch the constellation in the sky.

"That's the Big Bear and Little Bear," Jenny said. "The bear is revered by the Chippewa; it represents courage and strength. It can also be a spirit guide in your dreams."

"Really," Jack said, recalling his Sleeping Bear Dunes dream that had haunted him for months. "And over there is Cassiopeia, or the Queen's Throne, although most people call it the 'W'. But, if you look closely, it looks like an upside-down chair. See it?"

"I think I see it!" Kristen pointed into the sky.

"Show me again," Jenny asked.

Jack took her hand and used it to point to the constellation and, in doing so, felt her close presence and familiar scent. "Right there," he said.

"Okay, I see it. It *is* upside-down. The queen will fall off her throne!" Jenny laughed.

"Now, look straight up in the sky. See those three brightest stars? That's the Navigator's Triangle; Altair, Deneb, and Vega. And that star, Deneb, is the head of the Great Northern Cross. See the cross bar, it's almost a straight line, and the bottom of the cross is right there." Once again, Jack used his pointed finger to sketch the summer constellation. "And the cross points directly in line with the Milky Way. It's so bright because we are looking at our galaxy edge on."

"You know, those stars are where we came from." Karl joined the conversation. "Or, as the song says, *we are star dust...*"

"What do you mean we are star dust?" Kristen asked.

"Karl's right," Tim said. "Everything in the universe comes from fusion reactions in stars, turning hydrogen into heavier elements. That would include carbon and carbon-based molecules, the foundation of life. So, in a real sense, we're all connected to the universe."

"Okay, where did the hydrogen come from?" Kristen challenged.

Karl turned to her. "Well, the prevailing theory is the Big Bang…"

"That's okay Karl," Kristen interrupted. "It was a rhetorical question. I just believe there was a Creator, a first cause. Something had to create the Big Bang."

As the night grew late, Karl excused himself and headed back to the cottage, leaving the couples alone on the beach. A bit later, Kristen leaned over and whispered in Tim's ear.

"You know, I think we'll call it a night too," Tim said. He stood up and grabbed Kristen's hands to help her up from their beach blanket. "I've got a date with Karl early tomorrow; we're getting close on the prototype."

"You got a flashlight?" Jenny asked.

"Yep, right here," Kristen pulled the small torch out of her pocket.

"Okay, see you guys tomorrow."

As they walked away, Kristen said "I'm so happy for those guys. They're falling in love and they share such a strong faith."

"Well, I have to admit they're a better fit than Jenny and Sean were. As far as their faith, I hope you don't hold my lack thereof against me. Hey, give me that!" Tim said as Kristen let the flashlight beam go astray of the path.

"I got it," she laughed as they hand-fought over the light. "No, I won't hold it against you, but I do have a question for you."

"What's that?" Tim asked.

"What if it's all true? What if there is a God? What if Jesus is the Son of God who died for our sins and was resurrected?"

Tim went quiet as they walked down the dark path toward their cottage. It was warm enough where the crickets were starting to chirp. Finally, Tim answered. "Well, the implications would be staggering. It would change everything. But there's no proof."

"Okay. I have a homework assignment for you. Study the

growth of the early church and report back to me," Kristen said, half-kidding. "And, for extra credit, research how many prophesies in the Old Testament were fulfilled by the coming of Christ."

"Yes, Ms. Campbell," Tim replied in a childlike voice. "Hey!" he yelled as Kristen turned off the flashlight and trotted down the path laughing.

Jack and Jenny sat next to each other at the fire, surrounded in silence except for the intermittent crackle and pop of embers. Jack broke the ice. "Tell me what happened to you Jenny. What made you come back here?"

Jenny remained silent for a moment. "I guess this is the closest thing I have to home. Things weren't working out for me downstate, with Sean and all."

"I'm really sorry about Sean."

Jenny threw a pebble at the fire. "Yeah, I really tried to make that work. Even tried to start a family—that didn't work either. I'm not so sure we were meant to be together."

"Tim said you had a job with the Conservancy. What happened there?"

"That was another mess. I went drinking one night with my girlfriends and got on the wrong side of the abortion argument." Jenny turned to face Jack. "Basically, I was shunned. I guess you can't be pro-life and liberal at the same time." She returned her gaze to the fire. "Anyway, it got ugly. I couldn't work there anymore. So, with the help of Sean's brother, Steve, I ran away to the U.P. And here I am."

"Well, you've surrounded yourself with some incredible friends."

"Yes, I've been fortunate. It was Mary DeVries who brought me back to the church. As you know, I'm a recovering Catholic." Jenny chuckled. "Talking about recovery, what happened to you?"

Jack used his hand to start digging a little hole in the sand. "Oh Jen, what a long strange trip it's been," he referenced the

Grateful Dead album. "When you knew me in college, I was pretty full of myself—but I guess you knew that. Anyway, my partying lifestyle didn't work out too well with a wife, a child, and work. I lost my way."

"Tell me about your daughter," Jenny asked.

A smile came to Jack's face. "Meg teaches downstate. It's been months since we've talked. I'm not sure it would be politically correct to have a dad who's off grid. Anyway, she's an adrenaline junkie like me, but super nice. You'd like her. Thankfully, she dodged the bullet that hit me."

"So, you just quit drinking?"

"Oh God, no," he turned to face Jenny. "I wish I had, but it took what it took. I lost my wife, I lost my job, and Meg was embarrassed by me. But, even then, I kept drinking, as much out of shame as anything."

"What changed?"

"Well, I got the shit kicked out of me, and finally asked for help. And, here's the thing; I thought by surrendering, by turning my life over to God, that I had lost my freedom and choice. But it was the exact opposite—I got my freedom back."

"I'm happy for you, that must have been painful. Did anybody help you through the process?"

"Oh yeah. I met a bunch of great guys through AA."

"I meant a woman." Jenny clarified.

"Oh. I guess I had some encounters, but nobody special—certainly not since I've been sober." Jack stared at the ebbing fire. "I've always been a one-girl type of guy."

"Look Jack," Jenny raised her hand toward the horizon. "Northern Lights!"

"Whoa! I haven't seen those in years."

They remained silent watching the ethereal waves of effervescent green pulsing in the night sky. Jack found his hand next to Jenny's. Feeling as awkward as a teenager on a first date, he grasped it. Her hand was warm and welcoming. Jenny leaned into him, nuzzling her head on his shoulder. Jack turned and kissed Jenny softly, unleashing a wave of sensual memories. She responded with earnest lips. Jack gently laid her down on the blanket and rolled on top of her. He embraced Jenny, enveloped by her warmth and life force. "You feel perfect," he whispered.

"Make love to me, Jack."

"Shouldn't we use some protect..."

"It's okay."

Joined as one, they were oblivious to a shooting star that etched a brilliant arc across the heavens.

FORTY-SIX

Aux Baie, MI – July 8

As the full warmth of July arrived, things were going well. Perhaps too well. The first signs of trouble came when two government sedans and a State Police patrol car parked in front of the church around noon. Word quickly spread through town that government officials had entered the church, without knocking.

Cindy Beers heard the commotion at the front door and left the serving line, wiping her hands on her apron. She entered the lobby and saw the five officials. Her heart skipped a beat as she asked, "How can I help you?" One of the visitors was a county inspector she had worked with in the past. She caught his eye, but he gave a quick shake of his head as if wanting to stay anonymous.

The apparent leader stepped forward. "I'm Trevor Godwin, Director of Federal Health and Human Services for this district. We're here for a spot inspection of your facility for probable violations of code." Godwin's high, nasally voice seemed well-matched to his pinched face.

"Do you have a warrant?" Cindy asked, her voice quavering.

"We've got more than that," Godwin said, shaking a piece of paper in his hand. "You were put on notice by Inspectors Furman and Johnson in March. This church is suspected of providing childcare, schooling, food and medical services, all without a license. If Pastor David DeVries and Ms. Jennifer Hernandez are present, you should advise them now."

"Yes sir," Cindy said as she quickly exited the lobby heading for the church offices. Tim and Kristen were walking toward her and saw her panicked expression.

"What's wrong?" Kristen asked.

"There are inspectors at the front door. You know I wasn't able to finish the applications..."

"What's going on?" Pastor DeVries asked as he and Jenny exited his office.

"There are inspectors at the front door and they're asking for you and Jenny!" Cindy said, her face contorted in fear.

"Okay, okay. Calm down. We have nothing to hide," Pastor DeVries said. "On second thought, Tim, you and Kristen might want to leave the premises."

"If it's just the same to you, we'll stay," Tim said.

"Your choice. Let's go greet our visitors," Pastor DeVries said as he led the entourage toward the lobby.

A couple miles away, Jack was at Johnny-B's cabin along with several other hunters. They had gathered around a six-point buck that was hanging by its hind legs from a rope attached to a nearby maple tree. A weathered tribal elder, Sam Aishkebay, approached the deer with a sharp fillet knife. Sam had already made an offering of tobacco at the site of the kill to thank the buck's spirit for giving itself to the hunter. Now it was time to dress the deer. He started by cutting around the anus, careful not to puncture the colon. Sam then respectfully cut off the buck's private parts. He worked the knife into the cavity of the animal, so he could reach inside to grasp the colon with his rubber-gloved hand and pull it out of harm's way. With that clear, he took a gut hook and ran it down the length of the animal until he reached the rib cage. After a little trimming in the cavity and down the backbone, the guts rolled out and hung down the front of the carcass. Finally, Sam reached deep in the cavity down toward the neck to find the trachea, cut it with the knife, and removed the guts in one steaming heap that he placed in a wheelbarrow. It took all of five minutes.

This was not the first time Jack had seen a deer dressed, but it still made him a bit squeamish. He was not sure if it was the smell, the blood, the guts, or just the whole experience. Jack knew this was an instructional moment; he would be expected to dress his own game soon. He wasn't looking forward to it, but knew it was a rite of passage.

With temperatures warming, they decided to forego hanging the deer for days. Instead, they were going to quarter it and use a refrigerator to age the meat. Sam was preparing to do so when a truck came speeding up the two-track toward Johnny-B's cabin. Startled at first, the men relaxed when they saw it was Aishkebay's pickup. The vehicle came to an abrupt halt and Sam's son, Jimmy, jumped out.

"There's trouble at the church," he said, "some Feds and troopers are there!"

"How many?" Johnny asked.

"I don't know, three cars, maybe five or six guys."

The men jumped into action. Johnny ran to his cabin while others grabbed their rifles and ammo. Johnny came out of his cabin with a sniper rifle, a bag of 2.4 GHz walkie-talkies, and an illegal police scanner. Jack grabbed his lever-action Marlin and a box of shells to put in his pocket. Johnny addressed the hunting party.

"Okay, we don't know what's going down, so we play this carefully. Sam, you and Jimmy cover the back of the church. Stay undercover. I'll keep you posted on the radio," he said as he threw one of the yellow walkie-talkies to Jimmy. "Don't do anything without my orders. Joe, go over to Brogans and let them know what's going on and watch the road for any cops coming from the south. Luke, you do the same thing over at the gas station for anybody coming from the west." He threw both a walkie-talkie. "Keep me posted, but don't do anything without my orders, got it?"

"Yep," both men replied.

"Jack, you're coming with me," Johnny said as he climbed into his pickup and started the engine. "Plug this in," he said as handed the police radio scanner over to Jack who had entered the passenger side.

Soon, four trucks were speeding down the two-track heading for the main road and town.

"This is Jenny Hernandez, our church's president, Cindy Beers who is working on our certifications, Tim Kelly who is a volunteer instructor and Kristen Campbell who is a volunteer nurse," Pastor DeVries finished his introductions.

"I need to see your PIVs," Godwin said.

DeVries handed his smartphone over to Godwin, who handed it over to one of the state troopers. "Scan it," Godwin said. "What about the rest of you?"

"Last I heard, we don't have to have PIVs," Tim replied, narrowing his eyes.

"Oh, a bunch of OGs." Godwin smirked. "Well, last I heard, you still have to have IDs and present them on demand."

Tim hesitated. He knew this would create a blip on the grid but saw no alternative. He pulled out his wallet, removed his license, and handed it over to the trooper who scanned it. The others followed suit.

"You know, those IDs will be obsolete soon," Godwin said. "Anyway, I presume you are certified to teach, and you are certified to nurse, in Michigan?" Godwin alternatively looked at Tim and Kristen.

"As a matter of fact, we are," Kristen replied.

"We'll verify that later," Godwin said. "Let's start with the kitchen."

Cindy led them to the kitchen, having to pass through the fellowship hall that was beginning to fill with patrons for the midday meal.

"I submitted our application weeks ago," Cindy pleaded. "You can see we've had a food license for years." She pointed to the old certificates still stuck to the corkboard in the kitchen. "We just got behind with The Crash and all."

"That's no excuse. Other facilities have had no problems," Godwin said. "Trooper McKay, please advise everyone in the dining hall to clear out. This kitchen is closed until further notice."

"Yes sir," the trooper replied. He went through the swinging door into the fellowship hall with Cindy trailing behind trying to assure the guests, "No need to worry, this is just temporary."

"Is that really necessary?" Pastor DeVries protested. "These people are hungry."

Godwin ignored his pleading. "Okay, where's the daycare located?"

"Follow me," Jenny said, leading them back through the fellowship hall and down the hall to a set of classrooms full of infants and preschoolers.

"What's the matter?" Tina Cutler asked as they entered her room.

"The matter is your church is an unlicensed daycare center." Godwin sneered. "Johnson, show them the regs."

The MIOSHA official handed Jenny a thick packet. She leafed through the 50-page document in bewilderment.

"Pardon me, but as a church we are exempt from these regulations," Tina said. "We've been holding vacation Bible school at this church for years!" Tina's loud voice had awakened Noah who now started to cry, clearly irritating the officials.

"Wrong," Godwin replied. "Vacation Bible schools are for summer vacation and, besides, they're to run no longer than four weeks during a 12-month period. We warned you in March. This daycare center is now closed. You need to contact the parents or guardians to retrieve their children."

"You've got to be kidding me," Jenny said, clenching her fists. "These people have nowhere else to go for food and daycare!"

"It's a matter of safety. You're not responsible for these people, the government is," Godwin replied.

"There are no government services around here!" Jenny blasted back.

"Well, then they should move to the city," Godwin said.

"They're all a bunch of OGs, aren't they? Maybe we should check their IDs too!"

Johnny and Jack had just parked their truck behind a hedge on the other side of the street from the church when the walkie-talkie came to life.

"Johnny, this is Joe. The Sheriff just sped by heading for town. You want me to follow?"

"No, he's cool. Stay put and keep me posted."

They got out of the truck and found cover to watch the front of the church. It looked like people were being ushered out of the building. Johnny went back to the truck and re-trieved his sniper rifle. He used its scope to get a close-up of who was doing what. A state trooper was now in the parking lot taking pictures of people's license plates and asking for IDs. Johnny turned on the laser rangefinder.

"I'm heading in," Jack said. "Jenny's in there."

"The hell you are," Johnny countered. "You'll only make things worse."

Inside the church, Tim couldn't take it anymore. "On whose authority are you acting? Isn't the County responsible for health and safety inspections?"

"The federal government has temporarily taken over health and human resources under the state of emergency," Godwin said.

Tim looked over at the two county officials for support, but they simply shrugged. They looked sympathetic, but power-less.

"Okay, where's the medical clinic?" Godwin asked.

Kristen walked them further down the hall to a small office that had a makeshift exam table, some rudimentary instruments, and shelves stacked with medicines and supplies.

"Closed," Godwin said. "Johnson, take pictures of this entire room. And scan some of the supplies—I want to know where this stuff is coming from."

Kristen gasped.

Goldwin turned on her. "So, you think we can't trace your black market suppliers? They'll be in for a surprise! And I don't care about your nursing license, this is an unlicensed medical facility that we deem to be a threat to the community."

Tim moved closer to Kristen who looked to be on the verge of tears.

"Pastor DeVries and Ms. Hernandez, in front of these witnesses you are hereby served this Cease and Desist Order from 25th Circuit Court," Godwin said in his nasally voice. "If you do not comply, you and your associates will be subject to arrest." Godwin handed the multipage document over to Pastor DeVries.

Tim got in Godwin's face. "Remember, you work for us, you petty little apparatchik!" Kristen grabbed Tim to hold him back.

"What did you call me?" Godwin shot back.

"Look it up on the Internet."

Sheriff Larson pulled his cruiser into the church lot and parked next to the state trooper's vehicle. The scene looked chaotic with people being ushered out of the church, children crying, and vehicles pulling into the lot. Larson walked over to Trooper Andrew McKay.

"Hey Andy. Looks like a real cluster. What's going on?"

"No shit, Jim. Trooper Harris is helping HHS serve a Cease and Desist on the church. Boy am I glad you're here. I was about to call for backup."

"Let me give you some advice. Don't call for backup, in fact, you should back off," Larson said.

"No way, who's the law around here anyway?" The trooper's attention was focused on some pickups that had rifle racks mounted in their cabs. Several men stood next to the trucks and they didn't look happy.

"Well Andy, I think they are," Larson waved his hand at the crowd congregating in the parking lot. "They're the people we're sworn to protect. Look at it from their eyes; we come in here and threaten their children, threaten their church, and threaten their way of life—as miserable as it may be. How would you react?"

McKay loosened the leather strap restraining his side arm.

"I wouldn't do that Andy," Larson said, getting in position to bodily intervene

"Why not?"

"You like to walk?" Larson asked.

"What?"

Sheriff Larson pointed to McKay's right leg. A tiny, red laser beam was wiggling in a tight, one-inch pattern on his kneecap.

"Oh shit!" McKay looked up toward the parking lot.

"Don't worry, if they'd meant to shoot you, they would have by now." Larson said.

"What happens next?"

"I would suggest we keep our cool and escort your HHS guests off the premises. I would also stay quiet about this; the Resistance knows who we are, what we're doing, and monitor our radio channels. Believe me, you don't want to get on their shit list. There might come a time when you'll have to decide whose side you're on. Understand?"

"Yeah, I guess."

"One more thing. Next time you state troopers come into my county, you let me know. You might have statewide authority, but I'm the top law enforcement official in this county. And remember, I was elected, you weren't."

"Sure Jim."

"Good, follow me. Let's de-escalate this cluster before things get out of hand."

Washington DC
The Bureau Surveillance Room
Before heading home, Tommy checked on his secret subroutine surveilling Tim Kelly. There had been action! Tommy pulled up the record. Kelly had been scanned by the State Po-

lice in Aux Baie, Michigan, as well as his girlfriend, Kristen Campbell. Several others had been scanned too, including Jennifer Hernandez... Hernandez! Tommy quickly confirmed the link, Jenny Hernandez, aka Jennifer *Bennett* Hernandez! What the hell! As a one-off from Steve and Scott Bennett, why hadn't Hernandez triggered a major alarm?

It took only a minute for Tommy to find the answer. It was so simple it was laughable. The Michigan DOMV only had a record for a Jennifer Hernandez—her maiden name. They never made a link with Bennett, Tommy chuckled, at least not in this database. But the picture was becoming clearer: Karl Schultz, Tim Kelly, and this Jack Conrad went off grid on April 20. Kristen Campbell crosses the Mac Bridge on the same day. And now Kelly, Campbell and Hernandez are scanned together in Aux Baie. They are hiding in the U.P.! Looks like they had dodged another bullet, but how long could that last?

FORTY-SEVEN

Grand Rapids, MI – July 9
District School Office

Meg arrived early. There had been no traffic. In fact, the business district of Grand Rapids was eerily deserted. In contrast, the District School Office was a beehive of activity, the parking lot full of late-model hybrid and electric cars. Burning time in her dilapidated Honda, Meg felt a growing unease. She looked out her window and realized she was parked under a light pole with an attached surveillance camera. Crap! They'd probably been watching her for some time. She took a deep breath and exited the car. Meg felt some relief in just taking the physical action of walking into the lobby to be screened.

"I see you're PIV registered," the guard said looking at his computer terminal. They were in the middle of implementing the new identity and electronic access program. Meg, like most tech-savvy young adults, was an early adopter.

"Yes sir," Meg replied.

"Please scan your finger and enter your PIN," the guard said, gesturing to the reader and keypad on the counter.

Meg complied, and a green light came on indicating that the fingerprint and PIN number she entered was the same as embedded in her smartphone as well as in her permanent record in the Cloud, and that her identity certificate was still valid and showed no holds. It was a three-way match: what she had—her PIV, what she knew—her PIN, and who she was—her biometric fingerprint and facial image. Meg thought it was ingenious, combining the functions of communication, identification, and purchasing all on one device.

"Okay, all items in the container, including your belt and smartphone." Meg followed as instructed and then walked through metal detector. She presented herself to the woman at the registration desk in the lobby.

"Megan Conrad to see Principal Peters."

"Please sign in here," the attendant said as she picked up the phone and connected with Principal Peters' office. "Someone will be with you soon." Meg took a seat on what looked to be brand new furniture.

"Hi Megan, I'm Janice, Principal Peters' assistant." They shook hands. "Come with me, they're expecting you. Did you drive or take public transportation?"

"I drove. The roads were practically empty," Meg said.

"Yes, no more traffic jams. People must be using the new bus system."

Soon they entered a plush office suite. "Just a second," Janice said as she walked down a hall and poked her head into a conference room. "Megan, they're ready for you now." Meg walked down the hall and entered feeling a mixture of excitement and dread.

"Hi Megan! How are you today?" Principal Jean Peters rose from the conference table and shook her hand. There were two strangers around the table who also stood up.

"Fine, thank you."

"Megan, this is Gwen Roach from District and Derrick Edwards from the Department of Education."

"Nice to meet you," Meg said as she shook their hands and they all took their seats.

"Coffee, water?" the Principal asked.

"No, I'm fine."

"Okay then. We have reviewed your application for a fulltime position. We have a few questions before we make our final determination."

"All right," Meg said. She started to twist a ring on her finger.

Derrick, the federal guy, jumped in first. "Megan, we noted on your personal data that your father is off grid. Can you provide us more information on his status?"

Meg was taken aback by the question. She scrambled for an acceptable answer. "Well, I haven't seen my dad for almost a year," she lied. "My mother divorced him, you know, and I remained in her custody until I was of age. I saw him only on rare occasions. I don't know where he is or what he's doing."

"I see," Derrick said. "We do have records of him calling you back during The Crash. Can you expand on those conversations?"

Meg felt herself flush and hoped it wasn't visible to her interrogators. "He was just checking to make sure I was okay with all of the rioting and looting back then." Meg searched her memory for the last time she had a phone conversation with her dad. "I don't think we've spoken for maybe eight months or so."

"That's correct, Megan. As you know, the government tolerates off-gridders, but they remain a threat to the state. We can't have them influencing our teachers in any way. Any further communication with you father is prohibited under our regulations. I know that's tough, but you understand the necessity, don't you?"

"Yes sir," Meg replied, knowing they were probably monitoring her smartphone anyway.

"Good," Derrick said.

"Megan, another item that came up in our background check was your relationship with New Hope Church," Gwen said with a gratuitous smile. "The IRS says you donated to the church. Are you a member? Have you ever worked there?"

Once again, the question caught her off guard. As Meg tried to frame an answer, she noted how much makeup Gwen had on; you could see her foundation crack as she feigned her smile. "Um, that was really nothing. I did some volunteer work in their daycare last summer. I believe I did give some money at a fundraiser for a kid with cancer. I can't remember the amount, maybe $20."

"Actually, it was $40," Gwen corrected. "So, you're not a

member?"

"Oh no. I'm agnostic," Meg lied again. "I just had spare time on my hands, and they needed help."

"Good," Gwen nodded. "You know that New Hope was a sponsor of the Christian School. We can't have a public school teacher being biased, can we?"

"Of course not. I stopped volunteering with them months ago," Meg said, hoping that they hadn't traced her sporadic attendance at church over the last year. At least she was too broke to give regular offerings that they could trace.

"Megan, we were very impressed with your essay on our new Common Course." Principal Peters steered the conversation away from more contentious matters. "Perhaps you can share some highlights for Mr. Edwards?"

"Sure, um." Meg hesitated, trying to recall the essay she had concocted for this liberal audience. All she had to do was regurgitate what they wanted to hear...

"Well, my main point is that Common Course must extend beyond standardized teaching to include a new, common morality. We can no longer endorse individual, capitalistic goals at the expense of the common good. For too long, capitalists have exploited the disadvantaged—slaves, immigrants, minorities, even child labor. And, they have raped our common environment for their private benefit. We need to instill in our children that all private enterprise and property is dependent on the state. It is the state that created the infrastructure. It is the state that embodies our common will. It is the state that must remedy social injustice and inequality. Clearly, we need to teach our children that the individual is subordinate to the collective good." Meg paused for effect and looked around the table. She had them sniffing the bait, now for the hook.

"This goal is impossible under the current, splintered education system. We have parochial, charter, and home schools that are at odds with our common purpose. They focus on the individual and narrow, parochial goals. They divide, not unite. They siphon taxpayer money away from public schools. They need to be eliminated so we can have a single, public school system that focuses on the common good, the Common Course."

"Excellent!" Derrick said with a big smile.

"Your writing is inspirational." Gwen agreed. "We've posted your essay on the District's website."

Principal Peters looked at Meg. "Megan, could you please step out in the hall while we deliberate?"

Meg stood and exited the conference room, closing the door quietly. It was only a minute or two before they summoned her back.

Principal Peters was smiling. "Megan, we have great news! We would like to extend to you a full-time position teaching fourth grade at Middleton Elementary. Do you accept?"

"Of course, thank you!"

"No, thank you Megan," Derrick said. "Our country is at a crossroads. We can no longer fall back on the failed practices of the past. You are the vanguard of a new movement to make America fair and just." He finished with a smug smile.

"Janice will help you with the paperwork and your orientation," Principal Peters said. "But let me highlight a few of the benefits you will receive working for the school system and the state. Assuming you pass DHS clearance, you will be elevated to Gold status. Your income will increase to 100,000 credits which we will automatically load to your PIV account. After your probation period, your income will double to 200,000 and, with tenure, you can even earn more!"

Meg was dumbfounded at her newfound wealth. She currently earned only 40,000 credits at the base Bronze level.

"Of course, as a government employee, you will automatically be enrolled in our own, special pension and health plans." Peters added. "Also, as a Gold, you will be PreChecked for priority access to all travel, entertainment, and sporting events. In addition, the District will pay your union dues and as well as expenses for continuing education and conferences." Principal Peters paused as she waded through Meg's file.

"Okay, it looks like we already paid off your student loans—almost 30,000 credits." She looked back up at Meg. "What car do you drive?"

"I have an old Honda Civic," Meg said.

"Well, we can't have our teachers running around in rust buckets, can we? The District will lease a new Green Car for you from United Auto. Also, you will get a government-issued PIV smartphone for all your security, data, and financial needs." Jean picked up her PIV unit to show it off. "Anyway, Janice will get you started with the paperwork and finish orientation. But, do you have any questions for us?"

"No, I'm good. In fact, I'm thrilled!" Meg put on the expected happy face.

"Great!" Peters said. They all stood and shook hands. Meg confirmed her first impression that Derrick Edward's hand felt like a cold, dead fish.

Meg exited the room and addressed Janice. "May I use the bathroom first?"

"Sure, down the hall on the left."

Meg went down the hall and entered the unisex bathroom. At least she was alone in the multi-stall room. She looked at herself in the mirror. Meg felt elation over her unexpected windfall but sickened by her deceit and sellout. What would her father think about all this? She walked over into a stall. Some guy had left the toilet lid up and there was dried pee staining the rim. Meg leaned over the porcelain bowl and threw up her breakfast of granola and yogurt.

FORTY-EIGHT

Aux Baie, MI – July 10
Community Church

The church called a full congregational meeting two days after the HHS raid. Despite the gas crisis, the church parking lot was jam-packed with cars, trucks, and dirt bikes. Inside the chapel, it was standing room only. Johnny-B helped resurrect an old closed-circuit TV to broadcast the proceedings inside the fellowship hall which was handling the overflow. No one could remember a turnout like this for any church event.

Pastor DeVries was at the pulpit to open the meeting. The Church Council sat in chairs between the pulpit and the altar. The Pastor started with a simple prayer: "Let the words of our mouths, and the meditation of our hearts, be acceptable in Thy sight, O Lord, our strength, and our Redeemer. And all God's people said..."

"AMEN," resonated throughout the church.

"I have a confession to make," DeVries said. "When I was called to this church almost three years ago, I saw it as my off-ramp to retirement. A nice, small church to maintain as I ended my productive days in the ministry. Meet on Sundays, deliver a good sermon, nurture the flock, call on the sick and elderly, and focus on our ever-shrinking community of believers. Well, God had different plans for this church. Maintenance was not enough. Our Lord has guided us to be a missionary church; growing, thriving, and reaching out to transform people's lives. Not by promotion, but by attraction and providing services freely to those in need. And, with The

Crash, there has been so much need." Pastor DeVries paused to look over his congregation.

"Before we get to our main agenda item, I want to recite some statistics." DeVries looked down at his notes. "First, membership. Two years ago, 112 members; today, over 225 active members. That's amazing! Number of meals served; two years ago, none, today 350 meals per week and growing. Daycare attendance; two years ago, zero, today over 20 kids. Church school attendance; two years ago, nada, today over 35 students. Home conversions for off grid energy; 25 since March. Mission trips to surrounding counties; 12 since December. Patient visits at our medical clinic; 975 since April. AA attendance; averaging 18 people per meeting. The list goes on." DeVries paused and took another sheet out of his pocket.

"Please stand as I call out your name," DeVries said. "Johnny-B, Cindy Beers, Linda and Bryce Brogan, Cal and Tina Cutler, Kristen Campbell, Sam Aishkebay and all tribal hunters, George Russell and the tribal fishermen..." The congregation started to spontaneously clap as one after another of the congregation stood. "...Tim Kelly and all teaching assistants, Jack Conrad and his construction team, Jenny Hernandez and her co-op gardeners, all of the 4H kids, Bobbi Holt and the outreach team, all members who participated in a mission..." The applause became thunderous as more than half of the congregation remained standing, some turning red in embarrassment at the unexpected adulation. "Thank you, thank you all. And thank you to the entire congregation for making this happen. It is your church. You are the Body of Christ." The applause finally dwindled, and people sat down in anticipation of the real purpose of the meeting.

"All right then," DeVries continued. "I am going to turn the pulpit over to your president, Jenny Hernandez." DeVries extended his hand to where Jenny was sitting. She rose and approached the pulpit, receiving a quick hug from the Pastor as they changed places.

"Good morning," Jenny said.

"GOOD MORNING." The congregation responded in unison.

"First of all, I would like to thank Pastor and Mary DeVries for their leadership during these tough times. Pastor and Mary, please stand." Jenny started to clap, and then the entire congregation joined in as Pastor DeVries stood and motioned to his wife who stood up from her position in the front pew.

"Okay," Jenny continued. "For the record, it is obvious we have a quorum, so we will forgo a count. There is only one agenda item for today's meeting. By now, you are all aware that our church was raided two days ago. We were served a Cease and Desist Order to stop all services that Pastor enumerated—food services, childcare, schooling, and medical care. I presume the federal authorities would expand their list to include home conversions, construction, and hunting if they were aware of those unlicensed activities." Jenny paused to collect herself. "So, the choice facing this congregation is simple. Do we shut down these activities? Or, do we continue to serve our community and risk legal action, including arrest and incarceration?"

A hush fell over the congregation. Finally, Cal Cutler rose and spoke. "I move that we continue to provide church services, as is, and that we seek an injunction to stop what is clearly an unconstitutional overreach by federal authorities."

"Okay, we have a motion by Cal Cutler. Do we have a second?" Jenny asked.

"I second," Bryce Brogan said as he raised his hand.

"Bryce Brogan has seconded the motion. Okay, the floor is open for discussion. Please raise your hand to be recognized," Jenny instructed the congregation. She pointed to a woman waving her hand. "Yes, Liz?"

"When you say arrest and incarceration, who would that include? The congregation as a whole?"

"Liz, we don't think the congregation is at risk. The Cease and Desist cites Pastor DeVries and me. The Church Council may also be at risk since they are officers of the church. However, to be brutally honest, we don't know the risk. This is unfamiliar territory for all of us." Jenny recognized a man sitting near the front of the chapel, "Tom?"

"If a member, or his family, has PIV privileges, do we risk losing those?"

"I don't have an answer to that, but I do have a warning. During the raid, they were scanning store-bought items in hopes of tracing the buyer. So, if you have been donating items to the church, you may be at risk." Jenny paused, waiting for the mumbling to die down. "If you are concerned about PIV privileges, you can disassociate yourself with the church until this is resolved." Jenny pointed toward a man standing near the rear, "Michael?"

"First of all, I want to thank you, Pastor, and the Council for your courage in the face of this governmental oppression. However, speaking as a retired lawyer, I wouldn't hold my breath about getting an injunction. If my former associates in Marquette are correct, the Feds have usurped the powers of the state courts. Anything they don't like they take right to a federal judge under the state of emergency. It's total bullshit! Pardon my French."

"Thank you, Michael. Sam Aishkebay?"

"Our people have seen this before. The federal government changes the rules when they want to, and we lose. I had a dream," the tribal elder said, silencing any remaining noise in the chapel. "It was sunrise, but instead of light, darkness approached from the east. A mother bear saw the darkness and stood up on her hind legs to protect her cubs. She was confused, not knowing whether to run or stand. And where would she run? Across the waters to Canada? I say we make a stand and fight."

Jenny stood transfixed at the pulpit, mesmerized by Aishkebay's vision. It resonated at some deep, instinctive level she couldn't fully understand. She knew the bear was a powerful totem not to be easily dismissed. And the threat was real. Should we stand and fight?

Seeing Jenny's paralysis, Pastor DeVries returned to the pulpit. "I'll take this one Jenny. Sam, I appreciate your sentiments and I understand your people's history. But we, as a church, can't endorse violence. However, we can all participate in civil disobedience, such as Martin Luther King, Jr. and Gandhi supported. But, as Jenny said, we don't know the risk. You could be putting yourselves in harm's way."

As DeVries finished answering, Jenny could see Johnny-B looking down his pew toward some fellow hunters and Sally Larson. What are they thinking? Jenny wondered.

"Then Pastor, what are you asking from us?" A woman's voice blurted out.

"We are asking for your prayers and support. The Church Council is prepared to take the brunt of this, but we can't guarantee the outcome. There could be risk for the congregation. We will not proceed without your support. It's your church." DeVries sat down, leaving the pulpit to Jenny.

The entire congregation was now murmuring. Jenny had to yell to be heard. "Are there any more questions?" The crowd went silent. "Okay, we will take this to a voice vote. Cindy, could you please repeat the motion."

Cindy looked down at her notes. "That the Church will continue to provide services, as is, and will seek a judicial injunction to halt unconstitutional actions by federal authorities."

"All in favor of the motion say aye," Jenny said.

"AYE!" The response shook the rafters of the old church.

All against the motion say nay." A muted handful of nays could be heard.

"The motion passes. God be with us."

FORTY-NINE

Aux Baie, MI – August 14
Jenny's Camp

It had been about a month since the HHS raid on the church. Everybody was waiting for the next shoe to drop. Sensing that they were working on borrowed time, Karl had redoubled his efforts to complete the plasma drive prototype. Today would be the big test. He hoped for success!

While Karl was excited to show off his invention, he kept the audience to a minimum to ensure secrecy. Besides Tim and Johnny-B, Karl had invited his tool & die accomplice, Argus, and his nephew, Alex, who had access to the industrial lasers at Michigan Tech. The only person missing was Jack—his former roommate. Karl walked from the garage laboratory to Jenny's cabin and knocked on the screen door. "Hey Jack, we're ready," he yelled. As Karl walked back to the garage, he smiled. Jack had come a long way since they had first met; from unemployed laborer to running construction teams and AA meetings. And now, he and Jenny were together. Oh, to be young again!

Once Jack had joined the team, they circled around the prototype sitting in the garage laboratory. It was horizontally mounted on ground brackets with a length of about four feet and weighing only 80 pounds. The exhaust was pointed out the garage opening. Karl made introductions.

"I think you all know Argus. Without his help, the concave input port would have not been possible. And this is his nephew, Alex," Karl nodded toward a studious, young man wearing glasses. "Alex was kind enough to borrow some laser time over at Michigan Tech, so now we have an exacting micropore in the input port. Those elements are key to the compression chamber. With respect to the combustion chamber, you can see we have a pulsed, electrical array to ionize the micro-jet of air. The array should temporarily bend the plasma's magnetic fields to form plasma bubbles to throttle the reaction within thermal limits. Finally, Tim helped reengineer the exhaust to flare around and shield the inline crank shaft—don't want to melt the crank shaft!"

Karl handed out safety glasses to all and returned to the control panel. "All right, are you guys ready?" He was greeted by silent nods, but he did notice that Tim and Jack took a step back—they had witnessed the pyrotechnics of the first prototype. "Here goes nothing," Karl said as he flipped the switch. To everyone's delight, the new device gently hummed before releasing a controlled, blue flame out the exhaust. Karl's eyes were transfixed on a multimeter to determine if the amperes, volts, and wattage being produced were within expectations.

Johnny-B was the first to react. "Holy shit, this thing really works!"

Argus couldn't control himself, "Karl, this is incredible! What is your nominal output?"

Karl turned around with a wide smile. "Gross output of 55 kilowatts. And net output of 11 kilowatts," he yelled. "Did you hear that? Eleven kilowatts net!" I wish Uncle Jacob were alive to see this, Karl reflected. It was his dream and they had all scoffed at him. But he was right!

Despite the excitement, Tim had a frown on his face. "What's the matter?" Jack asked. "You guys are going to be zillionaires! Is this thing patented?"

Tim remained silent as the plasma drive continued to hum. Karl came over to join the conversation. Tim shook his hand. "Congratulations."

Karl looked at Tim's face and read his mind. "I know, I know. This changes everything. This is an invention for the world, not just us. But how do we protect it?"

"I don't know," Tim said. "Our best protection might be to put it in the public domain. Maybe a nominal license fee?"

Johnny-B joined them. "Karl, do you have the specs on this? You might want a separate copy in case your team gets compromised."

"I think that's a great idea." Karl agreed. "But what do you mean by 'gets compromised'?"

Jenny could see the guest of honor fidgeting. "You okay Karl? Did you want to check on your prototype?"

"Yes, if you don't mind. It's like a baby you know, it needs constant attention."

"Well go ahead," Jenny said. "We'll join you after tea." Jenny smiled as Karl darted out the door. Their little dinner celebration had been a success and it was nice to have some good news for a change. With Jack serving tea, Jenny returned her attention to the remaining guests; Pastor and Mary DeVries, Kristen, and Tim. "So, Tim, do you think we can use the generator this winter?"

"Absolutely. In fact, Karl wants to have a couple more prototypes up and running by year end. Might need to buy some more turbines on the black market."

"Maybe I can help with financing," Jack offered.

"That would be great!" Tim said. "My biggest fear now is being discovered."

"Our lips are sealed," Pastor said, moving his fingers across his pursed mouth.

Tim smiled. "I'm not worried about you guys, but someone else might blow the whistle. You know, they're encouraging snitches—just like they did during COVID-19."

"Nobody would do that," Mary DeVries said. "At least not from our church."

Jenny frowned. Tim was right and Mary was naive. It was her biggest fear now that the church was openly breaking the law. One call from a disgruntled congregant and they were done. Just the thought made her queasy. Time to change the subject. "Tim, how are your classes coming along?"

"I've got the kids working on a Better Government assignment. Everyone is reading the Declaration of Independence and the Constitution. Then we're going to brainstorm how to tweak our government."

"We hold these truths to be self-evident," Kristen said. "That all men are created equal, that they are endowed by their Creator with certain unalienable Rights, that among these are Life, Liberty and the pursuit of Happiness."

Jack was impressed. "Not bad. So, why can't liberals admit that our country was founded on spiritual principles?"

"It doesn't fit their narrative," Tim replied. "You know, our Founding Fathers were like fish that don't know they live in water. They were so immersed in a Judeo-Christian ethos that the existence of a *Creator* was never in question. It was on this firm, cultural foundation that a secular Constitution could be built." Tim paused and adjusted his glasses.

"On the contrary, progressives would prefer to focus on the term *self-evident* in the Preamble. These intellectual elites think they can drain the water—in their eyes the oppressive traditions, authorities, and religious dogmas of the past—and replace it with secular enlightenment. They believe abstract reasoning can address all societal problems. If they could just impose the right mix of laws and regulations on the ignorant populace, then they could achieve secular nirvana! Problem is, they collapsed our ethical foundation, so we now have coercive law resting on the shifting sands of moral relativism."

"I get it," Jack said with some satisfaction. "Our current politicians are fish living in different waters, the swamp!"

"That's right," Tim said. "And they're surrounded by swamp creatures: lawyers, regulators, lobbyists, activist celebrities, journalists, and rich donors. The so-called cultural elites of our time. But here's the irony; these same secular elites who want to control your thoughts and behavior have given you a free pass on morality. Want to hook up? No problem, you're free to have premarital sex. Oops, got pregnant? Don't worry, you're free to get an abortion. Tired of your marriage? That's okay, you're free to get a divorce. Kind of bored? No big deal, you're free to visit porn sites, gamble, or fog your brain with marijuana. These are self-centered wants, not virtues."

"What's with the newfound religion?" Jenny asked. "You're not suggesting we make those choices illegal, are you?" She looked at her old friend with new eyes. Was his worldview changing?

"No, but some cultural taboos might help," Tim replied. "We used to have internalized codes of conduct, but that common ethic has been gutted and replaced by what?" Tim let the question dangle before continuing.

"It's the same with our politics. Many partisans now believe the end justifies any means, regardless of the damage done. They view government as a weapon to be wielded, not limited as our Founding Fathers had envisioned. Some are political arsonists. They fan the flames of racial and class discontent and then demand government action to extinguish their media-amped firestorm. All in the name of social justice."

"There's nothing wrong with social justice," Mary De Vries said.

"Of course not," Tim agreed. "It's a lofty ideal. But the means of achieving that goal can be disastrous. Just ask the people of Russia, China, Cuba, and Venezuela how top-down edicts of what's just and fair are working for them. It's a very slippery slope that can drag everybody down. No, fairness and justice are best enacted at the community level by individuals who consider it a societal norm, a virtue."

"Tim, what you call a societal norm is what Christians would call having the law written on our hearts," Pastor DeVries said.

"I think people of faith and agnostics can agree on that one," Tim said. "But I'm afraid that identity politics in this country has hardened hearts. It's become adversarial and vindictive. I've never seen our country so polarized and pessimistic."

"Excuse me," Jenny said as she got up from the table. "I'm not feeling too well." She walked off toward the hallway.

"I'm sorry Jen, did my ranting upset you?" Tim asked.

"No, not at all, reminds me of old times," Jenny called out as she went toward the bathroom, Jack following close behind.

***

Jack was leaving church on Sunday when he pulled one of the summer residents aside. "Hey Chuck, I heard you're going downstate to visit your father-in-law."

"Yes, I'm afraid he's on his last legs. I want to get Carol down there before he passes."

"I'm sorry to hear that. Could you do me a big favor and mail this postcard when you're there? It's for my daughter, but I don't want it to be traced to this zip code."

"No problem." He took the colorful postcard and stuck it in his shirt pocket. "Wasn't that a great sermon today?"

***

After feeling sick for more than a week, Jenny finally made an appointment with Kristen for a checkup. Jenny was sure it was some sort of stomach bug. After giving Jenny a careful exam and talking her through her symptoms, Kristen remained perplexed.

"I don't know, Jenny. It might be acid reflux or the beginning of an ulcer. I'd like to get a urine sample."

"What for?"

"A pregnancy test," Kristen replied.

"That would be impossible!"

"Just humor me, Jenny."

FIFTY

Washington D.C. – September 25
The Bureau Surveillance Room

85% complete...

Tommy watched patiently as the HHS database link to the Bureau continued to upload. He leaned back in his chair, put his feet on the desk, and started to unpeel his next candy bar. Things were slowing down. Another 9/11 had come and gone without an event, so the Bureau was off high alert. While Tommy's caseload remained constant, the cases that held his interest were now on the backburner.

91% complete...

Congressman Steve Bennett's case was now playing out in endless committee investigations and court hearings all staged for the evening news. Tommy felt tainted by association. His department had help dig up dirt on Bennett, including the unfounded allegations of infidelity that were leaked to the press. How sick was that?

96% complete...

The Plasma Drive Technologies case had gone dormant after the HHS hits in Aux Baie back in July. And those hits, including the link to Bennett's sister-in-law, Jennifer Hernandez, were only visible to Tommy. With Scott Bennett still on grid in Grand Rapids for all to see, the case had become stagnant. Chalk one up for the good guys, Tommy smiled.

98% complete...

Today's mundane task was to link the HHS database to the Bureau's Operation Heartland database. Although routine, this task was particularly repugnant to Tommy. They were going to use the HHS database to target churches and faith-based organizations for providing social services without regulatory license or permission. The media continued to paint the religious as wingnut wackos. Only gullible morons fell for this propaganda. Regretfully, there were a lot of gullible morons nowadays. Why persecute good people who are just trying to help?

100% complete.

Finally, Tommy thought. Simultaneously, a major alarm went off on his tracking monitor. He isolated the event and double-clicked for the details. His jaw dropped. Oh shit! It was a double alarm both for Steve Bennett and his son, Scott. He traced it back to the July 8 raid on the Aux Baie church. Besides being scanned, Jennifer Hernandez had been served a Cease and Desist Order and was put on an active HHS hot list. When the HHS database had linked to the Bureau's, Jennifer Hernandez had matched Jennifer *Bennett* Hernandez, and the alarms went off. This hit would certainly make it up to Reggie and others. Even worse, the event record included a scan of Tim Kelly, linking Plasma Drive Technologies to Hernandez. Damn!

Tommy propped up his head on folded hands trying to come up with a plan. There was no way to cover up this hit. It would be just a matter of hours, maybe minutes, before the shit hit the fan at DOJ and Energy. Tommy made a painful decision; by being the messenger of this surveillance breakthrough, he might stay in the loop. And, if he stayed in the loop, he might be able to help these poor guys. Tommy reluctantly keyed his intercom.

"What is it?" Reggie answered.

"I have a breakthrough on the Bennett and Plasma Drive Technologies cases. You'll want to see this."

Twenty minutes later, Reggie sat back in his chair with a smile on his face. "Excellent work, Tommy. Particularly your suspicions about Hernandez's greenhouses. Hunter at DOJ and

Kohl at Energy are going to be thrilled. We might have killed two birds with one stone! This is going to help both of our careers."

"Thanks, but I need your help." Tommy went into suck up mode. "What does this plasma thing have to do with national security?"

"I don't expect you to understand all this," Reggie said. "You're an analyst, and a good one. But let me help you with the big picture. What are the four basic needs of people?"

"You mean like food, water, shelter, that kind of stuff?" Tommy played along.

"That's close." Reggie conceded. "Actually, its food, shelter, healthcare and education. Shelter includes energy, like electricity. You control those four needs then you control the country. Well, we've nationalized healthcare and, for all intents and purposes, education. And we just nationalized food distribution and utilities. So, we're close to securing the country. But what would happen if everybody had their own little power generator in the backyard? Or worse, what if they were producing their own food in greenhouses throughout the country? We could lose control of the heartland. And this bitch might have both!"

"I see," Tommy replied. "But how do we prove that? Should we raid her place? It looks like HHS is on her ass too."

"This is where my political experience pays off, Tommy. We can't just barge in there with guns blazing. Remember, this is Congressman Bennett's sister-in-law. Bennett might be on the ropes, but he is still a force to be reckoned with. No, we need hard proof before we roll her up along with her collaborators. So, sit tight and I'll show you how it's done." Reggie picked up his smartphone and hit a speed dial icon.

"Reggie Woods for Assistant AG Hunter. It's concerning the Bennett case." Reggie took a sip of coffee as he waited for Hunter. He didn't have to wait long. "Yes sir. We may have a breakthrough on both the Bennett and Plasma Drive cases, but we could use some satellite time to confirm our suspicions...

The Upper Peninsula of Michigan, we may need visible and thermal imaging… Yes sir, I'll contact Under Secretary Kohl at once and we will get the coordinates over to you within the hour." Reggie hung up and smiled. "That's how it's done. Now, I need the coordinates for Aux Baie in the next fifteen minutes. Okay?"

"Yes sir." Tommy stood and left the office. What an arrogant asshole, he thought, as he walked back to his room.

***

The scene reminded Tommy of a Hollywood movie. Bigwigs from DOJ, Energy, and HHS sat at conference table in a darkened room waiting for the satellite imagery to appear on the big screen. Even though this was a top-secret meeting, Reggie had thrown Tommy a bone and got approval for him to attend. Tommy suspected the real reason was to cover Reggie's ass if there was a problem or a question. The first image came up and the Energy analyst, Sarah Wong, used a laser pointer to highlight the image.

"For your bearings, here is the general area with no magnification. Here's the Mackinac Bridge connecting the lower and upper peninsulas of Michigan." She swirled the laser pointer around the Straits of Mackinac. "Okay, up here is Lake Superior and this is Marquette, the closest big city to the target. Over here is the target area itself, Aux Baie, Michigan, at the base of the Keweenaw Peninsula. This is a remote area consisting of coniferous forest, glacial moraines, and surface swamps. The population density is less than 20 people per square mile, and that was before The Crash. Marquette, where our HHS office is, has less than 20,000 people. So, it's a great place to hide, but a curious place to conduct high-tech research. Michigan Tech is nearby, and they're doing some splendid work up there, but we haven't found a connection." Wong paused and brought up the next image.

"This is from last night, 22:00 Eastern. For reference, this small cluster of lights is Marquette. From this image, you can see just how deserted this area is. Okay, let's zoom in on the target area." As the image zoomed, pinpricks of light became more pronounced, some larger than others. "Once again, what you would expect for a rural area. This little cluster is downtown Aux Baie. You can also see a few stand-alone mercury vapor security lights around barns and houses. Okay, let's switch to thermal imaging." The screen dramatically changed into a kaleidoscope of colors. "Now, let's filter for natural, ambient heat sources." The screen changed to a dark blue with a scattering of red and one yellow-white dot.

"What are all those red dots scattered around?" Assistant AG Hunter asked.

"Sir, those are primarily wood burning furnaces that are increasingly in use by rural populations, particularly since The Crash." Wong explained.

"Max, we're going to crack down on those." Energy Under Secretary Kohl added. "It suboptimizes utilization of the grid, not to mention the pollution. However, this is the boonies, so it's hard to enforce."

"I see. Keep going Ms. Wong." Hunter ordered.

"Okay. I want you to concentrate on this spot of yellow-white light." Wong used the pointer to highlight the spot. She zoomed in until the spot filled the center of the screen. "What you're seeing is a rather intense energy plume, certainly uncharacteristic for the rural surrounding. We estimate the energy output to be in the range of 50 kilowatts. That's enough power to back up a small building, say 2,500 square feet or so."

"So, it's just a backup generator?" Hunter asked.

"Oh no," replied Wong. "It might be used for backup, but this isn't your typical diesel or gas generator. The next slide will explain." She brought up a graph with the vertical axis showing electromagnetic intensity and the horizontal axis wavelength. "Look at these spikes," Wong used her pointer to highlight the 700 to 900 nanometer range. "The primary signature of this power source is nitrogen and oxygen, not carbon-based signatures you would expect with a gas or diesel engine." The analyst paused as if she had answered the question.

"Sarah, could you please put that in layman's terms for the audience?" Kohl said.

"Oh, I'm sorry. I guess it's obvious to me. Those electromagnetic signatures are consistent with a plasma discharge. It's quite amazing!"

"It's also a threat to our national security," Kohl said. "Please pull up the last image."

Wong complied, showing the power source overlaid on a visible, daytime image of the target area. "This shows the exact physical location of the generator," she said. "It's coming from this small building right here—maybe a garage?" She highlighted the grainy structure with her laser pointer. "The structure is on property owned by a Jennifer Hernandez. Apparently, she uses greenhouses, here and here, for year-round cultivation." Wong expanded the image. "You can see the property abuts Lake Superior and is several miles from the nearest paved road."

"Okay, thank you Sarah," Kohl said. "You've all seen the intellectual property. If this got out it could disrupt our entire energy sector, not to mention IP piracy by China or other enemies. We must contain this, but we must do it very, very carefully. I can't overestimate the importance of secrecy here." He looked up and surveyed the attendees in the room. "This completes the formal meeting. You're all dismissed except for the senior HHS representative. Reggie why don't you stay too."

After the subordinates had left the conference room, Kohl turned to Hunter. "Max, what's your plan to roll them up?"

"We've looked at all sorts of options including simultaneously hitting the property from the road, air, and the lake." Hunter explained. "The problem is, we can't guarantee where the conspirators will be located. They're all off grid. In the end, we decided the most discrete path is to roll up Hernandez first, using HHS violations as a pretext. Her church has exposure to multiple infractions and she's the church president. Once in custody, we can use her to nab anybody else who is connected to the operation. We can also use Hernandez as leverage if anyone tries to intervene, including her father-in-law, Congressman Bennett."

"What's your timetable?" Kohl asked.

"We're shooting for mid-October," Hunter said. "We've already reached out to the HHS field office in Marquette to get the lay of the land. And a SWAT team is being assembled for the actual operation." Hunter turned to the HHS representative. "Who's the Director of your Marquette office again?"

"His name is Trevor Godwin."

Out in the hallway, Tommy approached the DOE analyst. "Nice presentation. I'm Tommy Sutton, Domestic Counterterrorism."

"Thank you. Sarah Wong, Department of Energy." She shook Tommy's offered hand.

"I had a question but didn't want to interrupt the meeting. Is this plasma energy clean?"

"I've only seen their patent application, but it looks clean. They claim that the plasma exhaust is quasi-neutral where the ions and electrons exist in roughly equal numbers. So, the ions and electrons should easily recombine to neutralize the exhaust with no release of ozone. They may have literally captured lightning in a bottle!"

"Why are they so concerned about this invention?" Tommy asked. "It sounds so promising."

"It is promising, but totally disruptive. Can you imagine the impact to the fossil fuel industry if this was commercialized? Not to mention our huge investments in solar and wind energy. With decentralized heat and electricity, you could change the lives of everybody in the northern latitudes. Utilities, agriculture, electric vehicles—it's mind boggling. No, we can't let this genie out of the bottle."

"Thanks Sarah. Once again, great job!" Tommy walked out the door shaking his head. What planet are these people from anyway?

FIFTY-ONE

"I got this one," Meg said as she offered her PIV to the waiter who had brought another round of drinks. The waiter waived his POS device over her PIV to record the sale. As he turned to leave, he looked at the transaction record and muttered under his breath, "Bunch of Gold bitches."

Meg sat at the round table with four of her associates, a small retirement party for her mentor, Doris. The rest of the teachers had passed on the invite. Doris and her friends were pariahs at the school, protected only by union seniority rules. The authorities weren't sure about Meg yet. In her two short months of teaching, she had successfully straddled the competing philosophies at the school.

"You can't go!" Meg implored. "What am I going to do?"

"Oh Meg, you'll be fine," Doris replied. "You've got these guys figured out. Just keep your nose clean and go about teaching the kids. You're one of the few that actually gives a damn."

"I don't know. My class is out of control," Meg said as she took another swig from her beer.

"Well, pardon my critique, but you can't negotiate with them," Doris said. "I know you are all about collaboration, but these are undisciplined kids. You need to establish clear boundaries. Remember what I told you on your first day? Make an example of a troublemaker right from the start. You've got to get their attention! Oh, and no smiles before Christmas."

The other teachers chuckled in knowing agreement.

"It wasn't like this when I was in school," Meg said.

"Listen sweetie, I'm 60 years old. You wouldn't believe the changes I've seen! My heart goes out to you rookies. You've got to deal with three, huge societal changes. First, this is the entitlement generation. Most of these kids have been given everything. Including unending praise by their parents thinking it will build self-esteem. But it's just the opposite; they have no coping mechanism for failure. They never had to earn anything—everybody's a winner! When things don't go their way, they go berserk." Doris took a sip from her wine. She was holding court and had her friends' rapt attention.

"Second, there's no respect for authority anymore, parental or otherwise. There are few role models now for acceptable behavior. Most of the kids have been in daycare since they were infants. Many of the parents have abdicated any discipline to us. Not only do we have to instruct them, we've got to socialize them as well. I call them dry-clean students; parents drop them off in the morning and expect them to be cleaned and pressed when they come home."

Meg interrupted. "You know, I was discipling Billy Thompson the other day, and he just walked away from me! I caught-up with him and asked him 'do you do this at home with your parents?' and he said 'yes' and continued walking."

"Just another case in point," Doris agreed, taking another sip before continuing. "Finally, you are dealing with the first Internet generation. They expect instant gratification from their devices, another entitlement. They use social media and video games as their societal touchstones —their new role models, peppered with gratuitous sex, violence, and vitriolic tweets. It's almost the exact opposite of the Protestant ethic. Who wants deferred gratification and pious living?" Doris asked.

"But it's subtler than that. Many of these kids don't even know how to interact with real people. They're cyber-deranged. Instead of taking away their electronics, we label them as victims of ADHD, low self-esteem, ASD, a broken fam-

268

ily, whatever. But don't worry, the state is there to help with counselors, child psychologists, and individual lesson plans. Well, either our gene pool has gone to hell over the last 50 years, which I doubt, or our culture has. And I think we've finally hit critical mass." Doris let that hang in the air while she took another sip of wine.

"What do you mean by critical mass?" A compatriot took the bait.

"Well, back in the day, we might have one or two trouble-makers or challenged kids in the class. With just a couple of kids, we could cope. Give them extra attention, send them to the principal, provide reasonable punishment. We had the authority back then. But now, you might have a quarter of the kids screwed-up. With those types of numbers, it's like a chain reaction with kids bouncing off each other until the class explodes. Meg, how many troublemakers do you have?"

"You know, you're right. I've got about five or six kids that are out of control, and they disrupt the class for everyone. But most of them are good kids, they just can't seem to help themselves. I think a few have deep behavioral issues."

"Yeah, and I bet you spend 80% of your time trying to control 20% of your class. Our teaching and socialization are now calibrated to the lowest common denominator of the class; and our whole educational system and society suffers. The sad part is the solution is simple. You see it with our well-adjusted students; instill an attitude of gratitude, love and attention from a positive role model, firm boundaries that are enforced, and non-cyber activities and socialization. Pull the plug on the Internet!"

"Thanks for the inspiration," Meg replied with a rueful shake of her head. "You sound like you're endorsing home-schooling."

"Oh, honey, you'll do fine," Doris responded as she finished her glass of wine and ordered another.

***

The last straw came several weeks later. Trying to find a way to reestablish control of her class, Meg decided to implement a team structure. She picked out her five best students and made them team leaders over four or five other students. Just as Doris had said, these leaders came from strong, engaged families. She grouped the students' desks, so the teams formed islands. This forced attention on the team, and it allowed her to spread out the troublemakers. Meg hoped the team leaders would act as good role models and enforce positive peer pressure. She would rotate leaders once the kids got the idea. It took a while, and she had to intervene on occasion, but it had started to work. Meg saw improvement across the board. Students were more engaged. Loud outbursts or attention-getting stunts subsided. The kids were even more polite to each other. For Meg, it was a breath of fresh air. Even her fellow teachers remarked on the improvements in her classes. And then, it all fell apart.

About a month into her experiment, Principal Peters unexpectedly monitored Meg's class. Meg was sure that the Principal wanted to see how the environment had improved so dramatically. And, her kids didn't disappoint. They were energetic, but courteous. They stuck to the lesson plans. And there were no emotional outbursts like there had been in the past. It was one of the most gratifying days Meg could remember as a teacher. When she was asked to meet with Principal Peters, she was looking forward to positive feedback and some sort of recognition.

"Come in," Jean Peters said after Meg's light tap on her open door. "Hello Meg. Have a seat," she waved her over to one of the two chairs facing her oversized desk. "I wanted to give you some immediate feedback on your performance. Mind you, this is not a formal performance review, but more of a midcourse correction."

Meg's heart dropped along with her expectations of this meeting.

"Meg, we have had several complaints from parents and students about your new teaching style. Almost to a person, they call it elitist."

"I'm not sure I understand," Meg replied.

"Well, they claim you are showing favoritism to a select few in your class, your team leaders. And I saw the same thing with my own eyes when I audited your class. You just can't do that. I remind you; you are the leader and you must treat everybody the same. No favorites!"

"But I was just trying to provide some positive role models for some of the more challenged kids. It also allows me to physically separate the troublemakers," Meg explained.

"Meg, we have specialists and counselors for challenged kids. It's not your responsibility. Remember, many of these kids come from broken homes. They have low self-esteem and don't need that reinforced by placing a peer leader over them. How do you think it makes them feel?" Principal Peters didn't wait for an answer. "It makes them feel like failures, and that's not acceptable."

Meg thought about offering a defense but saw where this was going. She remained silent.

"Now, I want you to return to our Common Course teaching practices and lesson plans. No more teams and team leaders. No more elitism. You must treat everybody the same. If you can't handle the challenged kids, then engage our school counselors, that's why we have them on payroll. Do I make myself clear?"

"Yes, Principal Peters."

"That's not all," Peters continued. "We know you have been meeting with some of the reactionary teachers at our school. Your PIV log shows several off-premises meetings. Also, we know you have conducted various Internet searches related to traditional teaching practices. Let me remind you that these reactionaries and their traditional solutions are the problem, not the solution. Remember, we need to teach our children that the individual is subordinate to the collective good. You know who said that?" Meg remained silent, stunned by the spying that had occurred. "You did, during your interview," Peters answered her own question. "No more team leaders."

"Yes, Principal Peters."

"Excellent, you're dismissed."

***

A week later, Meg got out of her car, dejected. Same shit, different day, she thought. Since her meeting with Peters, her class was back to chaos. It was even affecting her physically. She used to jog when she got home after work, now she just wanted to hole up and have a beer or two. Her digestion was a mess.

"This sucks," Meg muttered as she walked toward her front door. Before entering, she habitually checked her mailbox, even though mail was practically nonexistent nowadays. Much to her surprise, she found a single postcard. The front was the classic, dayglow poster from the movie *The Endless Summer*. On the back was a simple message. *Surf's UP. Going to see an old flame. Join me. Love, Moondoggie*. It was from her dad! She broke down and started crying uncontrollably.

She knew exactly where 'U.P.' was.

FIFTY-TWO

Washington D.C. – October 8

Tommy finished the handwritten note, folded it in half, and slipped it into his back pocket. He doubled-checked where Mrs. Bowden's PIV was located—Joann's Salon. Perfect! And she had just gotten there. After a quick DOMV check, he had her car make, model and license plate. A quick call to Reggie and he had time off to pick up a prescription.

Fifteen minutes later, Tommy made a pass in front of Joann's Salon. Bowden's car was there all right, and no surveillance cameras were in sight. He parked around the corner and walked toward the store front, senses on hyperalert. The salon had a large picture window but, thankfully, Bowden's car was parked on the side. Tommy approached the car, pulled the note out of his pocket, and stuck it under Mrs. Bowden's windshield wiper. Taking extra precaution, he walked around the entire block to return to his car. Tommy was back at his office within an hour, making sure he checked in with Reggie upon his return. Now, all he could do was wait and hope.

It was late afternoon when Steve Bennett reached the DHS offices. John Bowden was waiting for him outside. "Let's take a walk."

"Sure." That sounded more like an order than a request, Steve thought.

Bowden remained quiet until they were a few blocks away. "I've got a note in my pocket. I'm not going to give it to you, I'll just repeat what was written, it's short."

"Okay." If this wasn't coming from John Bowden, he would

have chuckled at the cloak and dagger of it all. Instead, he felt a creeping sense of dread.

"*Scott B. on DOJ/DOE hit list. Jenny H. on HHS hit list. Cases linked and hot.*" Bowden concluded, still walking straight ahead. "Hot was in caps."

Steve's heart skipped a beat. What the hell? "Who was the note from?"

"Anonymous. But it was handwritten, which was stupid, or the person was in a rush. It was left under my wife's windshield wiper. Crude, but effective."

Steve tried to think straight, but his mind was frazzled. He reached out to his friend. "What do you think?"

"Well, we know Scott's company was on Energy's shit list before. And we know Hunter from DOJ is gunning for you. Not sure where your sister-in-law comes into this. Doesn't she live up in the U.P.?"

Steve didn't hear Bowden's last question. His mind had become clear. "Didn't you say Scott's business associates went off grid some time ago?"

"Yes, I think that was back in the spring," Bowden replied.

"I've got to see my son—right away!"

FIFTY-THREE

Leaving Washington DC Airspace – October 9

"With this headwind, should be a bit over four hours," Dan Fisher said through the intercom. He was flying Steve Bennett to Grand Rapids, Michigan, the next day on the single-engine Cessna.

"Well, let's hope my bladder holds out," Bennett shouted, and laughed. They both wore headsets to drown out the engine noise. Steve sat in the copilot's seat.

"You can always use a pee bottle if things get bad." Dan chuckled. "So, what's going on with Scott to warrant this unplanned trip? Is it that plasma thing?"

"Yes, I'm afraid it's raised its ugly head again. To make things worse, Scott might have gotten my sister-in-law, Jenny Hernandez, involved."

"I remember Jenny, nice woman."

"Yeah, she's a gem. Jenny didn't get much of a fair shake from my brother. It wouldn't be right to get her mixed up in this mess. Problem is, I can't call, email, or text anybody to unwind this thing. So, I need a face-to-face with Scott."

Dan turned to face his boss. "You know, there are still a few ways to communicate that the Feds are having a tough time monitoring."

"What do you mean? I thought everything was bugged."

"Listen, for your own sake, I am not going to get into detail," Dan said. "I think you need plausible deniability. But there are some legacy radio systems that can be used to cloak data, at least for a while. Some of us veterans are networking on it. So, in an emergency, I might be able to get a message out to someone. Of course, they would need to be physically close to a network operator."

Steve turned to address Dan whose eyes were hidden behind aviator sunglasses. "How the heck can you pull that off? Aren't all radios monitored?"

"That's the beauty of it," Dan replied. "We are doing everything open channel. But we can still cloak some data."

"Okay, I won't ask anything more. I think you're right; plausible deniability might be wise right now. I'll keep that in my hip pocket in case the shit hits the fan."

"No problem boss. I've got your back."

Scott picked up his dad at the municipal airport on the outskirts of Grand Rapids a bit after noon. His father hadn't given any reason for his visit. Judging by the frown on his dad's face as he got into the car, it was not a good news visit.

"Scott."

"Hey dad. Okay flight?"

"Yes, everything went well. I plan on heading back after we get a bite to eat. Dan is fueling up the plane right now. Why don't you drive us over to Stella's, they've got a good burger."

"Sure. You're heading right back? What's going on?" Scott said as he pulled away from the curve and headed for the exit to the airport.

"Well, I was hoping you would tell me. I just got intel that says you're still on Energy's shit list and that Jenny may now be involved. What the hell is going on? I thought I told you to drop that plasma stuff!"

Scott remained silent, trying to frame a response. He exited the airport merging onto the access road heading for the expressway. "It's not that big of a deal. We weren't doing anything illegal, just research."

"Listen son, this is dead serious. With the state of emergency, people are getting locked up for even looking the wrong way, and there are snitches everywhere. You've got to give me the full story, for your sake and Jenny's. What the hell is going on!"

"Well, I kept you out of the loop on purpose; I thought that would give you plausible deniability." Scott remained silent about his father's connections with the oil industry. Perhaps his dad had other reasons for shutting down the company?

"You know, that's the second time I've heard that term today. I'm not buying it this time. This is family. Tell me everything."

Scott paused, thinking of a way to spin the response. "Well, following your advice, we shut down our website and Cloud server in September. But we let our top scientist keep working on a pro bono basis. Anyway, he had some success with a prototype. To be safe, I withdrew, and we shut down the facility in October."

"So, you did shut it down?" Steve asked.

"Not entirely. The team headed up to Jenny's place in April to continue research. It wasn't just my decision. Tim has a relationship with Jenny too, you know." Scott regretted his answer. It sounded lame.

"Well, you might have gotten Jenny into a real mess. She's on HHS's hit list, and now they've connected her case to your DOE case. So, I presume they know about Tim and your team collaborating with her. That's not good."

"I'm sorry dad. I made a mistake, but I can fix this." Scott wondered if he could regain his father's confidence. "Why don't I just fly up there today and warn them in person? Maybe get them out of the country to Canada? Besides, Dan is already here with the plane."

Steve frowned. "Son, I'm already under investigation for evacuating you during the attacks. You know that. Taking the plane to Aux Baie would be like sending up a distress flare. I'm sure they're tracking the plane right now."

Scott could hear the irritation in his dad's voice increase. He needed a plan and quick. "How about I just drive up there tomorrow? I can get there in under eight hours, warn Tim and Jenny, and be back by midnight."

"I don't know. You could be walking into a trap. I've still got some pull, but the game has gotten a lot nastier. Not sure I could help you up there. If you do go, I'd give Marquette a wide berth. That's where the HHS office is. Of course, they'll probably be tracking your PIV anyway."

Scott took that as a green light. "Listen dad, this is my responsibility. I need to fix it. Besides, I have every right to visit my Aunt. It might provide a plausible..."

"Don't say it," Steve interrupted.

PART 3

We must know, at the same time, that capability at any time could be turned around on the American people, and no American would have any privacy left such is the capability to monitor everything—telephone conversations, telegrams, it doesn't matter. There would be no place to hide. If this government ever became a tyranny, if a dictator ever took charge in this country, the technological capacity that the intelligence community has given the government could enable it to impose total tyranny, and there would be no way to fight back because the most careful effort to combine together in resistance to the government, no matter how privately it was done, is within the reach of the government to know. Such is the capability of this technology.

Senator Frank Church (D-ID)
August 17, 1975 Meet the Press

FIFTY-FOUR

Present Day

St. Ignace, MI – October 10, 8:10 am
U.P. Side of Mackinac Bridge

Just as the attendant had promised, there was a mini-mart on the other side of the bridge. Scott checked his PIV map—only four more hours to go before he could warn his friends in Aux Baie! He entered the deserted oasis and pulled up to one of the gas pumps. It took a second or two for the pump to query his PIV and acquire Scott's GUID, Globally Unique Identifier, to access his citizen status, credit level, and vehicle registration from the Cloud. As the download completed, the pump display lit up: *Scott Bennett, Gold, Credits ∞, 1971 Porsche 914-6, Premium Gas + Carbon Penalty = C10.55. Commence fueling.* Scott opened the fuel lid mounted on the front of the Porsche and started to pump the gas.

Not too long ago, 10.55 per gallon would have floored Scott. But he was now used to the excessive fuel and carbon taxes. Besides, he had plenty of credits. But it was killing the automotive industry. Nobody could afford to drive these days, pushing everybody into public transportation or bicycles.

The pump came to an automatic halt. The screen popped up 10.7 Gal, C112.89, Thank You. Scott knew the transaction had been duly recorded in his database, credits had been deducted from his account, and certain algorithms were being applied to determine any anomalies. For instance, was the gas purchased consistent with the mileage driven since his last fill up? The Feds were always on the lookout for gas hoarding and black market activities. Not a problem, Scott thought, he was sure he was clean. Fueling done, Scott took his PIV out of the dash mount and headed into the store. He was hungry

"Good morning Mr. Bennett." The sole, male clerk greeted him. "How can I help you today?"

"Just taking a break," Scott replied and headed to the rest-room. He soon exited and the clerk picked up the conversation. Probably bored out of his gourd with so few customers, Scott figured.

"That's quite a car you've got there! A Porsche 914-6? Never seen one of those before."

"It's a collector's car, totally restored. Porsche made less than 3,500 of them," Scott said as he walked the sparsely stocked aisles of the mini-mart looking for a breakfast snack. "The dash 6 means the car was equipped with the flat-6 racing engine from the 911 Targa, except it is center-mounted in the 914 so it has perfect balance and a top end of 125 miles per hour." Scott had no problem warming up to talk about his car. He grabbed some granola bars and scanned their barcodes to purchase. Barcodes still made sense for small food items and had not gone to RFID chips yet.

"Well, they certainly are killing you on the cost of gas," the clerk said. "I think that's the highest I've ever seen for a car."

"Yeah, huge carbon penalty," Scott replied. The coffee looked like mud, so Scott went over to the cooler and picked out a cola. He scanned it and his PIV gave an audible chirp to alert him of a junk food tax. Besides the tax penalty, this purchase would hit his healthcare record too and might impact his insurance rating. However, the biggest irritant was going to be the barrage of pop-up advisories that would hit his PIV for the next week or so advising him of the perils of junk food. Feeling a bit guilty, Scott looked around for some fresh fruit but there was nothing on display. "Any fruit?"

"No sir, I'm sorry. We don't carry fruit, not enough traffic to keep it in stock," the clerk replied. "There's a chance you might see a fruit stand on your way, local farmers looking to barter. But most have been shut down by the black market laws. Where you headed?"

"Aux Baie," Scott replied as he approached the counter. "I'm going to take U.S. 2 over to 141 and then 41 up through Baraga."

"I've seen fruit stands on 41 before," the clerk said. "But, be careful, there are reports of militia in that area."

"Militia?"

"Yeah, the Michigan Militia, the Resistance—you know, off-gridders. The Feds are trying to hunt them down."

"Interesting." Scott gave the clerk his food items to bag. "I'll keep my eyes open."

"Thank you, Mr. Bennett. Have a great day!"

Scott got into his Porsche and pulled over to a parking area. He opened his cola, unwrapped one of the granola bars, and started his snack. Michigan Militia. Scott was sure he'd heard of them before. Maybe his PolySci class in high school? Of course, the Toledo War! "Toledo War," he verbally queried his PIV. A soothing female voice responded:

"The Toledo War, also known as the Michigan-Ohio War, was waged from 1835 to 1836..."

As Scott ate, he listened to the improbable story of the war between the two states. While it was a war with no deaths, blood was actually spilled when a Michigan county sheriff had tried to arrest an Ohio militia major. The major and his sons had resisted arrest and one son stabbed the county sheriff with a penknife before fleeing to Ohio proper.

"...certainly, none of the participants could have foreseen the continuing war between Ohio and Michigan as waged by the Ohio State Buckeyes and the Michigan Wolverines on the gridiron each fall. In fact, the nickname Wolverine is said to have originated from the Toledo War with Ohioans claiming the Michiganders had come at them like angry Wolverines."

Scott let out a guffaw. It sounded like the Wild West back then, with competing sheriffs and militia. But it dawned upon him that not much had really changed. The cities were pacified, but rural America was up for grabs. If fact, he was headed for the booby prize of the Toledo War—the remote Upper Peninsula. With that thought, he finished his snack, pulled out of the mini-mart, and officially entered the U.P. People from the lower peninsula called the U.P. natives "Yoopers" who ate pasties and had their own accent and dialect. Conversely, the Yoopers called the lower peninsula population "Trolls" because, on the map, they lived beneath the bridge.

Scott hadn't gone far before his PIV started chirping now and again. He disregarded the incoming emails. Scott already knew what they were. He was sure his Toledo War inquiry had triggered several keywords, including militia. Scott guessed the incoming spam would be extolling the virtues of gun control while pillorying militias and sheriff's posses. Maybe even a think-piece from an Ivy League professor on how the Second Amendment had been misinterpreted. Scott muted his PIV.

Aux Baie, MI – 8:15 am

Jack had been awake since early morning listening to the sound of wind whistling through the pines and the distant, crashing surf. A warm front had come through during the night and he knew Lake Superior would be lit up. A familiar excitement and apprehension took hold of him. It had been over a year since he had been kiting or windsurfing. It was now October and the season would be ending soon.

Jack slipped out of bed, trying not to awaken Jenny. In the dim morning light, he could see her resting peacefully, her long dark hair spilling across the pillow. We should get married, Jack decided. He fought the urge to crawl back into bed. It had been a while since they had made love. He couldn't quite put his finger on why. Maybe it was nerves—everybody was on edge about what the Feds might do next. Anyway, it gave him further incentive to go kiteboarding and let the physical exertion bleed off his anxieties and frustrations.

After a lean breakfast of fresh eggs and homemade salsa, Jack took his coffee cup with him and went back in to check on

Jenny. She was awake in bed with the nightstand light on, reading the Bible. Jenny looked up as Jack entered the room. "Good morning, sleep okay?" Jack asked.

"Pretty well," Jenny said. "Are you heading out?"

"Hear the waves? I've decided to go kiteboarding before I lose the season. If it's blow'in, I'm go'in!"

"That sounds great. Where will you be?"

"With a south wind, I think I'll walk around the point and setup on the thin beach there. Might have to do a hot launch by myself."

"Do you need me to help or watch?"

"No, I should be fine. Besides, I'd have to teach you how to hold the kite," Jack said. "We'll save that for another day."

"Okay. I'll be doing some gardening this morning. Maybe I'll check on you later."

"Sounds good. I left the coffee on for you. Love ya."

"Love you. Be safe!"

***

"Good morning Tim," Pastor DeVries said as he stuck his head into the fellowship hall. "You're in early."

"Good morning! I'm just preparing for our Better Government finale. We're wrapping it up today," Tim waved at two whiteboards showing a dozen or so bullet points that the students had come up with as recommendations.

DeVries perused the proposals and a smile crossed his face. "Out of the mouth of babes," he said.

"Yes," Tim agreed. "It's quite fascinating. I facilitated the discussion, but the kids did everything else."

"What time is your class?"

"10:30. We want to be done before midday meal. Can you join us?"

"It would be an honor. I'm sure Mary will want to attend too." DeVries turned and headed down the hall toward his office.

FIFTY-FIVE

Washington D.C. – 8:20 am
The Bureau Surveillance Room

Tommy was about to sneak out of his office when a loud chirp from Bennett's tracking monitor stopped him in his tracks. "Damn!" He didn't have time for this; he had no idea how long Reggie's meeting would last. Tommy pulled up the alert, it was a keyword alert for Michigan Militia. But it wasn't from a call, email, or text message; it was a simple Internet inquiry for the Toledo War. He took a quick glance at the Wikipedia response and chuckled. Reality is stranger than fiction, Tommy thought as he quickly turned and exited his office.

His heart beating fast and his palms clammy, Tommy tried to act nonchalant as he walked down the hall to Reggie's office. He gave a quick knock and entered. As suspected, the office was empty. He walked around Reggie's desk and looked at the monitor. He was in luck. Reggie's computer had been biometrically unlocked. Tommy sat down behind the desk and typed in Reggie's password he had easily hacked months ago; *NOTSNIW@398*. It was the name of Reggie's bulldog spelled backwards and his street address—how lame was that! He was in.

Tommy did a quick search and found the Do Not Detain email that went out to the State Police and PIV Checks. He clicked on the forward icon and pulled the scrap of paper out of his pocket with the email addresses. With shaky hands, Tommy entered the addresses for the sheriffs of Baraga, Iron, Keweenaw, and Houghton Counties. Knowing the raid was coming from Marquette, he excluded that sheriff's office.

Tommy took a deep breath and clicked send. He waited until the email was sent and then deleted the message and emptied the trash. As an extra precaution, he wiped the keyboard clean with his shirtsleeve.

The hallway was clear as he walked back to his office. Once inside, he sat down and let out a deep sigh of relief. He looked at his watch. 8:30. It had taken all of seven minutes to complete his secret transmission. Now, he would just wait and hope that one of the local sheriffs would smell a rat. It was a long shot, Tommy conceded, but it was his only shot.

Tommy's relief was short-lived as he came to a full realization of the risk he had taken. Perhaps it was time to get out of this shithole, he thought. He had been planning it for months. It would mean leaving town and going off grid. His original plan had been Texas to meet up with his brother Ben. But the Upper Peninsula of Michigan was becoming intriguing. He wondered what was going on up there with the Resistance and this new plasma engine.

Two floors upstairs, Reggie Woods sat in the secure conference room ready to brief his superiors on Scott Bennett's status. Given the early hour, he was surprised to see Assistant AG Hunter and Energy Under Secretary Kohl at the table—this must be more important than I thought! The Health and Human Services representative, Trevor Godwin, had joined the conference remotely from Marquette Michigan.

"Bennett just cleared the PIV check at the Mackinaw Bridge," Reggie said, starting the briefing. "His ETA for Aux Baie is around midday. We've put out a Do Not Detain advisory to the State Police and we've shared our data link with Marquette."

Kohl leaned toward the speakerphone. "Godwin, you sure you can pull off this raid?"

"Yes sir," Godwin's voice came through loud and clear. "The team is already mobilizing. They should be ready to deploy at 11:00. We'll trail Bennett and snatch him once he reaches his destination."

"Good. What assets are you deploying?" Hunter was fidgeting with his pen, every now and then clicking it on the table.

"Twenty men in all. Two HHS officials including myself, two DOE techs for the generator, and a 16-man SWAT team for security. We'll be driving five Suburban SUVs. We have commandeered a Fish and Wildlife boat to be positioned offshore and there will be a chopper on hot standby. However, we don't expect much resistance," Godwin said.

"With Bennett in the picture, what's your new ops plan?" Kohl asked.

"The plan remains basically unchanged," Godwin said. "We have two targets for apprehending Hernandez, the church and her property. Our intel says she often attends the illegal, midday meal at the church. That's our primary target and provides legal pretext. If Bennett shows, we roll him up there with the others. If Hernandez is a no-show, or if Bennett heads for her property, we conduct the raid there. Either way, it's a small town. Should be a cakewalk."

"Listen Godwin, it's imperative we secure their generator, computers, documents and Chief Scientist Schultz, understand?" Kohl seemed uneasy with the unexpected change in plans. No one had expected young Bennett to come into play, forcing them to move up the raid.

"Yes sir," Godwin replied. "We'll have four of the agents monitoring egress to the property. Nobody comes or goes without us knowing. As planned, we'll use Hernandez as leverage to roll up the co-conspirators, including Bennett."

"Nabbing Bennett would be a *huge* bonus." Hunter jabbed the table hard with his pen to emphasize the point. The room went silent.

Watching Hunter, Reggie realized he was sweating. This mission had become serious—a career-changing mission.

"Okay then," Kohl broke the silence. "Keep us posted as the operation proceeds. And remember, this is all off the books. We want complete secrecy as to the nature and capacity of the generator. Got that?"

"Yes sir!" Reggie said, hearing Trevor Godwin echo his words on the speakerphone.

FIFTY-SIX

On the Road to Aux Baie, MI – 9:00 am

Heading west on U.S. 2, Scott had forgotten how immense the U.P. was; more than 300 miles from east to west. The route offered sweeping vistas of Lake Michigan, now a mosaic of waves driven by a strong southerly wind. But Scott wasn't in a sightseeing mood.

To distract his worried mind, Scott turned on the radio and searched for some news. AM talk radio was now extinct, eliminated by the FCC which resurrected and corrupted the so-called Fairness Doctrine. Of course, that left American Public Radio, APR, as the only source of news. They claimed that they were committed to airing both sides of a controversy. Well, that was a frigging joke unless you viewed progressive versus far left as competing world views! Case in point: the nonstop propaganda by the state-sanctioned media to push adoption of PivPal. It was a classic strategy of carrot and stick, flaunting all the benefits of PivPal while painting non-adopters as reactionaries and unpatriotic. And it was working. PIV had saturated the cities. Only the rural areas were offering resistance.

At first, Scott had been enraged at the censorship and progressive groupthink emanating from APR. But now, he found it slightly amusing to listen to the so-called journalists attack everything conservative. Scott had to admit that they had refined their pitch to a fine art. Each moderator sounded so articulate, reasonable, topical, and glib. Almost as if they were clones. But, if you listened objectively, it was clear there was no controversy being debated. They had selected the question, and they had the answer—an unassailable truth to broadcast, unchallenged, across America.

He finally found APR broadcasting out of Marquette. Before long, the subject matter became obvious. It was an attack on homeschooling. The moderator, whose voice had the pre-requisite vocal fry and intonation, tossed a softball, leading question to her guest.

"...so, given the lack of socialization by these home-schooled children, don't we risk generating social outcasts, or worse, sociopaths who can't adapt to our culture?"

"That's right Hannah. Our studies show that home-schoolers have a limited ability to integrate with their peer groups and, quite often, adopt antisocial or reactionary be-havior. In many cases, these children are isolated from the Internet and the free exchange of ideas. Most are off grid. Their parents wield complete authority which can often lead to abuse. It's really a shame, but we are taking steps..."

Scott just shook his head. Most homeschooled kids he had met were smart, considerate, well-adjusted, and multital-ented. Thank God their caring parents still had access to trad-itional educational materials; not the progressive rubbish that was coming out of Common Course nowadays.

With APR broadcasting an anti-homeschooling segment, Scott knew cable and Internet news would be piggybacking with similar diatribes. Online mobs would join the chorus to vilify homeschoolers. The progressive media had perfected their echo chamber to relentlessly hammer home the social cause of the day—or at least that day's news cycle. Scott leaned over and turned off the radio. He could only take so much.

As bad as radio and TV were, Scott was more concerned about the Internet. It was insidious. With the PivPal suite, the state had vastly simplified the user's experience to navigate essential apps because the suite was the only choice! At the same time, the Web had become a thinly veiled propaganda machine. If you strayed off the progressive path, there were Bots to publicly shame you or endless pop-ups to bombard you with the liberal perspective. Add that to the socialist indoctrination of students, and you had the recipe for one-dimensional thinking. No skepticism. No debate. Just progressive dogma to fundamentally transform the country and its founding principles.

Many conservatives placed the blame on The Crash. But Scott realized the country's demise had been brewing for years. The symptoms now seemed obvious. An electorate that was ignorant of basic civics—only 25% of Americans could name all three branches of government or explain the Bill of Rights. Or college administrators turning a blind eye to censorship of conservatives on campus. The brazen attacks on religious institutions as if they were outlawed, not protected, by the Constitution. The incessant whittling away of the Second Amendment right to bear arms by regulatory fiat or judges legislating from the bench. And now PIV, which left your entire life open to unreasonable search by authorities. Sure, you could opt out of this 24/7 electronic dog collar. But if you did, you lost your rights to participate in the new society and economy. You became a pariah in your own country. I guess if you don't know the Bill of Rights, Scott brooded, you don't miss them when they're gone.

Marquette, MI – 9:20 am
Health and Human Services Facility

The SWAT team assembled in a large conference room at the HHS offices. They were good, well-trained men who had been picked from the various federal agencies in the area: FBI, ATF, Border Patrol, and Marshals. Since this was a covert mission, state and local law enforcement had been excluded. The agents had already been briefed on the mission days ago, but the acceleration of timetable required some explanation.

"We have a co-conspirator heading toward the target area," Trevor Godwin said. "So, we've moved up the mission to entrap him along with the others."

"Who is he and is he armed?" asked the lead FBI Agent, Gary

Pulaski.

"Scott Bennett, a nephew of Hernandez." Godwin left out the political connection. "Bennett is not considered armed or dangerous. Remember, our primary target is a church so resistance should be minimal. However, during our last raid, we did encounter some pretty irate OGs, so we need your team for security."

"That shouldn't be an issue," Pulaski said. His black tactical garb, flak jacket and assault rifle offered visible assurance.

"The only change in the op is to wait on Bennett to determine his location," Godwin continued. "If his destination is the church, it remains primary. If he diverts to the property, that becomes primary. Once again, taking Hernandez into custody is the priority, followed by securing the generator, computers, and scientists at the property."

"Is this generator hazardous?" an ATF agent asked.

"We don't believe so," Godwin replied. "However, just in case, two DOE technicians will be traveling with me for deactivation. Any other questions?"

"What's Bennett's ETA?"

"At his current rate, he should arrive around noon. We plan on departing at 11:00. Each vehicle is equipped with a standard geolocator to track Bennett's status. The other co-conspirators are off grid." Godwin replied.

"What's the tactical channel?" an agent asked.

"Channel 4," replied Pulaski.

"Anything else?" Godwin asked.

"No, we're good to go," Pulaski answered for the group as they started to inspect their weapons.

FIFTY-SEVEN

Aux Baie, MI – 9:30 am

Once he reached the beach, Jack put his face to the wind to fully absorb the sensual assault of gusting wind and crashing waves. He could feel his excitement grow as he went through his prelaunch routine: pump up the 9-meter kite, attach the control lines, don his full wetsuit including booties and gloves, attach his harness. Even though the air and water were both in the low 50s, Jack decided to pass on his hood, preferring to keep his ears unfettered.

After checking all his gear, Jack considered his self-launch options. The small strip of beach was hardly wide enough to accommodate the wingspan of his 9-meter kite. The adjacent steep bluff prevented the use of a self-launch/landing line. The shore break prohibited a drift launch. That left two sketchy alternatives; walk out into the water until the lines became taut and pulled the kite into a powered-up position or try a hot launch from the beach. Jack could tell there was a deep drop-off from the shore which would make a water launch extremely difficult. That left the hot launch as the lesser of two evils.

In a normal launch, the kite is at the edge of the so-called wind window, where the kite is at equilibrium between stalling out or lofting. The control bar and lines can then be used to finesse the kite up into the air. With a hot launch, the kite is dead center in the wind window, creating tremendous force. Occasionally, kiters become human slingshots or are unceremoniously dragged across the beach during this maneuver, risking severe injury.

Jack approached his fully inflated kite which had its leading-edge to the wind to keep it depowered. Jack carefully swiveled the kite about 45 degrees, enough to have the backside start to fill with the wind, but not too much where the kite would power-up and tumble down the beach. As a precaution, Jack scooped up a couple handfuls of sand and placed it on the kite canopy to keep it earthbound. He then ran back up the beach to his control bar, attached his safety leash, attached the chicken loop, and inserted the donkey dick. He was ready.

Jack slowly stepped backwards to bring equal tension on the control lines, which caused the kite to complete its swivel into the wind and...WHAM! The kite caught the full force of the wind, shedding the sand from its canopy and pulling hard on Jack's harness as it remained in an upside-down position, leading-edge down. Jack dug in with his heels and leaned back hard to counter the force. He was fully committed now. Jack pulled on one of the outside steering lines and brought the leading edge of the kite up so it would face the water and...

The force of the hot launch caught Jack by surprise. It took all his strength and leverage to offset the power of the kite, dragging his heels through the sand as the kite raced upwards. He quickly ran out of beach and had to slide across the water until the kite finally came to a neutral 12 o'clock position. "Holy crap!" Jack waded back to the shore to retrieve his kiteboard, his heart beating fast with the adrenalin rush. In the shallows, he slipped his feet into the board straps, dropped the kite a bit into the wind window, and gracefully came up on plane. Jack used the first breaking wave as a launch for an epic jump. A smile crossed Jack's face. He was back in his element. All his worries—the HHS raid, his daughter's well-being, Jenny's sudden reticence—faded into the background as he became one with the wind and water. One last conscious thought crossed his mind: if that was the launch, how the hell am I going to land this thing?

Despite her morning nausea, Jenny forced herself to finish breakfast. She was eating for two, she reminded herself. The whole experience was slightly overwhelming. She had been convinced she was infertile, but the pregnancy test and her body told her otherwise. Jenny felt unbridled joy and elation, but a nagging fear was just under the surface. I'm 42. What if I miscarry? Jenny had no choice but to turn her life, and the emerging life in her womb, over to the care of God. It was too much for her to handle alone. She had Kristen as a confidant but had decided not to tell Jack until she was sure the pregnancy was viable. Still, Jenny could hardly contain her gratitude for being given a second chance. Thank you, Lord!

After cleaning the dishes and completing her morning ablutions, Jenny undressed and looked at herself in the mirror. She pivoted to view herself sideways and saw the beginnings of a baby bump. Her breasts were tender and definitely larger. Well I'll be, never had that problem before, Jenny chuckled. She was at a loss as to why Jack hadn't seen the changes yet—men! She finished her self-examination and dressed in her work jeans and a hoodie sweatshirt. In the hallway closet she retrieved her trusty down vest and headed to the door.

"Come on Toby, back to work," she said as Toby roused and ran out the open door with Jenny following behind.

It was a beautiful, high energy day with the sun peeking in and out of fast moving clouds. The sound of the surf added to the sensual delight. Jenny soaked it all in, but soon her mind turned to her dilemma—the summer growing season was over. She would have to depend on the greenhouses to meet the increasing demand of the church and community. But the output of her greenhouses would be subpar during the cold and dark of winter. She was hoping that the new power generator was the answer. Before venturing to the greenhouses, Jenny decided to check on the garage laboratory to see if Karl was up and about. Sure enough, he was in the corner tinkering with the generator.

"Hey Karl, how's my favorite engineer today?"

"Oh, not too bad. If I could only tweak this compressor, I'd be better off." Karl put down his tools and gave Jenny a hug. "You look radiant today," he commented as he bent down to give Toby a scratch underneath his collar.

"Well, thank you Karl. It's such a beautiful day." Jenny wondered if he knew her secret. No, she concluded. Kristen wouldn't tell. "So, do ya think we have a chance to use this for the greenhouses this winter?"

"No doubt in my mind," Karl replied. "We should have enough power before the snow flies. Johnny says you'd like to add some more grow lights too. That shouldn't be a problem. We'll have plenty of power."

"What about uptime?" Jenny asked. "Can you keep it running?"

"Well, we don't have much of a track record, but I think with a little babysitting we should be able to keep her humming." Karl gave the prototype a loving pat. "We're almost done with the second prototype so we can keep one on hot standby if need be. We're talking mass production here!"

"Have you thought about going public yet?" Jenny asked. "I've got some environmentalist friends over in Marquette who would flip out over this. I also want to encourage greenhouse farming in Aux Baie—we need to expand our food supply."

"You know, we were just talking about putting this in the public domain," Karl said. "Perhaps you could help."

"I'd love to. Just let me know." She gave him another hug and continued her stroll toward the greenhouses. As an afterthought, she turned and yelled, "Don't work too hard!"

"Hardly working!" Karl shouted back as he watched her leave with Toby at her heels.

As Jenny approached the first greenhouse, she could hear the cheerful laughter of her church ladies as they worked. She smiled. Both Donna and Carol greeted her with a "Hey Jen!" when she entered. They were harvesting some of the lettuce today and Jenny took time to help. They worked together as a group so they could converse and, on occasion, sing. But before long, Jenny was feeling a bit nauseous. She excused herself and started for the door.

"Are you going to the meal today?" Carol asked.

"Yes, I was planning to."

"You can carpool with us."

"Great, I'll meet you back here around 11:30," Jenny said. Gas was becoming a rare commodity, so everybody was carpooling. She figured she could get a ride back with Tim and Kristen if necessary.

Once outside, Jenny felt better and decided to head toward the lake to look for Jack. She followed the old familiar path to her favorite overlook with the osprey nest and clinging birch trees. As she wound her way through the forest, the whispering pines gave way to the noise of crashing surf. When she finally crested the high bluff, the strong wind made her long black hair stream out behind her. Jenny looked out toward the glistening lake and saw Jack's red kite darting up and down through the air. Below the kite, Jack was carving a wake with his board, white water flashing in the sun. Every now and then, he would line up a wave and jump in the air, letting the kite give him wings. He's so strong and graceful, Jenny thought. She sat down to watch, Toby by her side. Soon, Jenny was mesmerized by the sensory overload of the wind, waves, and clouds that were racing by the sun. Gazing at Jack, she realized she needed to tell him about the pregnancy. It was time. He needed to know. She prayed that he would be as joyful as she was.

FIFTY-EIGHT

On the Road to Aux Baie, MI – 10:00 am

There was no traffic and Scott made good time traversing the western expanse of the Upper Peninsula. Soon, he turned off U.S. 2 and was heading north again on 141. Scott was lost in thought when he came over a rise in the road. "Damn," he yelled as he saw a dirt bike in his immediate path. Nimbly braking and swerving the Porsche to avoid a collision, Scott gave the motorcyclist a prolonged dirty look. To his surprise, the guy gave him the stink eye back. Flushed with anger, Scott almost stopped the car to turn around and confront the idiot. Then, in a flash of self-awareness, he laughed at himself—road rage in the middle of nowhere!

After he regained his composure, Scott accelerated back to cruising speed and passed a sign advertising a roadside park in one mile. As he approached the park, Scott saw an object on the side of the road. He quickly braked and downshifted, realizing it was a motorcyclist down on the road's shoulder, a female judging by the long hair. The Porsche gears moaned as he stopped one-hundred feet beyond the sprawled victim. Reflexively, he grabbed his smartphone, got out of the car, and ran toward the woman. As he approached, he didn't see any signs of blood and then, in the distance he saw a bright reflection of a light or mirror. Oh no, is that a signal? Scott wondered as he turned and started to run back to his car...

"Stop! Drop the PIV!" A young man in camo was next to his car holding a 12-gauge, pump shotgun aimed directly at Scott's face.

Scott obediently bent down and dropped his smartphone

on the shoulder of the road and raised his hands. He took a chance. "I already pushed the panic button," he lied.

"Don't think so," another young man came out of the brush by the road. He waved what looked like another PIV in his hand. "You didn't do shit, Mr. Scott Bennett, Gold elite."

Caught in his lie, Scott turned red. Obviously, these were not your ordinary crooks. The guy must have a universal receiver or something that could not only detect outgoing signals but also read unencrypted data from his PIV. Not good.

"Nice car, Mr. Gold." The woman victim had miraculously recovered and was now sizing up Scott. Even with her dingy camo outfit, there was no disguising her beauty; trim body, long brunette hair and twinkling green eyes. Scott remained silent, not sure how to play this.

"I know what you're thinking," the techie with the receiver said. "In another minute or two your travel plan will trigger a dead man alert. I don't think so. If I recall, the programming for a dead man alert is a full 15 minutes when stopped at a rest area. Takes time to take a dump!" he laughed. "So, you have about 10 minutes to tell us who you are, what the hell you're doing up here, and what did you bring for us in your hot little sports car?"

Yes, these guys were sophisticated, Scott thought, but they had their limits. They couldn't hit the Cloud to know his full background. He decided to play it straight. "I'm Scott Bennett, Congressman Steve Bennett's son. I'm on my way to Aux Baie to visit my Aunt, Jenny Bennett."

"Can you prove that?" the woman asked.

"Yes, but I need my PIV."

"Sure," she reached down, grabbed the smartphone, and handed it over to Scott. "Don't be stupid."

Scott scanned his fingerprint on the embedded reader and then entered his PIN to unlock the bio and Cloud access. He quickly called up his personnel profile and handed it back to the young woman.

She quickly scrolled through the profile and checked out a

few other screens including his travel log. She gave a nod to Mr. Shotgun who lowered the weapon from Scott's face. Meanwhile, Mr. Stink Eye came up the road, the loud exhaust of his dirt bike heralding his arrival.

"What do we have here?" he asked. "Richie Rich lost in the wilderness?" He got off his motorcycle and approached the group, a semiautomatic in hand.

"Says he's Congressman Bennett's son on his way to see his Aunt in Aux Baie. His PIV profile checks out," the woman replied. "We're wasting time here." She turned and looked Scott straight in the eyes. "I'm from the Aux Baie area, don't know a Jenny Bennett." Mr. Shotgun raised his weapon again.

Scott was taken aback for a moment, then recovered. "Her maiden name is Hernandez – Jenny Hernandez Bennett." He looked at the young woman expectantly.

"Okay, tell me something about Jenny Hernandez that only a nephew would know," she demanded.

"Well," Scott paused. "She's part Chippewa, her former husband, my Uncle Sean, committed suicide a couple years back, she loves yoga and is a greenhouse…"

"Stop," the woman interrupted. "Why are you visiting her?"

Scott realized that the group was becoming agitated as the minutes dragged on. The techie was transfixed on his universal receiver. Mr. Stink Eye was getting back on his dirt bike, maybe to act as a scout? Once again, Scott stuck to the truth. "She and her co-op friends are being monitored and are in danger."

The woman walked over to Mr. Shotgun and whispered something in his ear. He nodded. "Okay, I'm coming with you," she said to Scott. "We need to leave now. If what you say is true, you're probably being monitored, and this unplanned stop will be noticed." She trotted over to her dirt bike still lying in the margin, picked up a backpack next to it, and returned to Scott.

"Let's go, now," she ordered and started to trot toward the Porsche. Scott obediently followed.

"Be careful, Sally," Mr. Shotgun yelled, revealing her name. "His car has *Stop Me* written all over it and the Feds are becoming thick as flies."

"Got it, CJ," she replied. Sally pulled a small revolver out of the backpack, opened the passenger door, and sank into the low-slung seat of the sports car. Scott got in and turned to appraise Sally in close quarters. "Go," she ordered, wagging the revolver now resting in her lap.

Scott started the engine and expertly accelerated through the gears. In his rearview mirror, he could see that the rebel bushwhackers had already disappeared. The surrounding forest had regained its serenity as the telltale whine of a fully powered Porsche receded into the distance.

Washington D.C. – 10:05 am
The Bureau Surveillance Room
Tommy switched over to geospatial mapping to check Bennett's progress. It looked like he was stopped somewhere on U.S. 141. A soft chime indicated Bennett was approaching dead man limits for nonmovement. Tommy zoomed in on the map and saw a rest area icon. The surrounding area was free from any PIV or electronic footprints—just Bennett. Probably taking a crap, Tommy concluded. Another five minutes and a dead man alarm would go off and Tommy would have to alert Reggie, which he really didn't want to do. Thankfully, Bennett's icon started moving again, heading north on 141.

On the Road to Aux Baie, MI – 10:10 am
"So, are you part of the Michigan Militia, the Resistance?" Scott tried to break the awkward silence.

"Ya think?" came the snide reply. "Are you a Fed, or just a Gold suck-up?"

This wasn't going well, Scott thought. Time for more honesty. "Listen, if you know who my father is, you know we're some of the good guys, we oppose the federal takeover." He downshifted as he navigated a sharp curve.

"Oh, I see, part of the loyal opposition," Sally said with a smirk. "Must be tough with unlimited credits, your own Gold healthcare plan, your own Gold pension plan, and having to drive around in an old Porsche. Gosh, maybe we can help you before you choke on your silver, or should I say Gold, spoon." She started playing around with Scott's smartphone, pulling up various screens and navigating through all the apps.

"Hey, could you leave that alone! It's always transmitting; you press the wrong button it might trigger an alert."

"Oh, poor illiterate me," she mocked him "I don't know what to do with a Gold PivPal – oh, with Star." She took off the rubber boot and looked at the back of the unit. "A Mach 5. Hmm, all the regular features plus 3-factor verification, intuitive GPS, and multitier syndication. Let's see, I wouldn't want to pop off the backplate and trigger the panic button."

"Okay, I get it. You know what you're doing, and I am just the spoiled, rich kid from downstate who came up here for vacation. Oh, and maybe tell my Aunt that she's about to be busted by the Feds".

"All right. Tell me all about that," Sally turned to face Scott. "We have plenty of time before Aux Baie."

"Okay," Scott said. "First of all, whatever you think, there is a rearguard in the government trying to resist the Feds. My father is in the middle of it, but it's a dangerous game we're playing. The amount of surveillance going on is shocking. Our only saving grace is there's too much data for them to process. But, if they want to, they can narrow their focus and do deep data mining on select targets, like my dad."

"How did Jenny get caught up in this?"

"Apparently, she was already on a watch list as a suspected rebel sympathizer, helping out OGs through her church." Scott replied. "I might have amped the situation by sending some associates up here to conduct some unauthorized research and development. Anyway, it looks like the Feds connected the dots between Jenny, my associates, myself and my dad." Scott braked the Porsche and downshifted as the came through a small town in the middle of nowhere. A tiny store front had Pasties advertised and underneath that a sign; *For Sale – Make Offer*.

"So, who are these associates and what are they researching?"

"It might be best for both of us if we just let that go," Scott replied as they exited the town, passing a road sign announcing that they were entering Baraga County.

"Let me guess, could it be Tim Kelly and Karl Schultz?" Sally asked.

"Damn, how much more do you know?"

"I know enough."

"Okay, what's your story?" Scott tried to turn the tables.

"My turn?" Sally teased. "All right. I'm Sally Larson, 24. Used to work with the DNR and had my own Gold PIV. Now, I'm a so-called OG. Unlike you, I decided to fight totalitarianism. We're not part of Jenny's co-op, but we've got her back. There are a lot of people up here who don't give a damn for the Feds, or Gold elites for that matter."

Scott was formulating his retort when he saw a vehicle approaching in the distance. Sally followed his gaze down the road.

"It's a cop," she said.

"Damn, get rid of the gun," Scott yelled as he rapidly braked the Porsche down to 55 mph. Sally didn't move.

"Throw it out the window, now!" Scott implored.

"It's too late," Sally said as they passed the sheriff's car.

Scott kept his foot off the brake and stayed at a steady 55 mph as he looked in his rearview mirror. Sure enough, the cop was turning around, and had hit the flashers on the light bar. Crap!

"Put the gun under the seat. Let me handle this," Scott said as he pulled over to the shoulder and stopped. The sheriff's car parked about fifty feet behind him. It took a while for the officer to get out of his vehicle and approach the Porsche. Scott rolled down the window.

"Officer." Scott greeted the sheriff, his heart pounding.

"Mr. Bennett," he replied.

"Do you need my PIV or prints?"

"No, that won't be necessary. I know who you are." The sheriff leaned down and looked in Scott's window. "Who's the young lady?"

"Just an OG. She had a motorcycle accident a ways back and I'm giving her a lift to town."

"I see. She doesn't look hurt. Ma'am, can I see your ID?" the sheriff asked.

Sally fumbled in her multi-pocketed fatigues, pulled out a State of Michigan ID, and handed it over Scott to the officer's outreached hand. Even though off-gridders weren't required to have PIVs, states still required some form of identification for undocumented citizens.

The officer peered at the card and then bent down to look in the open window at Sally. "Ma'am, could you please exit the car."

"I don't think so."

Damn, what is she doing? Scott wondered.

"Get out of the car, I am not going to ask again," the sheriff ordered.

"Why?" Sally asked.

"Why? So, I can give my favorite niece a hug, that's why!"

Sally jumped out of the car and ran around to jump in the sheriff's arms. "Uncle Jim!"

He gave her a big bear hug and then turned back to Scott. "She didn't kidnap you or something, did she?"

"Well, uh, not exactly," Scott said.

"I see," Sheriff Larson said with a chuckle. "Listen, Mr. Bennett. You probably already know this, but there's an active track on you. What's a bit strange is that I just received a Do Not Detain order on you this morning. Looks like they want to follow you somewhere or to someone. What's your business up here?"

"He's Jenny Hernandez's nephew." Sally blurted out. "And he works with Tim Kelly and Karl Schultz. Sorry." Sally shot an apologetic look at Scott.

"Is that true?" Sheriff Larson asked.

"Yes sir." Scott paused a second, weighting the merits of full disclosure. "Actually, I'm here to warn them. My Aunt Jenny is a target of the Feds as are my associates, Tim and Karl. They came up to Jenny's to finish work on an invention, a new power generator that the Feds also have in their sights. It looks like they connected the dots all the way back to me and my father, Congressman Bennett."

Sheriff Larson frowned, working his chin with his hand. "I don't like this; I don't like this at all. Sounds like a trap to me." Larson paused. "I'm sure they know I've stopped you, so we have to act quickly. Here's what we're going to do. As Sheriff of Baraga Country, I am putting you under protective custody..."

"You're arresting me?" Scott interrupted.

"No, no, no. Just listen to me. You're coming back to my office with me. You'll be safe there until we figure out what's going on with Jenny and your associates. My guess is that they plan to nab you and your friends in Aux Baie. Not sure about this invention of yours. Is it important?"

"Yes, it could fundamentally change how energy is produced."

"Really?" Larson arched his eyebrows. "Okay. Sally, I want you to drive Mr. Bennett's car, with his PIV, to the outskirts of town and ditch it. You drive a stick, right?"

"Yep, dad taught me before I had a license," Sally said.

"Okay. Next, I want you to contact your Resistance cell and y'all meet me at my office. Bring your weapons. If my hunch is right, the shit's about to hit the fan. Can you do that?"

"Sure, Uncle Jim."

"Good, now we've got to move before they target us."

Washington D.C. – 10:15 am
The Bureau Surveillance Room

Tommy couldn't believe his eyes. Bennett's icon had stopped in the middle of nowhere and was co-located with a law enforcement icon. Could his plan be working? He double-clicked on the LE icon to retrieve the header: *Squad 1, Sheriff James Larson*. Yes! But what is Larson going to do? Tommy wondered. For that matter, what was he himself going to do? This data would get to Reggie eventually. They might move on Bennett now. Tommy just stared at his monitor trying to divine what was going on and figure out his next steps. He accessed the sheriff's data net and pulled-up Baraga County's CAD feed. It showed Bennett was pulled over for speeding. Tommy frantically alternated between his monitor and the dispatch feed waiting for a change in status.

Finally, almost simultaneously, Bennett's Porsche separated from the sheriff's car and the dispatch feed updated. Bennett had received a warning for speeding. Is that it? Tommy wondered. Maybe not—what would I do if I were a friendly sheriff?

Baraga County – 10:20 am
With Scott sitting in the passenger seat, Sheriff Larson reached over and keyed the radio mic. "Brenda?"

"Good morning Sheriff," the central dispatcher replied. "What can I do for you?"

"Have we heard back from Houghton and Iron County on tickets for our pancake breakfast?" Larson hoped that Brenda remembered the code words.

There was a slight pause before Brenda responded. "No, no we haven't."

"Could you please do me a favor and reach out to Sheriff LaFontaine and Sheriff Griggs? We need to lock in attendance ASAP. Over."

"Yes sir, shall do."

Larson could tell by the tension in Brenda's voice that she had gotten the message. Now all he could do is hope all worked out as planned.

Washington D.C. – 10:25 am
The Bureau Surveillance Room

"Sutton, what the hell is going on with Bennett!" Reggie screamed through the intercom.

"I was just about to call you. He was pulled over by a sheriff and..."

"Tell me something I don't already know!" Reggie interrupted. "This could have screwed-up everything! Who was the officer?"

"James Larson, Sheriff of Baraga County."

"Those damn sheriffs! Remind me to get this guy fired."

"Sir, I believe sheriffs are elected, not appointed," Tommy said.

"Well, that's stupid! Listen Sutton, if you can't keep me up to date, I'll find someone who will, and you'll be in front of a judge this afternoon. Got it?"

"Yes sir."

FIFTY-NINE

The fellowship hall was full of school-aged children, but also a sprinkling of adults who were curious about the results of the Better Government project the students had been immersed in for weeks. In the back stood Pastor and Mary DeVries as well as Kristen. Despite the friendly church setting, Tim was surprised at how nervous he felt as he walked to the front of the room by the whiteboards. He cleared his throat and adjusted his glasses.

"Okay now, let's get started," he clapped his hands to quiet the audience. "For those of you who are visiting, the last several weeks our students have concentrated on what can be done to improve our government. This culminated in a brainstorming session where the students narrowed down dozens of ideas into a short list of recommendations, which are listed on the boards behind me." Tim waved his hand toward the two whiteboards. "Now, I'm tired of doing all the talking, so we are going to have students summarize the main points for me. Of course, I might make a comment or two." That got the students laughing. Tim gave a shrug and smiled—they were on to him.

"Okay, let's start at the top. Who wants to explain Remember E Pluribus Unum?" A bunch of hands went up. "Lauren, why don't you take this one," Tim pointed to one of the middle school girls.

"E Pluribus Unum means *out of many, one*," Lauren began. "It's our country's motto 'cause we had thirteen colonies that came together to be the United States." Lauren paused to check her notes.

"Excellent Lauren. And what did we mean by remember?" Tim prompted.

"Well, we felt that people have forgotten we're all Americans. Now we have all these groups that hate each other." Lauren glanced at her notes again. "You said that diversity is great, but we need a common denominator—kind of like math." Lauren let out a nervous giggle as she finished and sat down.

"That's right Lauren, we need a common morality," Tim said. "Great job!"

Lake Superior Near Shore Waters

Johnny-B stretched over the rail with the gaffe hook and snagged the buoy and pulled it in to access the anchor chain. He attached the chain to the net lifter and engaged the motor. The chain slowly wound its way up until the lead anchor of the gill net was on board. Johnny attached the lead line and float line in the grooves of the net lifter and started the lifting process. The captain, George Russell, kept his 30-foot fishing boat parallel to the net line, allowing a bit of slack in the net to reduce the strain on the lifter. With the strong southerly winds, it was a chore to keep the boat straight. Every now and then, a wave would break over the gunwale splashing Johnny and George's son, Will.

The nets had been set the night before to take advantage of the Whitefish nocturnal activity. Now came the payoff. As the net came over the outboard roller, Johnny and Will jumped into action, removing the fish from the meshes and sorting them by size and species. Any immature fish were thrown back overboard to further grow. As usual, the catch was mostly Whitefish with a stray Lake Trout and Cisco here and there. It was a good catch. They would take their haul back to port, put some on ice for local use, and smoke the rest. It would keep high-quality protein on the plates of the community for at least a week. In exchange, the crew would barter with the church co-op for goods and services. Following the church's lead, they would apportion ten percent for the poor or infirm. Several members of the Tribe would help untangle and repair the nets for the next outing.

"Look at that!" Will pointed toward the horizon. "What is it?"

Johnny threw a nice two pound fish in the box and looked up to follow Will's gesture. Toward shore, he saw a red kite darting up and down in the wind like a massive warning flag. Johnny could make out the kiteboarder below the colorful airfoil, carving a frothing wake. "That's got to be Jack Conrad!" Johnny said. "Hey George!" Johnny yelled over the noise of the engines and pointed out over the water. "Ever see that?"

"Crazy white man!" George said. "It must be 25 knots out there!" All three of the crew stood transfixed watching Jack kite toward them.

"Whoa!" Will yelled as Jack took a large jump, hanging in the air like he was flying.

"Look!" George shouted. "There's an eagle following him!" Sure enough, hovering over Jack's kite was a bald eagle effortlessly keeping pace, gliding into the wind. George and Will were mesmerized by the sight. Johnny knew the eagle was a sacred symbol for the Tribe, a prayer carrier often invoked for healing. They watched in reverence as Jack and the eagle retreated into the distance.

"Guys," Johnny interrupted their trance, "we're falling behind!"

George and Will took one last look and then refocused on their duties. Johnny and Will picked up their pace before the net and fish were hopelessly tangled. Soon the catch and tackle were safely put away in boxes. George was about to move on to the next net setting when he saw another boat by the shore. "Johnny, who's that?" George pointed in the direction of the boat.

Johnny got the binoculars out of the cabin and focused on the other vessel. "It's Fish and Wildlife. They've got their bow to the seas."

"What the hell are they doing out here in this rough weather? They know we have rights to these waters." George narrowed his eyes. Will joined his father to gaze at the distant boat.

"I don't think they're here for us," Johnny said. "They're anchored off Jenny's property. Something's not right. How about we hightail it back to the harbor? We can pull the other net later or tomorrow."

"You want me to radio in?" George asked.

"No, let's keep radio silence."

"All right boys. Batten down the hatches, it's going to be a rough ride."

Within minutes, the *Peggy Sue* was racing toward shore, slamming into 6-foot waves. They took shelter behind the cabin as spray cascaded over the boat. It was nasty, but they had seen worse.

Marquette, MI – 11:00 am

The SWAT team gathered around the command vehicle in the Health and Human Services parking lot. Trevor Godwin used his tablet to pull up a map of the area. "All right, Bennett just entered Baraga County on 141. There was a screw up and he was stopped by the county sheriff who gave him a speeding warning. But he's back on his way." Godwin used a stylus to highlight where Bennett's icon was on the map. "ETA around 12 noon. We are going to intercept 141 here, near Covington, but wait for Bennett to pass. We'll give him a 10-minute lead and then trail. We want to give him a clear path to his destination. Understand?"

"Yes sir," the team responded in unison.

"All right then, let's saddle up!"

Aux Baie, MI – 11:15 am

"Okay, who wants to explain Preach the Preamble?" More hands flew up. "Mark, give it a shot."

"We hold these truths to be self-evident that all men are

created equal, that they are endowed by their Creator with certain unalienable Rights, that among these are Life, Liberty, and the pursuit of Happiness," Mark said.

"That's right. It comes from our Declaration of Independence. So, what were our Founding Fathers trying to tell us?" Tim asked.

"Well, um, we have a creator, you know, that's God. And all life is special, even babies who haven't been born yet. Liberty means the government shouldn't spy on us and tell us what to do—they're not our parents you know," Mark said, eliciting a chuckle from the audience.

"What about pursuit of happiness?" Tim prompted. "What makes you happy?"

"I like to fish and hunt and just have fun," Mark said. "But we also talked about keeping our water and earth clean and helping our neighbors, just like Pastor tells us."

"Very good Mark. And what did we say about all men are created equal? Does that mean everybody is the same?" Tim asked.

"No, of course not. We're all different. Like, I'm a guy and Lauren's a girl. Some people are stronger or smarter or nicer. Like, I'm a better shot than Cody, but he's smarter. And Lauren is nicer than both of us and she can draw. I can't draw, my mom says it's not in my nature." The laughs from the audience brought Mark up short. "What I mean to say is that God loves us all the same and the government should treat us all the same."

"Well said, Mark."

***

For over an hour, Jack's body had been on autopilot—reacting to the challenging conditions of Lake Superior without conscious thought. An upcoming wave told his knees to bend to absorb the shock. Sensing a wind gust, his arms instinctively extended to depower the kite, while his body leaned back to counterweight the force. Jack's eyes deciphered the seemingly random undulations of wave and trough to anticipate a crest, angling his board upwind to launch off the emerging peak as his arms simultaneously sent the kite overhead to create loft. Now airborne, an internal gyroscope sensed his height, speed, and direction to keep the kite at the perfect angle of attack to stick the landing. He was in The Zone...

It was some time before Jack realized an eagle was trailing him. Concurrently, he was jolted by a premonition; something bad was about to happen. And it wasn't about him or his kiteboarding. He thought about Jenny. Jack angled the kite toward land and went to full speed, skipping over the swells as he rapidly approached the shore.

***

Trevor Godwin stepped out of his Suburban and gave a hand signal for the other drivers of his convoy to collect. Once they circled Godwin, he gave final instructions. "Bennett's 10 minutes down the road and 30 minutes outside Aux Baie. Squad 5 position yourselves off 550 right at the entrance to Hernandez's property, right here," Godwin used a stylus to tap the county map on his tablet. "The rest of you follow me. We will converge on the church to search for our primary. If she's not there, we will leave Squad 4 and the remaining units will divert to the property. I'll have eyes on Bennett, and, with any luck, we will roll him up at the primary or secondary. Channel 4 in case of an emergency, otherwise, comms-out. Questions?"

The four drivers, fully clad in tactical gear, remained mum.

"Good, let's go."

***

Sally pulled the Porsche into a short two-track that dead-ended at the lake. It was an old party beach she had frequented as a teenager. The car would be invisible from the road. As instructed, she left the PIV in its cradle. She walked back to the road, which was deserted. With no chance of hitchhiking, Sally jogged to Johnny-B's cabin, about a quarter mile down the road. She rushed up Johnny's porch, knocked on the door, and barged into his entryway. Johnny sat on a chair in his small mudroom trying to pull off his clingy fishing gear. He looked up at Sally, "Hello?" he said in shocked response.

"Johnny, we've got a problem!"

"I thought so! What's going on?"

***

"Who wants to explain this next bullet, Follow the Constitution—Stupid." Once again, more hands shot up in the air.

"Terresa, why don't you start," Tim said. "There's a lot here so I might call on several students."

Terresa, a young Native American, stood and addressed the audience. "Well, the Constitution was made to limit the powers of the federal government. The Founding Fathers were afraid the government would grab all the power like they did in Europe. So, they made a list of what the federal government could do, and the rest was left to the states and to the people—which is us!" The young girl smiled and sat down.

"Excellent Terresa. And what were the original, enumerated powers given to the federal government? Michael?"

"Okay, I memorized these," Michael said as he stood up and blushed. "Maintain the army, coin money, collect taxes, hmm... foreign relations, interstate trade. That kind of stuff."

"Very good Michael," Tim said. "These activities are called natural monopolies and are best suited for a central government. As Terresa said, the remaining rights were left to the states and the people via the 9th and 10th Amendments, part of our Bill of Rights. What other rights are irrevocable? Ava, you look eager to answer this one."

"Yes, Mr. Kelly. The Bill of Rights are the first ten Amendments of the Constitution. The key ones are the First Amendment, which is freedom of religion, speech, assembly, and the press. The Second Amendment, which is the right to bear arms. The Fourth Amendment, which is protection against unreasonable searches. You already mentioned the Ninth and Tenth Amendment which give power to the states and the people. The rest of the Amendments, except the Third which is weird, protect people against abuses by the government and judicial system. You know, like guaranteeing a quick trial

314

with a jury."

"Excellent summary, Ava. And what rights are being abused by the federal government or others? Give me examples if you can."

"Well," Ava continued, "they're closing down churches. Also, if you are a conservative, you can get beat up at college just for saying what you think. And they won't allow conservative news anymore, not even on the radio."

"Randy, what about the Second Amendment?" Tim challenged a boy who hadn't raised his hand.

Randy stood, obviously anxious at being called on. "You can still have a rifle or a shotgun, you know. But you gotta register it every year and, you know, pay a big fine. And they can take away the rifle if they don't like you. So, you know, people are hiding their rifles like we're criminals."

"Good job Randy! Who wants to talk about the Fourth Amendment and PIV? Emma?"

"The government is using our smartphones to spy on us. They listen to what we say, they look at our emails, they know where we are. The Founding Fathers didn't have smartphones, but if they did, they wouldn't let you spy with them. They say you don't have to have a PIV, but if you don't, you can't get a job, you can't vote, and you can't drive. It stinks!" Emma grimaced. "But I wish I could still have one for Facebook!" Several people in the audience laughed.

***

As Sheriff Larson entered his offices, he saw that Brenda had read his mind. All five of his deputies were waiting in the large anteroom.

"All, this is Scott Bennett, Congressman Bennett's son." The deputies nodded. "Scott is under our protective custody. I have reason to believe that federal agents intend on raiding Aux Baie today with the probable targets being Mr. Bennett, Jenny Hernandez, the church and maybe Jenny's camp. Without getting into detail, there may be an experimental power generator at Jenny's place, and it appears the Feds want to get their hands on it. Anyway, this is our county, our jurisdiction. Nobody is coming in here and arresting our citizens or taking their property without our agreement. Unless it is a clear federal violation under the Constitution, these federal agents have no standing here. Does everybody understand?"

Everyone nodded.

"Good. Brenda, were you able to reach Sheriffs LaFontaine and Griggs?"

"Yes sir. They said they would get right back to us."

"Okay. I don't know what we might be up against, so I'm taking no chances. I've also put out a call for temporary deputies. So, don't be surprised if some of the local Resistance shows up. Brenda, start a full scan of all public safety bands and command channels. Let me know if we have any unusual chatter out there. The rest of you get into tactical gear." Larson looked at his watch. "I'm showing 1130. I want to be ready to roll at 1200."

***

Tim looked up and saw that Jenny and some of the co-op gardeners had sneaked in the back of the fellowship hall. He also saw the clock—it was 11:45. Time to wrap things up before the midday meal. The smell of soup permeated the room, and they were monopolizing the dining tables. "All right. How about Balance the Budget—Stupid? Lisa, we haven't heard from you yet."

"This is really simple," Lisa said. "You can't spend more than you make. Just like a family, the government's gotta balance its budget or even save some money for tough times. If you don't, you're going to pass down debt to your children. Our government is passing down over $30 trillion in debt to its children. That's stupid and not very nice."

"Nice job, Lisa. Next on the list is No Government Elites. What did we mean about that? Samuel?"

"That means government workers should get the same benefits as regular people. That includes the same healthcare, job security and retirement benefits as regular people."

Samuel referred to his notes. "You said 'politicians should be forced to drink their own bath water.' Which is kind of gross."

"Uh, thanks for the excellent note-taking Samuel," Tim said with a chuckle. "Okay, just one more on the list. What did we mean by Tax Reform for Dummies? Tonya, I'm sure you know this one."

Tonya stood up with a big smile. "Well, all members of Congress should be given their tax documents, pencil, paper and a calculator. They should then be locked in a room by themselves with no lawyers or accountants. They will get one day to complete their tax forms. If they can't complete them, or if there are any errors, then they can never run for office again. This will guarantee immediate tax reform!" Everybody in the fellowship hall broke out in laughter and started to clap.

As the clapping died down, Pastor DeVries joined Tim at the head of the class. "I just want to congratulate all of you on an excellent presentation," DeVries said. "Tim, you have lit a fire in these students! Thank you. I also want to remind everybody here that, despite tough times, we have received so many gifts from God. Gifts of life, our freedom, work and recreation, our community, and our faith. But remember, to keep our gifts, we must give them away and share them with others."

Tim looked at the attendees and wondered how many fully understood the Pastor's parting words—the paradox of having to give it away to keep it.

SIXTY

The Resistance members started to show up in dribs and drabs at the Sheriff's Office on the outskirts of town. Some dressed in camo, others in hunting gear, blue jeans, and Carhartt jackets. They carried their scoped hunting rifles and shotguns comfortably, as if they were appendages of their bodies. Many were from the Tribe, others ordinary citizens: Ben and Jimmy Aishkebay, George and Will Russell, Bryce Brogan, Cal Cutler, Sally Larson and two other women, Johnny-B with his illegal assault rifle, and other residents. The Sheriff's staff freely mingled with the citizens, renewing old acquaintances.

"I think this is it," Johnny-B told Sheriff Larson. "There might be a few stragglers. I think Jack Conrad is out on the water."

"Okay, listen up," Larson got everybody's attention. "There is a high probability that Aux Baie will be raided by the Feds today. Don't know the timing, but it could be imminent. We have reason to believe they may be timing their raid to coincide with the arrival of Scott Bennett," the Sheriff nodded in Scott's direction. "He's the nephew of Jenny Hernandez and an associate of Tim Kelly and Karl Schultz. Anyway, we believe the targets may be the church and Jenny's camp. I would like to deputize you to protect our citizens." The Sheriff paused, waiting for any pushback. "If you agree, please step forward and line up in front of me."

The ragtag army of 15 lined up as ordered.

"Okay, raise your right hand and repeat after me." Sheriff

Larson administered the oath to them all and then instructed everyone to pick up their badges from the table.

Several of the hunters couldn't hide their disdain as they picked up their dayglow green vests with Sheriff's Dept. stenciled on them. "You might as well write *shoot me* on them," one of the hunters said as he donned the vest.

Washington, D.C.

Tommy watched the mission unfold on his multiple monitors. As expected, Bennett had driven to Aux Baie and was now stopped just outside the small downtown. He had not gone to the church or to Hernandez's property as expected. Tommy homed in on the satellite screen where Bennett's icon had stopped. It looked like a short two-track or beach park. Maybe taking a break? But why there? Bennett's PIV had been quiet for a while, so he wasn't communicating with anyone. Strange...

Tommy zoomed out to look at the big picture. The icons for the SWAT Team were moving rapidly toward Aux Baie on 141. They should be there within 10 minutes. Sheriff Larson had sped back to his office where the icon for his squad car remained. This should all be over within an hour, Tommy figured. What a tragedy. He was about to switch screens when he noticed two additional icons on the periphery of Baraga County. He zoomed in on the western icon, which differentiated into three separate icons. A quick click produced identification; *Houghton Country Sheriff Squad Cars 1, 3 and 4*. And they were making tracks! Tommy focused on the southern icon which also differentiated into three icons; *Iron County Sheriff Squads 1, 4 and 5* speeding north following the same route as the SWAT Team. "What the hell is going on?" Tommy asked out loud. The minute he said it, he got it.

Aux Baie, MI – 11:55 am

While his convoy closed on the GPS position of Bennett's PIV, Trevor Godwin made a command decision. He put his arm out the window and gave the halt sign as his Suburban pulled into

319

the two-track. The other Suburbans parked on the shoulder blocking any possible escape. In a matter of seconds, Godwin had boxed in the Porsche and two agents were out and rushing the car, weapons drawn. As the agents lowered their weapons, it became obvious it was a bust. One agent opened the car door and pulled out Bennett's PIV, checking the screen to confirm the ID.

"He's not here," yelled the agent, holding up the PIV as if proof.

"Check the bushes," Godwin yelled back.

Agents from the other vehicles had converged on the spot and they all did a quick search of the immediate area. No sign of Bennett; just some beer bottles and a pair of underwear.

"Okay, let's get to the primary ASAP. Squad 5 head to the property and give me Bennett's damn PIV," Godwin ordered as they rushed back to their vehicles.

***

"Ralph, you stay here with Sally, Scott, and Brenda to hold down the fort," Sheriff Larson said.

Sally walked across the ante room to stand next to Scott as the Sheriff continued.

"Stay comms-out unless there's an emergency. Whatever you do, don't let anybody nab Scott."

"Except me," Sally teasingly whispered to Scott.

"Sheriff," Johnny-B said, "these might help." He threw one of the 2.4 GHz walkie-talkies over to him. "Range is only a couple miles; nobody monitors them."

"How many do you have?" asked the Sheriff.

In response, Johnny emptied his backpack on the table—10 yellow walkie-talkies.

"Great Johnny! Okay, here's the plan. I'll take the main force over to the church. That's where our highest civilian risk is. Lou, Randy and Trent, load your squads and follow me." The deputies nodded in agreement. "Johnny, take a vehicle and two newbies to check out Jenny's camp. Mike, take Squad 3 and a newbie to provide support for Johnny. Are these walkie-talkies on a party line?"

"Yes sir," Johnny replied.

"Okay, each Squad carries one. I want a sitrep every 10 minutes. Newbie deputies, you take orders from my staff. One last thing, no gunfire unless there is a clear and present danger. I don't want to start a shooting war with the Feds. Got it?"

***

The fellowship hall was a flurry of activity as the patrons lined up to be served. Kristen, Tim, and Jenny joined several students to move tables and chairs back in place. Kitchen helpers came out to place pitchers of water on each table along with salt and pepper shakers. Pastor and Mary DeVries placed some homemade centerpieces on each table. The soup, potato leek, smelled delicious.

"What's that?" Tim put his hand up to quiet everybody. A pounding noise was reverberating down the hall from the Sanctuary, followed by an ear-piercing splintering sound from the adjacent kitchen. Before they could react, the outside door of the fellowship hall came smashing inward...

***

As the Sheriff and his convoy drove off toward the nearby church, Johnny-B pulled Deputy Mike Ramsey aside. "Listen Mike, why don't I enter Jenny's property first with my pickup. You follow a couple hundred yards back in case it's an ambush. I'll keep you posted on the walkie-talkie. Okay?"

"Sure Johnny," Mike deferred to the senior veteran who knew Jenny's camp inside out. "You taking your banned assault weapon?" Ramsey asked half-kidding.

"Does a bear shit in the woods?"

***

Jack was still on an adrenalin high as he entered the cabin looking for Jenny. He found a note that said she had gone to church for the midday meal. As he walked over to the garage to look for a vehicle, Karl emerged with some tools.

"Hey Jack, I saw you kiting in the distance. That must be fun."

321

Jack disregarded the pleasantries. "I need to get to the church!"

"Is everything okay?" Karl frowned.

"I really don't know."

***

Jenny sat sobbing on the floor, her hands cuffed behind her back. Kristen and Cindy were moaning beside her. Tim was clenching his jaw, shooting angry daggers from his eyes. Pastor DeVries looked devastated.

"Where is Bryce Brogan?" Godwin demanded.

"He's not here," Tim said with a sneer. "If he was, he would have surrendered."

Jenny tried to recreate the last few minutes; first the deafening noise, then federal agents bursting through the main three doors simultaneously. The assembled diners gasping out of fear, grabbing their children and loved ones to shelter them from certain harm. The agents had corralled them into a shrinking, wailing circle. Jenny had tried to come to their defense, only to be butted in the ribs by a rifle. The physical pain was dwarfed by Jenny's emotional trauma—they had violated her church family. One by one, the Church Council had surrendered as ordered and were separated from their friends and guests.

Now they were determined to find Bryce. Why Bryce? Jenny had a fleeting memory of the Brogan clan gathered at the Christmas Eve church dinner in this very room. Bryce's cousin Kurt, the Colonel from the National Guard, had brought oranges...

Godwin walked around the captives who cowered as he approached. He compared each man to a photo he had on his tablet. Finally, Godwin seemed satisfied that Bryce Brogan was not present. He picked up a megaphone to blast the close quarters. "You must leave the premise now! Go home! If you linger you will be arrested!"

Jenny watched as everybody started filing out the fellowship hall's gaping door like frightened sheep, leaving the

Church Council alone with their captors. But the guests didn't get far, stopping in the church parking lot as a parade of sheriff vehicles sped up the main driveway from both directions to block the SWAT team's SUVs. Fifteen sheriff's deputies exited their vehicles. A few deputies shepherded civilians away from the scene. The remaining deputies trained their firearms on the federal agents standing guard outside the church. Sheriff Larson exited his squad car and approached the agents. He kept his side arm holstered, but his hand was near.

"Under my authority as Sheriff of Baraga Country, you are to cease and desist this action, or we will be forced to arrest you!" Larson shouted.

Trevor Godwin appeared at the door to the fellowship hall. "Sheriff, this is a federal matter! We have a warrant for the arrest of the church leadership for violation of federal HHS laws. You and your deputies are to stand down now!"

Upon hearing this, the sheriff's deputies spread out to find better cover and shooting lanes.

"That's not going to happen!" Larson yelled back. "HHS laws are a state and county matter. You have no authority here. I'm the highest law enforcement authority in this county and I order you to cease and desist!" It was dead silent.

Except for the clicking and clacking of various rifles being locked and loaded.

***

Johnny-B had almost completed the short drive to Jenny's property when his walkie-talkie squawked. "The church has been raided by a dozen or so federal agents. We're in a stalemate." He registered the message but was more concerned with the black Suburban SUV he saw tucked away in the bush down the road. It was an ambush! He turned his ancient Ford 250 pickup off CR 550 and headed down the two-track toward Jenny's camp. He drove slowly, waiting for the Suburban to follow.

"Mike, you got my 6?" Johnny used the walkie-talkie to contact the deputy that had been trailing him.

"10-4 Johnny. I've got eyes on a black Suburban that just turned to follow you. You were right, it's a trap. What's the plan?"

"Follow him but stay out of sight. When you hear the crash, make tracks." Johnny replied as he stopped his pickup on the other side of a bend in the two-track. He looked over at the two newbie deputies sitting next to him on the front seat, fear written across their faces. "You know why I don't use a last name?"

"Nope," one deputy replied.

"Because it's Goode."

"Johnny-B Goode? You got to be kidding me," said the other deputy, breaking the tension.

"That's God's honest truth," Johnny replied. "You two buckled up?" Johnny watched in his rearview mirror as the Suburban came around the bend and stopped.

Going full speed in reverse, Johnny's pickup slammed into the Suburban with a jarring crunch. The truck's trailer hitch punched through the SUV's radiator and pushed the engine block off its mounts. Twelve airbags deployed simultaneously, incapacitating the four agents. Before they could regain their senses, Johnny and four deputies had surrounded the vehicle holding shotguns and high-powered hunting rifles. The Suburban engine was steaming, and the smell of hot radiator fluid filled the air. "What the..." Deputy Mike disregarded the various curses from the four agents as he flex-cuffed them and loaded them into the crumpled bed of Johnny's pickup.

Johnny's mind was on fire as he navigated the long two-track to Jenny's cabin: How big was the federal response? What about the Fish and Wildlife boat offshore? How can we get some leverage over this situation? Upon entering Jenny's compound, Johnny saw Karl and Jack look his way, their mouths agape. I guess we are a sight! He parked in front of the garage and Deputy Mike pulled in behind him. Before Johnny had fully exited his pickup, Jack was in his face. "What the heck is going on?"

"The Feds have raided the church. Sheriff Larson is responding with force. These guys were waiting in ambush for us," Johnny said as he nodded his head toward his captives. "I think they're after the plasma drive—oh, your friend Scott Bennett is at the Sheriff's Office."

"Scott's here? Where's Jenny?" Jack asked.

"I don't know. Just a second." Johnny pulled his walkie-talkie out and keyed the mic. "Four federal agents under custody at Jenny's camp. Over."

"Still a stalemate here. Sheriff Larson is negotiating with the Feds. Over."

"Are there hostages?" Johnny asked.

"Yes, DeVries, Hernandez, Kelly, Campbell and Cindy Beers. Over."

Jack clenched his jaw. "I've got to get over there!"

"Hold on Jack," Johnny held up his hand. "Mike," he yelled at the deputy guarding the prisoners. "Check out the lake to see if there is a Fish and Wildlife boat offshore. If there is, let me know." He turned to Karl. "Did you ever save the plasma drive specs?"

"Yes. They're on a thumb drive over in the guest house."

"Get 'em now! We're heading to my place and then the church."

"But..."

"Just do it," Johnny ordered.

Washington DC – 12:20 pm
The Bureau Secure Conference Room

"The task force has reached the church." Reggie addressed Attorney General Hunter and Energy Under Secretary Kohl who had rejoined the meeting for the grand finale. Besides Hunter and Kohl, a handful of subordinates were seated at the large conference table. "I am waiting on a sitrep. Hold on one second." Reggie reached for the intercom. "Sutton, what are your monitors showing?"

"Director Woods, I think we might have a problem,"

Tommy replied.

"What do you mean?" Reggie asked, his voice rising in irritation.

"Well, I'm showing four of our SUVs at the church, but also four sheriff squad cars," Tommy said. "Also, our SUV at Hernandez's property is co-located with a sheriff squad. It looks like they are shadowing our units. There has been no communication from either side."

"Contact Godwin now," Hunter said, his face contorting. "We may need to send in reinforcements. Dammit Woods, you should have sent in an overwhelming force. This covert raid is bullshit."

Reggie grimaced. He hadn't made that decision. The committee wanted this off the books! But he couldn't argue, not with Assistant AG Hunter.

"Patch into Godwin's tactical channel now!" Reggie yelled at the technician coordinating the communication links. After a hiss and a crackle, Reggie said, "Godwin, this is Reggie Woods, we need a sitrep ASAP." Static.

Finally, Trevor's voice came over the comm link. "We have the church and our primary target secured. Secondary target has gone black. Bennett is missing and off grid. We have met significant resistance from local law enforcement and a citizen mob. Are we cleared to use lethal force? Over."

The conference room went silent. Everybody gave furtive glances at each other. Nobody had expected this!

Finally, Hunter spoke. "You guys were sent up there to retrieve the power generator. Now you're telling me that site has gone black and Bennett is missing? This is FUBAR! And, no, you can't use lethal force," Hunter said. "If that ever leaked out, just think of the optics; *DOJ massacres worshipers!* Use your head, dammit! You're holding hostages, right? Can't you exchange them for the generator?"

Before Godwin could reply, Kohl from Energy broke in. "Max, we do want the generator, but the inventors, specs, and IP are just as important. Can't you just send in reinforcements?"

Hunter stood up and started pacing around the room. "Woods, get your tech to bridge in Governor Davis and the Commander of the Michigan State Police. Godwin, get your damn helicopter in the sky and put the fear of God in these rubes. I'm going to have to brief Secretary Gould on this—the Department of Homeland Security needs to get involved."

"Yes sir!" Oh shit, Reggie feared. This thing is going south!

SIXTY-ONE

"WW5BT, WW5BT, this is K8JNB. Come in WW5BT," Johnny-B tried to conceal his urgency. Jack and Karl stood behind him as he worked the radio, fine-tuning the channel. The thumb drive had already been uploaded to Johnny's computer and was ready for encryption on the channel carrier. They had added a preface to explain the situation in Aux Baie. "WW5BT, WW5BT, this is K8JNB. Come-in WW5BT." Johnny knew that Big Texas kept a pretty strict schedule. He could only hope he had his ears up. "WW5BT, WW5BT, this is K8JNB. Come in WW5BT," Johnny repeated one last time.

The radio came alive with Ben Sutton's voice. "Well, hold your horses, Johnny. You caught me on the can! What's new in the U.P.?"

"Ben, I wanted to give you some feedback on that recipe you sent me." Johnny started the encryption program. "It turned out all runny. What are we doing wrong? Over."

"Probably undercooked," Ben replied. "I'll have to get back to you after talking to my wife. Over."

"Thanks Ben, I got a bunch of hungry kids waiting for your answer. Over"

"How's the weather been up there in the Arctic Circle? You getting snow yet?" It was obvious Ben was buying some time.

"Well, we had some flurries the other day," Johnny said. "But I know a guy that was out kiteboarding today on Lake Superior. I think he's one can short of a six-pack..."

They continued meaningless banter for a couple of minutes

328

until Sutton brought the conversation to an end.

"Listen Johnny, I'll get back to you with that fix. Can't have runny eggs. This is Big Texas, WW5BT over and out."

About 1,500 miles away in a ranch house near Midland Texas, Ben Sutton used his arm to sweep a pile of clutter off his desk and started decrypting the message. When he had finished, he read it out loud. "Aux Baie under siege by Feds. They seek new power generator. Specs attached. If you do not hear from me within 24 hours, release to public. JB." Sutton started wading through the tech specs running his hand through his hair. "What the hell is a plasma drive?"

Johnny was about to shut down his radio when he saw that Ben had also sent a message during their conversation. After decrypting it, he stared in disbelief; *RFH going live at 1 ET on 1010. Coming to the party?*

"Johnny, we've got to get over to the church, now!" Jack yelled.

"Yeah, sure." Johnny answered absentmindedly.

Karl looked over Johnny's shoulder and asked, "What is RFH? A new radio frequency?"

"No Karl, it stands for *Radio Free Heartland*."

Community Church – 1:15 pm

As they approached the church, Johnny, Jack, and Karl had to stop at a checkpoint.

"Where's Sheriff Larson?" Johnny asked the deputy in charge.

"Just beyond the church," the deputy said. "They're using a mobile home as the command post."

As Johnny drove past the church, they could see a crowd had gathered in the parking lot, some with firearms. After parking behind the command post, they all squeezed into the mobile home to brief Sheriff Larson.

"We have four Feds detained at Jenny's camp," Johnny said. "Mike's there with two deputies. I had to take out their vehicle in the process. A few scrapes and bruises, but nothing serious. We saw a Fish and Wildlife boat earlier, but it's gone—too rough on the lake." Johnny gestured to his friends. "I think you've met Jack and Karl before. Karl is the chief scientist behind this new power generator. Sheriff, I've seen it work. It's the real thing. I bet that's the real target here."

"That adds up," Larson said. "Doesn't make sense to sic a SWAT Team on a church for some HHS violations. Jenny was probably targeted for leverage."

"What's happening in the church?" Jack asked in a shaky voice. "Is everybody okay?"

"As far as I know," Larson said. "But I'm afraid Jenny and the church leadership are now hostages. After our first encounter, they backed off and are holed up inside. Probably a dozen plus agents in full tactical gear. Looks like a covert op gone bad. They didn't expect us!"

"Sheriff," Karl said, "if they're after the generator, they'll want me too. I'm willing to exchange myself for the hostages."

"Thanks, but let's keep that in our back pocket for now. Actually, this thing has escalated beyond a local dust-up," Larson said ominously. "But we should reinforce Jenny's camp. If you want to go back to Jenny's, that's your choice. There's a deputy outside that will take you there."

"Thanks Sheriff, I think I will," Karl replied. "Someone's got to babysit the generator." As Karl exited the RV, the sheriffs from Houghton County and Iron County leaned in through the door.

"Hey Jim, the cavalry's here." Sheriff LaFontaine joked.

"Tony, Nick, I'll be right with you," Larson said, returning his attention to his immediate audience.

"What are LaFontaine and Griggs doing here?" Johnny asked.

"Well, I was about to brief you," Larson said. "We've implemented our Mutual Aid Pact. All the sheriffs in the U.P. have signed on; an attack on one of us is an attack on all. We've seen this coming for a while. This is the fourth church raid in as many months. We're not going to take it anymore. We caught them with their pants down this time. Not sure where this is heading, Johnny, but we may need your help engaging the Resistance. Now, if you'll excuse me, I need to talk with them."

"One last thing," Johnny said. "We've uploaded the specs of the power generator to a safe site and can make that info public at any time. We're using a covert, national comms-net. I can brief you on it later. Anyway, the specs might give us leverage over the Feds."

Larson paused to consider this new wrinkle before replying. "You might have something there. If this generator is so important, we might offer it up along with the specs and safe passage in exchange for the hostages. Might be worth a try. But how do we put that offer on the table?"

"I'll volunteer," Jack replied, his voice now steady.

Sheriff's Office – 2:00 pm

Brenda was giving Sally an update on the Mutual Aid Pact when the walkie-talkie came to life. "Brenda, this is Jack. I need to speak to Scott Bennett. It's important."

"Just a second," Brenda said.

"I got this," Sally took the walkie-talkie and walked over to Scott who was pacing back and forth in the small office, muttering to himself. "Jack needs to speak with you, just push and talk."

"This is Scott."

"Hey Scott," Jack said. "Are you aware of the hostage situation?"

"Yes, I hear they have Jenny, Tim, and Kristen."

"That's right. We want to propose a swap: they give us the hostages in exchange for the prototypes, the specs, and safe passage out of Aux Baie. It's your Aunt and your business, are you good with that plan?"

"As long as we have Karl, I'm fine," Scott replied. "But they might not bite. How about I offer myself up? It's my fault this happened anyway. I never should have involved Jenny."

"I don't think that would be wise," Jack said. "They'd use you to take down your dad. We may need his help before this thing is over. Right now, by all appearances, you've been kidnapped by the Resistance and are off grid. We should keep it that way."

Sally grabbed the walkie-talkie from Scott. "You're right Jack. Move forward without Scott. He's too valuable to give up." With no objection from Scott, Sally ended the call.

Scott walked over to the couch and sat down, putting his head in his hands. Sally followed and sat next to him. She put her hand on his knee and gave it a gentle squeeze. "Listen Scott. Without your actions, the Feds would have been long gone with the generator and your team. Besides, this confrontation was inevitable. The Feds have been leaning on us since the Emergency Acts. They've usurped authority from our state and county officials. They've shut down our charter schools. They're seizing our firearms. And now, they're raiding churches and taking hostages. For God's sake, enough is enough!"

"But what can we do, what can I do?" Scott asked.

"Scott, wake up—you're the catalyst! The revolt has started. Resistance cells are mobilizing across the Upper Peninsula and the sheriffs are on our side. There's no turning back now."

Scott turned to match Sally's gaze. "You got to be kidding me. The Feds aren't going to just roll over and let this happen. What about the State Police and National Guard?"

"Not sure where their loyalties lie. But we should find out soon," Sally said. "Marquette could be the key. Do you know any politicians up there? Maybe through your dad?"

"Yeah sure. Why do you ask?"

SIXTY-TWO

"What do you mean he's staying neutral?" Assistant AG Hunter screamed into the speakerphone. "Fire his ass and get his second in command to move on Aux Baie." The dozen or so meeting attendees watched wide-eyed as Hunter spouted off.

Robert Gould, Secretary of Homeland Security, raised his hand to silence Hunter and continued his conversation with the governor of Michigan. "Governor Davis, what did the State Police Captain say, exactly?"

"Captain Malek said they're not going to take sides in the conflict and face off against their own citizens."

"You mean terrorists." Gould corrected.

"With all due respect, Secretary Gould, our citizens are not terrorists," Davis said. "It was your heavy-handed raid that precipitated this crisis. And on a church for heaven's sake!"

"That may be the case," Gould said. "But let me remind you that Michigan is now fully dependent upon federal revenue sharing. Your state's lack of cooperation would be unfortunate. Now, certainly you can bring in State Police from the lower peninsula. Also, you have a National Guard post in the area: the 107th Engineer Battalion out of Ishpeming. We strongly suggest you mobilize it to keep the peace in Aux Baie."

"All right, Mr. Secretary, I'll mobilize the Guard. As far as the State Police are concerned, I can give orders, but I can't guarantee compliance. There might be some split loyalties. I presume you know by now that the Upper Peninsula Sheriff's Association has implemented a mutual aid pact to, and I quote, 'protect the citizens of the Upper Peninsula'. At the risk of sounding rude, we have a real shitshow on our hands—and it's not my fault." The speakerphone clicked as the Governor hung up.

Gould turned to address all the meeting attendees. "What other federal assets do we have up there?"

Aux Baie, MI – 6:15 pm

The sun was low in the sky as Jack approached the fellowship hall, waving a makeshift white flag. He knew everybody was watching him; most of the town was behind him in the parking lot and he was sure the Feds had eyes and guns trained on him. He took a deep breath and continued toward the door.

"Stop right there," said the agent guarding the door. "What's your business?"

"I want to talk with your commander. I have a proposal to defuse this situation."

"Don't move." The agent retreated into the church.

After a couple minutes, the door opened to admit Jack. One of the agents patted him down and led him to the Pastor's office, which had been expropriated by a man who apparently was in charge.

"Who are you and what's your offer?" asked the man sitting behind Pastor's desk.

"My name is Jack Conrad and I speak for Sheriff Larson as well as Plasma Drive Technologies. We presume you are here for the power generator, not the church. In exchange for all the hostages, we will give you the power generator, the specs to the generator, and free passage out of Aux Baie." Jack took a breath before continuing. "If you don't free the hostages, or if any of them are harmed, we will broadcast the specs to the general public, to the entire world."

"Oh really!" The man stood up and leaned over the desk to confront Jack. "Well, I'm Trevor Godwin with HHS," he spat out. "You have a lot of nerve marching in here and demanding anything. You and your co-conspirators are going to prison for a long, long time. In any event, I'll need to talk to my superiors. Agent Pulaski, escort this criminal to the library."

As Pulaski grabbed his arm, Jack held firm in front of Godwin. "Also, I need to see the hostages, confirm they're unharmed."

Godwin frowned but relented. "Show him the detainees and then hold him in the library."

Without speaking, Pulaski led Jack back toward the fellowship hall and then through the swinging door of the kitchen. Jenny, Pastor, Kristen, Tim, and Cindy sat on the floor, handcuffed, backs to the steel cabinets. They all looked up at him in surprise.

"Jack!" Jenny cried.

"Shut up!" Pulaski said. "Or we'll gag you all."

Jack met Jenny's eyes and mouthed "Are you okay?" She gave an imperceptible nod. However, Jack could tell she was afraid, as were all the others. Jack was mouthing "keep the faith" when Pulaski yanked his arm and led him to the library.

***

The chopper came in low and fast at dusk. It was hovering over the church before most citizens had a chance to react. Blinding searchlights lit up the entire parking lot as a booming megaphone repeatedly announced, *"This is an illegal assembly! Disperse now or you will be arrested and detained!"*

Many in the crowd ran for cover expecting the worst. Several citizens were getting itchy trigger fingers. Sheriff Larson and his deputies implored the hunters in the crowd to keep their rifles shouldered. But after 15 minutes of the aerial harassment, Larson approached Johnny-B. "Johnny, do you have any tracer rounds?"

"Yes sir. Do you want me to fire across their bow?"

"Yeah Johnny, but let's first talk to our posse. Don't want anybody following your lead and actually shoot the chopper down!"

It seemed hot in the conference room. Reggie thought about adjusting the thermostat but didn't want to draw attention to himself. DHS Secretary Gould had excused himself leaving Assistant AG Hunter and Under Secretary Kohl as the senior officials. They were all waiting for an update from Trevor Godwin. The tech specialist finally secured the communication link and Godwin's voice could be heard over the speakerphone.

"They're offering up the generator, the specifications, and free passage out of the county in exchange for our hostages," Godwin said, the muffled chop of a helicopter could be heard in the background. "If we don't release the hostages, they threatened to release the specs to the public."

Hunter put Godwin on mute and turned to Kohl from Energy, "What do you think? Is that enough?" Reggie Woods watched in silence as the heavyweights took over. He knew he had become a bit player, which was fine.

"As long as they have their inventor and a copy of the specs, they'll be able to replicate the generator and hold the IP over our heads," Kohl replied. "No, it's not enough. Can't you get reinforcements up there and arrest the whole group?"

"We have alerted the State Police and we are mobilizing a battalion of the National Guard," Hunter said. "They should be there by sunrise. But things have gotten more complicated. The sheriff's association up there is actively supporting the Resistance. We risk losing control."

"Well, then I would respond in force," Kohl said.

Hunter put the speakerphone off mute. "Godwin, we have the National Guard mobilizing. They should be there by dawn. Can you hold out until then?"

"No problem, sir. We have plenty of firepower and we have the hostages. Their proposal was a sign of weakness. We…" Godwin paused while the speakerphone reverberated with the chop of the helicopter and another staccato sound. "Shots fired! Shots fired!" repeated Godwin.

Aux Baie, MI

Johnny's M16 left a trail of tracers in the night sky about 25 yards in front of the helicopter; just close enough to get the message across. The chopper banked hard right and cleared the area.

***

"Godwin said he relayed the proposal to his superiors." Jack briefed Larson, Griggs and LaFontaine who were gathered in the Command Post. "He promised an answer by tomorrow morning."

"Did you see the hostages?" asked Sheriff Griggs. "How about the number of agents?"

"Hostages were cuffed in the kitchen. They seemed to be okay, but Jenny looked scared. Anyway, I saw at least a dozen agents, all heavily armed and in tactical gear."

"Thanks Jack," Sheriff Larson said. "We have eyewitnesses who saw four to a vehicle, so probably 16 agents inside. Sounds like they are trying to buy time, probably for re-inforcements." He turned his attention to Griggs and LaFontaine. "What about Marquette? Is Sheriff Robbins holding firm?"

"He's hanging in there," Sheriff LaFontaine said. "Also, some good news. District 8 State Police has declared neutrality. Can't say about the local posts, but they'll probably follow Captain Malek's lead. We're also looking for a provisional leader, maybe a retired politician. We can't be the face of this revolt forever!"

"No shit," Larson said. "Well, if they're buying time, then we should expect a federal response soon. Maybe the National Guard. We need to get prepared. We need more deputies. Heck, I hate to use the word, but we need a militia. What about the approaches to Baraga?"

"We've got you covered on the west and south," Griggs

said. "Sheriff Robbins has your east flank protected. Marquette County is the key; that's where the headquarters of the State Police and National Guard are."

Sheriff Larson agreed. "Yep. We need someone in Marquette we can talk to and trust. We've got to transition to civilian leadership ASAP."

SIXTY-THREE

Mackinaw City, MI – 8:00 pm

It was dark as Meg approached the bridge, its gleaming towers rising high in the distance. She felt a growing excitement, as if the Mighty Mac was her bridge to freedom. Meg was done. Done with teaching. Done with the bureaucracy. Done with progressive groupthink. Done with indoctrination of her students. It was all bullshit! Meg had asked for tomorrow off to give herself a head start. However, since both her PIV and car had active GPS, her movements were being tracked. But was anybody looking? Anyway, she was so close, she could smell freedom.

As she came around a curve, Meg's heart sank when she saw an overhead sign with the message *Traffic Stopped Ahead*. What was going on? Meg immediately went into panic mode. Were they searching cars? Had she triggered a geofence? She didn't see any option but to continue forward. Soon, she saw brake lights ahead. Both lanes were backed up for a hundred yards from the toll booth and PIV checkpoint. A couple of state trooper cars had their beacons flashing. It looked like they were directing cars back through a U-turn. Now trapped between cars, Meg had no choice but to creep ahead.

"Officer, what's the problem," Meg asked as the trooper came up to her open window.

"Bridge is closed until further notice. You need to turn back over there," the trooper said and waved his flashlight toward the U-Turn.

Meg looked at the trooper with pleading eyes. "But my father is expecting me. Why is the bridge closed? Weather?"

"There's been a civil disturbance, now please move on, you're blocking traffic," the trooper said more forcefully.

Not wanting to push it, Meg complied and took the U-Turn heading back south from where she came.

Aux Baie, MI – 9:00 pm
Jenny's Camp

Karl stepped away from the group of deputies and the ambient light of Jenny's cabin to appreciate the night sky. With no moon and clear skies, the stars gleamed with unmatched brilliance. Karl marveled at the densely glowing swath of the Milky Way, our home galaxy comprised of more than 200 billion stars. Each star a plasma fusion engine transforming hydrogen into helium, and helium into denser elements, ad infinitum, until the very building blocks of life were formed. Although he was agnostic, Karl felt humbled by the Universe and its mysterious perfection. If there is a God, certainly this is his face, he thought. Karl watched in awe and silence, finally returning to tend to his plasma drive, an infinitesimal, but purposeful reflection of God's creation.

Washington D.C. – 10:15 pm

It was late in the evening when John Bowden was buzzed into Steve Bennett's condo. Marge mixed them both some stiff, scotch drinks as they exchanged pleasantries. Soon, the pair retreated to the study and shut the door.

"I presume you've had your place swept," Bowden said.

"Yeah John, we're clean. I assume this is more than a social call."

"Your son's car was found abandoned outside of Aux Baie around noon today. The PIV was inside, so he's off grid. Coincidentally, there has been a federal raid on the local church and hostages were taken. There's now a standoff with the local sheriff and his posse." Bowden paused.

"Is Scott a hostage?" Oh Lord, what have I done? I should have never let him go.

"No, but your sister-in-law, Jenny Hernandez, is. And the

shit is hitting the fan up there. Looks like the sheriff's association is supporting the Resistance. As a friend, I hope you're not involved in this."

"I knew Scott was heading to the U.P. to shut down any lingering aspects of his company. He was also going to warn Jenny to clean up her act. I was expecting him back tonight," Steve said. "That's all, I promise."

"Well, I wouldn't hold your breath. With no car and no PIV, Scott's probably not traveling tonight. Besides, roads are shutting down, including the Mac."

"Is there a full revolt?" Steve's eyes widened.

"Hard to say. I can tell you we're seeing a spike in rebel activity across the heartland. Not sure if it's coordinated or not. I'll keep you posted on Scott the best I can."

"Thanks John," Steve shook Bowden's hand and looked him directly in the eyes. "Scott means everything to me."

After Bowden had left, Marge tried to console Steve, but to no avail. He had let his son go into harm's way and he was powerless to help. Finally, Steve surrendered to Marge's suggestion that they offer up a prayer for Scott's safety.

***

After three tries on the intercom, Reggie Woods gave up and walked to Tommy's office. Without knocking, he burst in. All the monitors were still on, and candy bar wrappings were spread all over the floor, but no Tommy. Reggie speed-dialed Sutton using his PIV. No response. Off grid. "Son of a bitch!" Reggie yelled as he hit another speed dial button.

"Internal Affairs," answered the security specialist.

"This is Reggie Woods, Assistant Deputy Director Counterterrorism. I need an all-points bulletin out on Thomas B. Sutton, analyst. Probation violation at a minimum. Also, suspected of conspiring to commit treason. And he just went off grid."

Ten blocks away, Tommy Sutton blended into the crowds as he enjoyed an unusually warm October night. The area was called *NoMa*, for North of Massachusetts Avenue, one of the more dangerous areas in the city. As a white man, Tommy stood out. But, the vibe was good. Some hip-hop music drifted out of a local bar and he caught the waft of marijuana. People were getting on with their lives, oblivious to the escalating crisis across the country. The Feds will put a lid on it anyway, Tommy guessed. Keep the populace in the dark. He stopped in his tracks. "North or south?" he asked himself out loud. He already knew the answer. The question was how to get up to the Upper Peninsula of Michigan without being caught. Surveillance cameras were everywhere now, loaded with the latest facial recognition software. But Tommy still had a few tricks up his sleeve - he smiled as he patted his pants pocket and felt the top-secret thumb drive he had taken from the Bureau. Tommy turned north and continued his way down the poorly lit street, contemplating the journey ahead.

Mackinaw City, MI – 11:30 pm
Dockside Bar & Grill
Meg's instincts were right—martial law or not, others were still hoping to travel to the U.P. Several of her new-found friends at the bar were looking to join the Resistance; the word was out! They all sat in a booth drinking beer and waiting for their new acquaintance, Paul, to return. An old Clapton song, *I Shot the Sheriff*, was playing on the ancient jukebox. Finally, Paul came back, weaving his way between two pool tables.

"I found a guy. Says he's got a boat, but with the travel ban, it's going to cost us."

"How much?" One of the would-be travelers asked.

"That's the thing. He's not accepting PIV credits. Too easy to trace, he says."

"How about this?" Meg asked. "She placed a gold coin into Paul's hand. "A gift from my dad."

As they sped across the Strait of Mackinaw, Meg's spirits rose. Paul had family in St. Ignace and was willing to help with transportation. Meg exited the crowded cabin and walked to the front of the boat. In the distance she could make out the sparsely lit outline of the Upper Peninsula. The wind in her face and the swell of the waves brought back familiar sensations. She let herself smile as she pulled out her PIV and let it slip into the deep, dark waters.

On the Road to Marquette, MI – 12:50 am

Scott's pulse increased as their squad car was stopped at the county line. Their driver rolled down his window to address his peer from Marquette. "Got some VIPs headed for Marquette," he said.

"We were expecting you," the deputy replied as he leaned down and looked through the back window to inspect Sally and Scott. "Should be all clear to the city. So far, the State Police are standing down."

"Thank God," their driver said. "Don't want to get into a shooting war with our friendly troopers!"

"You're good to go," the deputy waved them through. "Safe travels!"

After clearing the checkpoint, Sally turned to Scott. "So, tell me more about this guy." Sheriff Larson had instructed them to open a liaison with civilian authorities in Marquette. They figured the Bennett name would carry some weight, so Scott was volunteered.

"I've met him several times at fundraisers. A big supporter of my father. He's a retired state senator, but also a former head of the Michigan Republican Party. Solid libertarian. Soft-spoken, but he doesn't tolerate bullshit."

"I like him already," Sally said, and then leaned forward to get the driver's attention. "Can you turn on AM radio? Johnny-B says there might be some sort of broadcast at 1:00 am. Channel 1010. Thanks." As Sally sat back, her thigh nestled against Scott's. He waited expectantly for her to move apart. She didn't, which was fine by Scott.

After the driver set the dial on 1010, they waited. At exactly 1 am the channel crackled, announcing a carrier signal powered by 50,000 watts. In a phenomenon called skywave propagation, the signal bounced off the ionosphere to reach over 85% of the continental U.S.

"*This is Radio Free Heartland, broadcasting on AM 1010 nightly at 1 am Eastern.*"

"Oh my God!" Sally blurted out.

"Shh!" Scott implored.

"*AM 1010 is dedicated to the 10th Amendment of the U.S. Constitution; The powers not delegated to the United States by the Constitution, nor prohibited by it to the states, are reserved to the states respectively, or to the people.*

Fellow citizens and patriots, our country is in peril. The federal government has trashed our Constitution to assume powers they do not have! I could spend all night listing federal infractions, but we all know what's been usurped. Our First Amendment rights of freedom of religion, speech, assembly, and the press. Our Second Amendment right to bear arms. Our Fourth Amendment protection against unreasonable search and seizure – and surveillance! Our rights to due process. The so-called Fair Deal has made a mockery of our Bill of Rights and imposes socialism.

Do not be discouraged, you are not alone. Grassroots resistance is growing across the heartland. Sheriff's departments and National Guard units are taking sides with the people. Counties, and even states, are offering sanctuary for off-gridders. But we need your help. Band together with like-minded citizens. Resist the Feds. Continue to worship. Throw away your PIVs. Remember, it's not a crime to defend the Constitution, it's our duty.

Before signing off, two shout-outs. First, to the patriots of west Texas who are reclaiming their rights. And second, to the brave citizens of Michigan's Upper Peninsula who are under siege. Our thoughts and prayers are with you. This is AM 1010, the Voice of the Heartland. Good night and God Bless America."

Midland, TX – 1:05 am

Ben Sutton quickly shut down the transmitter. No sense giving the Feds more time to home in on his signal. He grabbed a beer out of his refrigerator and cracked it open, taking a long swallow. Ben considered his options. He could continue broadcasting out of this site for a few more nights, playing Russian Roulette with the Feds. Or, he could bug out to one of his backup installations. And, after that, there were over a dozen backups spread across flyover country to carry the flame. Ben wondered how long they could hold out. But it really didn't matter—they had to try.

SIXTY-FOUR

As the night dragged on, the hostages could converse more freely, releasing their tension and anxiety. Tim, as usual, took the lead. He turned to Kristen.

"Remember my Political Ecosystems class? I never got a chance to get to the punch line."

"Well, you have a captive audience, so to speak, fire away," Kristen said. The other prisoners—Jenny, Cindy, and Pastor DeVries—all turned to listen.

"Do you remember the first words I spoke to the class?"

"I do." Kristen smiled. "You said, 'fear and control'."

Tim was pleased that she remembered. "That was supposed to be my teaser, but I never got a chance to circle back to it. Fear and control are the roots of all political ecosystems, for both good and bad."

"How can fear be good?" Kristen asked, tilting her head.

"Humans are instinctively hardwired with fear to ensure survival. It is the primary motivator to control one's environment. It was fear that drove early humans to organize families, clans, and tribes to provide food, shelter, and protection from others. Fear is also fundamental to capitalism, the drive to produce and earn more." Tim scanned his audience to make sure they were tracking.

"All right, I get that," Kristen said. "But what about the downside, the bad?"

"Just as fear is hardwired in the body, control is hardwired in the brain. But here's the rub; egged on by fear, the mind can become obsessed with control. And not just self-control—but the control of others. And how do extremists control others?" Tim paused as a guard passed by the kitchen door. "By restricting their thoughts and behavior."

"I'm not sure I understand," said Cindy Beers. "By extremists, do you mean progressive radicals or conservative reactionaries?"

"What's the difference?" Tim asked. "Underneath their ideological veneers, they both seek absolute control. They exist on a circular continuum—go far enough left, or right, and you meet your counterpart. For every Hitler there's a Stalin. For every Mussolini there's a Mao. For every Marcos there's a Castro. They're all *statists* who maintain control through fear-based propaganda, restrictions, and enforcers. They all promise The Garden but deliver The State. If you're lucky, your nation is rich, and you become the ward of a nanny state. If not..." Tim shrugged his shoulders.

"But this can't happen in America, can it?" Jenny asked. "Don't we have checks and balances?"

"We used to," Tim replied. "They're called the press and the Constitution. Regretfully, the press has become a mouthpiece for the ruling class whom they fawn over. And, sadly, the Constitution is now viewed as malleable, subject to the whims of our rapidly changing culture. Even more vexing, tyrants eventually die, but the state may live on forever, growing like a weed. Modern technocracies can institutionalize one-party rule—just look at DC and our big cities. While the private sector collapsed during The Crash, government has thrived." Tim stopped momentarily, squirming to relieve the pressure from his handcuffs.

"Meanwhile, PIV allows authorities to spy on everybody, friend and foe alike. And social media? It just further justifies government intervention as extremists spew hate at each other. There's no longer room for policy debate and compromise. The other is illegitimate, the enemy, evil. What radicals and reactionaries don't realize is that harboring resentments is like taking poison and waiting for the other to die."

"So, all is lost?" Cindy asked.

"I don't know." Tim frowned. "With common decency and social mores collapsing, people look to the state to fill the void. So long as they can enjoy their worldly pleasures, people *want* to be controlled. In a perverse way it's freeing—you're not responsible. Those who choose self-reliance, self-control, and a virtuous life have become the minority. Ironically, *we're* now the counterculture! Perhaps we're beyond the tipping point and have lost our free society." Realizing, for once, he didn't have an answer, Tim turned to DeVries. "Pastor, help me out here."

"Tim, you forgot one aspect of our basic nature—faith. The state isn't going to save anybody with fear and control. Instead of being politically woke, maybe we need to be spiritually awakened? The wounds to our body politic are too deep for legalistic Band-Aids. We need spiritual sutures that only God can provide. And they might hurt," DeVries cautioned, "just like a fever or childbirth are painful, but good. Thankfully, we have the Helper who will never abandon us."

Tim turned to Kristen who leaned over and whispered in his ear, "The Holy Spirit, who intercedes on our behalf."

Pastor DeVries bowed his head. "We need to pray. Lord, we lift up our country, its leaders, and its people to you. Open our eyes Lord, that we may not be deceived by tyranny. Soften our hearts Lord, that we may not succumb to hate. You are our light and our salvation; whom shall we fear? Bring us clarity of purpose to obey the words of Christ; *Thou shalt love the Lord thy God with all thy heart, and with all thy soul, and with all thy mind. This is the first and great commandment. And the second is like unto it, thou shalt love thy neighbor as thyself.*"

"Amen," Jenny spoke for all.

***

Jack soared over the lake enveloped in silence. In the distance, he could see the mother bear anxiously pacing back and forth on the shore. Finally, she stood on her hind legs searching for her lost cub. Knowing time was short, Jack stalled in the air and looked down. A small disturbance in the water was the telltale sign. He folded his wings and dove, hitting the water hard. Powerful frog kicks and strokes propelled Jack deeper and deeper until he saw the child and grabbed its arm. He looked up at the light above and used all his strength to regain the surface. Jack put the infant in a cross-chest carry and, with adrenalin coursing through his veins, started the long swim home. "Please Lord," Jack pleaded as he tried to detect a heartbeat under his supporting arm. And then, the baby moved...

"Jack, Jack," Johnny-B gave his friend a gentle shake until his eyes opened.

"What's wrong?"

"Nothing, it's okay," Johnny said. "You fell asleep. It's time for your watch."

"Oh," Jack sat up, rubbing the sleep from his eyes. "Thanks Johnny." He dangled his legs over the bunk in the command post RV. They were hot-swapping beds and it was Johnny's turn for a break. As Jack put on his shoes, he tried to remember his fleeting dream, but it was elusive. His thoughts turned to Jenny and her safety. Jack looked at his watch. It was 5 am. Just hours before dawn.

***

Jenny awoke with a jolt. Had she been dreaming? She waited in silent apprehension. Around her, she could see her friends with heads dangling in awkward positions of sleep. A dim light peeking through the kitchen window suggested it was predawn. Faint voices echoed down the hall, "The Guard should be here within the hour. Set up some sniper positions in case this goes hot. We can catch the protesters in a crossfire..." The dreadful reality of the situation came crashing down on her. Was this really happening? And then, Jenny felt it again, her hand instinctively reaching down to cradle her womb in wonder.

***

In the quiet of the early morning, the civilian militia could hear the National Guard convoy approaching from miles away. Their numbers had shrunk throughout the night, but still a hundred-odd men, women, and teens formed a cordon around the church. Squad cars had been positioned to block the driveways. In front of the squads, Sheriff James Larson, Bryce Brogan, Johnny-B, Sam Aishkebay, and Jack Conrad stood with a score of deputies. Standing to the side was Mary DeVries, clutching her Bible with eyes closed in silent prayer. Using their walkie-talkies, scouts provided reconnaissance for the Sheriff as the convoy approached. It was an overwhelming force.

The citizens had checked their firearms and ammo. They were locked and loaded waiting for the Sheriff's orders. Hidden around the property, several residents had their smartphones ready to record the conflict in hopes of broadcasting it to the world. The tension was palpable as the lead Humvee came into view, stopping just short of the barricade. The passenger door opened, and the battalion commander stepped out to confront the rebels. He walked up to face Sheriff Larson and Bryce Brogan, concealing something in his hand. The commander turned his wrist and tossed an object to his cousin. Bryce released one hand from his shotgun and caught the orange mid-air.

"Hey Cuz, hey Jim, how can we help?" Lieutenant Colonel Kurt Brogan asked as he removed his cap, smoothed out his hair, and gave a reassuring smile.

ABOUT THE AUTHOR

J. P. Redding

J. P. Redding is a first-time author, former corporate executive, and retired entrepreneur
in the field of software development. His passions include
extreme watersports as well as
a deep concern for the fate of
our nation, as founded, and the

God-given and constitutional liberties of its citizens.

REQUEST FOR REVIEWS

Thank you for reading OFF GRID! I hope you found it to be a good read and thought provoking. I am anxious to hear your thoughts. Book reviews also improve the visibility of my book relative to the millions of other titles out there.

Leaving a review on the Amazon product page for the eBook or Paperback version of OFF GRID would be deeply appreciated. Near the bottom of the product page is a section for Customer Reviews. Just below this section is a place to *Review this Product* and a prompt to *"Write a customer review"*.

Thank you for your consideration!

J. P. Redding
Author - OFF GRID

CAST OF CHARACTERS

Sam Aishkebay: Aux Baie tribal elder and hunter.

Johnny-B: Jenny's maintenance man. Veteran, fisherman, and Resistance leader.

Cindy Beers: Co-op member (goat cheese), church council member.

Jerry Belinsky: Legislative aide to Rep. Steve Bennett.

Scott Bennett: Co-founder Plasma Drive Technologies (PDT). Son of U.S. Rep. Steve Bennett.

Rep. Steve Bennett: Ranking member House Committee on Homeland Security.

John Bowden: Under Secretary Dept. of Homeland Security (DHS). Friend of Steve Bennett.

Bryce Brogan: Proprietor, Brogan's Farm and Feed. Church council member.

Lt. Colonel Kurt Brogan: Commander, local National Guard unit. Bryce Brogan's cousin.

Kristen Campbell: Tim Kelly's girlfriend. Registered Nurse.

Jack Conrad: Construction worker and avid kiteboarder/windsurfer. Jenny Hernandez's college lover. Father of Meg.

Meg Conrad: Novice elementary school teacher. Daughter of Jack Conrad.

Tina Cutler: Co-op member (chicken and eggs), new mother. Wife of Cal Cutler.

Pastor DeVries: Pastor of the Aux Baie Community Church.

Mary DeVries: Wife of Pastor DeVries and Jenny's confidant.

Dan Fisher: Private pilot for Rep. Steve Bennett. Desert Storm Veteran.

Trevor Godwin: Director, Health and Human Services - Marquette MI Office.

Robert Gould: Secretary, Dept. of Homeland Security (DHS).

Jenny Hernandez: Naturalist and church president. Jack Conrad's college lover. Steve Bennett's sister-in law/Scott Bennet's aunt.

Max Hunter: Assistant Attorney General at Dept. of Justice (DOJ).

Tim Kelly: Co-founder PDT. Brilliant agnostic. First-time professor.

Richard (Dick) Kohl: Under Secretary Dept. of Energy (DOE).

Sheriff Jim Larson: Sheriff of Baraga County. Resistance sympathizer.

Sally Larson: Resistance member. Niece of Sheriff Larson.

Principal Jean Peters: Principal at Meg Conrad's school.

George Russell: Tribal member, Captain of the *Peggy Sue.*

Karl Schultz: Chief Scientist of PDT. Retiree from Lockheed Martin.

Marge Stevenson: Rep. Steve Bennett's Admin. Assistant and companion.

Tommy Sutton: Bureau analyst under Reggie Woods. Sympathizer of PDT.

Ben Sutton: Veteran, Resistance leader, and HAM radio operator in Texas. Older brother of Tommy.

Ken Weaver: Dept. Chairman, Political Science, Traverse University.

Sarah Wong: Analyst, Dept. of Energy (DOE).

Reggie Woods: Assistant Deputy Director - Domestic Counterterrorism at the Bureau.

Made in the USA
Middletown, DE
18 January 2021